The Grid

www.penguin.co.uk

Also by Nick Cook

The Hunt for Zero Point

The Grid

Nick Cook

doubleday

TRANSWORLD PUBLISHERS
61–63 Uxbridge Road, London W5 5SA
www.penguin.co.uk

Transworld is part of the Penguin Random House group of companies
whose addresses can be found at global.penguinrandomhouse.com

Penguin
Random House
UK

First published in Great Britain in 2019 by Bantam Press
an imprint of Transworld Publishers

A CIP catalogue record for this book
is available from the British Library.

ISBNs 9781787632127 (hb)
9781787630383 (tpb)

Typeset in 11.5/14.5pt Sabon by Jouve (UK), Milton Keynes.
Printed and bound in Great Britain by Clays Ltd, Elcograf S.p.A.

Penguin Random House is committed to a sustainable
future for our business, our readers and our planet. This book
is made from Forest Stewardship Council® certified paper.

MIX
Paper from
responsible sources
FSC® C018179

1 3 5 7 9 10 8 6 4 2

To my forever guide star
Ali
and to
J & A and F & B.
Thank you.

Although you appear in earthly form, your essence is pure Consciousness. You are the fearless guardian of divine light.

Mawlana Jalal ad-Din Muhammad Rumi

Book One

What you seek is seeking you

1

WE ARE HALFWAY UP THE TOWER WHEN I HEAR THE JUMPER'S VOICE.

'M-*Mister* Cain? Is that you down there?'

Forensic Services reckon the accent is Tennessee, West Virginia or Kentucky. The stutter points to a bunch of other things too.

I cup my hands and call back up into the darkness. 'I'm here.'

'Alone?'

I look at Hart – 'Hetta', she'd announced as we were introduced ten minutes ago, and then gone the extra mile by spelling it. She holds me back with one outstretched hand. The other is wrapped around her automatic. A bare bulb swings from the ceiling on a length of frayed cable and does odd things to our shadows as she shakes her head.

'No,' I yell back. 'I have an agent here for my protection. She has relieved the Metropolitan Police Department negotiator.'

There's a pause.

All I can make out above us is the larger of the church's two bells and the bottom half of the ladder leading to the uppermost level, from which the jumper is threatening to throw himself.

We wait as the wind whistles around the chamber, whipping up enough dust and bird shit to make my eyes water and sting my throat. Then:

'Mister Cain? I told the negotiator and I'm telling you. What I have to say is for your ears only. Your colleague needs to *s-stay* on the level below.'

'Sir,' Hetta calls out. 'You up there. My name is Hetta Hart and

I'm a Special Agent with the United States Secret Service. Doctor Cain is under my protection. You are to stay in a position where I can see you at all times. If I cannot see you, I will not be responsible for your safety. Do I make myself clear?'

I have no idea she's planned this speech. I would have advised against it. But what's done is done. We listen for a second or two.

'Perfectly clear, Agent Hart. *P-perfectly.*'

He invites us to take up position on the next floor and for Hart to remain at the base of the ladder. From there she will have an unrestricted view of us both.

'But I trust, Agent Hart, that you understand *m-me* when I repeat to you that I mean no harm – and that if there is any *cheatin'*, I will not hesitate to jump. Do I make *m-myself* clear, ma'am?'

Hetta is momentarily taken aback. I am too. It's a display of respect for authority neither of us expected.

'Perfectly.'

She signals that it's OK to make my way on up.

I edge my way around the bell. It is old and big – at its base, the width of a small car, maybe – and so cold to the touch that it drives the remaining feeling from my fingertips.

A half-formed memory comes to me from my childhood: of a preacher at my father's funeral, talking about Jesus or God coming 'like a thief in the night'. I didn't understand it then and I'm not sure I do now, but it makes me think about the church. *Why here?*

The guy had been here for twenty-four hours, according to Lefortz. Maybe longer.

He'd avoided detection during three packed services, the last on a busy afternoon with two senators and their families in the congregation. Security must have already done at least one sweep.

As I place my foot on the bottom rung of the ladder, I get the strangest feeling. Like I've been here before.

Hetta looks at me. 'You OK?' she whispers.

I nod.

As I start to climb, the silence is replaced by the sound of sleet and freezing rain driven against the cupola above us. The wind brings with it the thud of helicopter blades and the crackle of police radios. Through the hatch above my head I see a searchlight playing across the wall.

I place my fingertips on the lip of the opening and haul myself up.

He is poised on the ledge by the north window. Office blocks are silhouetted against the black sky behind him, beyond the glare of the lights. He is wearing a black hoodie and Levi's; the hoodie is pulled tight over the mask, its rictus expression angled toward me. Lefortz had told me about it, but it still manages to catch me unawares. In silhouette the plastic has the texture of real skin.

The arched eyebrows, knowing smile and goatee have been made infamous by hacktivists, protesters on Wall Street and places where world leaders have gathered to debate climate change, globalization and the war on terror. It's a Guy Fawkes mask – so-called after an anarchist who tried to blow up England's Houses of Parliament in sixteen hundred something.

I have read, too, that protesters themselves refer to him – to it – as Guido.

He has smashed his way through the slats and is clinging to a large rusted nail that's protruding from the top of the frame.

They estimated in the command post that he weighs around 140 pounds, is five-ten, maybe a little shorter, and in his mid- to late thirties. From the things he says, and the way he says them, the consensus is he's military or ex-military. I agree.

He motions me to sit with my back against the wall.

The cops weren't kidding. There is barely room for us both. The floor is around six foot by six, with the open trapdoor in the middle.

He turns and looks out over the labor union next to the church, toward the office blocks beyond.

Lefortz briefed me during the thirty minutes it took me to get here. His call had woken me a little after 03.40.

Guido had used a pick-gun to unlock all the doors from the basement of the church to the roof. A cleaning contractor in an office across the street spotted what she thought was a flashlight moving around inside. The two patrol officers who'd arrived on the scene found all the doors and gates locked – no sign of a break-in.

When they gained access a half-hour later, they found food and a bottle of water in the janitor's cupboard, along with a map of Lafayette Square, and plans of the White House and North Grounds.

Almost every fence jumper who's ever gotten into the North Grounds – before Jim Lefortz overhauled Presidential Protection operations – has suffered from a depressive illness or psychosis; the kind of condition, whatever, that can make a person believe they'll get an audience with the leader of the free world by parachuting into his bedroom or the Oval Office.

I've dealt with a lot of unbalanced people in my career; many were military or ex-military. And when you get a soldier or an ex-soldier who's disturbed and has a grievance, you have a loaded weapon.

I have devoted the best part of my life to ensuring veterans are treated for the service they have given this country, not vilified.

So, if this guy says he means nobody any harm, and he'll come down once he's said his piece, I'm going to give him the benefit of the doubt.

Push comes to shove, there are only three things that matter.

Who is he?

What does he want?

And why did he ask for me?

I draw my knees to my chest and wait. The sleet has turned to snow, which starts to settle in web-like drifts around my feet and in the folds of my jacket. I can see Hetta at the base of the ladder, but not the weapon I know she's holding in her right hand.

A gust of wind threatens Guido's balance, and I resist the temptation to reach out to him. He appears calm, considering the shit-storm he's stirred. I'm not taking his 'normal' at face value, though; it's most probably evidence of dissociation – a barrier he's erected between himself and the world.

He turns to me and something neither of us can see tugs at his left hand.

'M-Mister Cain, d-do you b-believe in God?'

The question is followed by a spasm, an exaggerated version of what just grabbed his arm. A myoclonic jerk can be caused by a change in body chemistry – a caffeine-induced leg or arm spasm, for instance, as we drift off to sleep – but Guido's, if it is a myoclonus, could be down to a surplus of adrenaline, or evidence, alongside the stammer, of some kind of past trauma.

Whatever it is, I must get on with what I came here to do: convince him that the world he has lost faith in still holds hope – not so easy when I am not sure I believe it myself.

'I don't know how much you know about me . . .'

'A lot.'

This distracts me for a moment. I refocus. 'But I know remarkably little about you. Can we—?'

He cuts me off. 'Please, answer the question.'

With his free left hand, the one affected by the myoclonus, he makes a minute gesture, something that looks to me like a thumbs-up. His hand is hanging by his side and I am keen for him not to see I've noticed it, but it throws me for a second and I force myself back.

Do I believe in God?

'For all the terrible things we do, there is goodness in each of us, and it may be that that goodness has a source. I don't know what that source is. I wish I did. But some people call it God.'

The words sound ludicrous said out loud, because they aren't mine; they aren't even my thoughts. They're a mishmash of someone else's belief system, someone I once loved more than life itself. It's better than the truth, though, and seems to satisfy him.

'And do you believe the President to be a g-good man?'

'Yes, I believe so.' A truthful response, but, again, not the whole truth. He's a politician, for Christ's sake, is what I really want to say.

He glances at the scene below, and the myoclonus tugs at his arm again. Then, slowly, he extends the index finger of his left hand as well as his thumb.

'I told the negotiator there is a plot to kill the President. There is. It is well planned, advanced, and will be well executed, unless you move to stop it.'

He raises his head and looks out across the rooftops, which gives me an opportunity to glance down. Hetta cups an ear and shakes her head.

She can't hear us.

Guido turns back to me.

'President *T-Thompson* is our best hope and I know – because it is in your nature – that you will leave no stone unturned in your efforts to protect him.'

His eyes continue to watch me, and I think of something I haven't heard in a long time: the sound of a dial-up modem.

For the past fifteen minutes, Guido and I have been engaged in the equivalent of all that screeching and squawking, probing each other for compatibility, and suddenly we are hooked up.

I don't know why or how, but I feel it: we're in business.

I must complete the 'handshake' – exchange those last vital bits of diagnostic data – and begin the process that will bring him down safely: invite him to step away from the drop, ask him for his name, get him to remove his mask and lead him to a place of safety; somewhere I can continue to speak with him, work out what it is that he needs, and ensure that he gets help.

And yet I also know that when he steps into my charge he ceases to be my responsibility.

He will be arrested, slapped with a count of unlawful entry, grilled about plots against the President and forced to undergo a thirty-day mental health evaluation while charges are prepared against him.

At the same time, people like Hetta – maybe even Hetta herself – in the Protective Intelligence and Assessment Division, people responsible for gauging threats to the President and the handful of others for whom the Service has responsibility, will probe him for anything that might signify that the peace camps by the North Fence represent a threat to the President so that Director Cabot has the excuse he needs to remove the protesters from Lafayette Square.

Guido turns in the same direction as before: toward the office blocks beyond the roof of the labor union. The wind drops and I hear the distant wail of a police siren. His words are suddenly clear and unmistakable. Not a hint of a stammer.

'Does the term "ground truth" mean anything to you, Colonel?'

My screwed-up expression probably tells him everything he needs to know.

'It's a term we used to use – one that became important to me.' He takes in a lungful of air. 'I came here for ground truth.'

'And did you find it?'

'Yes, sir,' he says quietly. 'I'm looking at it.'

'I don't understand.'

'You will, Colonel, you will . . .'

Something tells me I need to get to my feet, but Guido suddenly staggers and lurches, his arms spread wide.

And time does that thing time does in moments of shock: it stretches impossibly.

It twists, too.

I hear the report, a muffled crack, far off and distorted by the wind, *after* he falls. After the blood sprays from his right eye and spatters across my jacket.

Then he is on me, face down, twitching and convulsing, head on my chest.

I roll him onto his back and the blood continues to flow, black and viscous in the dim light, from the right eyehole's enlarged, jagged opening.

I pull his head onto my shoulder and see the hole in the back of his hoodie. I tear it off and realize that his mask is like the ones wrestlers wear, laced at the rear.

I fumble at the knot, but it's slippery with blood and I know I'm not going to get anywhere, so I lower his head and cradle it and see from his eyes and from some spasmodic movement in his arms and hands that he's still alive.

I pull back. The blood bubbles up through his mouthpiece and his eyes bore into mine. He's trying to tell me something.

He raises his hand till it's almost in my face and then Hetta's there, ponytail swinging, knife in hand. She's cutting at the laces. The mask drops away.

I look down.

The bullet has passed through his occipital and temporal lobes and exited his right eye, removing a large part of his face.

There is nothing anyone can do for him.

There's so much blood I can smell and taste the metal in it. It's a taste and a smell I know well. It takes me right back.

I do the only thing I can.

I pull him to me, so close I feel his heart stop.

Hetta rolls away, touching the crucifix around her neck, like she did every time the jumper got a mention in the mobile command post. When I set his body down and see him fully for the first time, I understand why. It isn't just that the bullet has removed half his face; what remains has been so badly burned there is really nothing left of it.

2

I'VE SHOWERED AND SCRUBBED MYSELF CLEAN IN THE RESTROOM down the hallway, but there are some things I'll never be able to wash away and I'm struggling to take in some of what's being said over the white noise.

It's less than two hours after the shooting and we're gathered in the Director's Crisis Center on the top floor of the Secret Service's downtown headquarters. Cabot is laying it on about the inherent security risk of people like Guido – the 'church incident' – serving as proof that he was right about the peaceniks.

The President's Chief of Staff, Reuben Kantner, brings some necessary sanity to the proceedings. He sits at the head of the table with Cabot by his side, quietly probing for details.

Reuben has almost certainly been up for hours, but even manages to *look* good in a crisis: his white shirt is pressed to within an inch of its life and he has none of the gray that flecks my hair.

I'm unshaven and in clothes borrowed from one of Cabot's assistant directors.

Next to Reuben, his head in a notebook, is the director of Internal Affairs for the Metropolitan Police Department. I don't remember his name. He looks impossibly young and is dressed more like a corporate lawyer than a cop.

Beside him, and appearing older than he did when I last saw him in the mobile command post a block from the church, is Captain Anders.

His first name, I now know, is Tobias, and it's clear that he is

11

struggling. Although nothing has been said openly, it is only too obvious that the 'jumper' was shot by one of his men.

Special Agent in Charge Jim Lefortz sits between us, tugging thoughtfully at the tips of his gray moustache. I've known him for six months – long enough to appreciate why he commands such respect.

There were two routes into the Service when he joined: you were either an ex-cop or you came in via the military. Like me, Lefortz was military; he'd been a Special Investigator with Army CID.

Much of the rest was hearsay – like the cartel boss he was rumored to have shot and killed during a money-laundering sting in Jalisco; the two-inch scar on his neck from a piece of the bomb that destroyed the Oklahoma Federal Building. He says little, but when he does it is on point and delivered in his warm, authoritative New Orleans drawl. Not for nothing is he known as 'Gentleman Jim'.

He's a year past retirement, but was persuaded by Reuben to take on the job of White House SAIC while the Thompson administration was in transition, which many commentators still consider it to be.

The Department of Homeland Security will launch its own inquiry into the shooting, and Dr Ameline Kurtz, who heads up its Human Factors directorate, will lead it. She sits between Cabot and me, mildly anorexic and immaculate in cream and black. Like the kid-lawyer from Internal Affairs, she spends her time scribbling notes and every time I hear the scratch of her pen, I sense Anders flinch.

Cabot turns and asks him what procedures are in place for establishing the jumper's ID.

The Special Tactics Branch Captain clears his throat and his face flushes. I could smell his body odor in the mobile command post and I can smell it now. He is in his late thirties, with Teutonic features – blue eyes, blond hair, fair skin. 'The Chief Medical Examiner's Office is conducting the autopsy. If his fingerprints are in the system, we'll get an immediate match.'

'And if they're not?'

'Then we'll initiate a print search at the local level.' Anders slides a finger from his Adam's apple to the back of his neck to loosen his collar. 'The decedent had severe facial burns also. If he's from the activist community, it won't take long for someone to come forward. We can put the details that we have out on social media—'

'They're already on social media! Twitter's all over it. People are saying he's a vet and that he had mental issues. They're also saying that between us –' Cabot jabs his finger at Anders and glances at Lefortz, '– we couldn't organize a fuck in a whorehouse.'

Now it's Ameline Kurtz who twitches.

'No one gave any order to shoot,' Anders says, quietly but firmly. Cabot has to lean forward to hear him.

'We have a man's brains splattered all over a church tower less than a block from the White House. So either somebody gave the order, or one of your men decided to fire for the hell of it. Neither is helping me feel the love for you right now, son, so you'd better get used to the fact you are going to be hung out to dry.'

Cabot sits back and grunts. The Crisis Center is a high-tech situation room next to his executive suite, paid for with money some say the Service should have spent on recruiting new agents. TVs occupy every spare inch of wall space, printers chatter like crickets, and telephones pepper the large mahogany table that occupies the center of the room.

Director Cabot is short, pug-nosed, with small, penetrating eyes that dart around the room, giving the impression everyone's under suspicion. He's sixty-odd, gray-faced, with, ironically, more than a look of J. Edgar Hoover. He was appointed by the previous administration on the strength of his unblemished record for fixing broken organizations. I can see why. He's one of those people with absolute faith in his convictions – something of a rarity right now.

'Isn't it a little unusual, your acting as negotiator in a situation like this?' He turns and fixes me with his pig eyes.

'Not really. In the six months I've been at the White House, I've got to know SAIC Lefortz well. We've a close working relationship. Plus I have a background in combat medicine; I know how to handle myself. And this man may have been a patient.'

'Oh?'

'He asked for me personally.'

'And you have experience of this type of situation?'

'The point was to avoid bloodshed.'

'I asked if you had experience.'

'My experience lies in the treatment of combat veterans – so, yes, I do.'

'How do you know *this* guy was a vet?'

'Because I know a combat injury when I see one. And some of the terminology he used was military.'

'What did he want?'

'He said there's a threat to the President's life.'

'They all do, son.'

'He said we should take this one seriously.'

'Fuck's sake!' Cabot pushes his chair back and looks at Lefortz. 'You got anything you want to contribute?'

Lefortz sits up. His face creases as he chews on the question.

'Josh – Doctor Cain – said it. It was my call. The guy asked for him. I asked if Josh'd be prepared to step up. He said yes.'

'That it?'

'Pretty much.'

Cabot draws breath for another tirade, but is stopped by the opening bars of Elvis's 'Suspicion', Lefortz's distinctive ringtone. The crooning builds until it fills the room.

'Sorry,' the White House SAIC says. It takes the whole chorus for him to find his phone and kill the call.

'The President isn't going to restrict the First Amendment rights of anyone who wants to demonstrate their grievances,' Reuben says before Cabot can regroup. 'But let's be real clear. If there is any threat to his safety, we need to know about it.'

He turns to me. 'Josh, I want a report on my desk by midday detailing everything. Names. Dates. Places. Everything our John Doe told you.' He looks at Anders, whose demons appear to have all but overwhelmed him. 'I need the same from the MPD. Some ammunition for when the shit seriously hits the fan – which, trust me, Captain, it's about to. Unlawful killing. Use of excessive force.

The militarization of our police departments. It's all going to crash down on us like a fucking tsunami.' His tone softens. 'You will be judged by what was going on inside your head at the moment of the shooting, Anders, so my advice is: take your time – get it all down while it's still fresh.'

Two minutes later, I am walking with Reuben down a staircase that offers a vertiginous perspective of the nine-story building's central atrium. At the end of the meeting, everybody dispersed except for Lefortz, whom Cabot had ordered to remain.

Reuben is tall and dark, a precise and graceful individual. He's a year or two older than me, but works hard – a lot harder than I do – to keep himself in shape. Knowing his intense dislike of Cabot, I congratulate him on a powerful closing speech.

He laughs somberly. 'Nature abhors a vacuum, right? The President's in Texas so he and the communications team can finish up on the State of the Union and then—'

He stops abruptly.

'I'm sorry, Josh, what happened up there must have been truly horrific.'

I tell him I'm OK, and turn the spotlight back on Thompson. 'The incident will have had some impact on his mental state, Reuben. I'll need to have a session with him on his return.'

Beyond the atrium I see snow driven by mini twisters swirling in the yellowy-gray light. The flashing lights of a plow bounce off the glass walls of the offices around us. It's the only vehicle moving on the street.

Reuben checks his phone, glances at the sky and nods. 'I'll set it up.'

With the airports and train stations closing, the capital is heading toward shutdown, and Andrews Air Force Base with it.

After too many years of back-and-forth, sledgehammer politics, not everyone had been convinced the Democratic Senator from Texas, Robert S. Thompson, was the man for the job. The election had been exceptionally close – the popular vote won by a margin of less than 200,000, and for a year, it seemed Thompson himself couldn't quite believe he'd done it.

There was shock, paralysis even, at the heart of his government in those first months. But now Reuben wants his boss back. Thompson needs to reassert his authority on what could be the most important address of his career. I'm not privy to what the President's State of the Union will contain, but anyone who's ever glanced at a TV or news site during his campaign could take a pretty good swipe at its messaging points: terrorism, conflict, humanitarian crises, poverty, disease and environmental catastrophe abroad; education, civil rights, racism, immigration, the war on gun-crime, the drugs trade and healthcare closer to home – not to mention tackling the multi-trillion-dollar federal budget deficit.

'Want a ride?' Reuben presses the button for the elevator that leads down to where the Beast lurks – the President's armor-plated, ten-ton limousine. 'I'm headed for the Hill, but I can drop you off at the Northeast Gate.'

'Thanks. But I could do with the walk.'

He glances at the sky again and gives me a suit-yourself shrug. 'Sure you're OK?' he asks again. There is something sad about his smile, but that's nothing new these days.

'Seemed like you were coaching Anders back there. What's going to happen to him?'

'To stay out of jail, he will need to convince a whole lot of people that his use-of-force decision was reasonable – from the perspective of a reasonable officer on the scene and not with the twenty-twenty vision of hindsight. If he gave the order, it will be on tape. If he didn't, the Keystone Cops accusation will stick. Either way, I'm sorry to say, Cabot is on the money.'

The elevator doors open. He steps into it.

'Reuben?'

He turns and holds the doors.

'What do you think—?'

'Relax,' he says. 'Lefortz knows what he's doing and you can leave Cabot to me. Get that report done, then go home. Get some rest.'

The doors close and I am left standing beside the foot-high silver letters that proclaim the motto of the United States Secret Service to the handful of people in the atrium: 'Worthy of Trust and Confidence'.

It's an eight-block, twenty-minute walk to the White House and, despite the sub-Arctic temperature on the streets, I really could do with it.

When trauma strikes, traumatic stress follows, generally because we fail to process what has happened. Thinking about the events of the past six hours, much as I don't want to, will help me come to terms with them.

Whilst the sequence of actions that led to the shooting is still unclear, my subconscious has been replaying the sights, sounds, smells and emotions of the encounter. And something has bubbled up to the surface: the handshake moment – the moment I knew Guido and I were in business, that there was trust between us – was triggered by his telling me that I would leave no stone unturned in my efforts to protect the President. *No Stone Unturned*. The promise that Reuben, Lefortz and I made when this thing started – nine months ago, when Thompson's nightmares began.

3

'IN THE WHITE HOUSE, THE PRESSURES ARE BEYOND ANYTHING THAT human beings are designed to handle,' a presidential adviser once said. Presidents are made of the same stuff as you and me and, occasionally, they break.

A recent study by one of our leading medical faculties concluded that nearly half the presidents between 1789 and 1974 met the Diagnostic and Statistical Manual of Mental Disorders' criteria for mental illness.

By most definitions, Robert S. Thompson was in rude mental health when he took office, if you ignored the madness that would make one want to be president in the first place.

But four months into his administration, he had a dream – the kind that sticks to you for days, like smoke. He told no one – to begin with, not even Jennifer, his wife.

Then he had another.

And another and another.

They took on many different forms, but always ended the same way: with his assassination.

Soon, he was losing sleep – to the point where he was getting maybe a couple of hours a night – and people began to notice that he had lost his campaigning sparkle. That was the point at which he opened up to Jennifer.

Reuben was the second person in whom he confided. Relieved that the changes he'd seen in his boss had an explanation, he urged Thompson to see the White House Doctor.

Thompson refused: *The doctor was an appointee of the previous administration. He might even be in on it.*

Reuben knew then that he had a problem: what had manifested in the President's dream-state had now been pulled into his waking reality. So he picked up the phone and rang me.

Reuben and I have known each other a long time. We've served together and fought together.

Two years after returning from Iraqi Freedom, George W. Bush's war against Iraq, he landed a job in Washington as a security adviser to Senator Tod Abnarth, an old friend of his parents, and the first politician to back Thompson for the White House.

For as long as I've known Reuben he's been ambitious, but I don't hold that against him. He's motivated by a deal more than fame and power. Like me, his sensibilities have been forged by war, but Reuben's strengths lie in administration – mine in hands-on medicine. After Iraq, we each chose a new path.

For reasons that are still hard for me to examine, let alone discuss, I chose to retrain. I returned to the Uniformed Services University of the Health Sciences in D.C., known as USU, where I undertook a four-year residency, which included a year at Georgetown University. I graduated as a fully qualified physician and psychiatrist.

By then, Reuben's political career had started to take off, so we got together less often.

With a specialism in the treatment of the mental and physical impacts of trauma under my belt, primarily in the military sphere, I returned to active duty. I ended up as the head of the medical facility for US Central Command and US Special Operations Command at MacDill Air Force Base, on Florida's Gulf Coast.

Embedded within the hospital was what I like to think is now one of the premier trauma units in the country, so when I first got the call from Reuben, I wasn't wild about the idea of coming back to Washington. I wasn't wild, either, about working for the President.

Thompson is young, moneyed Texas, clever and unblemished by scandal. He speaks eloquently, and has a picture-perfect family.

His wife, Jennifer, is a strikingly beautiful and successful attorney and a former human rights lawyer. She is intensely proud of her African American roots. Their three kids – five, eight and ten years old – are so stereotypically cute and well mannered they could have won Thompson the election on their own.

It wasn't hard to see what those who'd voted for him had bought into: the promise of a better world, a world without division.

But for my money, and evidently a fraction under half the country's voters, there was something a little *too* slick about Bob Thompson.

So, to begin with, I said no.

Reuben flew down to see me, drove me out to a secluded beach somewhere south of the base, and in the course of a long walk, told me about the breadth of Thompson's ambition and what he wanted to achieve. The dreams, he said, threatened to derail it all, and there was no one else – *no one* – he could trust to see Thompson, to examine him, and not have it leak.

'See him, Josh, see him once, and offer him the benefit of your advice. Of all people, I understand what you had in D.C. – what you had and lost. But it'll only be for a day. Two at the outside. Then you'll be back on a plane and back with your patients.'

So, I flew up, only for a day – two at the outside – to see Thompson; to give him – to give them both – the benefit of my advice.

'One man's paranoia is another man's due caution' remains a particularly helpful adage for anyone in Washington with political ambition, but I felt the President's increasing wariness was most probably adaptive: a means of coping. It wasn't, in my opinion, evidence of anything pathological, like an underlying illness.

For a while, my diagnosis made the President feel better. I saw him breathe a sigh of relief when I told him this, and his health, according to Reuben, improved steadily from that moment.

Inside of two days, I was back with my patients in Florida and Thompson was soon pretty much back to his old self.

But while the nightmares diminished in frequency, they did not go away. And when they came for him, they were brutal.

Reuben flew to Florida to see me again and, after some back and forth, offered me a new deal. The incumbent White House Doctor, an Army brigadier-general who was coming up for retirement anyway, would be let go. If I'd agree to it, I'd replace him. There would be no fanfare; no approvals had to be sought; the appointment was entirely at the discretion of the President.

When I said no this time, he threw Iraq at me.

'You and I do what we do because of what happened over there,' he said. 'Thompson is the real deal, Josh. I swear.'

Whilst campaigning, Thompson had vowed to do away with the machinery of what the previous president called the 'deep state' – that dark, unknowable part of government that exists below the waterline of accountability.

In Thompson's eyes, especially since the war on terror, it had gotten out of control. He wasn't against increasing military expenditure – but wanted to target the causes of conflict, rather than expanding the armory.

In the shadow of the dreams, however, Reuben noticed that Thompson had become increasingly wary of the people he needed to win over for his reforms to take effect.

The dreams seemed to come from a place of genuine fear.

Of our forty-something presidents, four have been assassinated. Almost a one-in-ten hit rate. Not good, statistically or personally.

I'd asked Reuben what exactly he wanted of me.

'To be the President's doctor, Josh – but also to be his eyes and ears.'

When I'd asked him if anyone else thought that Thompson was at risk of assassination, his answer came as a shock: his head of security, a long-time Secret Service veteran, White House Special Agent in Charge Jim Lefortz.

Reuben had worked with Lefortz on the campaign trail. Both ex-military men, they'd quickly forged a strong relationship. Thompson immediately bonded with him too.

After his wife and Reuben, Lefortz was the third person in whom Thompson confided about the dreams.

Christy Byford, his trusted National Security Adviser, was the fourth.

When I accepted the job, I became the fifth.

Reuben, Lefortz and I agreed we would pay special attention to any unusual threats so that if Thompson ever did ask, we could tell him we had them covered.

We'd labeled it *No Stone Unturned*.

Is Thompson the real deal? Is he, as Guido asked me, 'a good man'?

I don't know.

But his tapping into our code for the President's illness demanded my strong attention.

4

THE SQUARE HAS BEEN TRANSFORMED BY ITS BLANKET OF SNOW. Heavy, wet flakes continue to fall from the low overcast sky.

I show my pass, join a small line at the White House's Northeast Gate, and watch the statue of General Lafayette and the federal court building turn white.

To its right, I can make out a group of peace protesters being shifted from their tents by the White House North Fence and held at one of the cordons.

There's a low hubbub of excitement at the gate. My coworkers swap notes about what they have seen or heard as they warm their hands on take-out mochaccinos. I know no one here, so pass through the gate unremarked and make my way across the east side of the North Lawn. There are more uniformed Secret Service than usual in the trees and by the North Portico entrance.

When I finally access the first floor of the Residence, I pass the Vermeil Room with its gilt-framed portraits of First Ladies and the China Room, where, if she were here, it's possible I'd bump into the First Lady, who uses it for informal meetings and receptions.

I hear voices raised, one of them Molly's, as I turn the handle and open the door to my office. There is a look of relief, tinged with concern and possibly exasperation, as she realizes it's me.

She is sitting behind her desk, receiver jammed to her ear, remonstrating with whoever is on the end of the line and the person standing in front of her, too – a guy in a suit with his back to me.

'No,' Molly is saying down the phone whilst looking at the guy in the suit, 'it is not possible to speak to Doctor Cain at this time. No, I cannot give out the number of his cellphone. Requests for interviews have to be directed via the White House press office. Good day to you too, sir.'

As I close the door, the guy in the suit turns to face me. 'Doctor Cain, my name is Joe Seitz. We haven't met before.' He offers a hand.

I hesitate before extending my own, aware that Molly is getting to her feet. She looks angry. I'm not sure how old she is – I'd guess somewhere between sixty-five and seventy – but I do know that she is a fully signed-up member of the Daughters of the American Revolution, which lists the promotion of patriotism and the preservation of American history as prerequisites for membership, and that she is fiercely protective of me.

'Doctor Cain,' she says, 'I'm sorry, but this . . . *gentleman –*' she pulls a face, '– has been waiting here for the past half hour, and I told him—'

Before I open my mouth to tell her it's OK, Seitz jumps right in. 'I'm the Assistant Press Secretary, Doctor Cain. We have had multiple requests to interview you and I was wondering—'

I brush past him. 'I'm not giving any interviews. Sorry.'

'But, Doctor Cain . . .'

I leave him to remonstrate with Molly as I head through to my workspace and close the door. It's exactly the way I left it before the holiday, which somehow feels strange.

Molly calls me before I've even sat down, to apologize for Seitz's intrusion. This time I'm able to tell her not to worry about it. I'll get on to the Press Secretary, whom I've met a couple of times, and ask him to keep the reporters at bay. For the moment, all I need is a list of the appointments I have to keep and those I can shelve or cancel.

She duly obliges.

'I see that you still have your regular evening meeting with Professor van Buren, despite it being the first workday. Do you want me to reschedule?'

I shake my head. Today of all days I am going to need to spend some time with my old mentor. I just need a little space to write up my incident report for Reuben.

When I've finished, I push back my chair and stare across the South Lawn at the Washington Monument, a gray outline in the falling snow. Then I turn back to my screen and do a search for *ground truth*.

I find several meanings. The one that is most on point is: *a tactical situation on the ground that may differ from one that has been identified in military intelligence reports and mission objectives.*

It isn't a term I remember from my front-line service, but I agree with the consensus that Guido was most likely military or ex-military – his bearing and a certain formality in the language he used more than hinted at it. I add this to the ground truth memory.

I give my report one more read-through and am about to hit *send* when the phone rings.

'Doctor Cain? I have a Special Agent Hart in my office to see you. I can ask her to call back.'

I glance at my watch. It isn't yet midday, but it seems like a lifetime since we parted company at the church. I ask Molly to send her in.

In the daylight, her freckled skin has the pallor of milk and her hair seems blacker than black. She's a study in monochrome, but still striking, her cheekbones chiseled, her nose upturned. She spends a few seconds glancing over the Spartan details of my office.

'You OK?' I ask her.

'Sure,' she says. 'I'm fine.' She looks me up and down, then at the jacket slung over the back of my chair. 'You've changed.'

'It came with the stuff I borrowed off one of your boss's deputy assistants. What is it I can help you with, Agent Hart?'

'I need to know what you and the jumper spoke about.'

I show her the email on my laptop.

She scans my note to Reuben before sliding it back to me.

I can't help noticing that her fingernails are bitten.

'This doesn't detail what you actually *said*.'

'My recall is a little hazy . . .' *Because I was twenty meters up with a guy who's threatening to swallow-dive to the street.* 'This is, however, accurate in terms of flow and content. You want to hypnotize me to get the rest?'

'Not necessary.' There's no flicker of a smile. 'I'm intrigued, Colonel. The very last thing you said to me, shortly before you left the crime scene, was to search his body for some kind of list.'

'Did you?'

'Did I what?'

'Find one?'

She shakes her head. 'No. Because there wasn't one. And we looked everywhere. What made you think he'd make one?'

'Because he was counting down while we were talking. I think because he'd been brain-injured.'

'That's a pretty big leap.'

'He had memory problems, which would also account for the stammer. The list would have been some kind of *aide-mémoire*. He was checking points off one by one as he spoke to me.' I raise my hand and extend my thumb, my index and middle fingers: *One, two, three.*

'Please explain that,' she says. 'I need to understand everything you're telling me.'

'Diffuse axonal injury is often fatal. At the very least, it leaves the victim with persistent cognitive impairment, the most common being memory loss, and an inability to form new memories.'

She points to a chair in front of the desk and sits before I can reply. 'OK, so, let's say such a list existed . . .'

'Trust me. There *is* one.'

'Sure. So, how many items do you think were on it?'

'At least three.'

She waits for me to continue.

'First, he asked if I believed in God. I'm not religious, and it was important that I told him the truth, but we managed to get through it. My answer seemed to satisfy him. Item two was the plot to kill the President. He said it was at a highly advanced stage – ready to be carried out unless we did something about it.'

'And the third?'

'I think he was trying to tell me as he lay dying. He made a superhuman effort to do this.' I show her the three middle fingers of my left hand. 'He'd asked me if I was familiar with the term "ground truth". He said that's why he'd come to D.C. and implied, by looking at me, that he'd found it. I have no idea what he meant, but it sounded military – like a confirmation of some kind. A validation. As if *I* was the proof he was looking for.'

'Proof?' She types this onto her notepad. 'Proof of what?'

'That NASA faked the moon landings? Who the hell knows?'

Her eyes flash.

'Sounds as if you're taking what he said seriously.'

'In my business, Colonel Cain, we take everything seriously.' The look on her face hints at something darker: *and given what you do, maybe you should as well.* 'In PIAD we have a methodology. If this list is what you say it is, it would give an insight into his motivations, his thinking. It would also tell me he was calculating, precise—'

'Or obsessive.'

'Yes, or obsessive, and it would raise the whole question as to why this man picked you over everyone else.'

'Yes. But obsessive thinking is subtle. A great deal of mental illness is subtle. Sometimes, there's a paper-thin divide between sanity and insanity. I hate to say it, Agent Hart, but people who are mentally ill – or have a propensity toward mental illness – can latch on to protest causes, internalize them, and then—'

'Your report strongly suggests he *wasn't* mentally ill. And the Park Police and the MPD have no data on anyone with his kind of injuries. Thanks to Director Cabot's *fixation* –' she immediately regrets the use of this word, but it's too late: her rush of blood has made her feelings clear, '– we have compiled an exhaustive database on every single protester that has ever gone near the North Fence, and this man isn't on it. He's absolutely clean.'

She pauses to consult her notes. 'What else did he say?'

I point to my screen. 'That he knew a lot about me, that President Thompson was our best hope, and that I personally would spare no effort to protect him, because it was in my nature to do so. If you want the precise words, I can write them down too.'

'Not necessary.' She picks a paperclip off my desk, places it slowly and deliberately in the penholder next to the phone. 'I just need to know what he said and what he didn't.'

I look out the window, pausing to consider whether I should mention *No Stone Unturned*, but quickly decide against it. I don't want to go down a road that's going to prompt questions I don't want to answer. 'None of those comments were accompanied by the hand gestures, which tells me they were supplementary to the list. If you want a focus for your inquiries, I would strongly suggest you make finding that list your priority.'

She taps on her notepad and slides it across to me: *God. Threat. Proof.*

'If such a list were to exist, is that what it might say?'

I consider the words for a moment. 'Yes. Pretty much.'

'Good.' She gives me a thin smile. 'I'm glad we can agree on something.'

What a prick I must have sounded.

I'm about to apologize when the phone goes. It's Molly warning me that Joe Seitz is on his way back, so I haul myself to my feet and ask Hetta whether she might need any assistance identifying the body.

5

THE CORPSE IS STRETCHED OUT ON THE TABLE, COVERED BY A green sheet that exposes only the head and feet. Kate Ottoway, a highly experienced doctor of osteopathic medicine, kicks off by telling us that death was near instantaneous. The shell narrowly missed the victim's brainstem before dumping the rest of its energy into his skull cavity.

'DJ' Wharton, a bull-necked FBI agent who attended the autopsy on behalf of the Feds and the US Attorney's Office, who are leading the investigation into Guido's death, has already told Hetta that it was a Sierra MatchKing 30-caliber, 168-grain hollowpoint boat-tail bullet: the ammunition used by the MPD's sniper community.

DJ's thick head of hair matches the stainless steel furniture and fittings. He says little, but has not been unhelpful. He's built like a lineman and looks like an old-fashioned gumshoe. There is nothing remotely CSI about him. It's no accident that he and Lefortz turn out to be drinking buddies.

Guido was a healthy thirty-five to forty-year-old male carrying no detectable traces of recreational or prescription drugs or alcohol at the time of death. But there's no hiding the fact that he's really been through the wars, the most visible evidence of which is the knotted, red and purple scar tissue that covers his upper body, face and head.

I have seen plenty of keloid before, but this is particularly livid and as hard as vulcanized rubber. Kate reckons the burn occurred around five to seven years ago, and postdated a second serious injury.

The bullet delivered three impacts: the relatively small entry hole in the occipital bone; the pressure wave caused by the expansion of the bullet within the brain tissue, ripping the top of the head in two; and then the explosive exit wound around the right eye.

His skull was held together by the mask, but effectively unzipped.

She invites us to examine a depressed fracture in the top rear area of the skull – visible as a spider's web of hairline cracks – that caused severe bruising and hemorrhaging to the posterior parietal cortex. From the healing patterns, she estimates the injury to be around fifteen years old. Though skillfully re-elevated by a neuro-surgeon, one of its consequences would have been memory loss.

Hetta glances at me. 'What causes damage like that?'

Kate removes her eyeglasses, takes a moment to massage the bridge of her nose then replaces them. Her face is strong yet fragile, her hair long and prematurely gray. I guess she's in her early forties. I want to ask what made her devote her considerable surgical talents to the dissection of the dead, but I don't.

'It's difficult to be precise,' she says. 'But we're talking a blunt trauma. I've seen injuries like this in car accidents when the victim has hit the dash. It could also have been caused by a pressure wave. An explosion. If that's the case, then he was close to the blast and remarkably lucky to have survived. Fewer than ten per cent of people with severe diffuse axonal injury ever regain consciousness.'

The explosion theory is reinforced by our exchange in the tower, and by what Kate shows us when she pulls back the sheet to expose the torso.

Prominent on the upper right arm is a tattoo, sleeve art, a large, intertwined motif that includes an eagle's wings, a skull, a globe, the Stars and Stripes, and some lettering that's hard to make out where it has blended with the blood that's pooled and congealed in multiple hues of black and blue on the entire underside of the body.

Hetta leans forward. 'No Greater Love . . .' She traces the words with a finger held just above the skin. 'He was a Marine.'

'The tattoo is confirmatory evidence regarding the age range,' Agent Wharton pipes up. 'In 2007, the Corps banned sleeve tattoos – any large tattoos or collections of tattoos, in fact, on the arms or legs. So our guy appears to have joined the Marines prior to 2007 and most likely left – if the burn is anything to go by – around five years ago, having sustained a brain injury along the way.'

'I wish it were that simple. If he sustained the brain injury on combat operations, it's unlikely he'd have been allowed to return anywhere near the front line.' I don't want to sound unduly pessimistic, but at MacDill we treated thousands of veterans with traumatic brain injuries. Half a million US service personnel have returned from Iraq, Afghanistan and other theaters of war in the past two decades with some kind of TBI. 'The dozen or so Defense and Veterans Brain Injury Centers around the country, including the one I established at MacDill, will have records of the injuries. But it will take time to crunch through the data. We should run his DNA through the Armed Forces DNA Identification Lab too.'

The lab has swabbed samples from anyone who's served in the military since 9/11, but their results won't come in overnight either. Which leaves fingerprinting or a visual identification – somebody, somewhere, who will recognize the description of his burns – as the best short-term route. We're back to square one.

I wait for Kate to replace the sheet, but before any of us can look away, she takes the back edge of Guido's scalp between her thumb and forefinger and gently lifts and repositions it on what is left of his skull.

Hetta doesn't move, but Wharton bounces his not inconsiderable weight from foot to foot, as if he is contemplating escape.

With the blood almost drained from it, the knotted scar tissue of the dead man's face reminds me of Halloween masks we used to buy as kids. It's hard not to be drawn to the jagged starfish of bone, flesh and skin that stares back in place of the right eye, though the doctor is trying to direct our attention to something else: a set of small lesions on the surface of the keloid that run around the head, fractionally above the ears and several centimeters above the eyes – roughly the line a hat would rest on. They are barely noticeable, but unmistakably there: six of them, evenly spaced and roughly the size and shape of a dime.

'What do you think made those?' Hetta asks.

'I really don't know – but whatever it was, it went on long enough to leave a lasting impression on . . .' Kate stops. There is no medical vernacular – no language of any kind – to describe what is left of him.

Hart and I walk out into the fading light. It has stopped snowing, but the low cloud seems to indicate more on its way.

As I turn my phone back on, it vibrates with a dozen messages, one of them from Molly, reminding me of the Deputy Chief of Staff's Moscow planning meeting that's about to start in the Roosevelt Room.

The other message I pick out is from Lefortz. He suggests we meet for a drink at the usual place, a sports bar between the Whitehurst Freeway and the Georgetown Canal. I'll go there after I've finished my weekly meeting with my mentor, Ted van Buren. TVB's study is in the Medical and Dental Building, part of Georgetown's Department of Medicine. The bar is a fifteen-minute walk.

Hetta is heading to her office several floors below Cabot's suite and offers me a ride. She is as silent as I am. Perhaps we're thinking the same thoughts. I see the look in Guido's eyes, the blood bubbling in his throat; his effort to signal me with his hand.

The informal term amongst pathologists for what we have just witnessed is a 'human canoe' – a body with nothing in it.

Of Guido's three manifestations of trauma, only his memory lapses could be deduced from the pathology.

I'm missing something, a connection between the brain injury, the stammer and the myoclonus, and it's only when I'm sitting in my office after the Moscow planning meeting that I finally see it.

Shortly after our new trauma center opened, we received a soldier who had been running away from a suspected roadside bomb when it detonated in Sarwan Qala, a godforsaken hole in Afghanistan.

The blast blew him clean off his feet and threw him against the side of a building, which then collapsed on him.

He suffered a severe TBI, and was placed in an induced coma and flown back to MacDill. When we started to bring him out, he began kicking off all the bedclothes. Every time we replaced them, he kicked them off again, as if his life depended on it.

The nurses were quietly infuriated, the doctors baffled. It only stopped when we brought him back to full consciousness. And then we realized he'd been sprinting, as he had been when the bomb had detonated, because his life *did* depend on it. He was returning to his primal objective – survival – when he'd been robbed of consciousness.

Cognitively, he made a near full recovery. But he was left with a reflexive tic in his right leg, because the trauma had imprinted: the messaging had locked deeply in his body as well as in his brain.

For a while, he was rendered speechless, too, but we sorted that out through cognitive behavioral therapy. He was left with a mild stammer. The myoclonus, though, remained defiant, until we treated it subconsciously.

Doctor Mo Kerchorian, a genius I studied with alongside Ted van Buren, had developed a technique that cured his affliction. Some psychotherapists dubbed them 'cell memories'. Part physiotherapy, part hypnosis, it had been right on the edge of the medical mainstream. Mo went on to establish a clinic within the Department of Neurosurgery at the Stanford School of Medicine, part of the Veterans' Association Health Care System.

I glance at my watch. It's coming up to four o'clock on the West Coast. I get three rings before going to voicemail. His youthful, heavily accented voice invites me to leave a short message.

I ask if he had ever come across a Marine on the system, probably from the Appalachian region – Kentucky, West Virginia or Tennessee, maybe – who had been treated for flashbacks that presented as cell memories.

6

I HAIL A CAB ON 18TH STREET AND ASK THE DRIVER TO TAKE ME
to the Medical and Dental Building on the Georgetown campus.
The falling snow, which has started again, forces the traffic to
move slower than usual on the E Street Expressway, obscuring my
views of the Capitol Building, the museums and the memorials.
The Potomac is a wide, black lagoon beyond the lights of the Kennedy Center.

After my combat experience, it was a foregone conclusion that
trauma and PTSD would be my thing, and that at Georgetown I
would receive a year of expert tuition at its renowned Department
of Medicine, where van Buren was the Associate Professor.

His specialism is trauma and cellular level treatment at the
micro- and nano-scales. A dozen years ago, when I arrived as an
ex-military physician ten years older than the other students, a lot
of it was beyond me. But I liked the fact that he thought way outside the box.

TVB was a giant in every way, with a cheerful, ruddy face, wavy
white hair and blue eyes that twinkled beneath an earnest, inquisi-
tive brow. He wore a trademark tweed jacket and red moleskin
pants, and had a habit of sharing shots of Bulleit Bourbon with his
pet students in his Old Curiosity Shop of a study on the top floor
of his Georgetown home. Like the rest of the house, it was piled
high with papers and periodicals, dog-eared textbooks, stuffed
birds and antique maps, many of his parents' native Holland,
which they left hours before the Nazis invaded.

Ted had been born in Boston a couple of years later.

I'd always been drawn to a snapshot – in color, faded with age – that he kept on a shelf behind his desk. It had caught him at a moment when everything must have seemed possible. Ted, arms outstretched, is holding Jo up to the sky, while his wife Susan looks on. His expression, bursting with love, reminded me of the way Eric Abram had looked at Hope on our porch in South Tampa.

Hope had been planting aloes in the front yard with the sun in her hair when she spotted a frail and confused old man across the way. She'd asked if he was all right, and, hands trembling, he'd shown her a scribbled address and a black-and-white photograph.

The address – in our street – had belonged to Colonel Paul Tibbets, the pilot who'd dropped the bomb on Hiroshima. The photograph was of Eric's wife, Lola, whom he'd lost several weeks earlier, after nearly sixty years of marriage.

They'd met while he was in Reno, Nevada, on his way to a remote airfield near Wendover on the Utah border where he'd maintained the *Enola Gay* in the months leading up to the action that ended the war in the Pacific. They'd married pretty much on the spot.

When Tibbets got to hear about it, he summoned Eric to his office. Eric had told Lola nothing, but believed he was going to be court-martialed. Their mission was deep black before deep black was even invented.

Instead, Tibbets put him on an overnight train to Reno with a forty-eight-hour pass and an order to make the most of his honeymoon. It was an act of kindness he and Lola never forgot.

Hope had sat there holding Eric's hand while she told me the story. I knew how she felt about the military, about Tibbets, the bomb and war in general, but right then the poignancy of this old man's pilgrimage – his desire to find the house of the man who'd helped to change his life – was all she cared about. Eric felt her warmth, and so did I.

He started to tell us about the house he and Lola had owned on the beach, close to a point where the waters of Tampa Bay meet the Gulf. Much to his distress, he'd had to put it up for sale, so he could move north and be looked after by his daughter.

He reached into his pocket and showed me the sepia image of a radiant Lola under a bright sun.

'Her hair was blonde and her eyes were this beautiful gray-green, but the guys on the base said I'd found me my very own Rita Hayworth.'

He took my hand as soon as Hope left to get more lemonade. 'I came here to be reminded of what Lola and I had.' His eyes sparkled. 'And I found me another angel. But I guess you don't need me to tell you that.'

Not long after, Hope and I cashed in everything we owned, and with some help from her mother, bought Eric's house.

It wasn't much more than a shack a few meters back from a secluded beach on the point of a causeway, but we loved it. And we told him it was still his to return to, anytime he wanted.

On the three occasions he did come to stay, he never stopped telling us how much he loved what we'd done to the place. How Hope still had Lola's eyes. And how we needed to cherish every moment together, because in a blink it was over.

Hope and I walked the beach there, arm in arm, and swam in the ocean, for which she'd continued to have a longing ever since, as a child, she'd left her native California. And on long summer nights, we lay there in each other's arms, usually beside a fire, and discussed the life we planned to build together.

But that was before the war. Before a lot of things I have spent the best part of the last fifteen years doing my utmost to forget.

I clamber out of the cab, pay the driver and negotiate a path through the piles of shoveled snow. As I cross the threshold of the Medical and Dental Building, I glance up at its classical columns and finely pointed brickwork. I see the glow of van Buren's study from his third-floor window. One of the promises I made myself when I accepted the job of White House Medical Director was that I would see Ted every week. Not that he knows it, but Thompson gets two world-class shrinks for the price of one.

Ted is a polymath, but the mind is his real passion, and many an evening at the dinner table in the rambling brownstone at the eastern edge of the campus had been spent discussing the things that propelled his sizeable frame out of bed every day; none more so than his ceaseless exploration of the nature of consciousness – of what makes us 'us'.

He is currently working on a funded experiment with a device he's developed which uses ultrasound to manipulate tiny vibrations within the brain's neuronal structures – vibrations he believes to be the origins of brain waves, about which so little is known a century-plus after their discovery. He believes that tuning these vibrations will lead to new treatments for a range of neurological, mental and cognitive disorders, including depression and anxiety, two of the core mood states underlying PTSD.

In typical style, he has rigged up a clinical trial at his home. Volunteers for treatment are invited to stay while he monitors the results. He has tried many times, and failed, to explain to me what the treatment involves – all I'm able to remember is that it's required hefty investment from some big-shot venture capitalist and involves a computer developed by a tech start-up in Silicon Valley that crunches the almost infinitely complex data.

Susan is a professor of archaeology, and vanishes into the wilds for weeks, sometimes months at a time, leaving TVB in charge of their two dogs, three cats and a skunk they rescued from a pet store that was closing down on Wisconsin Avenue.

Jo is married to a surgeon and living abroad. The animals and students are their remaining family, in the environment you'd cherish if you were participating in a clinical trial or suffering any kind of depressive illness.

I know, because I was. And I still am.

7

THERE ARE TWO ASPECTS TO SECONDARY DEBRIEFING. THE FIRST IS to get the facts. The second is to ask the victim how he or she *feels* about them. I have told TVB that I am upset, profoundly so, by what happened in the bell tower. But, oddly, I can't tell him why.

'What did you do over the break?' he asks.

'Read. Walked. Caught up on some movies.'

'You've been all right?'

'Never better.'

'I'm serious.'

'So am I, Ted.'

'Any dreams? Flashbacks?'

'None. I'm sleeping fine. And I'm eating. And, not that it's any of your damn business, I haven't even looked at a drink.'

I started to drink soon after the war. Then, after the accident, I became one of those people I'd read about but never treated: a genuine, high-functioning alcoholic. And I must have fooled a lot of people, because I kept on working and no one seemed to notice.

But when I retrained as a shrink, I kicked the booze. I threw myself into psychiatry mostly because I wanted to know what had happened to me, but found, along the way, a desire to help anyone who ever had a traumatic experience, under fire or elsewhere.

And I thought I was doing well, until the morning I shut down.

I had been reading, studying, writing for eighteen, sometimes up to twenty hours a day. I went to bed one night and didn't want to get up the next morning. In the space of a few hours, the world seemed different. I lay with the drapes drawn, staring at the ceiling, for two, maybe three days. When I heard a knock at the door, I told whoever it was to fuck off. When I finally opened it, I was met by the uncharacteristically unsmiling face of van Buren.

TVB had devised his program for burnouts – bankers, lawyers, doctors, politicians, mainly. It didn't work for everyone, but it worked for me. He knew I needed sleep, lots of it, so he knocked me out – not in the sterile, hospital-like environment where most people go to rehab, but in his home, where I could still hear the dogs barking, the phones ringing, meals being cooked.

Slowly, the smell of Susan's freshly baked bread, the sound of TVB's Count Basie records, the drugs, and a desire to make sense of everything that had happened, did what they needed to. After three days, I was well enough to study again. For anyone who bothered to ask, I'd simply been under the weather.

'Perhaps you'll allow me to tell you what I think you're struggling with,' says the man who put me back together. He has lost a lot of weight since I first knew him, but his ice-blue eyes still sparkle beneath those wayward brows. He's wearing a well-worn sleeveless sweater and an old checked shirt – everything you'd want from your favorite Dutch uncle.

'If you set aside the trauma of the shooting, which between us we will deal with, what this man has done is shine a light on you. This would have happened sooner or later, Josh. There is no way as the President's doctor you could hope to stay out of the limelight for long. And, if you'll permit me to say so, placing yourself in the front line in the way that you did today was, well . . .'

He stops short of saying it. There have been plenty of times when I've come to TVB for refuge, but today isn't one of them. I don't want to talk about Guido anymore, nor do I want to talk about Hope or Iraq. I need to stay focused. So I change the subject and tell him – not for the first time – about the conflicted feelings I hold for my boss, the Commander in Chief.

He asks me to give an example of what I mean and I describe Thompson's behavior during the Pope's trip to the East Coast last spring.

After a scheduled visit to a Jesuit seminary in New York City, the President suggested that they should go back inside the church, just the two of them, for a moment of reflection. The Pope accepted and there was an awkward moment for the Secret Service as two of the most influential men in the world disappeared from view.

Then, *miracolo*, a paparazzo, who happened to be on the right floor of the building opposite, snapped an intimate portrait through the window of the two men holding hands as they prayed together.

The picture made the front page of just about every newssheet in the world and the following day Thompson's popularity ratings went through the roof. Two days later he confounded the commentators again by attending a closed conference of leading American Islamic clerics. To the media's infuriation, no insider divulged what had taken place, although there were rumors that Thompson had prayed with them, too.

So, it's very safe to say, not everybody loves him, but some now speak of '*Slick* Bob Thompson' as if he's JFK.

'The President wouldn't be the first politician to plant a vote-catching kiss on a baby's head. And I think it's good that someone, somewhere, has decided that the leader of the free world should be looked after holistically. Even better that the person charged with that responsibility is you.'

I mention tomorrow's appointment. In the six months I've been at the White House, I've met the President three times. He has regular check-ups, of course, but I've promised Reuben I will do them from hereon in.

TVB reaches into a drawer, pulls out a bottle and pours himself a slug of bourbon. 'Your job is to see to it that he functions to the very best of his ability, and in the four or eight years he gets to save the world, that he is as fit as he can be.'

He pauses. 'At the risk of being a little bit pompous, Josh, this befits your oath of office.'

He's right. But here's what I'd really like to ask TVB, if only I could: Does the dream mean Thompson is vulnerable – that he has a twist of paranoid personality disorder – or does it mean that he's a legacy merchant, fueled by narcissism?

Narcissism is the more interesting of the two, because it would suggest a non-classical form of the disorder.

Acquired narcissism, as opposed to the developed variety that forms during childhood, is fueled by fame, money and power. Hitler had it. It's also known as the God Complex.

A God Complex is neither here nor there if you're a rock star or a Hollywood celebrity. But if you hold a briefcase full of launch codes, it's a totally different scenario.

The night of the New Year's first working day, in the aftermath of a winter storm that's closed many of the city's streets, there's only a handful of people in the Blue Barge, Lefortz's local, a seedy throwback with a wood floor, a jukebox, a couple of pinball machines and staff who don't give a shit.

Lefortz is sitting in the corner. He slides a bottle of water at me.

Despite the best efforts of the double-glazing, the drone from the overpass drowns out the Rita Hayworth movie playing on the TV above our heads.

He chinks my glass and takes a pull of his beer. 'You all right?'

I nod. It's been a long day, and from the look on his face I can see that he doesn't want to be here any more than I do. I ask him what Cabot wanted to speak to him about after the meeting.

'Well . . .' He tugs at the tip of his moustache. 'He sure has a fuckin' bee buzzing around in that darkly suspicious bonnet of his.'

'Who was the jumper, Jim?'

'MPD still don't know. But they're working on it.' He shakes his head. 'You know what they say about this place. Too damn small to be a state, but too large to be an asylum.'

I nod. Something like that. I tell him about the many uneasy feelings I have, not least Guido's use of *No Stone Unturned*.

'A common enough expression.'

'But it was like he knew me.'

'Well, maybe he did.'

I shake my head. Burns or no burns, I remember every single one of my patients.

41

We sit in silence for several moments. I know Lefortz. He won't admit to being troubled, unless he can quantify it with names, dates and places. But he is. It's all over his face. I'm about to ask him which of the four investigations into the shooting is likely to report back first, when he asks me about Hart.

'She's . . . intriguing.'

He laughs. 'And then some.'

'Where'd you come across her?'

'She used to be in Presidential Protection. Got herself into some trouble, which I helped to . . . resolve. Transferred to the intelligence division. She's a one-off.'

'Why?'

'Because in this city of monuments to power and loss, Josh, she's about the only person I've come across I can trust.'

He looks at his watch. 'We just got word. Thompson's on his way back.' He drains his glass and sets it down on the table. 'Got to go.'

There's more snow coming and he needs to assign Thompson extra security because of what's happened. It's going to be another long night.

'Reuben's going nuts,' he says. 'And it's my ruby wedding on Wednesday.'

He gets to his feet.

'Why, Jim?'

'Because we've been hitched forty fuckin' years.'

'Very funny.'

'Why did I ask to see you?' His smile disappears. 'Because I'm sorry about what happened, Josh. If I'd known, I'd never have . . .'

He doesn't finish. As I watch him go, I think about those rumors. Lefortz's deeply lined face masks things I haven't seen in him before.

If it is true he was at the Oklahoma Building, only now do I gain some insight into some of the truly terrible things he must have witnessed.

8

I FULLY INTEND TO DO SOME WORK BEFORE I GO TO BED.

Three weeks ago, shortly before the holiday, Thompson announced his administration's determination to forge better relations with Russia and its new president – a bold play, given the contempt with which every spook, diplomat, soldier and politician holds what they have come to stand for these days. So I now have to ensure that the medical safety nets are in place for a Moscow summit in April. My team has drawn up a shortlist of hospitals capable of treating the President in an emergency, and tomorrow I'm due to discuss the protocols with Colonel Dmitri Sergeyev, their defense attaché.

I flip open my laptop and catch up on the damage inflicted by the storm: the counties left without power around the capital; a train that's derailed somewhere south of Baltimore; Thompson's impending return to D.C., just announced, following the re-opening of Joint Base Andrews and the city's airports; and, of course, the Guido shooting.

The chief of the MPD announces what everyone else seems to have known for most of the day – that, pending the results of ongoing investigations, the MPD's actions are '99.9 per cent likely' to have been responsible for the death of 'the peace protester' and that a single tactical officer – not the entire squad, as had been tweeted earlier – has been suspended while the inquiries continue.

There's a smattering of foreign news. A bomb has gone off in

Oslo, stock markets all over the world have been veering wildly on the year's first day of trading, and China has unveiled a solar farm the size of a small city.

The Middle East remains ablaze, with several moderate Arab countries teetering on the edge of conflict as warring factions in the remainder of the region continue to tear each other apart.

American warplanes have bombed a terrorist camp in northwest Africa . . .

It's coming up to 2 a.m. when I shake myself awake.

I step into the bathroom, splash my face, run my fingers through my hair, and marvel at how so much can be going on behind my eyes that the world never gets to see.

I move – as I do on restless nights – to the smaller of the two guest rooms and push back the door.

The portrait of Jack is mounted on its easel. Hope never got to complete it, but captured the essence of him as he was in the days before his death – quiet, composed, still. His shoulder-length hair is the color of gunmetal, and his old Shawnee blanket is wrapped around his shoulders. An ankh, the cross with a loop beloved of the hippy community, is hanging from his neck at the end of a leather cord, alongside his 'tree of life', framed within a circle, and a star, also in a circle, which he told people was some kind of Native American good luck charm. Hope depicted the three pieces of jewelry in intricate detail, unlike the rest of the painting, so they always catch my eye.

With his clapped-out Chevy Impala, they amounted to his sole possessions, aside from the clothes he stood up in. Well into his sixties, Jack hadn't carried an inch of slack. He was part Shawnee on his mother's side, and for all his kindness and otherworldliness, there was something hard and primal in his spirit, too – something of his ancestors.

He'd grown up on a reservation someplace in the Midwest and taken refuge there after Vietnam, until the day he'd climbed into the Chevy and found his way to the care home owned and run by

Hope's mother in Pennsylvania. He soon became part of Pam's furniture – a Mr Fixit who did the books, paid the wages, mended the electrics and tended to the yard.

Over time, he also became Hope's surrogate dad, and taught her how to paint. I didn't think there was anything going on between him and her mom, but seeing them together, you could be forgiven for disagreeing.

Standing there in front of Jack, I can still smell the oil and the paint thinner and see Hope, too, as she was the day she began work, standing on the porch she used as a studio when the breeze off the ocean allowed.

I came home early, snuck in the side gate and made for the fridge we kept by the hot tub, where three or four beers would provide the prelude to oblivion.

But something about her that day had made me stop and catch my breath. Something about the way her hair caught the wind and the light. Something about the way she was focusing on the brush-work, head tilted to one side.

It was like seeing her for the first time.

She was crying, and smiling too. As if, in the midst of that stillness, she was having a conversation with him.

Tattered and leached of almost all its color – except around the border where the green and yellow threads in the running motif seem as vivid as the day they were stitched – Jack's blanket is now draped on the back of a nearby armchair. I haven't been able to bring myself to throw it out.

A part of me is tempted to go and sit in the chair, to wrap myself in it and conjure up Hope's serene presence; to see if I can drift back to sleep as I gaze at her finishing Jack's unfinished portrait.

But I head for bed instead, where the dark will cocoon me until another day begins, another day when the thing that I *do* thank God for – my work – stands between me and the mind-numbing relief offered by the Triazolam in my bathroom cabinet.

*

I have no idea how long I have been out when my phone goes.

It takes me a second to realize where I am, a beat longer to focus on the screen, the time and the caller ID. It's Reuben. And I've been asleep for less than an hour.

'It's happening again,' he says. 'How long till you can get here?'

He doesn't do panic, but there is an edge to his voice I haven't heard in years.

9

LIGHT SPILLS FROM THE ELEVATOR INTO THE CENTER HALL ON the ground floor of the Residence. Reuben is holding it open with one hand, with his phone in the other. He hangs up as soon as he sees me.

When there is business to attend to, he sleeps in a room next to the east stairwell, across the hallway from the Master Bedroom. He is the only member of the inner circle allowed on the second floor at night.

The three children are looked after by Jennifer's widowed mother. When the dreams took hold, they were all moved into the East and West Bedrooms on the third floor.

The door slides open. I turn left and immediately right. The drapes in front of the half-moon window in the West Sitting Hall are backlit by the mute glow of the West Wing. The decor is Texan Chic, a reflection of the pastel hues of the Lone Star State.

The President is sitting on the edge of the bed with his head in his hands. He seems to be staring at his feet. His chest rises and falls rapidly. His T-shirt is ringed with sweat. The bedclothes lie in a heap on the floor. His head must have barely touched the pillow when it happened. Was his lack of sleep following the flight up a factor in this?

The First Lady emerges from the bathroom, dressed in a red silk robe and holding a glass of water. Her hand is shaking so badly that several drops spill on the carpet by her husband's feet. Without her make-up, she looks frail, ghostlike and ten years older.

I sit beside Thompson and take hold of his wrist. 'Mr President? Joshua Cain here. Your physician, sir. Can you hear me?'

I gently raise his head with my free hand. He holds it there like an automaton. His eyes are open, but glazed. The seconds tick by on my watch. His pulse is high, but regular. One hundred forty beats per minute, ten short of 'severe'.

I listen to his heart, then take a flashlight out of my case and shine it in both eyes. They move from side to side, metronomically. The good news is that the pupils are equally sized, which means his oxygen levels are as they should be. His heart is functioning normally; he has experienced no irregular or missed beats.

I switch off the light and snap my fingers. Thompson remains listless. He stares straight ahead.

'Mr President? I need you to tell me where you are and who is in this room.'

'Water,' he whispers, so softly I barely hear it.

Jennifer raises the glass but his eyes remain unfocused. She lifts it to his lips, but the water dribbles down his chin.

Wherever he is, the drink that he needs is there, not here.

I take the glass and put it on the floor. I then look her in the eye and tell her that, frightening as this is, her husband's life isn't in any danger.

I slip a cuff onto his arm and pump up the pressure. I wait till I get a reading. It's 150 over 100: officially Stage One hypertension, just short of Stage Two. Stage Three is when you call the paramedics.

Thompson is a fit man of forty-three, with little excess weight. His normal BP is 120 over 80. I release the pressure and remove the cuff. I ask him again, but still don't get a response. His head drops onto his chest. His eyes close.

I take my flashlight again, lift a lid, and get the same rapid eye movement. I glance up when Reuben touches my arm. 'He's in REM state – still dreaming.'

Reuben swears softly. The President had been doing well – three months, by my count, of good, solid sleep after that initial bout.

I haven't seen anything like this before. It's like a night

terror – the thing kids get when they are awake but not awake and paralyzed by something only they can see. Night terrors, however, are different from dreams. They occur when you wake abruptly from non-dream sleep. Thompson is very clearly in dream sleep.

Jennifer isn't handling it well. I'm about to suggest to Reuben that he remove her to the living room when Thompson's body shudders and his left arm flails so violently that the back of his hand hits my face.

The President throws back his head, his body arches and every muscle goes taut. His eyes open and he stares at the crystal chandelier above the bed. The muscles of his face contort.

He takes down a lungful of air and hurls himself backward, but not before he has expelled a single word at the top of his voice across the room.

'*Bomb!*'

I suspect that the dream is an expression of a deep-seated fear playing out with the intensity of a flashback. Flashbacks and dreams are different animals. Flashbacks are predominantly daytime events; dreams rarely, if ever, incorporate flashbacks. There is very little science on the point where the two meet. I have no idea what's going on, but the clues will be held in the dream itself, so I ask him to describe it – everything he can possibly remember.

Thompson gets to his feet and makes his way to the wing-backed chair to the left of the concealed door that leads to the living room. Jennifer and I remain seated on the edge of the bed. Reuben moves to the stool in front of the dressing table between the windows.

Thompson brushes a strand of his famously jet-black hair away from his startlingly blue eyes. 'The first time I'm aware of the danger is when this guy stands up. Beard, dark hair. He's several rows back from the stage. There are hundreds of people in the room, thousands maybe. The dream starts – my memory of it, at any rate – when I'm close to finishing my address.

'My mouth goes dry. I look at the lectern and I know I'm there. That this is for real. There's a glass of water in front of me and it's so cold I can see every drop of condensation. It's *that* real. I try to reach for it, but I can't. I'm frozen to the spot. There's absolutely nothing I can do.'

He drops his gaze, plays with his wedding ring.

'Suddenly I'm up near the roof. Everything is laid out below: the auditorium, the audience, the stage, the lectern. I can see me too. But I'm not *just* an observer. Everything I'm feeling onstage I can sense from that elevated perspective: the air conditioning chilling the sweat on my brow; my mouth bone dry. My fear. Because I know what's going to happen.'

'And what's that?'

'I'm going to die.'

Jennifer gets to her feet. 'Does he *have* to do this now?'

'It's better that he does, yes.'

'Why?' When she met Thompson, she was a human rights law-yer based a few blocks from here. She flashes me the kind of look that must once have decimated her opponents on the witness stand.

'The precise memory of a dream doesn't last.'

Thompson stands up, walks over to his wife and wraps his arms around her.

I ask him what happens next.

'The guy makes his way down the aisle toward me.'

'What's he wearing?'

'A suit. Open-necked shirt. Loose jacket. I'm fixated on the jacket.'

'Because of what it might hide?'

He nods slowly.

'Can you see his face?'

'No, not at this point, because everything now comes to me from this God's-eye perspective.'

'Where's security?'

'I don't know.'

'And the audience?'

'On their feet. Some don't seem to notice he's there. Others are transfixed.'

'They don't react?'

'Not to begin with. Only when it's too late.'

'When's that?'

'When he gets to the stage. Then everything unfolds in slow-mo.'

'How so?'

'There's shouting, yelling. Panic. I'm just standing there, rooted to the spot, staring at this guy, who's now no more than a meter and a half away. I want to speak, but I can't. I'm hypnotized by what I'm seeing – from this view above the stage. The guy looks at me for a moment, then turns to the crowd and spreads his hands wide.'

'Do you see the bomb?'

'No. But I'm imagining straps and wires, duct tape. Some kind of device.'

'Do you get to see his face?'

He nods. 'The guy has these killer eyes.'

'Who is he?'

'I have no idea. I have never seen this man before.'

'And that's when you scream.'

He looks embarrassed, but nods. 'A fraction of a second before he triggers it.'

He takes a step away from his wife and stares into the gilt-framed mirror above the fireplace.

'What the fuck's happening to me, Josh?'

'Nightmares are a survival mechanism, Mr President. Your brain may be running you through a host of imaginative threat scenarios in order to increase your vigilance. It is, in a sense, rehearsing you for something it believes may happen, based on a fear that at present is without form.'

When I look up, the President is facing me again.

'Is that good?' His eyes plead with me.

'It's not *real*, sir.'

'Lincoln dreamed of his assassination. He saw a corpse in the East Bedroom surrounded by a crowd of mourners. The corpse turned out to be his.'

'It's a story,' Reuben says. 'Nothing more.'

51

'He's right, Mr President. Your dreams are unusual in that they have the qualities of a flashback – the sights, sounds, smells, emotions of a traumatic event – except there's been no traumatic event: no guy with a bomb-belt, no killer with an assault rifle, no assassin with a knife.' I pause. 'These are all projections of your subconscious. We need to know what's projecting them.'

Physiologically, the President is OK. From a neurological and cardiovascular perspective, no harm has been done.

I give him a mild sedative – five milligrams of benzodiazepine – and advise him to get his head down, and to cancel any appointments he has before lunch. I give the First Lady a half dose of the same good stuff and advise her to do likewise. I inform the President I would like to check on him during the afternoon. Reuben and I confirm that we'll meet before I do – in his office at three.

I ride the elevator to the first floor and step across the lobby. There's no sign of Molly in the outer office – she won't be in for another hour and a half – so I'm surprised to see the light's on in mine. Hetta is in the chair opposite the window, her back to me. She is scrolling down her iPhone and scribbling in a notebook. A Styrofoam cup rests on the edge of my desk.

She stops writing and looks up. Her eyes narrow. 'If you don't mind my saying, Colonel, you look like shit.'

I thank her for her candor. She doesn't look too good herself, but, unlike Hetta, who seems to filter little between her brain and her mouth, I manage to stop myself from saying anything beyond the obvious. I ask her what she's doing here.

'There've been some developments overnight. First up, they found a partial list. You were right. I was wrong. I owe you one.'

She owes me one, but she's not sorry. 'Where was it?'

I put down my physician's bag and sit at the desk.

'In a drain hole two meters below the floor of the janitor's cupboard. Looks like he set up camp there before he made his move to the tower. They found spots of his blood on the tiles. It was twenty-four to thirty-six hours old. They think he cut himself eating. There was a knife in one of his pockets and, along with the bottle of water and maps of the White House, they found bread-crumbs and what analysis says are strips of deer meat.'

'Deer meat?'

'And traces of ash. When they pulled the drain cover off of the dirty water chute, they found more food debris, and the remains of a partially burned piece of paper with writing on it.'

'What did it say?'

'The top was destroyed. We may be able to get some of it back through analysis. But the fragment that was left said this . . .'

She picks her notebook off the desk and hands it to me.

The handwriting is spidery and it has a backward slope.

There are three words on what looks like the hashed lines of a damp and dirty page from a kid's schoolbook.

Proof.

Mac.

Jerusalem.

'FISH is running a check on it. If he's in there, we'll find him.'

The Forensic Information System for Handwriting database contains the tens of thousands of letters and documents that have outlined any kind of a threat to the Service's protectees.

'We can take a stab at the missing piece, based on what you and he discussed: God and Threat.'

She scribbles on a piece of paper: *God, Threat, Proof, Mac, Jerusalem.*

'Do Jerusalem and Mac mean anything to you – anything at all?'

'No.'

'You're quite sure?'

I begin to feel my hackles rising. It's early and I've had too little sleep. Lefortz had said something about rescuing Hart from trouble. I should have asked, but can only presume it was her mouth. 'Quite sure. I've got a load of work to catch up on, Agent Hart, and you said that there'd been some other developments.'

'There have. MPD has formally identified the guy. They've also charged two members of its Special Tactics Branch – Anders' unit – with his death.'

I see Guido lying on the autopsy table, and hear Kate Ottoway's unambiguous assessment that a single bullet had unzipped his skull.

'Two?'

'It's not yet official, but Anders is going to be charged too.'

Hetta drops her cup into the trash, wipes the ring left on the desk with a Kleenex, and disposes of that too. She takes a bottle of hand gel from her pocket, dabs some on her palm and works it into her fingers. 'Lefortz has a source on the Feds' investigation. No names, but you met him.'

DJ.

I ask her to go on.

'He reckons it's open and shut. Tactical Officer Jimenez took the shot. Says Anders gave him the order. Anders denies it.'

'He's consistently denied it.' I shared the post-shooting debrief in her boss's office – Anders, staring into his lap as he repeated his mantra: that no one gave any order to shoot.

'You saw how he was in the command post. The guy's an asshole.'

I take a seat behind my desk. 'There's audio of this, I presume.'

She nods. 'Special Tactics just upgraded to an encrypted system. The audio's clear. Anders tells Jimenez to take the shot. End of. An official memo will go out within the hour stating that –' she raises her notebook, '– the department's own review process will result in "a thorough assessment of the events that took place so that we may continue to move forward as a professional organization".'

'And the jumper?'

'A guy by the name of Voss. Master Gunnery Sergeant Matthew L. Ex-Marine. Transferred around a decade ago to the Army, where he had been in some kind of special recon unit.'

MPD found him in a DNA trawl on the veterans healthcare register – much quicker than I expected, too.

'Age thirty-seven. Dropped out after two tours of Afghanistan. We're looking for next-of-kin, but he was raised in an orphanage. Never featured in any investigation of a protest group. Discharge papers cite the skull fracture and the burn. I've asked for his full medical records. I'm guessing you'd like to see them too.'

I would.

Hetta slides a printout across the desk. I study it. Matthew L. Voss wasn't a good-looking man before the burn, but he had a face, at least.

'You're sure you never came across him? Maybe in your clinical work?'

'Positive.'

'In the tower, he spoke about *your nature*, Colonel. Why? Odd turn of phrase.'

I think about this. Being a perfectionist, hard on myself, and an inveterate multi-monitor, was *in my nature*, Hope used to say.

I rub my temples. 'I have no idea.'

'You OK?'

I nod. But I have a headache and it's threatening to become a migraine. I'm going to need caffeine – preferably intravenously. So I'm only half listening as Hetta starts telling me of a time she worked in some godforsaken field office way down south.

'When a thing weren't right there, the locals used to say somethin' in the milk weren't clean.' She gives the local accent her best shot, but she's no mimic. Her eyes narrow again. 'Well, somethin' in our milk definitely ain't clean, Colonel, 'cos there's no CCTV footage.'

'Of what?'

'Of our guy. Voss.'

The intelligence division, her department, receives feeds via the MPD's downtown control center from every CCTV network within a fifty-mile radius of the city. From every freeway, every school bus, every Metro and train station, every drug and liquor store – *anywhere* there's a camera.

Nowhere is this surveillance more tightly focused than in a two-block grid around the White House, an area that is picked over in real time for unusual activity. You bend down to tie your shoelaces, artificial intelligence is watching you, conducting a rapid facial pattern analysis against the digital imagery. To get to St John's Church, no matter what direction he came from, Voss would have passed dozens of cameras. Maybe hundreds.

Hetta gives me the name of a sixty-three-year-old preacher she is on her way to see. The Reverend Elliott Hayes is the director of the Georgetown Presbyterian Mission, a charitable shelter.

'A preacher?'

'Yes.'

'Why?'

'Got any better ideas, Colonel?'

A guy who seems to know about my nature.

Who uses an idiom that's shorthand for our sick President.

Who never leaves so much as a shimmer on a CCTV frame.

I get to my feet.

Maybe a priest is just the guy we need.

10

STEVE SITS RAMROD STRAIGHT. IF HE COULD, I KNOW HE'D salute me.

He's wearing a black sleeveless Puffa jacket that draws the eye to his amputated right arm. His head brushes the roof of his make-shift home, a piece of orange tarp suspended from a rope fixed between two trees. Steve is in a wheelchair. He doesn't want to get involved, so the meeting is off the record. I do not know his second name. I don't need to.

The only other things in here are a plastic chair and a shopping cart. The cart contains a plastic bag full of clothing, a prosthetic leg and an American flag. The night-time temperature has been cold enough to freeze the contents of a slop bucket beneath it.

Steve is clean-shaven, with closely cropped black hair, in his early forties, maybe. He calls Hayes 'Isaac'.

The Settlement is a two-hundred-strong community that has sprung up beneath an overpass on a patch of parkland between the river and 26th and K. Steve's tent sits right in the middle of it.

Hetta and I met the Reverend Hayes at a hole in the fence that has been erected around the site by the Department of Health and Human Services.

The whole place is like some Hollywood version of a Civil War tableau: men hunched in the mud and snow, government-issue blankets over their shoulders, staring into the embers of camp-fires. All it lacks is a guy playing a harmonica.

Steve motions Hetta to the chair. Hayes and I crouch by the

opening. The light comes from a battery-operated storm lamp that's running low on juice. It is still an hour before sunrise, but there's a steady rumble of traffic from the overpass.

Steve turns to me before the Reverend Hayes can introduce us. 'You were the guy that tried to talk him down. You were the guy in the tower.'

'Yes.'

'I read you're the President's doctor. That true?'

'It is.'

'*Slick Bob* for real?' He wipes his nose with the back of his sleeve.

'I'm just his doctor.'

'They said you were a combat medic.'

'Also true. What happened to you?'

'My Stryker got hit by an RPG. Mosul, 2004. I was the only one to get out. I was lucky.'

'Lucky?' Hetta says.

'Yes, ma'am. Lucky. I lost an arm and a leg. I cried when I saw the Towers go down. But the tragedy of my life is that I took it as an article of faith that my government knew more'n I did.'

I look to the Reverend Hayes, a softly spoken man sporting a clerical vest and dog collar beneath a plain green, Vietnam-style combat jacket. He is black, earnest and heavy-set, with deep lines in his forehead. His dusting of hair is almost entirely gray. He has been distributing food, water and essential medicines to the inhabitants of the Settlement for the past fifteen years.

At 17.24 yesterday, he called Health and Human Services to report a conversation that a member of his community had allegedly had with the protester.

The call was routed to the Virginia Fusion Center, one of a score around the country to merge intelligence from local, state and national law enforcement, as well as every three-letter agency, to provide threat data on anyone who has the potential to become a 'near-lethal approacher' – someone capable of killing the President.

'Just tell them,' Hayes says gently, 'what you told me.'

Steve takes the roll-up he's laid on the arm of his wheelchair, tamps down the loose tobacco at both ends, gives it a final inspection, and places it between his lips. He leans forward and lights it with a Zippo emblazoned with a blue and yellow unit badge. The 24th Infantry Regiment took a pretty heavy pounding in Mosul. I know, because I was there.

'What happened?'

Hetta leaves the talking to me. She doesn't need to compete with the connection between two combat veterans.

'It was Friday night. Couple nights before the storm. Someone had lit a fire an' it drew a bunch of new people. The guy stuck to himself, but he was watchin' everything. He was wearin' this mask . . . like a balaclava . . .'

He takes down some smoke and exhales slowly.

'The next night he's back. It's late. Two, maybe three in the mornin'. I don't sleep great, 'cos I sleep in my chair. Everybody else has turned in and it's just him an' me and he's starin' at the flames. I ask his name and he tells me it's John.'

'John?'

'Yeah. He says it in this weird way. "I, John", like it really means somethin', which is kinda funny, 'cos it's only afterward, when I see the news, I realize he's done given me the name of the church. But everybody here's runnin' from some shit or other.'

'What did you talk about?'

'He tells me he's ex-military, that he's picked up some injuries and that he's sick to shit with the fact we're fightin' countries we can't fuckin' spell. Well, I heard it all before. I may not like the government, but I love my country. When I ask him what he's gonna do about it, he tells me somethin' people are gonna remember. He's gonna mount a protest at the church where the President goes. He wants the world to know.'

'To know what?' Hetta asks.

'That things can't go on the way they bin goin'. That things gonna change.'

I glance at Hetta. 'Did he say in what way?'

'Yeah. In a way the whole world gonna know about.'

'I mean details.'

He laughs. 'Too fuckin' many. He tells me everything. He's gonna reach it through the sewer system. He's made a study of it and knows which parts to use and which parts to avoid. He's got tools for bustin' into the church. He knows how to cover his tracks. Ya-de-ya . . .'

He looks at me and holds up his hands. 'I'm sorry, man, truly I am. I shoulda told Isaac sooner, but I thought the guy was fuckin' nuts. I didn't know he was really gonna do it.'

Steve is a proud man whose world fell apart when his wife left him, taking their two children with her back to Columbia, South Carolina. He retrained as a bookkeeper, but he's been at the Settlement for three years now. He prefers it to the shelters established by the Mayor in a bid to rid the capital of its ten thousand homeless. They're rife with every kind of abuse, which gives an edge to my next question.

'The Reverend Hayes said that the guy made you touch him. Is that true?'

'Yeah. That's when I knew he wasn't just crazy, but *weird*.'

'Describe what happened.'

His smoke has spluttered out. He lights it again.

'When he's done tellin' me what he's gonna do, he gets up, walks over and squats down in front of me so we're eyeballin' each other. I have no idea what this guy is on, really I don't. But those eyes jus' keep watchin' me. And then, very slowly, he takes off his ski mask. Well, I seen some combat injuries . . .'

I wait for him to collect his thoughts.

'I look at him for as long as I can and then, when I can't stand it no more, I turn. He grabs my hand real hard an' pulls it to his face an', like, holds it there . . . against the knots an' the scars. I ask what the fuck he thinks he's doin' and he just stares back at me and says: "Remember".'

'Remember?'

'Yeah.' He shakes his head. 'Like I'm ever gonna forget.'

Hetta and I stand on a spit of land overlooking the river between the Settlement and the Watergate complex.

To the south, the early morning commuter traffic is building on the Theodore Roosevelt Memorial Bridge. To the northwest, the face of the Healy Clock Tower shines across the Georgetown University campus. The snow on the rooftops gives the oldest part of the city a fairytale quality I've never seen before.

Scarcely a breath of wind plays on the river's surface. The reflection of the lights from Arlington and Rosslyn is disturbed by a lone rower who's plotting a course against the current toward the Alexandria Aqueduct. Blocks of ice bob in the reeds by the water's edge.

Hetta is convinced Voss entered the capital by boat – most probably a collapsible canoe. She's asked Lefortz to authorize the Service's uniformed branch to search for it along the riverbank, called for a review of all imagery of the river, and for a forensics team to survey the culverts, sewers and drains between the Settlement and the church.

Four or five miles away, the Potomac hits open country. It would have taken Voss a couple of hours, if that, to navigate to where we're standing, ditch the canoe and make his way to the Settlement and then the church.

The corridor is normally well served by CCTV: the systems within the Watergate complex, the Kennedy Center, and an office building that backs onto the land beneath the overpass all provide a measure of interlocking surveillance.

Camera systems regularly go U/S, but the pattern-mining software the Service uses showed the glitch at the office block had never previously occurred, and was momentary: a few hours at most, but long enough for Voss to have made his way from the river to the camp. So either it was accidental, or it was orchestrated.

When she asks me what I make of Steve's story, I tell her I just know the assessment I filed for Reuben – that the discussion Voss and I had was lucid and cogent and, on balance, that he probably wasn't mentally ill – may need revision.

'That thing he made him do was almost ritualistic,' she says.

'Or it had religious significance.'

'And that "I, John" shit. That's pure Koresh.' She looks at me. 'You're the shrink. What do you think?'

I cast my mind back to the list she showed me: *God, Threat, Proof, Mac, Jerusalem.*

Memory, or the lack of it, is important to this guy.

'How well you remember something depends on how quickly and clearly your senses take in an experience. Seeing and hearing are key, but so too are smell, taste and touch. Getting Steve to run his hands over his burns – especially burns to his face – is powerful because there's revulsion there. You saw it. Revulsion runs deep. It imprints.'

'Why would he do that?'

'I don't know yet. I also have no idea why he would outline all his plans to a total stranger.'

I look at my watch. It's coming up to seven o'clock. I've a couple of hours to prepare for my appointment with Sergeyev. It doesn't pay to keep the GRU waiting.

But there's something Hetta needs to show me first.

Marty is a contractor security guard whose duty belt comes with a can of mace and a baton in its holsters. He's a heavy-set lunk in his late forties with impressive jowls and bushy sideburns.

'I think we had an open circuit issue,' he says. 'It's done that a few times.'

Hetta scans the rooftops. Dawn is breaking. An aircraft dips behind the Washington Monument on its descent into Reagan. Fast food wrappers skitter across the concrete floor of the empty fourteenth-floor office suite behind us. 'I need for you to explain to me what that means,' she says.

I know Marty is grating on her nerves. He grates on mine for sure. But Hetta's irritation is palpable. I can feel its heat.

'The tamper circuit is a loop that connects all the infrareds, the shock sensors, the pressure pads and the magnetic contacts throughout the building.' He rearranges his ill-fitting, company-issue pants by digging into the crotch and giving it a sharp tug. 'It does what it says on the can. Anyone tries to fuck with the system, the alarm goes off. But occasionally, because ours is brand new and the building isn't finished, it goes open-circuit – the current stops flowing and it trips.'

This triggers an alert at the dispatch office within the MPD's First District station on M Street.

'Was it or wasn't it a false alarm?'

Marty pulls a face. He doesn't want to be categorical. There was no one guarding the building Sunday night – there isn't on weekends – but the system is also linked to his firm's HQ, so it would have prompted a response. Somebody would have come by and swept the offices.

Once the guy was satisfied it was a false call-out, he would have keyed in his user number, killed it and reset the system. Somehow or other, there must have been a gap between the alarm registering down at the First District and its reclassification as a false positive. Which is how it came to be picked up by the Secret Service's pattern-mining algorithm.

Marty tilts his oversize head. His gaze shifts somewhere beyond the balcony. 'I guess MPD had other things on its mind that night, what with that shooting over at the church.'

Lefortz woke me in the middle of the storm. A quarter of four. Six and a half hours after the system tripped.

'And you say your colleague would have *physically* swept the building?'

'Yes, ma'am, he surely would have.'

Hetta gestures to the shell of an office behind us. 'But not these offices, because these offices are unoccupied.'

'Come *agin*?'

'I want to know whether somebody could have physically accessed the building – these floors up here – while the system was in reset mode.'

Marty doesn't hesitate. 'There are multiple sensors, including a hundred or so CCTV cameras, from the ground floor all the way to the roof. It's physically impossible for someone to get up here without being detected, even with a malfunction in the tamper system.'

'How come?'

'Because every camera has a battery back-up unit; they continue to record throughout.'

Hetta lets him know she's going to pass by later so she can examine the footage, then instructs him to leave us alone. Marty doesn't need to be told twice. He takes off like a whipped dog.

As the sun comes up, it hits the gold cupola on top of the bell tower, two hundred fifty meters distant. I walk out onto the balcony. It offers a clear line of sight to the church. Police tape crisscrosses the portico. Lights burn within the tower. Forensics teams are still at work inside.

Again I ask myself: why?

St John's, 'Church of the Presidents', is a stone's throw from the White House.

Why did Guido – *Voss* – pick it rather than the fence by the North Grounds for his protest? A protest that wasn't a protest but a warning.

I scan the area between the church and the tall buildings across the street.

'Hetta? What's over there?'

She comes and stands next to me.

'Next to the labor union? Offices. Nothing special.'

'In the tower, he looked at them. A number of times.'

'So?'

'Where was the sniper?'

'There were multiple snipers.'

'The guy who shot him.'

'Not a part of my jurisdiction, Colonel. And the official report isn't in yet.' She looks at me. 'Why?'

I outline the facts, such as they are:

- Voss was killed by a single bullet.
- We know where that bullet came from.
- Anders has denied giving any order to shoot.
- We appear to be dealing with a loner, who knows some things about me and is obsessed with the President.
- And he may or may not have been crazy.

A cold wind blows up from the street.

But here's the kicker: Voss couldn't have been in two places at once – the church *and* Marty's brand new office building.

And if he had an accomplice, the 'sad loner' piece flies out the window.

11

I'M HAVING A MORE GROUNDED CONVERSATION WITH A RUSSIAN military intelligence officer than I've had with anyone else in the past twenty-four hours.

Before getting down to the business that has brought me here, I study the framed pictures behind Sergeyev's desk. Of Putin. Of the new Russian president. Of Sergeyev looking slim, tanned and Soviet-heroic in his uniform – with Fidel Castro. With his family at Walt Disney World. Smiling at the camera through a cloud of cigarette smoke as he sits on the back of a tank, with cam cream on his face and an AK-47 in his lap.

If the pictures paint a thousand words, I still have no idea what they're trying to say. Whether he's old guard or a visionary reformer like his energetic new president.

I point to the photo of his family and compliment him on his pretty wife and his blonde, blue-eyed daughter and son.

'Do you know how much a nurse in Moscow takes home every month?' he asks.

I place my cup on the edge of his desk. His eyes are almost turquoise, his hair quite black.

'I don't, no.' I glance again at the photo. 'Is your wife a nurse?'

'She used to be. The answer is about eight hundred bucks.' He leans forward. His tendency to use slang when he shouldn't under-lies, I think, a desire to impress me. He doesn't need to. His English is exceptional.

'You know what a *doctor* gets? No, why should you? Around

sixteen hundred a month. Two grand, if he or she is really lucky. I'm trying to give you a little context, Colonel, before your visit.'

He leans back, adjusts his cufflinks and straightens the lapels of his blue Armani suit.

'It goes without saying, Colonel Cain, that we want the President's trip to go well and hope that it will lead to an entirely new era of cooperation between us. President Thompson is an interesting man. And yet we feel we still know so little about him.'

His eyes reflect the sudden drop in temperature.

'I have been tasked by my government with facilitating your visit. Your visa has been approved by me personally and I will ensure that the things we discuss and agree will be implemented.

'You and I know that, whilst there are two or three hospitals in Moscow that might conceivably be acceptable to you and your president, I know this is a purely cosmetic exercise. If, God forbid, there is a genuine medical emergency while President Thompson is in my country, any necessary procedures will be performed on *Air Force One*.'

This isn't what I expected. In the silence that follows, Sergeyev presses a button on an old-fashioned intercom and speaks to his assistant, who I can hear tapping away at her keyboard in the outside office. A moment later, she enters and replaces the silver coffee pot on his desk with another.

'So,' he says, when we're alone again, 'come to Moscow. Review our hospitals. We can, between us, come up with an acceptable list – the Burdenko General Military Hospital, the City Clinical Hospital No. 50 and the American Medical Center on Prospekt Mira, for example.'

He pours two more cups of black coffee. As he hands me mine, he asks what I think of the threat of Islamic terrorism that plagues our two countries and whether, as a military man myself, I believe the administration's Roosevelt-like policy of speaking softly and carrying a big stick will bear fruit.

I know he's questioning how Thompson's pre-election pledge to restart a Middle East peace initiative sits with wave after wave of well-targeted and highly successful air, land and sea strikes by our military against jihadi terror cells from Libya to Afghanistan and Lebanon to the South Sudan, while diplomats shuttle between Cairo, Tel Aviv, Riyadh and Tehran. The policy has attracted criticism from the Russians, which, in turn, has angered a good many people here, given their record in this same area.

Part of the reason for Thompson's visit to Moscow is so that he and his young Russian counterpart can reset their compass.

'Colonel, contrary to what most people might think, I don't have day-to-day dealings with the President. I see him when I need to, and I'm happy to report that, as he is in robust good health, I really don't get to do so that often.'

I pause. 'And, even if I were able to ask him about such things, he wouldn't discuss them with me.

'But what do *I* think? I think that the President's visit is a good thing and it will be a great success. I also want to thank you for your candor, and look forward to doing business with you.'

I get to my feet and smile broadly. He does too, giving me a glimpse of a shiny gold incisor.

He stands, and grips my hand warmly. 'The President is very fortunate to have a doctor who so selflessly puts himself in harm's way to protect him. I trust you are unscathed by your experience yesterday.'

I'm surprised it's taken him quite so long to mention this. 'I am a psychiatrist as well as a physician, and get to see many trauma victims.' I glance at the picture of him smoking on the back of the tank. He looks at it, too.

'Chechnya?' I ask.

'Yes.'

'Then you know exactly what I'm talking about. Yesterday's incident was, sadly, another reminder of the price we pay for conflict.'

'Quite,' he says. 'Well, I wish you the best of luck. I look forward to seeing you in Moscow. *Do svidanya.*'

He comes round the desk and calls out in English to his petite blonde secretary to escort me back to the embassy's vault-like reception area, where she will arrange for a cab to take me wherever I want to go.

I thank them both, but ignore the offer and wander out onto Wisconsin Avenue.

It's a fine morning – blue sky, bright sunshine, the snow crisp and crystalline – and, even though it's a little over a mile and still cold, I decide to walk to the Woodley Park-Zoo Metro station.

I read and process my messages on the way.

I have one from Reuben and several from Molly about appointments and meetings, as well as a missed call from a 650 Bay Area number.

Mo.

I listen to his voicemail. Born here to Turkish-Armenian parents, he has a thicker accent than Sergeyev's, and all I really catch are the profanities. I call him back.

'Josh, fella? My God, I'm talking to a fucking rock star.'

He laughs loudly.

'Listen,' he says, getting straight to it, 'about that guy. The guy you called about? On the news?' He hardly draws breath. 'The description you gave me – Marine, brain injury, stammer, the age range and the place he's from, which is West Virginia, by the way – it can only be one person. You were right. The injury that Gapes received to the skull produced a severe cell-memory—'

I interrupt him. 'Say again.'

'The injury he received to the brain. I said it produced a severe cell-memory reaction.'

'No. His name, Mo.'

'Sergeant Duke Gapes.'

I hold the phone a little closer to my ear. 'That's not the name put out by the MPD. They said his name was Voss.'

'Well, then, they're bozos.'

'They identified him through his DNA.'

'They're wrong.'

'You're sure?'

'I was the guy responsible for his treatment, Josh.'

I double-check I heard him right.

'TVB always said you were the natural and I was the guy who had to sweat my nuts off to keep up. Listen to what I'm telling you. Gapes is – *was* – a Marine sergeant who got blown up by a mortar in Iraq. He was a good-looking guy, too; nothing like that thick-set dude they released the picture of.'

'He was badly burned, Mo.'

'When I treated him, all he had was the brain injury.'

'When did you treat him?'

'Twelve, maybe fifteen years ago. We discharged him back east, to a veteran rehabilitation center in Maryland.'

'No doubt?'

'No doubt at all.'

I wait.

'Like you, Josh, I'm an anally retentive son of a bitch and I took the liberty of blowing up the picture they released. The guy in the photo's got a coloboma.'

A coloboma is a congenital malformation of the eye. It can manifest as a blemish on the iris, but I've only ever come across it once in all my years of clinical work.

'It's the classic keyhole shape,' Mo says. 'Take a look under enlargement. Then go check your corpse. If it's Gapes on the slab, he won't have a coloboma.'

I'm thinking about what I'm going to say to Hetta.

'Tell me about Gates.'

'*Gapes*. With a "p". The cell-memory issue needed repeat therapy. They gave it to him at the Maryland rehab center on a schedule we fed them from here. But then it went wrong for him.'

'In what way?'

'He was re-recruited to some low-level job in the military. Some place nearby. He flipped out. Couldn't take it. It surfaced in a compensation case. Some lawyer contacted me. Wanted to know if I would testify as an expert witness.'

She was trying to sue the government on Gapes's behalf. She was young, worked for a small-town firm close to where the family lived, a bit of a ball-breaker. 'Distinctive name. Eastern European – with a hint of the mortuary about it.'

Ever since I've known him, Mo has used mnemonics to remember names and places. He keeps telling me I should do the same.

She now works for a notable firm of litigators right around the corner from Lafayette Square.

I hang up.

I elect not to call Hetta, because, on top of the revelations from Marty, even I can't quite believe what I've just been told.

The MPD put out a picture of the wrong guy.

Guido isn't Matt Voss; he's Duke Gapes.

Nobody can be that fucking incompetent, can they?

Katya Dedovic is a good-looking woman in her early thirties with high cheekbones and a neat bob. She's at a table in back where no one is likely to see her from the street.

In the summer I pick up my breakfast here on my jog to work. The food's nothing to write home about, but the coffee's OK. I order two Americanos and sit down.

It's late lunchtime. There's a line of people waiting to be served and the noise levels are loud enough for our conversation not to be overheard.

We shake hands. Hers is very cold. The corporate front she tried on me over the phone is all gone. She looks like she's about to throw up.

'You sure it's OK to be talking about this?'

'Ms Dedovic, I told you. I'm from the White House. What do you want me to say?'

'Duke Gapes's case was a travesty,' she blurts. 'But we fought them and we got justice of a sort. Well, his family did. But if I'd known . . .' She stops. 'Let's just say I was younger and hungrier then.'

I study her more closely.

'You're saying you *wouldn't* take his case on now?'

She stares into the contents of her cup.

I try again. 'You people take on the federal government all the time.'

When I researched her, she'd popped up in a nanosecond. There is only one Katya Dedovic in D.C. Until a year ago, she'd been with a small firm in Heatherfield, West Virginia. Now she's with Collins Lovelock Land LLP, trial attorneys specializing in complex litigation.

'Doesn't matter how old or experienced you are when there's a refusal to declassify the information at the heart of the case you're fighting.' She pauses. 'Plus they terrified the living shit out of me.'

'Who did?'

'The people Duke got mixed up with.'

I wait for her to tell me more.

'Duke Gapes went AWOL because he was traumatized. He'd suffered appalling injuries. What they should have given him was veteran disability compensation alongside his Purple Heart. Instead they gave him a job he wasn't remotely able to handle.'

'After his neurosurgery?'

She nods.

'What job?'

'He worked for the Army's Intelligence and Security Command.'

I hide my surprise. 'What did he do there?'

'He was an office administrator. He worked in their headquarters complex at Fort Meade. Handled its IT.'

'You're sure?'

'He was certainly recruited as part of an initiative to get injured vets back into government work.'

'But?'

'For an office hack, he racked up a lot of air miles. Helicopters, mostly. One of them crashed.'

'How do you know?'

'A judge advocate from their legal team let it slip.'

'So that's how he got burned.'

'Yes,' she says. 'And the apartment.'

She sees my confusion.

'They fixed him up with a place on the Fort Meade site. Part of his rehabilitation. That was when his mother started getting the calls.'

'What calls?'

'He called three or four times to say they were sending him to the desert. Said he didn't want to go. Told her he was scared.'

'They foreign-deployed him – after what happened?'

She kneads her right eye. It was puffy when we started. Now it's red-rimmed too. 'Who knows? The negotiators wouldn't accept it as evidence. There was no trace of the calls and Lou – the mom – has dementia.' She pauses. 'But pretty soon after that, he ran.'

'How much compensation did you win for him?'

'I won compensation for the family. Duke was long gone when I took on the case. He'd been AWOL about eighteen months. Lou came to the firm I worked for then 'cos we were local. She had no money, but she wanted justice. She'd been diagnosed with Alzheimer's. I felt sorry for her. I did things like that then.' Her eyes cloud. 'I had no idea what I was getting into.'

'He never showed again?'

Duke Gapes had a history of mental issues following his combat injuries. She reckoned he most probably took himself off and killed himself. 'That's what I built the case on. After a year in which they told me I'd end up arrested if I persisted, or at the very least with my office sealed by a federal court order, I said I'd had enough. We agreed not to take it to the Supreme Court. We took their cash – one hundred eighty K, just enough for Lou's medical care – and promised it would remain confidential. That was fourteen months ago.

'So, what's the White House's angle? Does it have anything to do with what happened yesterday?'

'I'm not at liberty to discuss that, unfortunately.'

She frowns. 'So, what is it *exactly* that you want?'

12

THE LATE AFTERNOON LIGHT STREAMS THROUGH THE CHIEF OF Staff's three floor-to-ceiling windows.

Unlike his boss, Reuben was born into the Washington elite. His father was intelligent, driven and idealistic. His mother was intelligent, driven, idealistic and rich – a winning combination if you want to get things done here; and Reuben's parents, old-school Democrats, wanted to get plenty done.

By the time Reuben joined the Air Force, his father was already a state senator. Within a couple of terms, he had become the ranking member of the Senate Armed Services Committee. Then, in his early sixties, he dropped dead from an aneurism. Shortly afterward, Reuben left the Air Force to start his own political career. And with his mother's financial backing, and a little political influence, it didn't take him long to make an impact.

Reuben's first boss was Tod Abnarth, who recruited him for advice on military and security policy after the second Gulf War.

Abnarth was a friend of his parents, the senior Democratic Senator from Wisconsin and the most influential member of the House Intelligence Committee – unusual, given that he's a prominent Catholic. But D.C. has, for once, looked beyond its prejudice to embrace him as a doyen of the establishment. Reuben brought enough precision and discipline to his office for Abnarth to bequeath him to a young Texan senator who had his eye on the White House.

As I sip my coffee in front of Reuben's large, mahogany L-shaped desk, I look at a picture of him and Thompson flanking Abnarth in the senator's office, all three of them smiling broadly.

Abnarth is a big, rotund man in his mid-eighties, with a foxlike gleam in his eye; the most skillful negotiator on the Hill. I suspect he filled a hole in Reuben's life after his dad died.

I glance right, to a picture of Reuben and his wife, Heather, at a ceremony to commemorate her doctorate; his two daughters; shots of his mother and father; and several of his political heroes: King, Mandela, JFK.

There's also one of his old unit. Him and his men, assault weapons on their hips, beside a sand-colored HH-60G.

It's an odd thing to put on display, given what happened over there. I guess it must be because, as a recipient of the Distinguished Service Cross, it's what's expected of him, and it signals to Thompson's enemies that the man on whom he relies is no stranger to the sharp end of conflict.

'Hey, Josh . . .'

I turn. I don't know how long he's been standing there. He apologizes for being late, closes the door and flicks off the TV. I sit opposite him, in an armchair by the fireplace.

Reuben leans forward and runs a hand along his jaw. 'Give me your no-holds-barred, professional opinion on Hart.' He pauses. 'It's relevant, I promise.'

I tell him she's capable, methodical and focused, which may be down to superior autobiographical memory. The signs are subtle, but one of them is a link to obsessive-compulsive disorder, and she certainly exhibits some signature traits: reaching for her crucifix when she's stressed; placing the paperclip very precisely in my penholder.

'How do you rate her investigative skills?'

'She's smart. And she doesn't let go.'

He nods. 'That is starting to become a problem.'

'Why?'

'She may be using this investigation to manipulate an agenda.'

'Whose?'

'Her own.'

He reaches into the liquor cabinet beside the chair, takes out a bottle of Scotch and two glasses, looks at me, remembers, and puts one of the glasses back. He pours himself a good, strong measure.

'Just before you arrived, the President went to Seattle to address an engineering convention. Hart was part of the PPD team that deployed ahead of us. A couple of days before we got there they decided to kick back a little.' He holds up his glass. 'There was a lot of this stuff. And things became . . . rowdy.

'Two of the agents swung by her room and asked if she wanted to join the party. She took exception to some of the suggestions they made and got creative with the butt of her pistol. One of the guys lost most of his teeth; the other had to have his right ear sewn back on. Cabot got to hear about it, pulled everyone in, delivered a smack on the wrist to the shift-leader and kicked her sideways. Out of Presidential Protection and into threat analysis. He said it was locker-room stuff and she overreacted.'

'Is that what you think?'

'No.' He pulls a face. 'It isn't.'

'Then maybe I'm missing the point.'

'Cabot was looking to avoid another scandal. Lefortz is bound by his sense of fair play – he demanded he give Hart her job back. But Cabot refused. And now it looks like Hart is tearing up the city to make a point.'

'She may *have* a point, Reuben. There are aspects to the church incident that are really quite troubling.'

'Case closed, Josh, trust me. The police have their man and they've ID'ed the shooter. Cabot hates me and he'd love to get his teeth into Lefortz and Hart. There's unfinished business there. He knows he's using her for off-the-books stuff.'

'Off the books?'

'Things he needs to do that won't attract attention.'

'That doesn't make sense. The tower couldn't have been more high profile.'

'What are you saying?'

'Lefortz is the most seasoned professional I know. I can't

understand why he assigned Hart to me, when there were other agents on duty that night who're better qualified to protect me from some crazed guy in a church.'

Irritation flashes across Reuben's face. 'I still don't get it.'

'It's about trust.'

'What?'

'He told me he *trusted* Hart. That she was the *only* person he really trusted.'

'So?'

'Paranoia isn't something I'd ever have associated with him.'

'All Lefortz wants to do is go home and fish off a levee,' Reuben says. 'Or whatever the hell it is they fish off down south.'

He knocks back his drink. 'The point is, Josh, Cabot senses something's going on. He knows there's more to you than meets the eye. It was all over his face in the Crisis Center.'

He sets the glass on the table and gets to his feet.

'We need to cool this thing down. Please. Just focus on Thompson.'

George H. W. Bush and Ronald Reagan kept potted plants behind the Resolute desk. Eisenhower's drapes were blue; Nixon's yellow. Kennedy liked to sit in a rocking chair and, after 9/11, Tony Blair loaned George W. Bush a bronze bust of Churchill. Thompson's personal touch in the Oval Office is modest but poignant: a photo taken by satellite of Earth from space. It hangs on the northwest wall alongside the portraits of Washington and Lincoln, and it is beneath them that I conduct my examination of him.

I sit next to the President. Reuben sits on the other side of the coffee table.

Thompson's pulse and heartbeat have returned to normal and his systolic blood pressure remains slightly elevated at around 130.

'I would like to prescribe you an anti-hypertensive, Mr President. Prazosin. It's non-addictive and has no side effects. Its primary purpose is to lower blood pressure; it's also highly effective against nightmares. A nightmare is an energetic stream of thought. Remove the energy and the nightmares should go. The medication will help until we find out what's causing them. It will be most effective alongside psychotherapy.'

'Psychotherapy?'

'Yes, sir.'

'I don't know, Josh . . .'

'You and me talking. That's all.'

I look to Reuben for some support, but he keeps his eyes locked on his phone.

Thompson rests his chin on his steepled fingertips. Then he goes and sits behind his desk. He opens a drawer, pulls out a ring-file, walks back and drops it on the table in front of me.

The words *Daily Brief* are prominent, as is the presidential seal and a *Top Secret* stamp.

I open it.

An account of a public execution two days ago in a Yemeni town close to the Saudi border. The executioners were Salafists, extreme proponents of Wahhabism – a Sunni sub-sect. The people they rounded up were Shi'ites, Christians and Jews, and they were given a choice: convert to their particular brand of radical Islam or face execution.

Photographs show a pile of bodies in a mass grave. Men, women and children. Some have had their throats cut. Others have been decapitated.

Thompson taps the file.

'Those bastards started to cut off the heads of those kids in the certainty that their parents would beg them to stop the killing. And, you know what? Not one did. Not a single one. Better to join their children in that mass grave than denounce their religion.

'My parents were Southern Baptists and religion was the single most important thing in their lives. It nourished them until the day they died. But twist faith and it can be utterly destructive. It's the destructive impact of faith that I, we –' he turns to his Chief of Staff, '– that this administration is finally going to do something about.'

I glance between Reuben and the President. 'Wait a second . . .'

Thompson's eyes narrow. Reuben lifts his. I hold his gaze.

'When you told me what this administration wanted to achieve, you never said anything about taking on faith leaders.'

'Why does that bother you?' Thompson asks softly.

'Because it's a battle you can't win.'

'You think?'

'Yes, sir. I do. And it may explain something else.'

'Something else?'

'What happened last night.'

'Last night was an aberration.' He looks away.

'Which makes four aberrations, so far, on my watch.' He'd had nine assassination dreams before my tenure as White House Medical Director, which made last night's the thirteenth.

'You remember what I said, sir, about the brain being a survival mechanism. Well, I—'

'This is not a discussion we should be having here,' Reuben says.

'Agreed.' Thompson attempts a brave face. 'And besides, there is work to be done.' He stands up and returns the file to the drawer.

Fear has its own smell. Someone once told me it was somewhere between shit and spinach. I haven't yet been able to put a name to the scent of denial, but it's coming off him in waves.

Reuben speaks as he scrolls down his phone. ' "Pre-emptive Response", that's what we're calling this. We spend money on the problem before it degenerates into conflict. No more pork-barreling on weapons the military doesn't need.

'We spend instead on technologies that make a difference: robotics, predictive analytics, surveillance. And we plow the dividend into attacking the root causes of conflict: climate change, drought, famine, disease, mass migration, overcrowded cities, terrorism . . .'

I turn back to the President. 'And this is what you're going to announce in the State of the Union in two weeks' time?'

'Thirteen days' time. Alongside a roadmap to a lasting Middle East peace settlement.'

I don't know whether this is genius or insanity, but I can see that his call for a peace conference to which the world will be invited, where religious leaders will have seats around the table, will threaten the trillion-dollar revenue streams of our military-industrial-intelligence complex as well as the power base of local, state and federal politicians.

When I stand, the blood rushes from my head to my feet. The walls of the Oval Office close in on me. Did I give up a career in clinical practice for this? Reuben and I have a lot of history. Maybe I should have left it there.

'Mr President?'

He's scanning a memo Reuben just passed him. He lifts his head. The light glints on his reading glasses.

'In the dream, you were standing at a lectern. You said you could recall every last detail of it, down to the condensation on the glass.'

Thompson twists in his chair, suddenly wary. Reuben flashes me a warning glance.

'Can you describe what else was on the lectern, sir?'

He regards me over the top of his eyeglasses. 'The usual things.'

'I'd like you to describe them, please.'

His expression is somewhere between quizzical and irritated. 'Aside from the glass, a pen. A remote for the projector. And an ink blotter.' He thinks for a moment longer. 'Nothing else. That was it.'

'The blotter, Mr President. Please describe it to me *exactly*.'

'It was leather-framed. Dark green.'

'A presentational, ceremonial kind of thing, to commemorate your speech?'

'Precisely.'

'Was the name of the hotel on it?'

'The logo was clear. It was a hotel conference center.'

'A conference center in Jerusalem, Mr President?'

I don't wait for his answer. I just know.

Back in my office, I ask Molly what appointments I have tomorrow that cannot be postponed, switched or canceled.

We work on my schedule for fifteen minutes and finally iron it out. One of the things I love about her is that she never once asks why.

I tell her that I'm going on a trip, it will take a day, and I'll be on my cellphone. If I'm out of signal, I'll let her know. I'll call in on a landline when I can.

'Doctor Cain?' She stops me as I turn back to my screen. 'Special Agent Hart came by twice during your meeting with the President and the Chief of Staff. She wanted to see you. I said that wasn't possible, but she was most insistent. She . . .'

Molly searches for the right words, and for once they elude her. She passes me an envelope that's been lying on top of her out-tray. The handwriting, in black felt pen, is pure Hetta: precise, neat, economical.

'She said that I should tell you: "Opsec". Does that make sense?' I nod. Operational Security. I sit down at my desk and open it.

Been through CCTV with Marty. The break-in wasn't physical. Believe we have evidence of a second cyber breach. Need to speak with you. Need to speak with Lefortz. Don't call or text. H.

13

PATCHES OF DIRTY SNOW CATCH IN OUR HEADLAMP BEAMS ON A road that seems to unwind forever. The storm stayed east of the Appalachians and as we head west, the snow on the ground all but peters out. The occasional vehicle sweeps past from the opposite direction as we pass through a succession of small settlements. In the glow of the dash, Hetta's face remains a ghostly presence at the periphery of my vision.

She and I agreed last night that we're looking at a case of mistaken identity that's almost certainly deliberate. We met after we left work in the underground parking lot used by the Secret Service on the edge of Lafayette Square.

I stare out the window. Apart from the singing of the tires, there's little sound to disturb my thinking. Hetta doesn't like the radio. She doesn't like music. She was quick to let me know this when she picked me up outside my apartment at 5 a.m. She likes to use drive time to focus.

OK, so let's do that. I crack my knuckle joints and bring my tablet back to life.

I pull up Gapes's medical notes, which she has transferred to me.

The brain injury that Kate Ottoway identified caused Gapes crushing headaches, speech and walking difficulties and an inability to recognize everyday objects when blindfolded. In addition, he was wrestling with delusions and hallucinations, but didn't take well to a prescription of Clozapine, an anti-psychotic.

I scroll down, find very little else, and nothing at all about the evenly spaced lesions around his head. Was he receiving electro-convulsive therapy, perhaps? Did that account for his memory loss?

From the notes, it's impossible to draw any conclusions.

There's no mention of a coloboma either.

After we left the lot, Hetta went back to see Kate. Guido's eyes are blemish free. She and I checked the image put out by the MPD, however, and Mo's right: under intense magnification, you can see it – a small, keyhole-shaped flaw in his left eye.

Gapes's recovery support specialist makes no mention of how he came to be recruited by the Army from the Marines. He or she ought to have. Local Veterans Centers are concerned primarily with rehabilitation.

The fact that the Maryland center was just down the street from the Army's Intelligence HQ at Fort Meade . . . was that a factor, or just happenstance?

I can't escape the feeling that somewhere along the line, these notes have been doctored.

If that's the case, we also need to know what the military holds on Master Gunnery Sergeant Matthew L. Voss. Who is – or was – the guy they tried to palm off as Gapes? I've left this with Hart, though I guess Voss must be dead or something would have come up.

I close the file and open the next.

Boonchatz was set up so rural communities can monitor local news and events, but it has morphed into quite possibly the world's vilest bile and vitriol exchange.

'*Skylar Pyles is nothing but a two-bit piece of white poon trash . . .*'

'*Rylee McKibben has six dirty kids and counting. She spends all her husband's assistance money in bars . . .*'

Boonchatz is giving us a heads-up on Blacksoil, population 4,521, and the third worst crime index in West Virginia. If you're lucky enough to have a job, the median annual income is $23,575. If you're not, chances are you'll be out of work for a good long while.

The coalmines that had sustained the area for 140 years closed down in the late 1990s and the unemployment rate hovers around nine per cent.

On the city's eastern perimeter lies an almost road-free area of the Monongahela National Forest called the Laurel Forks. It's billed as one of the least visited federal wildernesses in the United States, but is less than three and a half hours from the capital by road. Hetta's 4WD Lexus is taking us there on US-48.

I turn back to *Boonchatz* and start reading aloud.

'*Cody Wyatt is the world's biggest deadbeat and a worthless ass druggie dad . . .*'

'*Makaylah Nuckles – let's just say it's not what you know, it's who you blow—*'

'OK,' she says, 'back up. Right there. That's him.'

To many, a connection between Cody Wyatt and Duke Gapes would appear paper-thin at best. Not to the Service, however.

The earliest it is possible to track their association is almost twenty years ago, when Wyatt friended him on Facebook. But we know they attended the same school – Boulder View – and that, during what Katya described as a dark period in Gapes's life, in the years after his father died, they hung out, did what kids in Blacksoil liked to do (and according to *Boonchatz*, still do): drinking beer, smoking weed, jacking cars and racing on the outskirts of town.

A trawl of the NCIC database throws up Wyatt's social security number, state criminal identification number and arrest record.

The Pentagon makes little effort to track down military personnel who abandon their posts in war or peacetime; it simply doesn't have the resources. It's barely able to keep tabs on the numbers. Hetta has pulled the data from the Pentagon's Office of Personnel and Readiness. I had no idea of the scale of it. None. Over the past fifteen years, they've listed in excess of 23,000 people as missing across the four services. The real figure is believed to be twice or three times that.

When the AWOL epidemic was at its height, shortly before our forces withdrew from Afghanistan, a Rutgers University research team set out to discover where people go when they run from the military. Almost eighty per cent of them end up in the area they regard as home.

After thirty days, the soldier's name is dropped from the rolls – the roster of personnel listed as duty-ready – and a federal warrant is listed for his or her arrest. The deserter becomes a felon. But the military doesn't have the personnel to pursue them, so becomes reliant on the civilian authorities.

The truth is, a whole lot of deserters never get stopped for running a red light or pulled over for parking ticket violations, which means they're left untroubled for weeks, months – decades, sometimes.

Gapes's personnel file shows that he was unluckier than most.

Several days after he was posted as missing, a couple of MPs showed up at his mom's trailer in the North Country Acres Mobile Home Park.

When they didn't find him, they looked around town for his known associates.

Cody Butler Wyatt, a thirty-eight-year-old, blue-eyed, white-skinned, six-foot-one, 260-pound male living half a mile away, dinged up in a beat when Hetta entered Blacksoil into the Service's Counter-Surveillance Unit Reporting database.

'Eight months ago, he was overheard in the Coalhole Bar 'n' Grill – a dive on the edge of town near the abandoned railroad depot – making threatening statements about President Thompson.'

She glances at me as we branch off US-48 onto the WV-42 South.

'He said Thompson's campaign pledge to disengage America from the multiple wars it was fighting against terrorism amounted to betrayal of his country. And that now that he was President, the only thing that was good for him was "a bullet through his worthless faggot brain".'

She trots out verbatim what Gapes had shared with me: that 'the plan', whatever it is, was *well planned, advanced* and would be *well executed, unless we moved to stop it.*

Is that what we're dealing with here, she asks me. A bunch of wacko nationalists?

The GPS tells us the dark smudge on the far horizon is the Monongahela National Forest and that Blacksoil lies beyond it.

I push my seat back and ask Hetta where she's from.

'Northeast Philly.'

'Your dad a cop?'

She glances at me. 'My dad a cop?'

'I figured you'd come from a family of them.'

'You going to send me your bill when we're done?'

I smile. 'It's called a conversation.'

Her eyes remained fixed on the road.

'My *brother's* a cop.'

'There you go.'

'My folks ran a bar. Had done since before I was born. Another brother runs it now. It's a family business. I helped out till I went to college.'

'You joined the Service from college?'

'I joined the Feds, then the Service.'

'What did you major in?'

'Computer science.'

Of course. 'Big family?'

She gives a shrug. 'We're Catholic.'

'And?'

'And what?'

'Tell me about them – your family. So, one's a cop and one runs the bar. That it?'

'There's seven of us.'

'Seven?'

'Another brother's got religion – he's a priest. My sister has her own family. And I got two other brothers, both still in school. *That's* it.'

We follow an old railroad and a boulder-strewn river, swollen by the recent rains and melting snow.

Fifteen minutes go by. I try again.

'So, why the Service?'

'When I was a kid, I saw patterns in things. I liked puzzles.'

'*That* was your reason for joining the Service?'

'No. I caught a guy my parents trusted to help them run the bar. He was skimming profits. It made me so mad I swore that's what I would do.'

'Hunt down fraud?'

'Big as it came.'

'So, it was the investigative side?'

'I guess.'

'But you can handle a weapon, too.'

She seems to grip the wheel a little tighter. 'It looks good when there are female agents protecting the President. I was a statistic in PPD's diversity quotas.'

'When Cabot came in?'

'Cabot is *all* about how things look. He doesn't give a crap about the President, honest to God. He was brought in to reform the Secret Service. He delegated the task of protecting POTUS to SAIC Lefortz.'

The silence stretches between us.

'You want to tell me what happened back there?'

She doesn't bother to ask how I know. My information can have come from one of two sources: Reuben or Lefortz. And Lefortz is too much of a gentleman to peddle gossip.

'They were taking bets. The jackpot went to the ape who could fuck me first.' She pauses. 'That was Director Cabot's idea of locker-room fun.'

There's a flash of pre-dawn light in the wing mirror as the road bends to the right. Then it straightens again and the white line unwinds into darkness once more.

14

THE FIRST SIGN OF HABITATION IS A SMALL, OUT-OF-TOWN MALL with a bar, an auto repair shop, a furniture store, a take-out pizza joint, a jewelry exchange and a payday loan facility, arranged around two sides of a parking lot.

We cross a bridge, hang a left and keep the railroad on our right till we find ourselves outside what was once a train depot: a long, low brick building with dust-caked windows, three-quarters of them smashed in.

Hetta pulls up in front of a corrugated-iron maintenance shed with *West Virginia Railroad* stenciled above the concertina doors. There's a steam locomotive out front, graffiti covering every inch of it. Between the shed and a warehouse is a single-story building with a flat roof and flashing signage. The Coalhole is open till midnight, serves beer, burgers and pizza, and is available for social functions.

There is no one around, so we make a U-turn.

Back in town, we turn into a street with a Pentecostal church at one end and a Baptist church at the other. Cody Wyatt's one-story house stands in the middle. It has a swing in the yard and a GMC pick-up with black windows on the drive. The drapes are drawn and there is no sign of life. We park up a discreet distance away.

The database holds a mugshot of Wyatt: a smalltime drug-dealer in a no-hope shit-hole with convictions for domestic battery and larceny.

When the coal company threatened to close down both Blacksoil's mines in the mid-1990s, Duke Henry Gapes Sr, known as Hank, mounted a spirited campaign to save them, rallying local people to march in defense of their vanishing pension and retiree healthcare rights.

The subsidiary of the company that owned the mines was declared bankrupt and most of its pension funds died with it. Years later, this was exposed as a scam. For Gapes Sr the betrayal was too much. Two days after the deal brokered by the mineworkers' union became a fait accompli, he died of a heart attack.

When Hetta told me this, I was filled with admiration for Duke, and compassion. He could have ended up doing a Cody Wyatt, but after three years kicking around the fringes of Blacksoil's petty crime scene, he took himself off to a recruiting office – the Armed Forces Career Center in Heatherfield – and signed up with the Marines.

Was there anger there?

Perhaps.

Enough to harbor rage against the system?

Unknown.

A twenty-year-old Ford pick-up with smashed wing mirrors and a West Virginia Black Bears sun-strip sits out front of the Gapes trailer. Its white paint is chipped and peeling, and the shutters have faded on the side that gets the sun. Shingles are missing from the roof. The lights are on behind the lace drapes, but there are no other signs of life.

Heavy metal rocks the trailer on the left. The one on the right looks like a junkyard. A pit-bull on a leash shivers and whines in the sub-zero sunshine. A pine forest sweeps down a wide, rock-strewn slope behind them. A pair of eagles soar above the ridgeline.

I close the window as the Gapes porch door opens. An overweight woman appears. She uses a stick and moves with difficulty. Tight gray curls protrude beneath her blue woolen hat. She is wearing blue slacks and a white windcheater. She looks around seventy.

Hetta and I exchange glances. This has to be Misty Buckhannon, Gapes's aunt, his mother's sister.

Hetta has pulled up the mother's medical records. The Alzheimer's is advanced. Louisa Gapes – Lou – needs Misty's full-time care. She is all but confined to the trailer.

Misty approaches the pick-up and puts her key in the driver's side lock. She wiggles it, removes it, looks at it, sticks it back in the lock and tries again.

Hetta shuffles in her seat. 'Lock's frozen.'

I open my door.

'What are you doing?'

'You got any hand gel?'

Course she has.

Misty turns around when she hears my steps on the gravel. She raises a hand and squints against the sun.

I step forward and squeeze some of the gel into the lock. This time, it opens.

She studies me more carefully. 'You from around here, mister?'

'No, ma'am. I'm from Washington.'

'*Worshington?*'

She turns back to the porch, then stops and says over her shoulder: 'Then I guess you're here about Duke.'

I'm sitting in a bay window at the rear of the trailer. Duke's mother, Lou, is beside me, her gaze apparently fixed beyond the chain-link that separates her yard from the trees.

Two framed photographs lie on the table in front of me. The first is of Duke in dress blues: the white cap, blue tunic, red piping, white belt of a Marine. The peak of his cap is low over his eyes. Mo was right; he had been a good-looking boy.

In the second photo, Duke is aged around twelve or thirteen; Hank in his late forties. They're both clutching fishing rods, and Duke, beaming, holds up two decent-sized trout to the camera.

Misty has already told us how much Duke loved his dad. And I don't doubt it. She knows that we know more than we're letting on. I can see it in her eyes. She also knows that we are not the people who showed up without warning to ask questions about her nephew. Those people carried no identification, wouldn't say where they were from, and appeared *after* Katya had agreed the compensation package.

'Do you recall the date?' Hetta asks. They are in the kitchen, Misty washing pans and dishes, Hetta drying them.

'It was the night before Lou's birthday.'

'When?' I ask.

'A little over a year ago. November 20th.'

'What did they do?' Hetta asks.

'Turned the place over good.'

'Sounds like they were looking for something, not someone,' Hetta says.

I don't have the first idea what to make of this. I just listen and observe.

When Hetta and Misty are finished, Misty comes over with a fresh pot of coffee and fills my cup.

Under Hetta's Opsec rules, we have implemented a few precautions.

The local field office, contrary to protocol, is completely in the dark about our visit. The only person that knows we are in West Virginia is Lefortz. I have told Misty no more than I told Katya: that the White House is interested in looking again at Duke's case. There is no TV here and no Internet. She seems unaware of the events in D.C.

Lou picks up the picture of Duke in his uniform and stares at it intently. She turns to me and says something. It sounds as if she's asking whether I know her son.

The clinical advice is easy to dispense. My training has given me the tools, supposedly, to deal with the victims of Alzheimer's. But now that Lou is focusing on me, her eyes searching mine for something – *anything* – I can tell her about Duke, I haven't the first clue what to say. And I don't have the heart to tell her the truth.

She takes my hand in her thin, bony fingers and asks me again. This time I hear her clearly.

'Do you *see* him?'

'Now come on, darlin',' Misty says. 'You don' wanna be talkin' that way . . .'

'Why does she say that?' Hetta asks.

Misty dabs at a bead of white spittle that is beginning to trickle from the corner of her sister's mouth. 'Because this is how life is, that's why.'

I hear her anger, bitterness and frustration.

'Katya told me your sister received some calls from Duke,' I say to Misty. '*After* he ran.'

'Uh huh. Did she also tell you they only ever happened when I was out?'

'No. Did you check with the phone company?'

Misty nods. 'There were no calls.'

She glances at her sister and taps the side of her head. 'She weren't ever the same after Duke got blew up in *A-rak*. She said Duke was callin' her 'cos he was in a place that made him *sceert*.'

If he was foreign-deployed, if he had been sent back to the desert, as Katya had maintained, it wasn't surprising that a return to the Middle East, with its memories of the war and the incident that gave him the brain injury, would re-traumatize him . . .

Misty shakes a finger. 'She said Duke was sceert 'cos he kept seein' his dad. She said he'd spoke to Duke – number of times.'

'But his father's dead.'

'Uh huh. Dead years.'

Lou has gone back to staring out the window. 'Duke . . .' she says suddenly, with heartrending sadness.

'I told you, Lou honey. You gotta stop talkin' that way. Duke's with our Lord now. He's at peace.'

Misty sets the milk down on the table and prizes Lou's hand from mine.

'Where does she say she sees Duke?'

And then, because I realize I'm not addressing the question to the person I ought to be, I take back Lou's hand. '*Where* do you see him, Lou?'

She points again toward the trees.

I re-examine the pictures on the table. 'Where did Duke and his father like to go fishing?'

Misty doesn't know. But it was somewhere up in the North Laurel Fork. They had a cabin up there. Sometimes they'd be gone for days.

'A cabin?'

'Old place, beat up.'

'Where?'

Lou gives my knuckles another squeeze. Her grip tightens. 'Creek Finger. That's where my boys go. That's where they *are*.'

We park in the out-of-town mall, next to the payday loan shop with the splintered window that radiates to the four corners like a spider's web. Hetta has managed to find a signal for her call to Lefortz and we're waiting for the encrypted feed he's promised her – a satellite image, downloaded from a database held within the Service's Intelligence Division – of an area of the North Laurel Fork, eighteen miles east of the North Laurel River.

The commercial satellite maps we've examined over the past thirty minutes show a lake fed by a tributary of the Laurel, shaped like a finger. It's unnamed on all the maps we've managed to access thus far.

The minutes tick by. Hetta produces her notebook. 'Can you function with post-traumatic depression?'

For a fraction of a second, I think she's talking about me. Long enough to wonder how much, with her access to every kind of Secret Service database, she *really* knows about me.

'It depends what you mean by "function".'

'I couldn't help hearing some of that stuff Misty was telling you about Duke's father. While we were in the kitchen, and you were with Lou, I asked about his mental state at the Veterans Center. You're the expert, but I can't get my head around the spooks wanting to employ someone with his kind of symptoms and history.

'His anxiety became depression. Then his depression seemed to morph into something more serious. Kind of bears out what Misty was telling you and what his medical notes said – if we can trust them at all.'

She knows what I think: that they've been altered, though quite why is anybody's guess. 'How serious is serious?'

'He heard voices. Saw things. Had hallucinations.'

'While he was in therapy?'

She nods. '*Before* they placed him in work.'

'Did anybody voice their concerns?'

'Yes. According to Misty, Lou did. Before she got sick. To his recovery support therapist.'

'When we get back, we're going to need to speak to him or her.' Then we'll know whether his notes are real or not.

'Best of luck with that. *He* was killed in a road traffic accident shortly before your friend Katya took on the DoD for compensation. She didn't tell you?'

No, she didn't.

'Where are you going with this?' she asks.

'A year, maybe eighteen months after he went AWOL, Duke allegedly called his mom. A number of times. Told her he was scared. It only ever happened, though, when Misty was out.'

'So?'

'Maybe he had eyes on the trailer. Did you see the way his mom pointed at the trees? The forest backs onto the yard. My guess is he had a prepaid cell and she really did see him there.'

'Where?'

'In the trees. Beyond the chain-link.'

She looks at me long and hard. 'The phone company said there were no calls.'

'If they can alter his medical notes, then they wouldn't have any difficulty manipulating the phone records.'

'And that shit about his dad?'

'In the kid's mind, he might not have been dead.'

She gives a slight shake of the head. 'Say that again.'

'Duke clearly did not want to be foreign-deployed. With his history, being sent back to the desert would have been a big stressor – severe enough quite possibly to have brought on a psych-osis in which he *believed* that he saw his dead father.'

'Like a hallucination?'

'If he was that sick, yes.'

There's a ping from her inbox. She detaches the sat-phone lead, and we open up the file to see what we've got.

I'm amazed by how much better the resolution is.

The lake is twenty miles from the nearest road. Rocks and trees pepper the desolate landscape.

We zoom in from space to a point where we're hovering just a hundred meters above its surface.

'There,' she says, pointing with her pen. 'There's something right there.'

I peer at the screen. It isn't easy to see. It isn't where I would have expected it, down by the water's edge, but higher, partially obscured by the trees, around two hundred meters above the shoreline: a cabin.

15

THE LAKE APPEARS AS IT DID IN LEFORTZ'S SATELLITE IMAGERY, only darker – a sliver of azure in the granite. It has taken a five-hour hike for us to reach it from the empty camping ground where we left the Lexus.

Hetta raises her binoculars and places the cabin under observation for several minutes before passing them to me. It's halfway between the lake and a jagged bluff that juts into the valley. Since the satellite pass that produced our imagery someone has carried out extensive repairs to it. The roof is newer than the walls; the lumber there has been freshly cut. The windows have been boarded over and the door seems to have been strengthened. I can see the last of the daylight glinting off the metal reinforcements.

It takes us another ten minutes to cross the valley. Hetta and I hunker down by a cluster of boulders. The cabin is now less than a hundred meters away.

The shrill cry of a night bird sounds from somewhere in the trees. The moon, three-quarters full, paints the lake and its surroundings blue, black and silver.

After ten minutes more of eyes-on, we're satisfied we're the only living souls out here beneath the crystal-clear star bed. But even though the cabin appears lifeless, we take the precaution of approaching in stealth mode.

From thirty meters away, there is an overpowering smell of creosote.

When I reach the door, I put my ear to it and run my hands over the reinforcements. A huge, industrial-size padlock hangs from a bolt that's as thick as my wrist. There is no rust on the screws. The work has been done recently, perhaps within the past month.

Hetta pulls out her Beretta and chambers a shell. I stand back.

The lock is no match for a .357 round.

The sweet smell of rotting tissue is so thick it makes me gag.

Hetta is standing just inside the door, her back pressed to the wall. Her hand covers her mouth and nose.

Her flashlight cuts through the darkness, the beam bouncing off of the walls and things that don't belong in a place that's twenty miles from the nearest road.

I struggle to take in what I'm seeing.

The cabin is maybe ten meters by eight. Just one room. I expected to see bare lumber; not this.

There are thousands of them. On the walls, strewn across the floor. I look up. They are even pinned to the ceiling.

Pictures, photographs, sketches, printouts . . .

Hart shifts the beam to the left of the fireplace. She moves it to the right. Up. Down. It's all the same. They're everywhere.

Images: *Of people, places, objects, things . . .*

Hetta retches and drops the phone. She runs outside.

The light remains fixed on the ceiling.

I look up and see a burning building, a blindfolded hostage with a knife to his throat, a power station belching smoke, kids at a rock concert, a train station, a fisherman staring at a dried-up lake, a plane slamming into the World Trade Center . . .

Hitler and Stalin and John F. Kennedy . . .

A volcano, the Eiffel Tower, an overturned battleship at Pearl Harbor . . .

The Kremlin, the Beatles, the Taj Mahal, a machine that looks like the Large Hadron Collider . . .

The Golden Gate Bridge.

And these are just the things I can put names to. There are hundreds, thousands, I cannot, because they are so ordinary, so everyday.

People in cars, sitting at desks, asleep in bed, walking, reading, laughing, crying; adults, kids, black, white, tall, short.

Houses, office buildings, slums, churches, cars, computers, guns, planes, tables, rivers, meadows, fish, mammals, insects, trees.

Some of the images are clear; some are fuzzy, like the grainy video you see of state funerals or politicians at rallies in the fifties and sixties.

Some are taken from ground level; some are like ones I had access to when I was in Special Forces: drone-camera, spy-plane and satellite shots.

It's like an exhibition of visual thought, at once random and connected.

Hetta walks back in. She picks up the phone. Neither of us says anything.

She swings the beam and it catches something to our right. The wall isn't the solid surface I initially thought it was, but a drape, a length of dark cloth, strung across the full width of the cabin.

Hetta signals me, nods, and starts toward it, weapon extended.

There's a moment during which she and I look at each other from both ends of the drape. Then, on her command, we throw it aside.

The inner sanctum is dominated by something red and oozing: a skinned carcass with a rope around its neck, tied to a butcher's hook that's bolted to a beam. It comes alive when I pan my flashlight along it, because it's crawling with larvae. A deer, I think; strung up, I guess, because it's food and Gapes had nowhere else to keep it from predators.

'You know,' Hetta says, her words muffled by her hand, 'they should do crazy wall kits at Kmart or someplace, because they'd fucking clean up.'

She's right. Every psycho, it seems, has to have one these days.

The light catches areas of meat missing from the deer's haunches.

She shifts her beam onto the wall behind the carcass.

I find myself staring at a poster-sized reproduction of a painting – an Old Master of Christ on the cross. To its right is some of the same grainy imagery we saw when we walked in, but devoted exclusively to the President – on the campaign trail, smiling, laughing, waving.

There are photographs of him in stadiums and on soapboxes at rural rallies – sometimes on his own, sometimes with Jennifer and the kids. Some are taken from a long way off: Thompson and the First Family tiny against large, cheering crowds and thickets of blue campaign banners. Others are about as close to the President as I've ever been. Gapes, or whoever took them, must have been standing only a couple of meters away.

To their right is a sketch of a bearded man with long black hair and pale, watery eyes. They stare at me with an unsettling intensity. Is that anger or passion? Does he hate or love me? He is about thirty-five years old and looks intensely familiar.

It might be the face of a 9/11 hijacker, or the priest who officiated at my confirmation. I haven't the first goddamn idea, although the script beneath the picture – in Arabic or Farsi – offers a clue.

Fuck.

Is this what a mind looks like when its switch trips?

I move on. At the far right side are images of an ancient and modern city, one with a familiar skyline: Jerusalem. They fill the circumference of the beam. But I've missed a section. I shift to the left, knowing, even before I do, what I am about to see.

'Whoa!' Hetta says. 'That is fucking incredible.'

I guess it is. I have my very own stretch of wall, with shots I've never seen before. A class photo from elementary school, me standing next to the teacher. I can't remember her name, but it's her for sure. A sketch of an Army officer. A little crude, but recognizable as my father.

I stare at myself on the school football team. I'm about thirteen, because I'm missing a front tooth, thanks to some asshole – Bertelsky – who knocked it out during practice.

Nearby I'm graduating from the Air Force academy – proud in my blue uniform, bow tie and graduation medal, flanked on one side by my commandant and on the other by my mentor, Senior Sergeant Deakins, who always said I could do it – that I had officer stamped across my forehead.

And here I am at USU, with some undergraduates, clowning for the camera with a guy in a long black wig: Dayno. We were going to a seventies party, I think. I look again. *Jesus*, I hope we were.

And I know what's next, because it's growing at the periphery of my vision – a sketch of Hope and her mother. Next to it is a snap of us on our wedding day. We're in the garden of the home – it must have been taken by one of the residents. Jack is holding Hope's hand as he gives her away. There are tears in his eyes. I'm starting to feel them in mine.

I move on quickly and suddenly I'm in Iraq, on the floor of a Black Hawk, kitted for action with my rifle and my blood bags. I don't remember anybody taking photos, but there I am giving them a thumbs-up. It was the night we went into Fallujah.

The next picture chills the shit out of me. Our backyard: a place that wasn't just inaccessible to the outside world but also invisible to it, because Hope and I liked to keep it that way.

I haven't seen it in fifteen years. There are the carved pieces of driftwood she used to collect, the ship's lanterns with the scented candles she lit on still nights, and the things she called her Pollyanna crystals – pieces of glass and translucent stones strung between the trees so they could catch the sunset.

Nothing, though, prepares me for the sight of our Jeep Liberty. It is so utterly crushed by the force of the truck that it's barely recognizable. The twisted wreckage is surrounded by flashing lights and a small army of first responders.

Somewhere behind them, I am fighting for my life.

And Hope is dead.

Outside, everything is as it was a second before we went in: the upturned bowl of black sky, the stars, the moon, the silence, and the bitterness of the creosote that manages to overcome the smell of death.

The world has continued to turn, but for me everything is different. I walk toward the lake. When I'm far enough away from the cabin, I settle on a log and breathe in the sharp air.

I have no idea how Gapes went about collecting his material. There's no electricity here, no phone signal, no Wi-Fi. It's as remote a spot as you'll find on the planet, and yet up on *my* wall, in addition to everything else, was a portrait of Jack. Jack in his Shawnee blanket. Not the one in my apartment, but unbelievably like it, and unquestionably painted by Hope. But completed. I have never seen it before in my life.

I hear a noise behind me.

'Colonel?' There is a surprising tenderness to her voice. She sits beside me.

I'm so cold that I feel the warmth of her body through the fleece of my jacket.

'How are you doing?'

'Needed a little oxygen. Sorry.'

'I guess that was your whole life back there.'

'The best bits. And the absolute worst.'

She passes me her bottle of water.

I turn to her. 'One to ten.'

'I'm sorry, I—'

'Crazy walls. On a scale of one to ten, where's that one figure?'

She doesn't answer. I guess we've had our Oprah moment.

A minute goes by. Then: 'Colonel?'

'Yes.'

'Did you notice the ordering? If you read the wall left to right – the Christ painting, the President, Jerusalem?'

It clicks. It follows the flow of our discussion in the tower and the words they found on the remnant of the note: *God, Threat, Proof, Mac, Jerusalem.*

'From the ordering and the content of the imagery, "Mac" must refer to you. You ever been called Mac? Anything like that?'

I shake my head.

'Your wife?'

'Her name was Hope.'

'I know.'

Of course she does.

She waits a moment. 'Could Mac have been a friend of hers?

101

Somebody she worked with? There's a lot of pictures of her up there – more than anybody else, in fact. Here.' She takes out her phone and starts scrolling.

Aside from the photo of our wedding day, there's one of Hope as a little girl – it must have been taken while she, her mom and her father were still living in California. She's giving the camera a gap-toothed smile and holding up a little china rabbit – her only possession to survive the west–east journey.

There's a picture of her and her mom sitting on the end of the bed of one of the old folk residents at the home, the three of them laughing over something Pam has said. But the one that pulls me up short is of Hope and the placard.

She's posing with it outside a cafe called the Artiste, a place where I used to study at weekends with my med-student friends. In the odd moments I'd looked up from my notes, I'd found myself drawn to one of the paintings on the wall. A painting of a beach. There was something magnetic about it. Something haunting.

'And I'd got you down as more of a Hopper or a Rockwell kind of a guy,' the waitress had said.

I'd looked up to find myself gazing into the most beautiful eyes I'd ever seen.

When I looked down, I noticed that she had paint on her hands.

The color of the sea.

I'd seen her before – once, a glimpse only, and from a distance: walking across the USU campus with an easel under her arm.

When she returned with my change, I asked her what she'd been doing at a military hospital.

She told me she was an art therapist.

I was twenty-three at the time and had no idea what that was.

She'd glanced toward a group of people outside. Some of them were holding placards. A couple of them stamped their feet against the cold. One of them, an old guy in a beanie, beckoned.

'Who are they?'

'They're protesting the invasion. You want to come?'

I'd laughed and pointed to my 'high and tight', my military grade crew cut. It was a couple of months after 9/11 and we'd recently invaded Afghanistan. 'I happen to believe in my country,' I said grandly.

She nodded. 'So do they.'

I peered a little closer. I recognized a few of them. I'd seen them on campus too. The university shared space with the Walter Reed National Military Medical Center, home to a number of out-patient clinics dedicated to the treatment of veterans.

Earle, the guy in the beanie, had defended a hill single-handed against hundreds of Viet Cong and received the Distinguished Service Cross.

Ralph, a Navy navigator, had been put through a double mock-execution after he was shot down over Basra in '91.

Keith, the youngest, still in his twenties, had driven his colleagues to safety, despite losing his right leg below the knee in an ambush outside Mogadishu.

'They're your patients?'

'I'm not a doctor, Josh.' She smiled. 'I'm an art therapist.'

She was halfway to the door when I realized I hadn't told her my name.

'How do you—?'

'Are you coming?' she called to me over her shoulder.

When I hesitated, she stopped and turned. 'I want to show you all the people who are going to live because of you.'

'Colonel?'

I look up. A cloud has begun to creep across the face of the moon. I return Hetta's cell.

She pulls out the sat-phone.

'Wait—'

'It's encrypted.' She dials a number, gets to her feet and walks back toward the cabin. Five minutes later, she's back to tell me that Lefortz is sending a helicopter and a PIAD forensics team. He's told her to stay and help secure the site, but I must go back.

Lefortz has no choice. He's told Hart that he has to let Reuben know that I'm here. He and Thompson are meeting with the Mayor of New York, then flying back into D.C. tonight.

'You want to know something?' Hetta says. 'Something weird . . .'

I am barely listening. For a moment, the idea of *something* weird in that cabin makes me want to laugh.

'I just calculated the number of images back there – five thousand, maybe, give or take a hundred.'

'And?'

'One of them is different.'

'In what way?'

'It's upside down.'

We start with the inner sanctum. I've tied strips of my shirt around my mouth and nose; Hetta has too. The rope holding the deer creaks.

Hetta shines her light. Christ, front and center, is nailed to the cross, skin so white against black storm clouds it's like his body is lit from within. Soldiers lift the cross upright.

The camera on Hetta's phone flashes. I set mine to record and start speaking.

'The Christ painting. We need to know everything about it: the artist, exactly what it depicts, if it's privately or publicly owned, what it means . . .'

I glance to the left and shine my flashlight onto a photograph of Thompson.

He's speaking to reporters. His plane is behind him. I recognize Hartsfield–Jackson Atlanta's terminal building and control tower.

I flick to another image: Thompson at the Iowa caucus. In another, he's shaking the hand of the Pope in Dallas – their much-publicized first meeting. Senator Abnarth, Reuben's first boss, is standing beside them. Gray and foxlike, Abnarth is wearing the smile of a man who knows that this is what will get his protégé into the White House.

I stand in the center of my section and avoid directing the flash-light at the image of the crushed Jeep. I scan the pictures. Move closer. A whole lot of people from my past, but none of them called Mac.

I focus instead on the portrait of Jack: old and at peace as he sat out under the big white oak in front of Hope's mom's home.

'Who is that?'

'Hard to explain. He was kind of like my wife's dad.'

'And him?'

I glance at the priest-cum-hijacker. I have no idea. I turn to the Jerusalem montage. I've never been to Israel, so it says little to me. But the fact that Jerusalem featured in Gapes's note and the President's dream is inescapable. The short hairs on the back of my neck stand up.

I don't need to ask her to take pictures of everything. She's already there. Superior autobiographical memory is often seen as a curse. Some people affected by it remember everything that ever happened to them. Hetta's is aligned to patterns in objects, which I suspect relates to something that once happened to her. In any case, she processed thousands of images in this section of the cabin in a beat, and determined one of them was different – low down and to the right of the fireplace: a print of an engraving, sixteenth century, maybe older; an old man at a desk.

I squat, hold the flashlight steady and tilt my head.

He has long hair and a beard. He's wearing a gown and a cap. I resist the urge to turn him the right way up.

He's writing something. And there's an inscription, in Latin.

The breeze drops. I get to my feet.

'Tell me what else you see.'

She looks at the wall again.

'There's something different about *those* images . . .' She points to a football team, a car license plate, a guy holding a lottery ticket, two or three others. They all contain numbers.

When we've finished recording them, I step outside to get some more air. Hart suddenly calls me back.

'What do you make of that?'

I follow her fingertip. To the left of the fireplace, an Auschwitz survivor has raised her hand so the camera can capture the six-figure ID tattooed on her forearm, but all I can see is the pain behind her eyes.

'Not that one, Colonel. The sketch to its left.'

Framed by an arch, it has the precision of a photograph. An office building, reaching into the night sky.

'It's the place beyond the labor union. The one Gapes kept glancing at when we were at the church.'

The viewpoint is almost exactly where I was standing, next to the trapdoor, looking over his shoulder, out of the bell tower.

I lean closer. There's a blur of light in one of the blacked-out windows. I point to it.

She nods. 'A muzzle flash.' Her face is a mask. 'Marine Sergeant Gapes knew how his mission was going to end.'

I remember Misty telling us about the people who showed up without warning to ask questions about her nephew. The ones who carried no identification and wouldn't say where they were from.

My mouth has gone dry. When I try and swallow, I can taste something metallic at the back of my throat. Something, until my encounter in the tower, I hadn't tasted since Fallujah.

16

LAST THING I DID BEFORE LEAVING THE CABIN WAS CALL LEFORTZ on Hetta's sat-phone and ask him to throw a protective cordon around everyone we've spoken to. I reeled off the list – Lou and Misty, Mo, Katya, Marty the security guard, Steve at the Settlement, the Reverend Hayes.

Gazing out the window as the LongRanger crosses vast tracts of forest, I make the most of one hour forty-five minutes of thinking time. Anders and his shoot-to-kill order swims to the forefront of my mind; the tone of voice he'd used to defend himself in the Crisis Center; Marty and his description of the processes that govern tamper circuits and call-outs; and the glitches that allowed Gapes to make his way unobserved from the river to the Settlement.

Pinpricks of light in the darkness below register the presence of the occasional town, like pockets of mental activity on a brain scan. Gapes's damaged posterior parietal cortex wouldn't even have shown a glimmer – and the parietal cortex is the brain's anchor to reality, the bit that provides us with spatial awareness. He must have been in a state of extreme dissociation.

During my time at MacDill we conducted a study of these dissociative states, common enough in PTSD. We failed to find a cure, but we did discover that Buddhist monks switch off large parts of their brain when they're in a highly meditative state. And psychics do too.

Lefortz cuts a lone figure in the pad lights as we drop behind a

107

group of low buildings in the northeast corner of Dulles Airport, which most people never see.

There's a double bump as the LongRanger touches down.

I slide back the door, duck below the blades and hold up a hand, ineffectually, against the spray from the pad as the White House Special Agent in Charge guides me to a black Buick sedan with its engine running. He points me to the passenger seat, then jumps in beside me. I hand him Hetta's USB, the full photographic record of the cabin's interior.

'You OK, Josh? Look like you've seen a ghost.'

I take a breath, and tell him about the images of Hope, the backyard of our place out on the point, the mangled wreckage of the Jeep. Then I tell him about the sketch of the muzzle flash.

'I was going to ask you to run this by your pals in the Agency, but now I'm not so sure. Let's stick with Byford for now.'

He nods. Thompson's National Security Adviser is a far cry from the buzz-cut generals and Cheney lookalikes that he believes are sharpening their knives for him.

We exit security and emerge on a back road through the trees, past the airport's western perimeter and a couple of isolated, blacked-out maintenance hangars, then go left on to US-50, heading toward Chantilly, Fairfax and Washington.

I figure Lefortz is saving his breath for when we get to Reuben's place, a private estate with its own security outside of Fairfax. But at the turnpike we keep going on the interstate, heading for the capital.

'Cabot knows, Josh. Don't ask me how. But he knows. About Gapes. About the investigation you and Hart have been running. About my involvement. They want me to bring you in.'

'*They?*'

'He and Reuben are on the phone right now. Cabot's accused the Chief of Staff of conducting an illicit investigation using Agency assets – of deliberately keeping him in the dark. They want to polygraph you. And they want to do it now. I'm sorry, but he has all three of us over a goddamn barrel. This is about damage limitation now. Protecting POTUS. Our mission, first and foremost, is to prevent Cabot finding out about *No Stone*.'

'Are the others secure?'

'We got to everybody except for the lawyer and your Armenian buddy.'

I sit up. 'Mo?'

'Relax,' Lefortz says. 'He's at the theater with his wife. Two of the FBI's finest are also enjoying the show.'

'The *FBI*?'

'An old buddy of mine fixed it. You met him. Big guy. Dave Wharton.'

'DJ?'

'I've briefed him on the key aspects. When the curtain falls, the agents will make themselves known. For as long as the threat persists, your pal Mo is going to be just fine.'

'And the lawyer?'

Lefortz's brow creases. 'Kind of weird, that. She told Wharton she didn't need protection, because the two of you never met.'

'We spent thirty minutes together in a coffee shop off Dupont Circle.'

'Maybe she forgot.'

'Since yesterday? I need to go speak to her.'

'Negative. You're not a part of the Federal Investigation. And besides, I just told you—'

'Where's Reuben?'

'Still with the President. In New York.'

'How easy is it to fake someone's voice, Jim?'

'What?'

'I've been thinking about Anders.'

'What about him?'

'His consistent denial that he gave the order to shoot.'

'If you were in the deepest shit, wouldn't you?'

'I don't think he's lying.'

'Christ, Josh. You listening to a word I been saying? We ran the tests. The voice on the tape was his, no question.'

'A kid with an editing tool can mash up a celebrity's voice, post the result online, and get a million hits. How easy is it to splice together three words?'

Take the shot.

'Cabot is screaming for your ass and you're thinking about Anders?'

'Just tell me, will you.'

'Splicing's a possibility,' he concedes. 'But the lab geeks have pretty much ruled that out too.'

'Why?'

'Because of the methods we use to detect it. Power on the electrical grid fluctuates the whole time. Any recording device that's near a mains supply – a CCTV camera, a camcorder, a cellphone – captures the fluctuations as background noise. We can evaluate the noise at every moment of a recording and date-stamp it.'

The orange sodium lights along the highway pick out the crow's feet around his eyes. 'The fluctuations can be erased, but only by state-of-the-art equipment not generally accessible to random white supremacists or crazy people.'

We agree that randomers and crazies don't get to alter Agency-held records or manipulate CCTV data either.

I tell Lefortz I forgot to put Anders and Jimenez on the list.

He hasn't. The plan is to drop me at a cab rank off the freeway while he delivers the USB to Byford. I'll warn Anders, and he'll go right on to take care of Jimenez.

15055 Catskill Drive is half brick, half timber, in need of attention, and, I suspect, on the outer limits of an MPD captain's capacity to finance. It's at the end of a semi-rural street in the small commuter suburb of Middleville, a few miles from the Metro in Falls Church. There's a light on above the porch and the garage door is open.

The cab driver does a three-point turn, parks up and waits, engine on, wipers working against the rain. I raise the collar of my jacket, drop my head and run toward the garage. I still have Appalachian mud on my boots.

Anders has two cars to his name: a Mazda CX-5 hatchback and

a Honda Odyssey. The Honda is in the garage; the CX-5 isn't. A kid's pedal bike with support wheels leans against a workbench.

I ring the bell. A sliver of light spills from a window as a drape slides back. I catch a glimpse of a woman's face. Locks tumble and the door opens – at least as far as the chain allows.

Her hair is scraped tight against her scalp. Her eyes are blood-shot, her complexion waxy.

I'm about to say something, but the words die the moment she looks at me.

'I know you,' she says. 'From the TV.'

'I need to speak to your husband, Mrs Anders.'

'You were in the tower . . .' She falters for a moment.

'Please, Mrs Anders, it's really important I—'

'He's not here.' Her tone is harsh. Maybe she thinks I'm on the tribunal that skewered her husband's career. She's skeletally thin, and has an accent. German, Scandinavian?

I look at my watch. It's past ten o'clock on a weeknight. Anders' file suggests he's not the type to drown his sorrows in a local bar, but 'administrative leave' and endless sessions with Internal Affairs will hurt a man like him.

'For what it's worth,' I say, 'I believe him.'

'Then go tell his boss.'

From upstairs, I hear the sound of a child crying. Before closing the door on me, she says: 'He took a call. Maybe thirty minutes ago. Sounded official.'

Back in the cab, I check my messages. Lefortz has delivered the package and is now en route to the second waypoint.

I try his cellphone. It's busy.

Jimenez's place is thirty minutes from where I am and maybe fifteen from Byford's gated compound on the Alexandria water-front. His file says he's recently divorced and living on the third floor of an apartment building in Clarke's Crossroads. The rent is part-paid by an MPD assistance foundation.

I am ten minutes closer when Lefortz calls. He's just parked up in a nearby lot.

I tell him about Anders. He calls a source at MPD HQ and gets straight back. No one knows about any interview request and, at this time of night, it's unlikely.

So his wife is lying, or he left the house to get some air – or someone is operating off the books.

Lefortz also has a draft copy of the FBI's preliminary account of the church shooting. He gives me the highlights.

Anders was where Hetta and I left him, in the mobile command post, monitoring the feeds. He is heard to say: 'Take the shot.'

The only other person in the CP, a Secret Service comms support specialist, didn't hear him. He was focusing on the monitors, not his boss.

Jimenez fired at 05.52. His body camera footage and weapon analysis puts this beyond dispute. Jimenez shot Gapes. And he admits it.

'Where was he?' I already know the answer.

'On the ninth floor of an office block behind the labor union headquarters.'

The place Gapes kept looking toward. The window with the muzzle flash.

'He's forty-one,' Lefortz continues. 'Joined MPD ten years ago. Been deployed across the Metro area for the past six on warrant service ops, crowd control, hostage situations – standard SWAT stuff. His bosses, Anders included, have all described him as a model tac officer. An expert rating marked him out for sniper duty.'

'And before MPD?'

'Marines. 24th Expeditionary Unit. Iraqi Freedom. More than 150 missions in the combat zone. Mainly around Baghdad.' He pauses. 'Gapes was in Iraq. So was the guy he data-dumped in the Settlement.'

And so was I. But Gentleman Jim doesn't go there.

I hear him swear softly. 'Son of a bitch just pulled up and went inside.'

It takes me a moment to realize he's talking about Anders, not Jimenez.

Two minutes later, my cab draws into the same lot.

The rain on the cab roof all but drowns out Lefortz's next call. I wind down the window and peer at the concrete tenement block. A light flickers in the second floor stairwell. It's Lefortz's cell. 'I'm going on up. Meet you on the third.'

I thrust some bills at the driver and sprint across the lot.

As I pass the first floor, I hear a woman shouting. In Spanish, I think.

Somewhere on the floor above a door opens and for a second or two house music pounds the fabric of the building. I carry on up. The paint on the walls, a lurid pistachio I've only ever seen in old movies, is chipped and graffiti-covered. The ceiling lights are all smashed.

It's more than fifteen years since I've been in combat, but the sounds of urban warfare have never faded. The two sets of shots come in close succession, and instinct kicks in. I take the steps three at a time. Moments later, I'm on the third floor.

Wire mesh hangs from a light fitting above my head. The neon tube is just about working and I detect the byproduct of its struggling electrics, ozone, above the acrid smell of piss and vomit.

There are ten doors down the hallway, five on each side, and I see traffic at the interchange through the end window. Lefortz is nowhere to be seen.

My stomach lurches as I hit recall.

I hear his ringtone. The opening bars of 'Suspicion' float toward me. I aim for the sound, my head filling with images I've spent too many years trying to forget. I can see them in the shadows – two guys, one each side of the door, weapons raised; a third, grenade in hand, preparing to kick it in.

The music stops as I reach the last door on the right. It's open a crack.

Lefortz's voice, thin and reedy, directs me to leave a message. I kill the call and push the door. It swings into the apartment. The room is dark and smells of cordite.

I step across the threshold and move briskly right so I'm not silhouetted in the frame. I run my hand up the jamb and find the switch.

Light floods the room. There's an armchair with a body in it. Jimenez's arm hangs down, an automatic a few centimeters from his fingertips, smoke still curling from the barrel. Two spent cartridges close by on the lime-green carpet. Between them, a single bloody footprint.

Jimenez's dead eyes stare at his blood and brains on the ceiling. A piece of him has narrowly missed a large crucifix hanging beside a crude portrait of the Madonna and Child.

A second body is face down in front of the chair. Anders has been shot at close range. The bullets have exited his back.

Lefortz's body is in the bedroom. I roll him over. Like Anders, two rounds, center mass. I touch his neck with a fingertip. No pulse.

A dirty nylon drape billows in the breeze. The window is open above his head. I stick my head out and see a ledge running toward the fire escape. Nothing moves below.

I turn back into the room.

I try to look at Lefortz, but can't bring myself to. So I close my eyes and a picture comes unbidden. Lefortz smiling as he gets up to leave the Blue Barge. *Wednesday is my ruby wedding.*

Wednesday is today.

I slump back against the wall. I have no idea how much time passes before I hear a noise behind and to the right of me. I look up.

A crouching figure, weapon raised.

'*Police!*' The voice is female, brittle, scared. '*Don't fucking move!*'

17

'NAME?'

'Colonel Joshua M. Cain, United States Air Force.'

'Age?'

'Forty-four.'

'Title?'

'Director, White House Medical Unit.'

'A position you have held for . . . ?'

'Six months.'

'How many years have you served in the United States Military?'

'Twenty-three.'

'You are a recipient of the Air Force Cross?'

'Yes.'

'For heroism in Iraq?'

'For *action* in Iraq.'

'Just answer yes or no please, Colonel.'

'Yes.'

The polygraphist sitting across the table stares at his laptop screen then taps the keyboard. His face is barely visible above the lid.

It is my second interrogation of the night. The first was conducted by a Major Crimes Division detective at a Fairfax County Police Department station fifteen minutes' drive from Clarke's Crossroads. The cop had barely hit his stride when two Secret Service agents showed up. I called Reuben from their Suburban, on my way to the White House. He'd heard the news and was on his way back to D.C. with Thompson in *Marine One*.

Behind the polygraphist is a two-way mirror, beneath which is a camp bed with two folded sheets, a blanket and a pillow. I am in a basement suite in the West Wing, several doors down from Room W16. The Oval Office is almost directly above me, which is ironic, because the room I'm in looks like a CIA rendition site.

A jumble of wires connects the laptop to the polygraph, and the polygraph to electrodes on the first and third fingers of my right hand, a blood pressure cuff on my left arm, a heart-rate monitor, and a pneumograph around my chest and stomach. I'm also wearing a headset that monitors the movement of my jaw – to prevent me biting my cheek or tongue, which would send my responses haywire during the control questions. By removing my shoes, they have made sure I can't press down on anything sharp to produce the same result.

The first of the control questions: 'Have you ever taken anything that did not belong to you?'

I see the pleading eyes of the woman in the *abaya*, feel my chest constrict and my pulse rate rise. I envisage the effect this will have on the electrodes monitoring my galvanic skin response.

'No.'

'Are you married?'

'No.'

'Were you married?'

'Yes.'

'Do you have children?'

I hesitate, but only for a fraction of a second. 'No.'

'Next of kin?'

'No.'

'Have you ever lied to someone who trusted you?'

Second control question. There isn't much to imagine this time. I think of Hope, her mother and Jack, and my heart begins to hammer.

'No.'

More tapping on the keyboard, then, except for the hum of the air-con, silence.

A beat later: 'Regarding your role as White House Medical Director, do you intend to answer each of the following questions truthfully?'

I breathe in and think of the waves lapping on the beach in front of our house; the view from the porch, out over the point. 'Yes.'

'Are the circumstances surrounding the death of White House Special Agent in Charge James Lefortz clear to you?'

'No.'

'Is Duke Gapes known to you?'

'No.'

'Did you and Special Agent Henrietta Hart undertake any follow-up investigative actions into the incident at St John's Church?'

Henrietta? My mind wanders for a moment.

'Yes.'

'Are you prepared to cooperate fully with all appropriate authorities in disclosing how you came to track down Duke Gapes?'

I picture the waves lapping around my ankles, feel the sand between my toes and wonder how Cabot knew 'everything', as Lefortz had put it. 'Yes.'

'Are you working for any foreign government or organization?'

'No.'

'Are you concerned for the health of the President?'

'Of course.'

'Yes or a no?'

'The question is ambiguous. Naturally, I am concerned for the health of the President. So is half the country – at least, the people who voted for him.'

Nothing, no hint of frustration or irritation creases the operator's brow as he recalibrates. Another pause. More taps at the keyboard. Then he asks whether I am responsible for ensuring the health of the President.

Bravo.

'Yes.'

'Is President Robert S. Thompson presently capable of fulfilling his duties?'

'That is a subjective question.'

This time, he lifts his eyes to mine.

I know what's coming and breathe in.

'From a medical perspective, is there any reason presently known to you why the President should be unable to fulfill his duties?'

'No.'

'Are you aware of any kind of plot to kill the President?'

'Beyond the claims made by Duke Gapes?'

'Do you have *definitive proof* of a plot to kill the President?'

'No.'

'Are there any reasons that might prevent you from legitimately fulfilling your duties as White House Medical Director?'

I let the feel of the beach flood my senses, look in the mirror and very clearly address my reflection. 'No.'

I am halfway to the door, still buttoning up my shirt, when Cabot walks in. As I knew he would be, he has been behind the mirror, watching on a back-up monitor. It is the first time we've seen each other since the meeting in his Crisis Center. His resemblance to J. Edgar Hoover – short, overweight, energetic and suspicious – hits me again. His pig eyes narrow as they adjust to the harsh lighting.

'You and I know that a polygraph does not constitute proof of any kind. It provides *indicators*. Even so, congratulations. For what it's worth, Colonel, you NDI'ed.'

I hold his gaze. *No deception indicated*. He's lying. And he knows that I know it.

'Am I free to leave?'

'Of course.'

'What'll you tell the media?'

'What we told the cops. The truth. That the investigation into the deaths of SAIC Lefortz, Anders and Jimenez is being handled by the Secret Service. And that Jim Lefortz was killed while conducting routine inquiries into the death of the protester.'

His darting, suspicious eyes narrow. 'Last time we met, Colonel, a man was shot dead right next to you. Now it's happened again. I know, for reasons that are not yet wholly clear to me, that your relationship with the President exceeds the regular duties of the White House Doctor. But that's OK, because we're on the same team now. Reuben Kantner and I are in agreement. Amateur hour is over. You guys are off the case.'

He looks up.

Reuben appears at the end of the lobby. He is still dressed in his overcoat. 'What the fuck has been going on?' He's looking at Cabot. I've never seen him lose it before, but he's right on the edge.

'The protesters by the North Fence and the –' Cabot considers his words, '– *residents* of the Settlement represented a threat to national security, as I've said all along. So, I have spoken with Mayor Phillips and as of this moment, the city authorities are evicting the protesters from the North Fence and bulldozers are leveling the Settlement. Both sites will be clear by morning.'

'Clearing the protesters was not a part of our discussion,' Reuben says levelly.

'Nor should it have been. It's the Mayor's jurisdiction, not the President's.'

For a moment it looks as if what's left of Reuben's sangfroid will exit stage left.

I stare at my friend. Lefortz is dead. Two cops are dead. And I have just been through an interrogation that threatened to reveal the President's fragility.

The thought that the pressure would get to Reuben of all people had never occurred to me before.

Our eyes meet and he seems to read my thoughts. He takes a deep breath.

'I'm sorry,' he says. 'The death of Lefortz has hit the President hard. Hit us all, in fact.'

'Quite. And I have a call to make – to his wife,' Cabot says. 'We'll leave the rest of this discussion till morning.'

He turns and disappears into the Secret Service command post down the hallway.

I look at my phone and see that I've got three missed calls from Mo.

When I glance up, Reuben is still staring after Cabot. 'Does he know about *No Stone*?'

'He knows *something*,' I say. 'But not that.' I pause. 'How hard is hard?'

Reuben rubs at the fatigue around his eyes.

I try again. 'Thompson . . . How's he doing?'

'As well as can be expected. He and Lefortz had been together a long time. Shit, he . . .' Reuben struggles for a moment.

'Lefortz made him feel safe. Which is why I'd like Thompson to reconsider what I said.'

'About what?'

'The psychotherapy.'

He nods. 'I'll talk to him about it. I promise.'

I wait for the reprimand I've been expecting since I landed, but it doesn't come. Instead, he asks me what happened. I tell him about the cabin, the crazy wall. Reuben listens, but says nothing. If it's possible, he looks even more tired than I feel. I ask if he's all right and he nods. Then I ask about Cabot.

'Leave Cabot to me.'

'He said you were in agreement.'

'We are. You're going to have to leave the investigation to him now.'

'Did you go public on the conference being in Jerusalem?'

'No.'

'Well, Gapes knew about it, Reuben. He also knew about Hope. He knew about everything. You. Me. Plus a whole lot more that doesn't add up, including a lawyer I spoke to yesterday who now denies that we ever met.'

'All the more reason to let Cabot handle this. Anything that'll keep that fucking nose of his out of the Oval.'

His phone pings. He looks at it. 'I got to go.'

I take a route back to the ground floor that avoids passing the Secret Service command post.

I check my voicemail.

Nothing.

I check my WhatsApps. One from Mo. 'You son of a bitch,' it reads. 'Call me.'

Book Two

*The wound is in the place
where the light enters you*

18

WORD HAS IT THAT HAIGHT GRAHAM IS CABOT'S FIRST CHOICE TO take over as White House SAIC. He is part of the investigative team that deployed to the cabin at the North Laurel Fork overnight. Graham and I are headed back there on a beat-up, eight-seat Citation Jet the Service uses when it needs to get in and out of D.C. in a hurry. Something – I don't yet know what – has required my presence urgently in West Virginia.

The interior reeks of cigarettes and take-outs. There are burns on the beige seat covers, the armrests and the matching Formica surfaces, and the john doesn't work. Within the Service, it's known, ironically, as 'Corporate Air' – a testament to the cutbacks Cabot was brought in to oversee – but the agents call it the Vomit Comet.

Reports of the Clarke's Crossroads shootings started to hit the wires just before midnight. Within a half-hour, despite a total news blackout, thanks to social media, the names of the three dead men were public. There is every kind of speculation, but the networks are already right across the connection to the church shooting. It's a shit-show.

Reuben and Cabot have been working through the night to ensure the party line, the murder–suicide narrative, is the one that sticks, and my involvement is kept away from it. Meantime, a covert manhunt is underway for the killer. The working hypothesis is that Lefortz stumbled across the execution and became a victim himself. I am lucky to be alive, but it doesn't feel that way. Like everyone else, I am mourning the loss of a friend. A friend who made me feel safe too.

Graham sits across the table from me, looking more likely to file the President's tax returns than to take a bullet for him. He is tall, wiry, and shaves his head. In his rush to act as my escort this morning, he's cut his scalp.

As the plane levels out, he gives the top of his ballpoint a double click.

'Army CID showed up at the site this morning. No warning. First we knew they knew was when three Black Hawks circled overhead twice and touched down by the lake. There must have been a leak from the Service to Army Intel or the Joint Special Operations Command.'

'JaySOC' is responsible for coordinating the activities of all US Special Forces and pretty much for executing the war on terror. Graham tells me that Cabot placed a call of complaint to its commander, General Zan Johansson, shortly after 9 a.m., only to be accused of withholding information about a fugitive from the Department of Defense. This forced a compromise: Army CID has been allowed on site, but only under supervision by the Secret Service.

'You know that the Army has consistently lied about its recruitment of Gapes, don't you?' It lied to his mom and aunt and it lied to Katya, their lawyer. I suspect that it lied to his rehab guru – his recovery support specialist – unless he was in on it, too, before the road traffic accident that killed him.

'I don't like it any better than you.' Graham picks at the scab on his head. 'But they want their pound of flesh. Gapes was their man.'

With two more clicks of his pen, he abruptly changes the subject. 'You served in Iraqi Freedom with the President's Chief of Staff.'

'Yes.'

'Can you tell me about the nature of your relationship?'

'The *nature* of our relationship?'

'If you prefer: how'd the two of you meet?'

'We trained at Patrick Air Force Base in Florida just before the

Gulf War. Kantner was Special Forces – Combat Search and Rescue. I was a combat medic with the 304th Rescue Squadron and attached to his unit. We fought together in Mosul, Fallujah and Tikrit.' I pause. 'Can I ask where you're taking this?'

'We have to assume, Colonel Cain, that Duke Gapes knew something about you we don't. Our starting point is your security check.'

Everyone who works for the President and Vice President needs Yankee White security clearance. I had to undergo a Single Scope Background Investigation, an aggressive, invasive review of my past.

He taps his iPad. 'Your wife was an artist?'

'Art therapist.'

'And what is that, exactly?'

'She worked with the emotionally distressed. Old people, mostly. People with cancer or in recovery. Stroke victims. Alzheimer's sufferers. Veterans. The art helped them to relieve symptoms of depression and anxiety. She was very good at it.'

'Might she have come across Gapes in that capacity?'

We hit some turbulence. The bulkhead rattles and a locker flies open. Several flight manuals spill onto a seat next to us. I wait for things to settle before returning my verdict: impossible.

Graham considers this. 'Before you married, she took part in several protest marches, didn't she?'

'Does the Secret Service have a problem with that?'

'Per se, no.'

I'm glad to hear it.

'Tell me.'

'About what?'

'The first time you met.'

He hands me a photograph. Hope and me sitting on the steps of the Lincoln Memorial. An hour, maybe, after we'd left the Artiste. A green placard with 'PEACE' emblazoned on it in big yellow letters sits on the ground by her feet.

'You were about to graduate into the Air Force. Why were you protesting the invasion of Afghanistan?'

'I wasn't. She was.'

Except she never did.

The protest had moved on by the time we got to the Mall, so we'd strolled into the Lincoln Memorial instead, a place I'd not set foot in since my dad had brought me to D.C. as a kid.

She asked what had happened to him.

'He died. Quite suddenly. When I was twelve.'

She reached out and touched my hand. I can feel the electricity now. The extraordinary sense of serenity that followed. And the lingering fragrance of what I later discovered was Ô de Lancôme.

'How did you know about the Rockwell?' I said.

'You *own* a Rockwell?'

'A print of a Rockwell. It was the last thing my father gave me.'

'Which one?'

'*Glen*—'

'*Canyon Dam*? I *love* that painting.'

That was when I knew for sure I'd met the girl I wanted to spend the rest of my life with.

'Hope worked in a number of hospitals and residential care homes across the Metro area. She also assisted at her mother's nursing home in Pennsylvania. If you're implying she might have forged some kind of relationship with Gapes via her politics, dream on. Far as we can tell, he was a dedicated Marine until he suffered his brain injury in Iraq in 2007 – the date listed in his medical records. Though they appear to have been tampered with, the year is consistent with the estimate made by the medical examiner. My wife was killed the same year.'

'Doctor Cain, Gapes's connection to you is the best lead we have. Why did he single you out? If you didn't come across him in Iraq or through your clinical work, perhaps he and Mr Kantner encountered each other during the war.'

'What has this got to do with my wife?'

He glances at his watch, a flicker of annoyance in his eyes. 'We'll be landing shortly, so I suggest we pick this up again when we're onsite.'

The engine note changes and the plane starts to descend.

*

North Central West Virginia Airport is a military-civilian field the Service uses when it wants its movements within the state to remain sub-radar.

We turn off the runway and aim for a hangar where a helicopter waits, beacons and blades turning. After a twenty-minute low-level flight, we pull up and over a ridge and throw a hard left turn. The rotors struggle for lift in the thin mountain air.

The lake is powder blue under the midday sky. It looks very different from when Hart and I got here last night.

Trees have been cut down to make way for a landing pad.

There's a small squadron of helicopters on the ground. To its north is an olive-drab tent big enough to house several platoons, linked to the cabin by a muddy trail. Cables snake their way up the hill.

On the ground, last night's silence has been replaced by the rumble of generators. It has rained here too. The scent of earth and fresh pinesap hangs in the air.

The filaments of an industrial heater glow bright red inside the tent. Graham guides me toward one of the smaller 'rooms' and closes the flap-door behind us. It contains two whiteboards, a table and four chairs. Hetta is sitting on one of them.

'Hey.' She puts down her coffee, gets to her feet and stiffly offers me her hand. 'How was the flight up?'

'Bumpy. How are you?'

'Cold.' She draws her camouflage jacket more tightly over her shoulders. She doesn't look at me.

'Hetta, I'm sorry—'

'Lefortz?' She wipes her nose with her sleeve. 'Bad call, I guess.' She pats the weapon on her hip. 'If he'd asked me to go to D.C. 'stead of you, maybe he'd still be alive.'

I'm back in Hetta's world of black and white and say-it-like-it-is.

I put my briefcase on one of the chairs.

The left-hand whiteboard contains a rundown of Gapes's career alongside mine. Arrows point to areas of intersection in Iraq.

The right-hand board is blank except for the words 'Layer 1' and 'Layer 2', and a vertical line between them.

'Hart suggested we subject the walls to infrared,' Graham says. 'To see if there's anything beneath the surface layer. And there is. In what you called the sanctum; the part he constructed behind the drape.'

He picks up a marker pen, draws five rectangles under 'Layer 1' and numbers them. They correspond to what Hetta and I ID'ed as the patchwork of themes Gapes had built around Thompson and me.

'Left-hand panel.' Graham turns to me. 'Panel 1A depicts an image of the Crucifixion. Panel 2A is devoted to nothing but images of the President.'

He writes '3A' on the next panel, the one filled with sketches of the 'hijacker-priest' and '4A' on the one that appears to lay bare my entire life. Finally, there's the area devoted to the Jerusalem skyline, taking in the holy sites of the three religions: the Dome of the Rock, the Western Wall, churches, dominated by two prominent towers atop the Mount of Olives. Above this, he scribbles '5A'.

'We're using your nomenclature. So, from left to right: *God, Threat, Proof, Mac, Jerusalem.*'

He turns to face us again.

'When we did the infrared scan we found a single image beneath each of the five panels. Under Rembrandt's painting of the Crucifixion is another of his, looks like Christ in Heaven I guess, but hey, I'm no fucking expert. You'll see it when we take you up there.' He writes '1B' in the right-hand column, beside 'God'.

'Next, beneath the pictures of POTUS, we have one word: 'Church'. Why a word and not an image? Church ... He chose a church to reveal himself to you. The Church of the Presidents. We're redoubling our efforts to search the area around St John's for anything that constitutes a threat.' He writes '2B' in the right-hand column, beside the word 'Threat'.

'Then we have our mystery guy, Rasputin hair and beard, killer blue eyes, and beneath him that one word in Arabic. The word transliterates as *Al-Mohandis.*'

'It means "Engineer",' I say.

Graham's expression tells me to shut the fuck up and leave this kind of talk to the experts. 'Underneath it there was another word, this time in Cyrillic. The word is *Pitnatsat*. Any idea why?'

'I don't speak Russian.'

'It means "fifteen".'

Graham scribbles '15ski' and '3B' in the right-hand column, next to 'Proof'.

He looks back at the board, clearly pleased with himself.

'I'm now going to skip to the final panel. I'll come back to panel four momentarily.

'Beneath Jerusalem, we found an image of a church – gold domes; ornate, like a wedding cake. Russian Orthodox, the Church of St Mary Magdalene on the Mount of Olives.' He writes this down next to 'Jerusalem', and labels it '5B'.

'Any of this make sense to you, Colonel?'

'No.'

Apart from the emergence of a Russian theme, the standout, for me, is the 'Proof' panel.

'Did you run the Engineer through face recognition?' I ask.

'Yes. Nothing so far. And maybe it *is* nothing. Gapes was here months. Possibly for all of the three years that he was on the run. And on his own the whole time. So, what did this place mean to him and how did he get a hold of these images? What are they? And where did they come from? But here's the thing, Colonel: *you* were integral to his thinking from the start. I agree with Hart, except "Mac" isn't shorthand for you alone. It also includes those close to you.'

He continues before I can get a word in. 'There's little hard science on what makes an assassin. Eighty-six per cent are men; seventy-seven per cent are white; forty-four per cent had a history of depression; twenty-three per cent had been evaluated by a mental health professional. Only ten per cent had voices in their heads. But nearly all had suffered a recent trauma. And more than fifty per cent of those strongly identified with *other* victims of trauma and perceived injustice. The road traffic accident that killed your wife, Colonel, also killed the driver of the truck. And there were questions, too – questions local detectives raised—'

'They were unable to reach a conclusion about the Highway Patrol's tire mark analysis.'

'I was referring to the Hillsborough Sheriff's Office's investigations into your mental state at the time.'

I struggle to maintain my composure. 'What has that got to do about anything?'

'A number of your colleagues referenced the fact you were stressed. You'd just returned from Iraq. There were reports of higher than usual alcohol consumption, of possible trauma reactions . . .'

For the first time since we've been together, Graham smiles to temper what he's just said. 'Look, Colonel, if it hadn't been for your diligence, we wouldn't be where we are with Gapes. Nobody wants to turn the spotlight on you. My director has made that very clear. We just want to get to the truth. So, if we can back up to the night your wife was killed, we can be done with it and move on.' He pauses. 'You'd been with the Kantners, hadn't you?'

'Yes. Reuben had just been hired by Senator Abnarth. We were celebrating at a restaurant near Lakeland, halfway between our two homes.'

'And this was . . . ?'

'Eight months after we both returned from Iraq.'

'You were at MacDill?' Graham looks at the timeline on the left-hand board.

'Yes.'

'So, this celebration, was it *really* only about Kantner landing a job in D.C.?'

'What do you mean?'

'Just answer the question.'

I look at Hetta, who avoids looking at me.

Then I glance at the empty fourth panel.

Whatever's beneath the surface layer is the reason I'm here. I ask Graham to get to the point.

'OK. This is a hard thing to ask, Colonel. And a lot harder, I guess, to answer. Your wife, sir . . . is there any way Gapes could have known she was pregnant when she died?'

130

19

BEFORE LEAVING THE TENT, I THROW A TYVEK SUIT OVER MY CLOTHES and, at Graham's request, hand over my phone. Hetta does the same. It's a secure site – no photographs, except by the forensic team. I didn't take any pictures. Hetta erased hers.

We put on latex gloves and plastic overshoes and head into the cabin. The odor of decay has been replaced by the smell of chemicals and powders. The deer carcass has gone. The creosote lingers. The light from four arc lamps, each directed into a corner, is blindingly bright. A female specialist, lying on her back, is shining the beam of her flashlight up the chimney. Another, looking for hairs, prints and fibers, directs a UV lamp across the floor. A male photographer, standing on a metal ladder, shoots away at a cluster of images to the right of the fireplace, close to the inverted printout of the old man in the engraving. I can't keep my eyes off the sketch of the office building which provided poor Jimenez with his vantage point, so have to turn before Graham spots my point of interest.

A catalogue is being made, I hear Graham explaining, as he gestures to the walls and the ceiling. Multiple cyber breaches and four deaths equals conspiracy, which has the Secret Service on high alert.

'Once the images have been digitized they'll be crunched through the PIAD mainframe, searching for patterns,' Graham says. 'Then we'll know what we're dealing with.'

Patterns . . .

I look at Hetta.

She hasn't told him.

Graham asks if anything is wrong.

'I was wondering if you'd reached any conclusions about the imagery.'

His eyes narrow. 'We've ID'ed three types. The bulk are printouts – images he's pulled off the Internet. We found a laptop, a printer and a prepaid cell under the floorboards, and reckon he must have had a place in Blacksoil, a lock-up, where he could plug in, download and print this shit. The sketches are unquestionably his. Handwriting's matched the strokes with known examples of his work.

'And then there's the third category.' He points to the banal, everyday stuff – people at work, lying in bed; men and women sleeping, talking, picking their teeth in traffic, watching TV or scrolling down their phones. 'They all lack definition, as if the device or sensor was lo-res or filtered.'

'Our best guess is that they were taken by a surveillance system, a very sophisticated one – nano-drones maybe,' Hetta says. 'So how did he get a hold of them?'

We follow Graham to the sanctum wall.

The surface layer of pictures has been carefully removed and stored, to reveal what Gapes had hidden beneath it.

Somebody has pinned printed labels in two-inch-high lettering to the tops of the panels. I stop when I get to 'Mac'.

Beneath the label is an intricate sketch of a fetus.

'We checked with the Hillsborough Medical Examiner. The autopsy did not reveal the fact your wife was pregnant.' Graham gives his pen another double click. 'But her medical records show she attended a holistic clinic close to the beach where you used to live. And that they scanned her.' He pauses, to give emphasis to what follows. 'Gapes couldn't have hacked the scan, because the clinic hadn't at that time digitized its records.'

'I told you, Graham – the dinner was a celebration of Reuben Kantner's impending move to D.C.' I look him in the eye. 'Nobody knew about the pregnancy apart from Hope and me.'

It's only in the helicopter on the way back to the airport that I realize that isn't true. Reuben and Ted knew. I'm sitting next to Hetta, in one of the bucket seats. We don't talk. We can't because of the rotor noise, and anyway, she's busy with her keyboard.

Graham sits opposite, his head against the bulkhead. As far as I can tell, he's asleep.

Hetta passes me her iPad and indicates I should scroll.

Colonel, I'm off the investigation – back to number-crunching at HQ. And someone is out to bury you also. If this isn't clear to you, it should be. Remember what I said about Cabot – about image, not substance? He doesn't trust you.

He knows there is something going on – something between you, Kantner and POTUS. Cabot needs a quick win on this, a scapegoat, and you need to tell me what's going on, about the deal the three of you made with SAIC Lefortz – then I can help.

I type: *What deal?* and hand it back.

She looks at me, pulls a face, then starts to type furiously: *Lefortz assigned me to you that night. He never said why. You have history with Reuben Kantner.* She stops, thinks for a second and adds: *You're the White House Doctor, but I don't see you doing a whole lot of doctoring.*

I type: *OK.*

She indicates I should scroll on.

Point Two. Did you notice anything different about the cabin?

I glance up. Graham's eyes remain closed.

No.

She leans across me. I smell her hair. She's showered – and used something a little more tantalizing than the stuff they provide in the field to fight off bacteria, parasites, fungus and chiggers.

Some of the images are different.

I respond: *More images with numbers?*

She shakes her head.

Different in what way?

She leans in to me again. *Some of them have been removed.*

*

They're huddled at the bottom of the stairs, between a fridge and a shrapnel-scarred wall. Three women, all in black, and five children: three girls, two boys.

Our flashlights pick out the torn flesh on their legs, heads, bodies and arms.

'*Shit . . .*' Reuben drops his gun.

They're all dead.

No, they aren't.

I sense rather than see the movement.

The woman is lying on her back in a pool of blood, several meters from the others. She's young. Eighteen or nineteen, maybe. She stares at me. Kohl is smeared across her face. She's trying to say something.

I don't speak Arabic, but I'm willing her to tell me.

She points to her stomach.

Reuben shines his light. I throw off my helmet and my Alice pack.

The guy who blew the hinges off the door is standing beside me. He's still holding the shotgun. The one who tossed in the grenades is standing beside him. They both look like ghosts in the darkness. I point to the pack.

'There's a plastic sheet in there. Spread it. Find my instruments, place them on the sheet and pour spirit over them.'

Reuben does so.

I make a small cut in the *abaya* with my knife, then rip a hole in it.

She has a one-centimeter bullet wound in her abdomen and two other injuries that I can see: a shrapnel entry site in her right hip and another in her right thigh.

At that moment, she arrests.

I start applying CPR, but thirty seconds in I know I'm not going to get her back. She's lost too much blood; she's gone into hypovolemic shock.

Two minutes later, I call it.

Time and place of death: zero dark thirty, Fallujah, Iraq.

I sit in the silence, my back against the fridge, and close my eyes.

When I get to my feet, Reuben is still standing over the body. He's numb with shock. Everybody is.

I can't rid myself of the look on her face before she died. Eyes wide. Pleading.

Pleading.

'Give me some light!'

For a moment, Reuben remains rooted to the spot. I yell at him again and he does so.

I make a vertical incision in her abdomen wall, from her navel to a point just above her underwear, then cut into her uterus. Hemorrhagic fluid washes out of it. There's a liter of blood in the peritoneal sac. An intestinal perforation, too, because I can smell it.

Her baby girl is almost full-term. The 5.56 round entered her jaw and exited via her thorax . . .

For a moment, I have no idea where I am.

Then I hear the whine of the engines and the rattle of the overhead bins and slowly pull things into focus: the cigarette burns on the seat opposite, Hetta asleep in the one beside it, and Graham, his back to me, across the aisle.

I have relived this scene many times, in flashbacks and dreams, but never in a dream that was a flashback; because, like I told the President, dreams that incorporate flashbacks are vanishingly rare.

I only just make it to the head before I throw up. I try to flush it, then remember: damn thing's broken.

The sights, sounds and smells of that night continue to haunt me as I sit in my office, trying to focus on the backlog of work that has built up in the thirty-six hours that I've been away. Molly comes and goes – she asks if I need coffees or sodas; if the thermostat is turned too high; whether I would like *her* to go talk to the Deputy Chief of Staff, who's chasing me for updates on the Moscow medical mission. She doesn't know I was present when Lefortz was killed – and, unless it leaks through the media, she never will. But she knows what's wrong with me goes beyond the shock, pain and grief I feel for him.

I press the intercom button. She picks up before I hear her phone ring.

'Is there still no word from Reuben Kantner's office?'

'No, Doctor Cain.'

'But he is in today?'

'Oh, yes,' she says. 'I spoke to his assistant. Five times, to be precise. He's in. And he's aware it's urgent.'

'And what about Admiral Byford?'

'Her office is aware you're trying to reach her, too.'

'Is she in today?'

'I do believe so, Doctor Cain, yes.'

'Would you take a letter to her for me?'

'I doubt she'll see *me*, Doctor Cain.'

'But you know her assistant, right?'

'Olive-Ann and I are on first-name terms. What may I tell her?'

'I have the results of her blood test.'

'Blood test?' Molly says. 'Was that an appointment you made through me?'

'No. Sorry. I should have told you, Molly. I took her bloods a while back.'

There's a pause. She knows as well as I do there was no blood test. The note conveys a message of a different kind.

'Very well, Doctor Cain. What should I say if Olive-Ann asks me about it?'

'That her boss has nothing to worry about. But I'd like to drop around to speak with her all the same.'

'At her office?'

'No. At her home.'

'You have her address?'

I don't. Just that she lives in Alexandria. On the waterfront.

Molly appears, hands me the address and picks up my envelope. I hear the outer door close.

I try Reuben again.

Still busy.

When I look up, a big guy in an ill-fitting suit is standing by Molly's desk. His back is to me and he has a phone pressed to his ear. The last time I saw DJ we swapped pathology notes over Gapes's tattooed body.

'Special Agent Wharton.'

He turns and hangs up.

'Lefortz said I should come see you,' he says.

'Sorry, you're going to have to back up.'

'He didn't tell you?'

'Tell me what?'

'That we got together before he picked you up at Dulles.'

'Anything I should know about?'

'Gentleman Jim and I go way back, Colonel Cain, and I know that he rated you highly. We shared a lot of data. I think I know pretty much everything he knew about the Gapes case. And I'm guessing you were there when he died.'

I say nothing. I promised Reuben and Cabot I wouldn't.

Wharton holds his hands in the air and smiles awkwardly. 'Listen, that's OK. Of course there are things he was working on he couldn't share with me. The President's probe, for example . . .'

'*Probe*, Agent Wharton?'

'All I'm saying is, if you need Bureau support . . .'

'Is that why you're here?'

'No. I'm here because Jim said I should come see you if the Assistant US Attorney and I got the proffer session in place.'

'Proffer session?'

'Between the Gapes family lawyer, Katya Dedovic, and the US Attorney's Office.'

He taps his watch and says he'll give me the details en route.

20

CHARLES LAND, SENIOR PARTNER AT COLLINS LOVELOCK LAND, forty years in the federal-slash-government litigation bullpen, is a large man who sweats profusely. He leans forward and the table tilts, slopping some of my coffee over Hetta's notes.

Katya, pale, frail, almost birdlike, her shoulders hunched, sits next to him. She's not said a word yet and avoids looking at me.

'Who is the target of this investigation?' Land addresses the question to the Assistant US Attorney, a pasty guy in his mid-thirties seated to my right.

He looks across at Wharton.

'The MPD is,' DJ says.

'And Ms Dedovic?'

'At this moment,' DJ says, 'she has subject status, which—'

Land lifts a finger to his cracked, fleshy lips. 'I agreed to this meeting owing to the deeply serious events at Clarke's Crossroads last night, and because my firm, Ms Dedovic's employer, is keen to assist in any way that it can. However –' he gestures to each of us, '– this is a proffer session, not a trial, and we're under no obligation.'

He draws breath to speak again.

'Mr Land?'

'Yes . . .'

Hetta dabs at the coffee on her notes with a Kleenex. 'Last year, Ms Dedovic met with an Army legal team in a compensation case involving Duke Gapes. We believe Gapes was involved in activity that may have a bearing on threats made against Ms Dedovic in order to secure her silence.'

'That is simply untrue,' Land says.

'She told Colonel Cain she was terrified.'

'Untrue again. My colleague denies she ever met with Colonel Cain.'

'May we put that question to Ms Dedovic?'

'No.' His lips thin. 'Ms Dedovic isn't the target of your investigation.'

Hetta turns to the attorney.

'We assert that Ms Dedovic's reluctance to tell us what she knows is based on a malpractice breach.' He shuffles his notes. 'The privilege between Ms Dedovic and the Gapes family was invalidated by Ms Dedovic's disclosure of confidential – possibly classified – information to a third party.'

He means me.

Land opens his mouth, but the attorney continues. 'Yes, we heard you, Mr Land. That meeting never took place. But if this serves as an incentive, we are offering Ms Dedovic a selective waiver that will grant her witness status, regardless of the—'

'Attorneys are covered under work-product immunity,' Land states confidently.

'Unless there is, as you know, substantial need,' the attorney says.

'OK, then convince me.'

The attorney turns to me.

I clear my throat. The air conditioning hums. 'Whatever Gapes was doing, it wasn't mail-merge programs in some Department of Defense back office. His recovery support specialist – who oversaw Gapes's rehabilitation in Maryland – is dead, and that may have had a bearing on his decision to go on the run.

'We also have reason to believe –' I look at Katya, who told me this, '– that there was a period in which he was foreign-deployed. He made a call to his mother while on the run to say he was terrified about being sent to the desert. Such pressures may also have tipped him over the edge.

'Whatever the truth, Gapes was desperate enough to go to ground for three whole years before surfacing at the church.' I look again at Katya, who continues to stare at the plush carpeting. 'Which is why it's absolutely essential we know what she knows.'

'So . . .' Land leans forward. 'We're agreed that there's more to this than meets the eye. And *I* need to know, Colonel Cain, what you were doing in that tower in the first place.'

Lightning flashes across the room. The networks warned that another storm was inbound. Rain. Hail. The works.

Everybody is waiting for me to say something.

'Mr Land, Doctor Cain isn't under the spotlight,' the Assistant US Attorney interjects. 'Our request couldn't be more straightforward.'

'Nor could mine.' Land gathers up his notes. 'I think we're done here.'

Five minutes later, we're out on Massachusetts Avenue.

The US Attorney's Office can subpoena Katya's 'materials' – the background to her negotiations with the Defense Department, as well as her phone and email records. Land, however, will simply appeal against it. This could go on for weeks, maybe months.

Wharton and his attorney buddy return to FBI headquarters to regroup, leaving us to find shelter from the rain.

'You OK?' Hetta asks.

'Fine.'

'You don't look so good.'

I move on. 'Did Lefortz ever tell you about some kind of probe he was conducting on behalf of the President?'

She frowns. 'No.'

I tell her about the cryptic conversation I had with DJ in Molly's office.

'Sure he wasn't talking about *this* investigation – Gapes and all?'

'Seemed like he was referencing something else.'

'Wharton and I go back a ways. Why don't I ask him?'

We duck into a doorway. There's another rumble of thunder. I ask if there's any news on Voss, the guy they substituted for Gapes.

She shakes her head. 'Nothing on any of our databases, but we're not playing with a full deck. If he was Special Forces, he could be on a classified register.'

I make a mental note. If that's true, Christy may be able to help.

'What about the cabin?'

'Upside-down man. Gapes's inversion of the old guy wasn't a mistake.'

'Who is he?'

'A Benedictine abbot. Johannes Trithemius. Sixteenth century. Lived in southern Germany. Invented steganography.'

'Which is what?'

'It's about disguising the message in a seemingly random piece of text or imagery, so that nobody apart from the sender and the recipient knows that it exists. The way I see it, everything on Gapes's walls is a message – the whole cabin is, in fact.'

'What about? Who to?'

'Still working on that. The code's wrapped up in the pictures with numbers.'

'And the ones that were removed?'

She shakes her head. 'Without my original photos we're fucked.'

'We're not fucked.'

She looks up.

'Byford has the USB I gave to Lefortz.'

'As in, *Christy* Byford? The National Security Adviser?'

I nod. 'She's on the inside.'

'The inside of *what*?'

This seems as good a time as any to tell her about *No Stone*.

Post Traumatic Stress Disorder is a curious beast. Two individuals can witness the same event and each be affected completely differently. It's the meaning you attach to the experience that determines the degree to which the trauma will kick in, or whether it kicks in at all.

Hope knew that bad things had happened to me in Iraq. She'd asked me to tell her about them. But how could I? We were good friends with the Kantners. Hope and Heather had looked after each other while Reuben and I had been deployed. If I'd opened up about Fallujah, the whole story would have come tumbling out. There would have been inquiries. Charges, maybe. Reuben didn't pull the trigger or toss the grenades into that basement, but he gave the order.

Even if we got off, I doubt his political career would have flourished with civilian atrocities in his resume. Mine either. But for me, that wasn't the point. Reuben, somehow, seemed to be able to live with himself after what had happened. I couldn't.

And every time I looked at Hope, it all came flooding back.

Before I went to war, we'd been trying for a baby. It didn't happen.

Not then, at least.

Ted knows, because I told him at the time of my breakdown. He also knows we'd traveled to meet Reuben and Heather in Lakeland – and that during the course of the meal, Reuben announced he'd landed his dream job as a senior staffer for Tod Abnarth, advising the senior Democratic Senator from Wisconsin on defense policy.

We'd all applauded and raised our glasses, but I could see, from the way Hope looked at me across the table, that there was something else going on.

Sure enough, on the way home, on the road to the freeway, she'd told me she was pregnant. I'd seen her expression in the glow of the dash and what it said: that this would change everything; that this was *our* new start. Instead of thinking about us, we'd have someone else to focus on: our own beautiful little girl.

Perhaps it was because I hadn't reacted in the way she'd hoped that she pulled the ultrasound image from her purse.

The photo of our baby at twelve weeks.

I open my eyes, half expecting to see the grille of the blood-red Kenworth: all fifty thousand pounds and six hundred horsepower of it.

Ted is sitting back in his chair. He doesn't speak, and, thank God, he doesn't judge either. The truck driver had made no attempt to brake because he'd been asleep. Analysis of the tire marks left by our Jeep, on the other hand, demonstrated that, at the very last minute, I *had* attempted to brake, but I hadn't attempted to swerve.

Because the last thing I remember is the glare of the headlights in the second before it slammed into us, I was at a loss to tell the investigating officers from the Florida Highway Patrol and the Hillsborough Sheriff's Office how this could have been.

Nothing was ever said officially, but background checks, of course, go way beyond. Hetta's warning and Graham's aggressive insinuations tell me that I am under a shedload of scrutiny, that Cabot and Co. are digging into the unofficial post-crash conclusions: that owing to some imbalance of mind, I had deliberately steered for the oncoming vehicle.

There's a knock on the door.

Ted says 'come' and Susan walks in with two cups of coffee. As she hands me mine, she gives my shoulder a squeeze.

She is preparing for another trip to Kenya, where she's working on a dig-site with her students. She's a decade younger than her husband, with long, gray hair and a smile that's wider than wide. She kisses the top of my head, tells Ted his dinner will be ready in fifteen, and heads back upstairs.

'Josh,' he says, as soon as the door clicks shut, 'these are the ripple effects of conflict.' The way he speaks, too earnestly, tells me, despite his claim to the contrary, that he's shocked by what I've told him. 'You have to allow yourself to let it all go.'

'I know.'

'Perhaps you will feel some improvement now that you've told me, but . . .'

I wait.

'Your guilt over Fallujah has been compounded by the guilt you feel about Hope. Of course you ruminate on these events. But it's fifteen years since she died. When you had your breakdown, I slapped a Band-Aid on you . . .'

I sense another 'but' coming.

'What is it you're not telling me?'

'The guy – the guy they shot – he knew everything, Ted.'

143

'What do you mean, *everything*?'

'He knew about Hope. He knew about our place on the beach. He knew she was going to have a baby . . .' I pause. 'There's nobody alive knows that, except for you and Reuben.'

Ted lifts his cup and sips his tea, watching me all the while.

'Where do we retain memory, Josh?'

'Memories aren't stored in any one area in the brain. You know that.'

'Explicit memory.'

'In the hippocampus, the neocortex and the amygdala.'

'The classical version. Science orthodoxy.'

'Is there any other?'

'From my research, there is growing evidence that our brains are physically incapable of retaining the quintillion bits of data we acquire in the course of a full life. So where do we store them?'

'There are only two options.'

'And they are?'

'First, that there are facets of the brain and its storage system we don't understand.'

He nods. 'Second?'

'That memory is held off-site, in a field of collective consciousness – much as Jung believed.'

He sits back.

'Your point being . . . ?'

'There are things out there, Josh – things about our innermost selves – that we're simply at a loss to explain.'

21

'YOU HART?'

'Yes, ma'am.' She extends her hand. 'Phone, please.'

Byford digs into her pocket. She knows my concerns. They were in my note about the non-existent blood test. Hetta places her cell in a briefcase with a wire mesh lining – a mini Faraday cage, impervious to signals, in or out. Ours are there already.

The waterfront complex where Byford lives used to be a tobacco warehouse. We're parked up just inside its heavy wrought-iron gates. I sit in back. Christy is in front, next to Hetta, still brushing the rainwater from the sleeves of her trench coat.

I've met Christy three times. She was retired and eking out a living as a lecturer at the Naval Academy in Annapolis when, in the face of one or two raised eyebrows, Thompson asked if she'd be his National Security Adviser. She hesitated before saying yes. She is divorced, has no kids, and there are rumors about her sexuality. She's smart, dresses smart and sports a fuck-you power hairdo that was probably last seen on Farrah Fawcett. And she and Thompson have known each other since he first arrived in Washington, when they worked together on the Hill.

She hands Hetta the USB.

It takes the spatial frequency pattern-monitoring software less than thirty seconds to compare the photos Hetta had taken on her phone with the 'official' imagery compiled by Graham's forensic unit.

We all lean forward.

On screen are three images that have been picked out by the algorithm.

All three have come from the main body of the cabin. When Hetta noticed that some of the images were missing, she couldn't, of course, say which – the unique way in which she processes things merely alerted her to the fact that *something* about the cabin was different.

Now we can see exactly what and where.

The first image to have been flagged appears to be a cutaway of a planet: an outer shell with inner shells that merge in what looks like an orange core. It had been in the top left corner of the wall, opposite the door, and has been replaced by a picture of a soccer stadium.

The second is a black-and-white photo of a man who looks like a young Napoleon – twenty-something, a little swarthy, a lock of lank, black hair across his brow.

The third is an overhead of a building – a drone or spy satellite shot. The resolution is as good as the picture that allowed us to identify the cabin. Unlike the cabin, however, this place appears to be bunker-like and is set in a sort of compound.

There's an odd look to it – and something familiar: it's the kind of facility that hits the wires when the Pentagon needs to persuade us that a rogue state has been developing WMDs.

'These were all removed overnight?' Byford asks. Like the other members of the National Security Council, she would have been sent the Secret Service's initial report on the cabin in the small hours, and then updates during the day.

'Yes, ma'am.'

'And you're sure it's just these three images?'

'The algorithm doesn't lie,' Hetta says.

'Who removed them?'

'We don't know. The Army muscled into the cabin as part of the forensic investigation. Gapes is their man and Director Cabot was under pressure to give Army CID access. In the end, it was agreed we both would have access. I'm hoping you may be able to help us here . . .'

Byford looks surprised. 'Me?'

'I was at the cabin when our relief team arrived. It got there when it was still dark; the Army CID team touched down six hours later. The cabin was a crime scene. Forensics all over it. Nobody entered unless they were suited and booted. Everybody changed and showered in a tent by the lake.

'As soon as I came off duty, I went down there to clean up. A couple of the Army CID guys had beaten me to it. One male, one female. The guy was in line to take a shower after me. I tried talking with him, but he didn't say much. There was something about him – about them both . . .' She pauses. 'I have this thing – I hate soap that's been used by anybody else, so I—'

'Hetta,' I say.

'Yes?'

'The National Security Adviser has a dinner appointment.'

'Of course. Sure.'

Hart reaches into her pocket for a small, transparent evidence bag. 'One of the three hairs he left in my soap. I ran another through our DNA database. Nothing showed. Unlikely, I guess, that he'd have a criminal record. I don't have access to classified Department of Defense databases.'

Byford holds the bag as if the contents might bite her.

'We also need to know what the military holds on the guy they tried to palm off as Gapes,' I say. 'Who is – or was – Master Sergeant Matthew L. Voss? I guess he must be dead, or we'd have turned something up by now.'

Christy pockets the bag and promises to come back with answers. She turns back to the screen. 'Whoever these people are, could they know we know these images have been removed?'

'I don't think so,' Hetta says.

'What about that misogynist son of a bitch?'

Hetta hesitates, unsure if she heard her right. 'Director Cabot?'

'Who else?'

Hetta shakes her head. 'Impossible.'

'Good. Then nobody else should, outside the three of us.'

Byford dons reading glasses and peers at the screen. 'So, what have we got? This shell-like thing? Your guess is as good as mine . . .'

She scrolls to the photo of Napoleon. 'Same with this guy. And the building? Again, no idea.'

I ask her about the Engineer.

'According to intercepts this past year, he's a bomb-maker. Something of a celebrity inside the intel community.'

I ask her why.

'Because every time we hear his name, we get a bunch of eschatology alongside it.'

'A bunch of what?' Hetta says.

'Allah's-going-to-come-down-and-blow-up-the-whole-world prophecy stuff.'

'I don't understand.'

'The intel that we have boils down to the guy being a bomb-maker who moonlights as an itinerant, miracle-working mystic who, in the fullness of time, will come out of the desert to smite down the unbelievers.'

'Is there any hard data on him?'

'Precious little. But we didn't know much about al-Sadr, al-Zarqawi or al-Baghdadi before they popped up on our screens either.'

'We're going to need everything our intelligence community has on him,' I tell Christy.

'Why? The intel says he's a joke.'

'A joke?'

'Propaganda. To get us looking the wrong way.'

'Gapes labeled his panel "Proof",' Hetta says. 'In the layer underneath, they found the word *pitnatsat*, the Russian for fifteen. Does that mean anything?'

Byford shakes her head.

'What about the bunker?' I ask.

'Locating this bunker is going to take some processing, but let's start by trying to get a match with overheads of suspected WMD sites within the usual borders.'

The Engineer. Gapes. Intelligence and Security Command.

Joint Special Operations Command. Weapons of Mass Destruction. Something clicks.

As a para-jumper, I was attached to Special Ops in Iraq. Our taskings came from JaySOC, with units like Reuben's: not black, exactly, but dark gray. The SEALs were a deeper shade. Then there were the CIA units. But one Army outfit – called 'the Activity' – was off the scale. It was rumored to answer to INSCOM.

'The shell-like thing is a component for a nuclear weapon.'

'How do you know?' Hetta says.

The rain on the roof seems to drum a little harder.

The answer is, I'm not sure. I just do.

'What else do you know?' Christy looks at us both.

We give her the short version.

'I'm going to need to get you both cleared,' Byford says when we're done. 'And then we're going to brief the President.'

22

MY APPROVAL FOR CATEGORY 3 SPECIAL ACCESS CLEARANCE, THE
highest there is, was authorized at midnight – just under eight
hours ago – on Byford's authority, and by the legal counsels of the
Secretary of Defense, the Director of the CIA and the President's
Special Counsel. It is being rushed through to enable me to receive
need-to-know intelligence on certain classified programs.

The lawyer behind the desk glances at me over the top of his
glasses as he reads from the document. He is keen for me to understand the penalties for breaching a Special Access Program request
form: a 150-year jail sentence and fines that would leave me with
several lifetimes of debt.

The Office of National Intelligence is the access control authority for the SAPs I am being cleared to know about. When we're
done, I make my way across the lobby, as directed, toward a reinforced door where I see the Attorney General and the CIA Director
deep in conversation.

I present my ID to a Marine. The watch team officer checks my
name against a list, asks for my phone, tags it, secures it in a
wooden locker, and asks me to follow him.

Like everything else in the 'Sit Room' complex, our destination
is much smaller than the carefully staged publicity shots suggest. We access it through a door next to what looks like a darkened
cubbyhole with video-conferencing facilities. The watch officer
shows me to my assigned seat – not at the table, but against the
wall to the right of the entrance.

The Secretary of State, the Defense Secretary, the FBI Director, the Vice President and the Homeland Security Secretary are already seated around the table – and so is Cabot, who smiles at me, briefly exposing his small white teeth. Christy stands behind a podium at the far end. I acknowledge her and she nods back as the Attorney General and the CIA Director take their seats.

The President and Reuben are the last to arrive. Thompson looks drawn. He mutters a greeting to no one in particular, from the head of the table. Reuben's expression is grave. With ten days to go before Thompson's State of the Union, his presidency is in crisis. The networks are still leading with extensive coverage of the shootings and their connection to the clearing of the Settlement and the North Fence camp eviction, which has resulted in multiple arrests overnight. The action is being widely reported as evidence of Thompson's double standards: a man who talks a good game when it comes to freedom of speech, but not when it impacts his own security.

Byford hits the remote. Along the top of the cover slide, above the seal of the National Security Council, run the words: *Top Secret – Special Access Required. Project Element.*

'We believe the deaths of Lefortz, Anders and Jimenez were linked to a serious cyber incursion; that a person, persons or agency unknown hacked into the MPD's comms network and that somebody masquerading as Anders – or a piece of software able to mimic his voice – told his tac officer, Raoul Jimenez, to take the shot.'

The room falls quiet.

'Efforts are being made to track back to the source of this incursion, as well as three others. In the first, a CCTV camera was repositioned to provide a view of the church from an office building across the street. In the second, a camera was disabled to allow the protester to make his way from the river to the Settlement, where he took refuge before making his way to St John's. We know that he accessed the church through the sewer system.'

She pauses before continuing.

'The most serious breach, however, involved the altering of

DNA, medical and personnel records on the veterans register, prompting the MPD to wrongly identify the protester as former Marine Master Sergeant Matthew L. Voss.'

She takes a sip of water. 'In the early hours of yesterday, the Secret Service was able to establish the protester's true identity beyond doubt. Until then, he was thought to be on the run, AWOL, very likely deceased.

'Night before last, we located a cabin in the North Laurel Fork, West Virginia, where he had been in hiding. Sergeant Duke Gapes – his real name, Mr President – was part of a covert effort involving our intel community at the highest levels.'

Cabot takes the podium and presents us with the cabin, floodlit, surrounded by cables. Tech support and forensics specialists obscure part of the shot, their white jumpsuits prominent against the trees.

'Mr President, what we have uncovered is complex.' He seems unusually pleased with himself, I guess because he can take credit for the breakthroughs of the past twenty-four hours and distance himself from anything that has gone wrong.

'We don't yet have a complete picture of where Gapes has been or what he's done since he went to ground three years ago. Neither do we know why Voss – the man originally identified as the protester – was chosen to divert our attention.

'It's partly with these questions in mind that I've been working with Mayor Phillips to clear sources of protest in the so-called peace movement. We're operating on the assumption that all this activity has been undertaken on the instruction of some foreign agency, but we shouldn't rule out the possibility the threat comes from within.'

The slide show flicks to an overhead of the Settlement and a map overlay showing the distance to St John's with dotted lines tracing Gapes's subterranean route, and then on to the cabin's interior.

Cabot acknowledges the murmur that greets the shot of the crazy wall. 'I know. There are more than five thousand images. Some photos. Some drawings. Many have been pulled off of the

Internet. Some come from a source that is particularly vexing, Mr President, because it tells us that Gapes had access to a source of surveillance imagery whose origins at this time are unknown.'

He beckons to the watch officer.

Hetta has also spent the morning getting cleared. She now makes her way across the room.

'Mr President,' Cabot says, 'this is Special Agent Henrietta Hart of our Protective Intelligence and Assessment Division. Hart was with Colonel Cain when he was called to St John's Church on Monday morning. Hart and Colonel Cain were also responsible for identifying Gapes and locating the cabin. She has been working on the data and has some early, critical analysis.' He touches her lightly on the shoulder. 'Go ahead.'

Hetta steps up to the lectern.

She touches her crucifix.

A section of the wall centered on the upside-down image fills the screen.

She flips it right side up and four rows of numbers appear:

17, 7, 21, 21, 6, 18, 21, 20, 25, 23, 21, 11, 20, 19, 11, 22
2, 11, 5, 7, 18, 25, 14, 14, 6, 11, 11
24, 21, 25, 8, 6, 8, 5, 21, 20, 25, 17, 6, 18
18, 11, 10, 21, 10, 8, 25, 2

'Johannes Trithemius was a sixteenth-century monk.' She focuses on the lectern, avoiding eye contact with her audience. 'For four hundred years, his book, *Steganographia*, remained an obscure text, but a few years back, an academic realized that it was riddled with messages. Steganography is a special kind of code – you have to know that it's there to begin with. The inversion of his portrait wasn't an accident. It was a clue, which I believe Gapes meant us to find quickly.'

She advances the deck to enlargements of half a dozen images. Arrows show where they were positioned on the wall.

The images containing numbers: one is a car license plate. Another is a street sign. A third is the registration of a commercial jet. In yet another, a man wearing a rhinestone shirt holds up a winning lottery ticket.

'We ran every single picture containing a number through our mainframe. The analysis showed that they do not match the originals, all of which can be found online. They've been doctored for a purpose. Together, they form the series of digits displayed in the last slide. Apply a simple reverse-alphabet system to it, and this is what you get.'

She hits the remote. The figures melt away, leaving a message:

I SEE THE FACE OF GOD
YOU SHALL TOO
BEAR TRUE FAITH
HOPE PRAY

'The sixteenth-century German alphabet didn't contain the letter W, so I think it makes better sense rendered as: "I *saw* the face of God." This may or may not be relevant, but Gapes tried to engage Colonel Cain in a dialogue on religion in the tower.

'The second line may be an implicit threat to you, Mr President.'

Even though she's now privy to *No Stone*, Hetta doesn't do soft soap.

'The third line has been taken from the oath an officer swears when commissioned – the oath you swore, Mr President, when you were inaugurated. The fourth line may be a reference to Colonel Cain's wife, who featured prominently in a part of the cabin that we've termed the sanctum, though we don't know for sure.'

'Tell me what you *think*,' Thompson says.

'I think every piece of information on these walls contains meaning, sir.'

'*Meaning*, Ms Hart?'

'Messages, Mr President. On the nature of the threat that Gapes outlined to Colonel Cain.'

'There are two distinct sections of the cabin.' All eyes shift my way as I get to my feet. 'The one you saw, Mr President, the main one, contains the seemingly random images. A second, roped off from the first in the sanctum, has five panels – five theme areas, each with two layers. One is dedicated to you, another to me. Mine is personal. Invasively so. It displays certain things I believed to be absolutely private. We don't know yet how Gapes managed to get a hold of this information, but we're operating on the assumption that he – or someone – hacked into my clearance document.'

'There is one last piece of analysis I would like to share, Mr President,' Hetta chips in as I sit back down.

'Go ahead, Special Agent Hart.'

'As my director mentioned, the images in the cabin taken in close proximity to you demonstrate one thing very clearly. If whoever took them wished to kill you, they had every opportunity to do so.'

'So?' Thompson says.

'Duke Gapes was a whistleblower, sir. Not a conspirator.'

I smile to myself. Only Hetta can give credit to Cabot for this insight and make him look like a complete idiot at the same time.

'A whistleblower?'

'Duke Gapes had insider knowledge of a plot to kill you. A plot that clearly remains extant. But for a reason we don't understand, he chose to present the data in the form of a riddle. Multiple riddles, in fact.'

Christy replaces her at the podium. 'Mr President, it is my wholehearted recommendation that you put your announcement about the peace conference on hold.

'Project Element is a covert operation undertaken by JaySOC to run down terrorist cells suspected of developing or seeking to acquire weapons of mass destruction. The tip of the spear is an Army action unit called the Activity.'

She pauses.

'The Activity's mandate for covert action was approved by the last administration, and that approval has been extended by oversight committees under your own. But even they are unaware of the precise scope of its mission.

'Gapes was part of a deeply secret cell, tasked, we believe, with providing the Activity with special intel on the WMD threat. His files contain no hint of this. We're not sure what he did provide. The compartmentalization and security surrounding this program is extreme. It was only when Colonel Cain deduced a connection between Gapes and the Activity that we were able to join the dots. My staff has spent the night working with lawyers to enable us – you and me, Mr President – to gain access to the files that confirmed the connection.'

Thompson's eyes narrow. 'And they still don't specify Gapes's role with this unit?'

'No, sir. JaySOC holds the tasking mandate for the Activity, and its commander, General Johansson, is overseas.'

She pauses again.

'For the past year, the Activity has been working with Russian Special Forces to track down terrorists plotting to use WMDs against our two nations. This may be significant, as there are a couple of allusions to the Russians in the five panels.

'On Monday night, a partial note found in the church included the words "Proof" and "Jerusalem". We believe the threat is linked to this man, the Engineer.'

She flashes up the sketch of Al-Mohandis in the cabin. 'We have very little on him, except that he appears to be a bomb-maker. Jihadists boast that he will deliver them from the "Far Enemy". That's us. Lately, that chatter has increased. I've asked for a maximum effort from each of our intelligence agencies, Mr President, to tell us why.'

'Jerusalem?'

'Yes, sir.'

'But nobody . . .'

Thompson gets to his feet. Faces turn to him. We need to hear something rousing, something reassuring. Something in future years, when the danger is long gone, we'll all read, and feel good about.

But the President looks like he's seen all four horsemen of the apocalypse. He picks up his briefing notes and walks from the room.

I know why.

The Engineer is the man with the bomb belt; the assassin from the President's dreams.

In the silence that follows, I see something else: ground truth. The term Gapes used right before he was shot.

A tactical situation on the ground that may differ from one that has been identified in military intelligence reports and mission objectives.

There *were* no intelligence reports. The intel community considered the Engineer to be a joke, a myth; that he didn't exist.

Gapes was attached to the Activity. He had some kind of special intelligence role within it. The Activity was tasked with hunting down terrorists seeking or armed with WMDs. The mythology said the Engineer was a bomb-maker.

I'm now in the helicopter that brought me back from the cabin, flying over that impenetrable black forest.

Dr Kate Ottoway. The dead white matter tracts in Gapes's brain. The voices and hallucinations. His medication. The clinical insights I'd received as I'd gazed into that void – the thought it had produced and I'd then dismissed: the parts of the brain that Buddhists shut down when they meditate, the parts of the brain mediums engage when they go into 'state' . . .

Something finally clicks. Gapes's knowledge about me; his pronouncements about my *nature*. Things he couldn't possibly have known by anything other than the most extraordinary means.

His employment by INSCOM wasn't an accident.

They needed him.

They recruited him.

Because he was psychic.

23

AFTER TWENTY-FOUR HOURS OF NON-STOP RAIN, SUNLIGHT, AT LAST, streams between the bare branches. Beyond the terrace, the ground drops away sharply past the swimming pool and the one-hole golf course toward a line of trees.

Hart and I are at Aspen Lodge, the President's Camp David retreat. It is the day after the Sit Room briefing. We have a kitchen, a sunroom, a living room where we've installed our temporary HQ, and four bedrooms, each with its own en suite. If we need anything, all we have to do is pick up a phone and ask.

The revelation that Gapes was producing psychic intelligence for the Activity has unlocked a wealth of new data. For the past day and night, Christy's team has worked to uncover all the elements of the Activity's ultra-classified WMD-hunting mission. It hasn't been easy. As Christy said in the briefing, each layer of secrecy conjures up another. And there are legal procedures for accessing each one. Special Access Programs aren't so called for nothing.

Each file we uncover is couriered to us from D.C. Our task is a delicate one. Our work has been rewarded with an official role in the ongoing investigation. My skills as a psychiatrist are sought in a bid to rapidly unlock the secrets of the cabin, now that we think we know what we are dealing with. But we must also continue to protect the President. No one must know about his vulnerability; about *No Stone Unturned*. Which is why, while answering to Cabot and Graham, who are leading the official investigation inside the White House, Hart and I will only go so far in revealing what we know.

As before, we will report our findings to the inner circle – Thompson, Reuben and Christy – before sharing them with anybody else. Hence our current seclusion.

After our analysis of the existing data, a ninety-minute drive on Monday will take the two of us to Fort Meade, headquarters of Army Intelligence and Security Command, where Gapes worked. Christy Byford has arranged for us to meet and interview General Zan Johansson there.

Thanks to the marathon efforts of Christy's legal team in the last twenty-four hours, we'll also be debriefed by Major Cal Offutt, one of Gapes's monitors during the years he spent with the Activity. Both Johansson and Offutt have effectively been subpoenaed to tell us everything they know. Project Element is so black, merely identifying and acquiring these files is an ongoing struggle.

The key point is that Gapes joined the program a decade ago, around the time the Activity and its hunt for WMDs transferred to JaySOC.

This part of the project – a subset of Element – had been code-named 'Chronometer'. Remote viewing – RV – was America's psychic-spying program. Initially sponsored by the CIA in the early seventies, it transferred to the Army, where INSCOM ran it through the eighties, moved it to the Defense Intelligence Agency before, finally, it was transferred back to the CIA, where it died a death in 1995. Upon termination and declassification, an official report made it plain to whoever came calling that there had never been anything in it.

This part was a lie.

INSCOM and the CIA were *so* desperate that, one year after 9/11, in their hunt to find bin Laden and his co-conspirators, they resurrected it.

In 2005, a small group of viewers left Fort Meade, where they had been based for the best part of three decades, to attach themselves to the SEALs and Delta Force. New recruits had been selected, too, via a program to evaluate veterans returning from

Afghanistan, Iraq and other recent theaters of war – the data having flagged up a correlation between psychic ability and certain categories of brain injury.

With Gapes, it got one of the best – until the helicopter crash that killed three members of the Activity and left him with burns that should have killed him outright.

This is the part I don't get.

Instead of letting him go, they dug their hooks into him more deeply.

I get to my feet and wander over to the window.

If we don't get a break before Thompson's State of the Union in a week's time, there will be no peace initiative – the Jerusalem conference will be canceled.

I turn from the window to *The Raising of The Cross* and *Ascension*, the paintings from the panel section of the sanctum Gapes had marked 'God'. They are projected on the President's eighty-five-inch, wall-mounted, flat-screen TV.

'You know how much those are worth?' Hetta says.

'They're priceless.'

'I got to tell you I never really understood that – *priceless*. *Priceless*. Doesn't everything have a price?' She frowns and shakes her head.

Miss Literal is determined to take her frustrations out on me today.

Whatever you believe it to be worth, *The Raising of The Cross* is an extraordinary work of art. The ray of light shining down on the broken Christ is almost too vivid to look at. As soldiers struggle to raise Him, a mysterious figure in a turban looks on – whether at us, or the scene that's unfolding in front of him, I can't be sure. In the foreground lies a freshly dug grave.

Along with *Ascension*, the painting Gapes hid beneath it, it's hung in the Alte Pinakothek in Munich, a gallery famous for its Old Masters. There are no obvious links to Gapes, nor do psychologists agree on any hidden meanings, except, perhaps, for one – that *The Raising of The Cross* is a metaphor for Rembrandt's struggle with his religious beliefs.

'The thing is,' I say, more to myself than to Hetta, 'Rembrandt is the turbaned figure. He's also one of the soldiers raising the cross. So, both observer and participant.' I pause. 'A remote viewer.'

Hart and I both battle with the idea of psychics producing data of value to the intelligence community, but we also acknowledge the military would not have spent millions if it hadn't been underpinned by results. I can hear Ted van Buren's voice at times like this. *There* are *things out there that science is still struggling to explain.*

I start again from first principles.

We have four layers of code. Four layers of unfolding revelation.

The first is what Hetta calls the welcome message: *I saw the face of God. You shall too. Bear true faith. Hope. Pray.*

I look at the face of Christ on the cross, and at Rembrandt's light, blindingly bright again, streaming through a break in the clouds, surrounding Him as He is lifted heavenward by angels. In the foreground, on the edge of darkness – the chasm that separates us from the risen Christ – the disciples are awestruck.

One of them, arms spread wide, is so overcome he seems to tumble backward, straight out of the painting toward me.

What is it that I'm not seeing?

I stare at a large sheet of paper Hetta has pinned on the wall next to the TV. On it, she's written, 'Layers 2 and 3':

*Panel 1. (Rembrandt) Crucifixion > Ascension = **God.***
*Panel 2. POTUS > 'Church' = **Threat.***
*Panel 3. Engineer (Mugshot) > '15ski' = **Proof.***
*Panel 4. Cain's Life > Fetal Scan (Hope pregnant) = **Mac.***
*Panel 5. Skyline > Church of St Mary Magdalene (Russian Orthodox) = **Jerusalem.***

The Jerusalem panel is of particular interest because it seems to suggest Gapes knew about the conference. If this is so, bizarrely, he seems to have known about it before Thompson did.

Much of the imagery is religious, Hetta points out, except for Panels 3 and 4.

I agree – up to a point. There is a possibility, I suggest, that Panel 4 could signify a more spiritual interpretation of 'birth'.

Hetta thinks about this for a moment, then jots on the page:

*Panel 4. Cain's Life > Fetal Scan (Hope pregnant/hippy shit/ birth?) = **Mac**.*

Panel 3 remains devoid of religious or spiritual meaning, leaving the five panels without any discernible thread.

Except for the two that have a Russian linkage.

And how the Engineer fits is anybody's guess.

Layer Four is the stolen imagery from the main body of the cabin: the photos of the individual we've dubbed Napoleon, the planetary shell and the bunker facility in the desert compound.

We're no further forward on them either.

'If he wanted to tell us something, especially about a threat to POTUS, why hide it?' Hetta says. 'And in code, but not good code?'

I have no idea. I also don't know why he had six evenly spaced lesions on his head, or why he chose to tell Steve at the Settlement about his plans for breaking into the church, only to use an espionage tool specifically designed to *conceal* break-ins.

Most of all, I don't know why he had a painting of Jack, which, unlike the one in my guest room, looked as if Hope had finished it.

We're still going around in circles several hours later when I hear a helicopter.

I get to the window as *Marine One* thunders over the lodge and touches down on the edge of the golf course.

24

THE PRESIDENT HAS HAD THIRTEEN ASSASSINATION DREAMS. THE
first, like a first panic attack, is the one I need to examine most
closely. He flew to Camp David alone yesterday, and we will have
him for the whole morning today, if we need it.

He's in the kitchen at 7 a.m. in jeans and a polo shirt, a sweater
over his shoulders, finishing his breakfast. He tells me he's slept
well. Since I prescribed the Prazosin, he hasn't had a recurrence of
the dream.

We're alone. Hetta has gone to the range to put in some practice
on her .357. I settle him in an armchair next to the fireplace. A
stool in front of it allows him to lie back comfortably.

The detail of dreams, which can reveal causes and triggers, can
be lost over time. Which is why I need to take this route. I know
he's under when I tell him his right arm is as light as a feather and
his hand starts to lift toward the ceiling. I ask about the first
dream, ask him to describe where he is.

'I'm in school.' He sounds a little drowsy, his voice younger, his
accent a little more Texan than the world has become used to.

'Good. Tell me what you see.'

'I'm in class. Carpentry class. Makin' something. We're in the
basement. Thick walls. Old place. Don't like it. Dark as hell.'

'How old are you?'

'I'm, ah, fourteen.'

'Who's with you?'

'I'm alone.'

163

'What are you making?'

'A box.'

'A box?'

'Yeah.'

'Why?'

'Put my tools in.'

'Your tools?'

'Carpentry tools.' He pauses. 'The box ain't finished yet.'

'Is that significant?'

'Think so, yes. Feel I need to finish it. Have to.'

I'm writing this down when his face clouds.

'What is it?'

'Somebody's coming. Footsteps. I can hear footsteps.'

'OK, stay with it. Tell me exactly—'

'The door's opening. It's him. Jesus, he's got a knife. He's coming for me. He's lifting it. I don't want to be here.'

He opens his eyes, sits upright and puts his hands to his face. 'God almighty, Josh.'

'It was real?'

'All too real.'

'And the guy with the knife?'

'Same as the guy in the Sit Room. Him. The Engineer.'

'You sure?'

'Never been surer of anything.'

'Then we need to talk about this.'

There's no end of stories online about Thompson's modest roots. He is the epitome of the American dream: the poor kid from a Southern Baptist family who went to the big city, and made a stash as a corporate lawyer before deciding to go into politics.

'I grew up with kids who weren't raised like we were. When I started hanging out with guys who liked doing the things kids do – music, girls, a beer or two – my folks did what a lot of church-goers did at that time in that neck of the woods: they sent me away to an all-boys boarding school, the Southern Cross. And when I say boarding school, I'm not talking about something you pay for. This place was run as a charity with a contribution from the state.'

'I didn't know that.'

'Yeah, well, it's not something I talk about much.'

I wait.

'The principal was a preacher, Pastor Green. He used to say woodwork was the Lord's work. Kept Proverbs 23:13, inscribed in copperplate, above his desk. "*Withhold not correction from a child, for if thou beatest him with the rod, he shall not die.*"'

The school was a converted warehouse – an ex-meat-packing factory. Thompson describes the maze of rooms beneath it. In one of them, they held carpentry classes on Saturdays.

'We had to make this box. Nothing fancy. Maybe thirty centimeters by twenty, fifteen deep. With a lid. To teach us dovetail joints. When we mastered the box, we could go on to bigger, better, more complicated pieces.

'Green put the older boys in charge of the classes and one of 'em, son of a bitch called Arturo, took a real dislike to this puny kid, Kit Harper. Every time Harper assembled his box, Arturo would pick it up, look at it, laugh, and smash it to pieces.'

Harper never complained, because Green had some saying in copperplate for that too. Until the day that Thompson told Arturo and Green they could both go to hell – and the pastor beat him so bad he ended up in the sanatorium.

'What happened after that?'

'My dad took me out. Sent me to a different school.'

'And Green?'

'He went to jail for embezzling church funds – not soon enough, though, for Kit Harper. He threw himself under a train.'

'When?'

'Two months after I left.'

'Mr President?'

He raises his eyes.

'Do you have any idea why Gapes would have placed the word "Church" beneath images of you on the campaign trail?'

We're so close, I see his pupils constrict.

'No,' he says.

'What did you major in?'

'Theology and law. My doctorate's in theology.'

I sit back. I still don't know what an Islamist bomb-maker is doing in his dreams, but I believe I know what he represents.

He is the darker side of Thompson's nature, an avenging angel righting wrongs he couldn't right as a fourteen-year-old.

And I have a further suspicion, after we have talked it out some more – that the Engineer, with his knife, his assault weapon and his bomb belt, isn't coming for Thompson. He's coming for Arturo and Pastor Green.

25

TRESCO IS TWO AND A HALF HOURS FROM WASHINGTON, BUT only an hour and a half from Camp David. A thought had been triggered by something Thompson had said – about the box in his dream having been half finished. I let Hetta know I'd be back by dinner.

The sun has slipped behind the trees by the time I pull up in front of the cottage. It has turned cold. The temperature on the dash says three below. Wood smoke from the chimney hangs in the air.

It is eleven years, incredibly, since I drove the U-Haul here, packed with Hope's stuff.

I climb the steps and knock on the screen door.

It opens and she's there, in jeans and a rollneck sweater. She's changed her glasses – they're smaller than they used to be. She has mitts under one arm, an apron under the other.

I feel the heat of the wood-burning stove on my face and smell baking.

Pam's face is more lined than it used to be. Her trademark Marlboro Reds have taken their toll. She gives me a long, hard stare, then steps forward and hugs me.

'Josh!'

I'm almost knocked off my feet by Poppy too.

'Not surprised?'

'Dog stopped her damn barking soon as you stepped out of the car. Only one person she does that for. What brings you here?'

'Came to see you.'

She takes a drag on her cigarette and smiles. 'Bullshit.'

It's a minute or two before my mother-in-law lets me go.

'I'll put on some coffee. You staying?'

'Not long. I should have called. I'm sorry.'

Pam ushers me inside. A rack laden with cupcakes is waiting to be iced by the sink. She orders me to take a seat and reaches for a pot of coffee.

A pan bubbles on the stove and a half-knitted sweater lies on the table. She makes them for each of her 'old folk guests'. There are jigsaw pieces on a tray next to it, and next to that, a sudoku puzzle, a crossword and a book on homeopathy. I never could believe her energy and, even now, in her seventies, she still has plenty of it. She'd be up before everybody else, the last to bed, and in between, she'd tend to the every need of 'her family', the Five Pines' twenty residents.

Pam trained as a nurse and has a gallows humor that sustained me during my years as a medic. What she has isn't much – a small nursing home that's become part of the community – but it's hers. She's worked hard. And she loves it too much to quit.

'Knew you'd come. Just didn't think it would take quite so long.'

I hear myself apologizing again.

'Got yourself into some trouble last week, I read.'

On a cork board, amongst numerous scraps of paper with the scrawled numbers of doctors, florists and funeral homes, are some photos of the residents, a picture of our wedding, one of Hope and another of Jack, and an overblown tabloid headline: *Prez's Doc Tried To Save Crazed Protester.*

We chitchat for several minutes, then suddenly she says: 'You can cut the crap, Josh. I get six cards and half as many emails from you in a decade. So, why *are* you here?'

'There's something I need to ask you.'

'To do with that?' She points to the headline.

I can't lie to her.

'OK . . .' She sits down slowly, watching me.

'When I brought down the U-Haul, there were only two things of Hope's I kept. Jack's old blanket, and her portrait of him. Lately, I've taken to looking at it. A lot. I mean, *really* looking at it. It's like having him in the room.'

'She could sure paint.' She sips her coffee, watching me. 'They both could.'

'This may sound strange, but have you ever come across another one?'

She leans back, studying me. 'Another portrait of Jack? By Hope?'

'Wearing that old blanket.'

'The one she was working on when she died?'

'This one's different. Finished.'

She shakes her head.

'No sketches? No preparatory drawings?'

She shakes her head again.

'Have you been through all her things? The boxes—?'

'Goddammit, Josh. You want to tell me the hell this is all about?'

I take my phone out and show her the picture from the cabin. Pam studies it a while, shakes her head and hands the phone back.

'Nobody's been here, asking questions, have they?'

'Questions?'

'About Hope and me.'

She reaches across the table and takes hold of my hand.

'Hope died a long time ago, Josh. You've *got* to let her go. God knows I adored my child, but she was complicated.'

'Tell me about it.' Complicated was one of the three million reasons I loved her. 'What about her things?'

'Her things?'

'The boxes from the U-Haul. Could anybody have gone through them?'

'Let her go, Josh.'

'Mind if I take a look?'

I drop to one knee and shine the flashlight under the door.

The light bounces off of the chrome fender of Jack's Impala – so close it's almost in my face. I sweep the beam across one tire, then another. Both flat. Breathe in dust and engine oil. The door, its hinges rusted to hell, has jammed a meter from the ground.

Pam is standing just behind me, waving a cigarette. The smoke drifts across the beam. 'You got a painting and an old blanket. I got his klunker. Good old Jack . . .'

The way Jack told it, two days after quitting the military, he was making for the coast, enjoying his newfound freedom, when the Impala died on him and, long after he'd fixed it, he and the car remained in Tresco. Jack put it down to fate – the area had once been Shawnee land. Pam had a more prosaic explanation – the Chevy, a '62 model, was a piece of shit that was running on borrowed time and wouldn't have made the coast anyway.

Irony is the car's now worth a small fortune and canny Pam is waiting for the right moment to sell it.

I roll under the door, haul myself to my feet, and dust down my pants and jacket.

Pam's voice, muffled, comes to me from the other side of it. 'Switch is on your left as you face the wall. Bulb's probably shot, though.'

She's right.

I raise the flashlight. Everything is covered in a thin film of grime. Spiders' webs hang from two sets of shelves above a workbench; behind the webs are jars with mottled labels filled with liquids and assorted bits and pieces. The moving boxes are stacked against the wall next to the Impala.

I'd shoved Hope's stuff into boxes four years after she died, and a year after I retrained as a psych. I couldn't bring myself to look at the paintings. I simply wanted rid of them. Shipping it all back here, I thought, would solve everything. Out of sight, out of mind.

I work my way through the boxes now, find the one labeled 'Studio', open it, wedge the flashlight between my neck and my shoulder and start rifling through it. A watercolor of the house, a couple of the beach, the sea beyond the point, a load of still lives, and some sketches: of me, of Heather Kantner, of a load of old people I don't recognize – her art therapy patients, maybe – and her mom.

But no sign of Jack.

I step back, and stumble over something behind me. There's an almighty crash and my shoulder hits the wing of the Impala.

'Josh?'

I tell her I'm fine.

I see the glow of my flashlight beneath the sump, kneel down, my forehead against the cold bodywork, and manage to roll it toward me with my fingertips.

The box I tripped over has split, its contents scattered between the Chevy and the wall. A scrapbook of the artists that had always inspired her: Klimt, Rothko, Picasso, Chagall. The small wooden casket in which she used to keep the things that had been most precious to her.

Inside it, there's a leather bracelet from Pam, the china rabbit that somehow managed to survive her childhood and make the journey east, a couple of CDs of bands she'd loved, some items of jewelry, a handful of heart-shaped beach pebbles, and her favorite photos. This is probably where she kept the ultrasound scan before taking it to Lakeland that night.

There's a shot of me taken the year we met, one of Pam smoking, and an envelope marked 'Jack' in Hope's loopy, distinctive hand. It contains a medal ribbon and his three pieces of jewelry: the ankh, the weird, stylized tree in the circle, and the silver star.

There's a photograph, too, in color, but so faded it could almost be sepia-tinted, of a couple of guys in flight suits and Aviators in the cockpit of a plane. It takes me a second to realize one of them is Jack.

I once asked him what he'd flown in Vietnam, but never got a straight answer. I knew forward air controllers hadn't had it easy. Their job had been to fly low and slow over the jungle, watching for enemy troop movements and calling down strikes.

I smile to myself. Before Jack grew his hair, before he smoked himself to death, he had really looked the part.

There's a motif on the fuselage, just below his right arm.

It's a mean-looking blade with a snake coiled around it, jaws open, fangs exposed, ready to strike. On the side of the cockpit is a single word: Jackknife.

The scrawled signature bottom right of the picture catches my eye. The writing is unmistakably Jack's.

I tilt it to the light.

It says 'Mac'.

26

BEFORE LEAVING THE FIVE PINES, I GO ONLINE AND FIND JACK'S
aircraft – a prop, long out of service, that had been designed for
the FAC mission. A Bronco. The Marines had used them exten-
sively in Vietnam.

I Googled Marine Corps Bronco recipients of the Navy Cross
and found only two: a pilot, Lieutenant Nelson Freeley, of VMO-
3, a unit based at a strip near Da Nang, and his observer, Sergeant
Jack Ackerman.

Jack's call sign had been Jackknife 13, which must have morphed into Mac the Knife then just plain Mac, which he abandoned as
soon as he came back Stateside and dropped out.

Jack and Nelson had both received the Corps' second highest
award for gallantry for an action in which Jack had guided a force
of Marine Corps/ARVN out of the jungle to a beach near a place
called Hoi An, where they were rescued by boat.

With no other air assets available, they'd remained on station for
as long as their fuel had allowed, advising the unit commander of
the exact location of the enemy – which had meant flying below
150 meters, exposed to ground fire throughout. Their ground crew
counted more than three hundred holes in the Bronco's fuselage.

They had severed electrics, hit black boxes, punched through
the self-sealing fuel tanks, drilled through the canopy, dented both
armor-plated seats and missed their bodies by a centimeter or two,
max. That they had both survived was a miracle; that neither had
even been scratched almost beyond belief.

I ask Pam if she knows any of this. She shakes her head.

But Hope must have done. Why else had she tucked away the photo in her treasure chest?

On the way back to Camp David, I rack my brains – somehow Duke Gapes connects me to the President and the Engineer, Hope's portrait of Jack and a nickname I didn't know he'd had.

The three pieces of jewelry, now on the passenger seat, trigger another memory. Three months before the crash, Pam called to say Jack was dying. The cancer had turned aggressive.

Hope and I flew up that afternoon. It had been a tough month. The workload had been intense. My drinking had gotten heavier. I couldn't remember the last time we'd touched, much less held each other, but she gripped my hand the whole way. In the dark of our hotel room near the airport where we stayed before driving up to Tresco, we'd made love with such tenderness I can feel it now.

When we got to the Five Pines the next morning, Jack, amazingly, had rallied. Hope took a photo of him sitting outside, beneath a tree, his blanket around his shoulders. News of her homecoming, Pam said, had given him something to stick around for. But we knew that we were witnessing a burst of light moments before it burned its last.

Four days later, we gathered around his bed. He gave my hand a squeeze, then asked for hers. I heard him whisper something – she never did tell me what, but moments after he died, she retrieved the ankh, the star and the tree of life from under his pillow. The following day, back in Florida, she started on his portrait, and kept working on it, out on the porch, using the photograph as her inspiration, silently, methodically, as, unknown to me, our child had started to grow inside of her.

OK. So Gapes is psychic. However it works in ESP-land, he'd worked out a bunch of things about Hope and me. But that doesn't explain the portrait. Or, as Hetta pointed out, why he chose to speak in riddles.

Unless that's the whole point.

The thought makes my blood pump a little faster.

I remember Steve describing the moment Gapes placed his hand against the knots and scars on his face.

Remember, Gapes had told the paraplegic vet.

Memory was important to Gapes.

But so was time. Time figures in this, too. It's like he was buying us time. Still is, maybe.

What for?

I'm wrestling with this as I grind through the gears on a twisty section of road on the home straight to Thurmont. It's close to midnight and I suddenly feel drowsy. But Thurmont is only a few miles from Camp David. I don't need to pull over. I don't need to stop for coffee. I'm almost there.

Then my head starts to hurt and my vision begins to swim.

I blink. Headlights. Dazzlingly bright. Belonging to something big – *something big on my side of the road . . .*

I peer through the windshield.

Coming right for me.

I throw the wheel and send the car off of a six-foot drop. As it starts to roll, out of the corner of my eye I glimpse a big silver grille and red paintwork as the truck thunders past.

The car hits the ground and my head snaps left, then right. Trees, rocks and earth fill my field of vision as it rolls. Then the belt clamps my chest hard against the seat and there's a bang as the airbag deploys.

A shriek of metal, the sound of glass breaking, the engine surging.

An enormous crash as the lights go out.

Then, at last, silence.

I'm alive, lying on my side, in the darkness.

I pull the airbag away from my face and become aware of the unearthly glow of the instrument panel. I smell damp vegetation and there's a loud hissing sound from under the hood. The windows have all smashed. My cheek is pressed against wet earth.

I release my belt and try to move, but I'm pinned against the door.

Then, beyond the windshield, beyond some trees that I can begin to make out in the weak ambient light, I hear movement.

I tell myself I've imagined it.

I know I haven't.

Something in the undergrowth. Getting nearer.

I lie there, listening, unable to escape.

Then, a voice in the darkness. 'Colonel? Colonel Cain?'

I breathe again.

What in God's name is *she* doing here?

27

HETTA FOUND ME, BECAUSE SHE'D FOLLOWED ME; STUCK A GPS tracker in the car I'd taken from the pool, and, maintaining a discreet distance, shadowed me all the way from Camp David to Tresco.

Why? She shrugs. A little dose of post-Lefortz paranoia, maybe. I tell her I know the feeling.

She was less than a quarter mile behind me when I was forced off the road. My abrupt halt had shown up on the tracker. But between there and the scene of the crash, she'd passed nothing.

What I saw was real, but I can't dismiss her version: that there had been no red rig on the road – no vehicle at all, in fact.

We take a left out of the dispensary. It's a clear night. The stars are out.

'Byford sent me some more files,' she says, as we head for the trail that'll take us back to the lodge. 'I thought you'd be interested to know that the lab found a match with those hair samples in the Armed Forces' DNA ID database.'

'Who is he?'

'Karl Dempf. Age forty-four. Wounded twice. First a decade ago, in Afghanistan, when he was an Army captain. A communications specialist. Second in Benghazi. He had the misfortune to be in our consulate when it was attacked by militants. Now he's a consultant with Triple Z Services. They're based in Herndon, outside D.C.'

'Never heard of them.'

'You won't have. They do a lot of sub-radar, security-related contract work. Byford's looking into it. And Voss, too. The file she's tracked down IDs him as Marine Raider Regiment. One of a fourteen-man Marine Special Operations Team that got ambushed on a covert attempt to take down some Taliban warlord. Whoever doctored Gapes's papers conflated his story with Voss's.'

'Voss had no dependents?'

'None. He *was* an orphan. And ugly with it.'

'And Gapes? What do Christy's files say about him?'

'Everywhere the Activity went, the viewers went too, as part of the assault unit. This was the subset of Element known as Chronometer. Sometimes, the unit worked independently; at other times, with the Russians – it depended on whose sphere of influence they were in. But the part about the viewers remained top secret, special access, highly need-to-know, until the helicopter crash that saw three of them killed and Gapes so badly burned that for a whole year it was touch-and-go whether he'd make it.'

'What about the Engineer?'

'Nothing back yet.'

'What's taking them? Myth or reality, they must have *something* on him.'

'I'm on it,' she says.

Up ahead, an old iron streetlight marks a fork in the trail.

We veer to the right and start downhill. My ribs are beginning to hurt.

'It took me a while to figure this part out,' Hetta says, 'but here's the news, Colonel: you and I have had a whole lot of smoke blown up our asses. If you were into something as covert as Duke Gapes was, and you wanted to go off-radar, what would you do?'

'Come on, Hetta, it's too damn late for twenty questions.' I move my hand to my ribs. 'And stop calling me that.'

'Calling you what?'

'*Colonel*, for Christ's sake.'

'I elected to maintain some formality between us,' she says. 'Because I didn't want things to become complicated.'

'Do you have any idea how you sound when you talk like that?' I laugh, then wish I hadn't. I place my other hand on my ribs.

'You're hurt.'

'Just some bruising.' I look at her in the dim light. 'You know what? Calling me by my first name and staying, just the two of us, in the President's hideaway, doesn't come under the heading of *complicated*. The world isn't always the binary place you imagine it to be.'

'Is that how I am?'

'Is what how you are?'

'Binary.'

'I didn't say that's how you *are*. I said that's how you see things.'

'Do I?'

I could cut the air between us with a knife.

'I'm a shutdown son of a bitch, Hetta. But none of us is perfect.'

We walk on. I look up. A plane, moving fast and high, tracks east against the star bed. I follow its winking lights for a moment or two.

'I'm sorry,' I say. 'Long day. I didn't thank you for coming to my rescue either.'

'No need.'

We walk on.

'You were saying . . . About the smoke . . .'

'It can wait.'

'No, it can't. Tell me.'

'INSCOM,' she says, 'proposed two pathways to the Executive Branch when remote viewing was resurrected after 9/11.

'One was for the Army to use it against what it called time-critical targets. This resulted in the quick and dirty recruitment of viewers and the coupling of RV to the Activity's search-and-destroy mission for the perpetrators of 9/11, initially, and later for jihadists seeking to take their game to the next level: the acquisition of WMDs.

'The other was the development of some rigor to allow them to get a better handle on the RV *process*. For all the years it had been an active program in the seventies and eighties, despite the involvement of the Stanford Research Institute, the science of it had remained a mystery. No one had had a clue how it worked. All they knew was that, somehow, it did.

'The intel community hated the "psychics", as they called them, because of the unwanted congressional attention they brought upon the whole intelligence community. That's what had killed the program first time around.

'This time, INSCOM knew that they had to keep it under wraps. So, when they persuaded the Bush administration to resurrect it, they also convinced it of the need for one hundred ten per cent secrecy. To achieve that, the administration used a presidential finding – a covert delivery mechanism for the President's executive order to the House and Senate Intelligence Committees. Stop me if you already know this.'

She plows on before I can tell her I don't. 'Under a presidential finding you're required to tell the Majority and Minority leaders and the chairs and ranking members of the oversight committees. Only, as with a lot of covert activity after 9/11, Bush's people rather conveniently forgot. The only person on the Senate committee they *did* tell was its Republican chair. But three years later, the Minority Leader, Tod Abnarth, got to find out about it.'

I tell her Tod Abnarth had been the senator Reuben had worked for when he quit the Army and moved from Florida to Washington. He'd also been an early supporter of Thompson.

'I know. It may be nothing. But good to check with your buddy, Mr Kantner, when we get back. Abnarth went ballistic and threatened to expose the whole program. Said there was no justification at all in classifying the science part of Chronometer.'

She stops.

I see two sentries up ahead, at an intersection a hundred meters before the lodge.

They recognize us, salute, and wave us on.

She continues when we're out of earshot. 'The covert action component was disguised within a $2.1 billion line item in the Department of Defense budget, which described Chronometer as

"Discreet Monitoring Capabilities", but the science investigation was suddenly in plain sight, if you knew what you were looking for.'

'Congress funded *science* to do with this?'

'Under the rubric of "consciousness research". INSCOM, through the Army Research Lab, contracted with the Neuroscience Department of the Baltimore Central Institute of Technology for a bit of kit called a "Holographic Information Transfer System". HITS was a prototype of some description. Helmet-based. You wore it.'

'The marks on his head?'

'Bingo.'

I see the lights of Aspen Lodge twinkling through the trees. 'This isn't blowing smoke, Hetta. In the world of covert ops, this is standard goddamn operating procedure.'

'Right,' she says. 'Going AWOL is too.'

I'm lying in bed, in the dark, staring at shadows on the ceiling, trying to focus on what she's told me, but all I see, all I can think about, is a stretch of single-lane country road swept by headlights.

It could be outside Thurmont, or it could be between Lakeland and the interstate. It doesn't much matter – they both look the same to me. The point is, I now know.

It came to me in that moment people say they see their life flash before their eyes. As I'd yanked the wheel, I hadn't seen a succession of images, I'd seen only one: Hope, beside me, yelling, screaming at me, as the truck bore down on us.

For all her serenity, Hope always did have a temper. It hardly ever surfaced, but it was there. As Pam had said, she was complicated.

This, though, was different. This was months and months of pent-up frustration and rage; and clinically underpinned by a label in the professional circles I moved in that was known as the 'ripple effect'.

She throws the scan of our baby girl at me and grabs the wheel.

I try to wrench it from her, but it's too late. The truck is upon us. She holds it there, holds it steady. Her strength is phenomenal. *Is this how passengers felt when the hijackers flew them into the Towers?* I'm in a state known clinically as tonic immobility.

Our combined closing speed, according to the accident report, had been one hundred twelve miles per hour.

Both of us should have died.

And a big part of me did.

28

FORT MEADE IS MORE LIKE A TOWN THAN A BASE, AND MARYLAND'S largest employer.

The route is dotted with faux plantation-style houses, boxy barrack blocks, offices and administrative complexes. The HQ building of the National Security Agency dominates the skyline, a dark glass Rubik's Cube four times the size of the Capitol where tens of thousands of analysts sift the world's emails and phone conversations for snippets of intelligence that allow America to stay ahead of her enemies – and her friends.

The Cube now hovers the other side of the trees as I park in front of the INSCOM facility. A sign directs me to 902nd Military Intelligence Visitor Reception.

The General is waiting two levels below ground, in a Secure Compartmented Information Facility with a table at its center, a couple of phones, and two flat-screen TVs on the walls. Like Hetta's fancy briefcase, it's totally impervious to electronic surveillance.

After stints with the Rangers and Delta, Alexander 'Zan' Johansson rose rapidly through Special Operations Command, juggling high-level strategy with protracted stints in the field. Having served in every theater of war in which the US has been engaged since 9/11, the General recently took command of JaySOC and the war on terror.

He gets to his feet and runs a hand over a pate that looks as if it's been sprinkled with iron filings. He's in combats, and taller and more greyhound-lean than I expected.

His grip is vise-like and he's clearly very pissed. Since his return from whatever war zones he's just visited in the Middle East and North Africa, he's been inundated with legal requests by Christy's team to divulge exactly what he knows.

He points to the bruises on my face. 'Been mixing it with the locals, Colonel?'

'A little car trouble is all, General.'

There's a knock at the door. Hetta looks hot and flustered. She's spent the morning back at her office in D.C.

'And this is Special Agent Hart of the Secret Service's Protective Intelligence and Assessment Division.'

'No apology necessary,' Johansson says. His sarcasm soars right over her head.

She places her phone on the table and switches it to record.

To accommodate us in his schedule, Johansson has flown up from Fort Bragg. After we've finished with him, he'll fly to the Pentagon, where he is due to brief the Chairman of the Joint Chiefs on his recent tour.

'General . . .' Hetta positions her two pens very precisely either side of her notebook. 'This session will be conducted in accordance with the United States Secret Service's investigation into the shooting of Duke Gapes, an intelligence operative under your command. Did you know Gapes, sir?'

'Never met him.'

'Perhaps, then, you'd explain the chain of command.'

Johansson doesn't refer to any notes. He casts a wary eye at Hetta.

'Our enemies know that to resort to conventional communications means we will hunt them down and kill them. INSCOM drafted a proposal to restart the remote viewing program in the wake of 9/11 and you can say what you like about the use of psychics, but the results have been spectacular.'

Hetta picks up one of her pens, scribbles something, then sets it back down and looks at the General. 'So, your command tasks Army Intelligence and Security Command, INSCOM, with providing special intelligence to the Activity, the unit Gapes was attached to.'

Johansson grunts.

'Shall I take that as a yes, General?'

A flicker of annoyance crosses Johansson's face. It's enough to suggest that, as far as he is concerned, Secret Service agents belong in the same category as politicians and news-hounds.

'Gapes's decision to go AWOL must have come as a blow, then.'

'A unit of this kind only works if it's secret.'

Hetta picks up her pen and starts writing again. 'We know that the order to shoot Gapes was a direct result of a hacked data breach within the Metropolitan Police Department's supposedly secure tactical radio net. That takes some doing, wouldn't you say?'

Johansson leans forward. 'We are fighting a sophisticated enemy, Miss Hart. For years, we've stopped nuclear weapons falling into the wrong hands, because between the Russians and ourselves we know the location of every last gram of uranium and plutonium on the planet. And if it moves, we track it, because uranium and plutonium carry signatures that are visible to our sensors. You want to know what keeps me awake nights? The thought that one day those sensors will blink and we fail to locate and track a weapon the Islamists have assembled.'

'The terrorists you describe would have the sophistication to mount an operation like this?'

'An operation like *what*?'

'Some kind of nuclear event.' She unfolds a piece of paper and sets it down on the table in front of him. It's the planetary shell from the cabin. 'Do you know what this is, General?'

Johansson looks at the sketch, then at Hetta. 'No.' His tone is level.

'What about the Engineer?'

Johansson stares at her. 'You think that is the key to this freak show?'

Hetta stops writing. 'Care to explain what you mean by that, sir?'

'Sure.' Johansson breathes in. 'Almost thirty years ago, we mounted a deeply covert operation to undermine the southern states of the new Russia – an area broadly described as the North

Caucasus. In amongst the Afghans, Saudis, Turks, Pakistanis and the whole fuckin' circus looking to continue the fight after beating the Soviets in Afghanistan, the CIA implanted this idea there was a new breed of leader in the region that would rally its inhabitants to an unstoppable cause. Russian clean-up operations in Chechnya were, to a large extent, a testament to the effectiveness of that operation.'

The General leans forward. 'The Engineer, Miss Hart, is what is known in the trade as "blowback": a myth come full circle to haunt us. What our beloved Agency did was to create leaders-in-waiting with superhuman powers, who have been folded into Islamist lore by desperate people in search of another bin Laden. The guy who is going to come back at the Last Judgment to save his people. Only he ain't, because he ain't fuckin' real.'

A bitter east wind is driving the clouds low and inland, obscuring our view of the Cube, as I check my messages on the steps of the portico two floors above the bunker.

I have a WhatsApp from Christy: *One down, two to go.*

OK. I now have some context for Hetta, the General and the shell.

'You were right. It *is* a component for a nuke,' Hetta says. 'It's called a ballotechnic, and it's an initiator. A trigger. A highly specialized one. Byford fixed me up with a proliferation expert who'd never seen anything like it. He's the reason I was late.'

'Go on.'

'A regular hydrogen bomb needs an atom bomb to trigger the fusion reaction. A Gen 4 nuke uses this instead.'

'How?'

'With difficulty, thank God. Basically, it's a material that's designed to explode when given a shock of sufficient intensity. But nobody has got one to work. Not even *our* weapons geniuses.'

'What if *he* authorized the removal of those images from the cabin?'

'Johansson?'

'Yes.' I decide to ignore for the moment what we agreed with Christy: that we'd keep our knowledge of the three excised images from the cabin to ourselves. 'You took a risk by showing it to him.'

'The bastard was playing poker with us. I just raised the stakes a little.'

'How?'

'Let's wait and see, shall we?'

When we take the elevator back down for Session Two, the General has been joined by a balding, heavy-set man with wire-framed eyeglasses.

Major Cal Offutt is thirty-eight, according to his documents. He looks older. He extends his hand. I'm set to shake it when I see he has three fingers missing and the two that remain are black and twisted like the roots of a tree.

'The General told me you'd been cleared and briefed,' he says.

'Partially. I didn't know you were with Gapes when he crashed.'

'Duke and I . . . we . . . we went through a lot together.'

'You OK to tell me what happened?'

'We were inserting a recon team on the Syria–Iraq border when we got daisy-chained by improvised bombs. One of them severed the tail boom and we went down. I pulled Duke clear just before the tanks exploded. There were no other survivors. If it hadn't been for—'

'Hadn't been for what?' Hetta says, far too quickly.

I shoot her a look. She doesn't get it, but Offutt does.

'It's OK,' he says. 'It's a story I need to tell, and there's not many I can tell it to. I dragged him into some cover and we lay low. By morning the insurgents had gone, but Duke was in a bad way. His burns were terrible. I carried him far as I could, but I could see he was going to die.

'If I continued to carry him, he'd die slow and in pain. If I went for help, he'd die, too, but maybe without as much pain. We reached a village – a place called Sweet Water in Arabic – and the locals seemed friendly enough. I left him there and went with an elder to see if we could find one of our patrols. Long story short, we got picked up by helo and I directed the crew back to the village, where I was sure we'd find Duke with his throat cut.

'But you know what? Even though those people had nothing – no medicine, little food, only that sweet water – they looked after him. And they prayed. They prayed all night. And by God's grace, they said, Duke would live if He so willed it. Well, Colonel Cain, He must have willed *something*, because against all the odds, Duke did survive.'

We get down to business.

'I will be leading this session, Major Offutt; Agent Hart will observe. You will have been told, I'm sure, that I'm a psychiatrist. You will also know that I was in the church tower seeking to talk your former colleague down when he was killed. It's clear from evidence we've drawn from the time he spent on the run that he had developed some particular obsessions – one of them being with me, another with President Thompson. I am especially keen to learn anything you can tell us about his mental state in the years he worked with you; also about the remote viewing process itself.'

'Yes, sir. Are you familiar with the protocols?'

'Not especially.'

'We still use a forty-year-old method called CRV – coordinate remote viewing – which involves my sitting in an insulated room with the viewer, reading out a set of coordinates and then listening to the viewer's impressions of the target. For the most part, as the monitor, I rarely intervene. But occasionally, I direct. If the viewer is having difficulty, for example, I might encourage him or her to look at the target from a different angle. Or at the prevailing conditions. Whether it's hot or cold. Wet or dry. If there are people in the vicinity. You get the idea. If nothing's happening, I can even ask them to go forward or backward in time to—'

'I didn't realize—'

'Oh, yeah. A good viewer can roam across time. Used in the right way, and in conjunction with conventional intelligence methods, remote viewing is a tremendous asset.'

'Gapes – was he good?'

'The best.'

'What makes a good viewer?'

'Good question. He and I used to discuss that a lot.'

'You were friends?'

'Yes, sir. You can't do something like this and not be.' He pauses. 'Even Duke didn't understand how he did the things he was able to do. He'd had the odd psychic experience as a kid – premonitions and such – but it was only after the brain injury his talent really kicked in. Nobody could access the signal line quite like him.'

He sees that I'm struggling and adds: 'Back in the day, they ran all kinds of tests. They put remote viewers in rooms like this one and found that they could still receive the target information.'

'So, this . . . signal line? This line between the viewer and the data they pick up from the target? It isn't electromagnetic?'

'It can't be.'

'So, what is it?'

'We don't know. But whatever it is, it has to be some facet of us – or of the world around us – that is very subtle.'

He hesitates. 'You take any physics, Colonel?'

'I'm a doctor. I have some.'

He sits up and it's like, suddenly, he comes alive. 'There are two aspects to quantum mechanics that resonate with remote viewers. When you measure the position of a particle – an electron or a photon, say – all information about its speed and direction, its momentum, vanish. And vice versa. Which is weird, huh? It's like we can't know both at the same moment, only ever one of them.

'Well, viewers will tell you that's what reality is. When they click into that other place, whatever that other place is, it's like they click out of this world. I wouldn't begin to know how to describe it, but hyperspace is a start, or another dimension. A good viewer, like Duke, can . . . could . . . flip seamlessly between the two.'

Johansson looks at his watch. Before he can interrupt, I ask Offutt about the second aspect.

'In the quantum field, everything is entangled. No matter how separated two particles become, once they've formed a connection, they communicate with each other instantly, whatever the distance, and continue to, whether they're next door or separated by an entire galaxy – and from now till the end of time. That's how remote viewing is. The viewer connects to the target instantly, no matter how far away it is, and we think—'

'Major,' Johansson says, 'if the Colonel and Agent Hart required a physics lesson, I'm sure they'd have gone to MI-fuckin'-T.'

'Sure.' Offutt glances from Hetta to me.

'We're trying to understand what made him run,' I say.

'Wasn't that established by the MPs?'

'The MPs were never made aware of the fact that he was working with the Activity. Did he ever share anything with you?'

'No.'

'You're sure?'

'Yes, sir.'

'He just left?'

He nods. 'One day he was here, right here. The next ...' He does this thing with the fingers of his good hand to show how Duke vanished into thin air.

I glance down at my notes. 'Would you describe Gapes as religious, Major?'

'Duke? Spiritual, perhaps. But not religious.'

'How would you define the difference?'

'It's hard to work in this area and not have a sense of connection with the great unknown. Duke did. I'm not a viewer, and I do. But the Christian thing? No. He wasn't into that at all.'

'Any affiliations with extremists? The far right?'

'No,' he says. 'No way. In any case, we were polygraphed every couple of months. If Duke had belonged to any kind of proscribed organization, the lie-detector Gestapo would have known.'

'What about his mental state?'

He describes some of the symptoms I saw in the tower: the speech and muscle spasms that were the result of the brain injury he received in Iraq. He confirms what I'd read in his medical report, that he got bad headaches, too. But when I ask if Gapes was delusional, Offutt shakes his head.

'You mean, like, serious mental issues? No way. Actually, I—'

Johansson cuts across him. 'The guy was clearly sick.'

Hetta looks up sharply from her notes. 'You said that you and Gapes never met?'

'Correct.'

'Then how can you know?'

'Know what?'

'That he was sick.'

'Check out his psych report. The guy was delusional and on medication. An anti-psychotic.'

'It's highly likely that his notes had been doctored,' I say. 'And besides, it's hard to be mentally ill *and* a bona fide traitor, isn't it?'

Johansson's expression drops another ten degrees. 'Your specialism is post-traumatic stress, correct?'

'It is, yes.'

'Do you know how much trauma my men get to encounter every day of the week?'

'I ran a center for the treatment of trauma-related illness, General. So yes, I do.'

'Then, under your classification, I have no doubt that half the men under my command suffer some form of PTSD. But you know what? They just get on with the job. They do it because they have a keen sense of patriotism. Duty, Colonel. Every day, they die to keep *us* safe.' He looks at his watch. 'This interview is now terminated. I have transport waiting to take me to the Pentagon.'

'General Johansson?'

He turns impatiently to Hetta. She doesn't move a muscle.

'As I made clear, sir, this is an official investigation into multiple murder and a conspiracy to kill the President. It will be over when we say it is.'

Johansson stiffens. The glint of steel in his gray eyes tells me that the appeal of Hetta's imminent rendition may have crossed his mind. But he maintains his silence.

I turn back to Offutt. 'When we were in the tower, Duke said something that I'm struggling to understand. He talked about *ground truth*.'

'Yes.' The Major glances uneasily at Johansson.

190

'What is it?'

'It has military, er, usage, of course . . .'

'Beyond that?'

'Duke and I . . .'

I wait.

'Viewers need feedback, Colonel. When you remote view, you're not always convinced that what you've seen is real. So feedback from the target becomes important. It helps the viewer to refine his accuracy. To know he's on the right path. It was the primary reason we started collocating viewers with the Activity's assault units – so that they could get near instant feedback.'

'Duke said that he'd found ground truth by looking at me. What could he have possibly meant by that?'

'Easy,' Offutt says. 'It meant you were the target.'

29

THE US ARMY RESEARCH LABORATORY IS SPREAD ACROSS VARIOUS centers around the country. Its East Coast contracts office sits in the basement of a large gray building in a tree-lined suburb of Bethesda, two minutes off Washington's Beltway.

Since emerging from the bunker a little over an hour ago, I've been hit by a stream of messages from Reuben, asking then demanding I get back to the White House. But he hasn't told me why, and, as Hetta points out, if we don't take advantage of this window of opportunity at the Army Research Lab, we may never get another.

I'll have to deal with Reuben when we're done here. Hetta has tucked our phones into her magic case, so that anybody interested in us can't track our movements. And she has taken the precaution of getting one of her colleagues at HQ to monitor traffic around us on automatic number plate recognition.

Betty the contracts officer keeps her eyes locked on her screen as she talks and types. She asks for the reference number again.

Hetta repeats the code Christy supplied. To view it online, we'd have to access the military's version of the Web. Onsite is a whole lot safer.

'Here you go.' Betty drops a wad of printouts onto the desk and we take them to the far side of the room.

The agreement covers an applied theoretical study into a helmet-mounted Holographic Information Transfer System by Baltimore's Central Institute of Technology, effective 1 March 2006, completion a year and a half later, value: $147,998.65.

The principal contact was a Dr Elliott Kaufmann.

Hetta hands me an attachment, a progress report with a picture of an oldish guy, sixties or seventies maybe, bearded, in an odd-looking helmet. *Stani Koori*, the caption reads, *testing the HITS unit.*

'Who's that?' I ask.

'The guy who trained Gapes. Once described as the world's greatest psychic. After 9/11, the CIA contracted him to train the remote viewers. Gapes was one of them.'

We move on.

Eight years ago there was a big funding jump, to $1.2 million, for a second-generation helmet. A delay in testing the Gen 2 system is put down to Koori's withdrawal from the program, and their search for a replacement.

The next image contains a dozen views of the helmet. In one of them, I can see six electrodes, evenly spaced on its inner rim.

Gapes was involved the following year, not Koori, but his name isn't mentioned, which is why none of this was picked up in our trawls, and why it was overlooked by whoever switched it for Voss's and altered his medical records.

There's another photo: Gapes in combats, wearing the helmet, giving the camera a thumbs-up – after the brain injury, but clearly before the crash.

Around this time, a Dr Joel Schweizer has joined Kaufmann, and the contract is renewed at $1.45 million, a relatively modest increase, for a Gen 3 helmet intended to communicate data from the holosphere – whatever that might be – on some kind of head-up display.

Their experiment appears to have failed. *'It is not known whether this was a hardware malfunction, an issue with the perceiver, or with the predicted theoretical approach.'* It also mentions some 'psychic disturbance' among the targets.

The contract value then dropped by more than half, and the year after to nothing at all. *'Project terminated due to inability of hardware/testing to corroborate theoretical approach.'*

'I've seen enough.' Hetta rolls up the paperwork and tucks it inside her fleece-lined jacket. 'OK, Josh. Let's go.'

Josh.
Wow.

Ten minutes later, we take an exit off the Beltway and park up next to a row of stores sandwiched between a garage and an office stationery outlet. It's raining a lot harder. Water pools on the road and the sidewalks.

Heads down, we run from the car into an Internet cafe, and Hetta orders two straight blacks from a guy with tats on his neck and quarter-sized gauges in his ears. He looks as if he's from a long-lost Amazon tribe. He starts to hit on her as she pays. She completely ignores him.

We retire to a line of shabby desktops at the back. Hetta spends a minute cleaning the nearest keyboard. An eye-watering bouquet of disinfectant and drains hits us from the nearby restrooms.

She logs on using a proxy IP address. 'OK, we got him. Dr Joel Schweizer. Computer scientist. Harvard 2001 to 2003. Founds Sub-Quantum Dynetics LLC down the road in Gaithersburg in 2005.'

She types some more then sits back and taps her teeth with her pen. 'Let's see . . . Nothing, nothing, nothing for several years. Then this: *Wired* tells us that S-Q Dynetics sells its first computer to Microsoft.

'Two years later, it reports the sale of a system to the Defense Advanced Research Projects Agency, and the year after, to an unspecified intelligence outfit . . .'

She punches in another name.

'OK, so you've been busy too, haven't you, Dr Elliott P. Kaufmann Jr? . . . Yup . . . Harvard again, 2002 to 2004, where he begins work on the architecture of a . . .'

Her nose wrinkles.

I lean forward. 'A phase-conjugate coupling device to the quantum holosphere.' I look at her. 'Any idea what that is?'

'No.'

'Thought you majored in computer science.'

'I did. But this is like another language.'

She scrolls down. '2007, Kaufmann gets a programming job with Baltimore CIT. I guess whatever he was working on at Harvard wasn't paying the bills.'

'Keep going. Schweizer shows up on the research contract seven years ago. And we know that S-Q Dynetics supplied equipment to DARPA and Microsoft as well as to an unspecified intelligence outfit.'

Hetta types some more. 'OK, so S-Q Dynetics doesn't have a website, because –' the logo of the Securities and Exchange Commission appears, '– it went out of business a little over three years ago.'

She keeps on going. 'They had aspirations to be the world's first commercial quantum computing company. What do you know about quantum computers?'

'Nothing.'

'They told us at PIAD that they can simulate in ten nanoseconds what it takes evolution to do in twenty years.'

'So, Kaufmann, back in the day, had written about something that couples to something called a holosphere. He leaves Harvard, takes a regular day job at Baltimore CIT, working away on what turns out to be the Holographic Information Transfer System. But he doesn't achieve a whole lot with it, until Schweizer shows up.'

She nods. 'Then, working together, they develop a third generation helmet, which, according to the contract, seeks to throw data from this holosphere onto some kind of visual display. But then the contract gets cut, because the system –' she picks up her notes, '– *fails to communicate data from the virtual quantum state* in the way it was meant to. There was a problem with something called the perceiver.'

'Not some*thing*. Some*one*. They used Gapes to calibrate it. Initially, they'd used this guy Koori, but that didn't work out, so they brought Gapes in instead. The marks on his head correspond to electrodes on the helmet. And check out those dates. The system starts to go wrong and they kill the contract the year before he goes AWOL. And I'm guessing Schweizer and Kaufmann will have disappeared too.'

And the Pentagon had paid compensation to Lou and Misty, buying their silence. That should have been the end of it. But then something happened that even the black world could not have been prepared for. Two years after the MPs first showed, the men in black arrived the day before Lou's birthday and kicked down her trailer door.

The first time was for show – what we were meant to see.

The second was because Duke Gapes had run for real.

The thirty-minute ride to the White House gives me some of the thinking time I need to assemble the case I'm about to put to Reuben.

Kaufmann, a physics prodigy, gave a speech discussing his work soon after he arrived at Harvard – a few months after 9/11.

He talked about the theoretical existence of a holosphere, in which *information*, alongside matter and energy, needed to be acknowledged as the 'fabric of existence' – a 'substrate' rooted in a 'sub-atomic sea' that science had yet to acknowledge.

He dubbed it 'nature's memory': an endless ocean of data held in the sub-atomic particles that subtend . . . well, everything.

It prompted a stream of discussion amongst his peers in blogs, forums and user groups, all of them quoting Einstein, Planck, Pauli, Dirac, Heisenberg and Schrödinger. If the theory was valid, they said, there ought to be evidence for the holosphere's existence.

Kaufmann said there was: in eastern mysticism. Sadly for him, he kept right on digging, and the hole he dug got bigger and bigger. Then he jumped right in. Hebrews, he said, referred to the holosphere as *The Book of God's Remembrances*. Early Christians as *The Book of Life*. Hindus as *The Akashic Record*. Jung's *Collective Unconscious* was evidence of it too.

Overnight, mainstream science vacated the building and ostracized Kaufmann for being too out-there.

But we'd found a retired Army intelligence officer and Cold

War-era remote viewer online. Paul H. Smith had come out of the woodwork after the remote viewing program had been trashed by the CIA, to describe the holosphere in much the same terms: as 'an infinity of information points, with each representing an object, entity, being, event structure ... an *archive* in the fullest sense: indifferent, dispassionate, with no capacity for judging; just data, pure and simple.'

This 'matrix', Smith wrote, 'catalogues human acts and events', with all other facts about the universe to be found there as well: 'information about animate and inanimate objects; about places, landscapes, substances, emotions, physical and non-physical qualities, artifacts, relations, things that are tangible and intangible, machines, history, personalities, everything ...'

When we'd read this, Hetta and I had looked at each other, neither of us saying a word, because we'd seen this matrix for ourselves: the pictures, photographs, sketches and printouts in the cabin – all five thousand of them: *Of people, places, objects, things ...*

When we'd met with Christy to discuss the three missing images from the cabin, we'd all assumed that Gapes's paranoia at being sent to the desert had related to a deployment in some far-flung shit-hole. And that she should focus the full might of her intel resources accordingly.

But everything we've just learned says her satellites have been pointing in the wrong direction.

30

I TRY TO FOCUS BEYOND THE WIPERS. IN THE HOMEBOUND rush-hour traffic I can hardly see a thing. '*Two* cars, you said?'

'Four, in fact. A couple of SUVs paralleling us. Since we left the cafe. A red Toyota six in front and a black Fusion five behind.'

I fight an instinct to turn as we head toward the next intersection.

'Oh, and a silver Tahoe, a block away, crossing . . . now.'

I nod, then check the wing mirror. See the Fusion. See the Toyota too. In the trade, it's known as a 'box'.

'You get an alert?' I haven't noticed her check her cell.

Her eyes dart between her mirror and the traffic ahead.

'No.'

So *she* spotted them. Well, she said she sees patterns.

The Toyota ahead drives on and makes his turn. The Fusion behind us follows suit. The SUV to our right slots in three vehicles back. The Tahoe on our left now takes the lead. Do it right, and it's almost impossible to get made. 'Which tells me,' she says, 'these a-holes aren't pros . . .'

'Betty.'

'Who?'

'Schoolmarm back at the Army Research Lab. She must have tipped them off. Or there was some kind of trip-wire on the file we accessed.'

She pulls an unregistered prepaid cell out of the glove box, hands it to me and reels off a number.

'Who am I calling? Putin?'

'No.'

'Did you know we were going to attract this kind of attention by heading to ARL?'

'I allowed for the possibility.'

'And showing Johansson the shell sketch?'

'Same strategy.'

'Christ, Hetta—'

'What's done is done, Josh. Please. Make that call.'

I hit dial, activate the speaker, and keep one eye on the mirror as we wait for the connection.

'Hetta?' A voice I recognize.

'Hey. Picked up some company.' She glances at her GPS. '17th and F in ten?'

'You got it.'

'DJ?'

'Yup.' His voice crackles.

'Josh will be in the Lexus.'

'What will you be in?'

'Let you know in a minute.'

She signs off.

The traffic starts to bunch as we approach a red.

I lose sight of the Fusion behind an articulated truck.

Hetta brakes.

'Undo your belt, Josh.'

I move too fast and she touches my arm. '*Slowly.*'

She opens her door and steps into the stationary traffic.

I make for the sidewalk. She motions me around the front of the car to tuck in behind her. Rain seeps down my neck. Hetta draws her .357. We walk the length of the truck.

The second we come into view, the guy lunges for something on the passenger seat. But Hetta is quicker. She smashes the window, opens the door, and by the time I'm alongside, she's snapped a cuff around his left wrist and forced him into the passenger seat. I reach in and fasten the other end to the grab-handle above his head.

She passes him the two-way radio he was going for.

'Tell your buddies we made you and they're more than welcome to follow us too, but – word of warning – when we get to where we're going, there's going to be a reception party.'

Up ahead, a car horn sounds as the lights turn green.

I run back to the Lexus and jump in behind the wheel.

Ten minutes later, with the Fusion right behind me, I approach Lafayette Square. There's an unusually heavy police presence. A protest is underway by the North Fence.

I weave through people making their way to and from the edge of the crowd, finally pulling up on 17th and F, as close as I can get to the Eisenhower Executive Office Building.

Fifty meters away, two squad cars, nose-to-nose, lights turning, block the end of the street. I'm wondering what next when a figure steps past the line of cops ranged across the street in front of them. DJ Wharton is dressed in a gray raincoat that looks uncomfortably tight across his lineman's shoulders.

Hetta, DJ and I gather in front of the Fusion.

Hetta hands over her captive's yellow two-way.

DJ glances at the guy, who's still tethered. He has to raise his voice above the noise of the protesters. 'Who is he?'

'No idea,' she says. 'I'm hoping you're going to tell me. Anyone follow us here?'

Wharton shakes his head, then turns and tilts it to study Hetta's captive in the streetlight. He appears white, gaunt and surprisingly young.

'Did he tell you anything?'

'No,' she says.

'He's Army CID,' Wharton says.

Hetta looks at him. 'How do you know?'

'This thing.' DJ holds up the Motorola. 'They've got a unique privacy code, which people think is unbreakable. It isn't. Last time I saw one it was in the hands of a CID sergeant on a joint case we investigated out of Quantico. He told me that Army CID bought a bunch of them because the shit they were meant to have got axed in the cutbacks.' He takes a step back, opens the door and takes a shot of the guy on his phone.

'I'll run this past some people I know. You?'

'There's somebody I've got to go see at National Geospatial.' She doesn't tell him who.

'Want me to send someone else along?'

'No,' she says. 'I'll be OK.'

She turns to me. 'How do I reach you?'

'Molly will let you know where I am. How long will you be?'

She glances down the street. 'I don't know. Quick as I can.'

She walks off without turning back and disappears into the crowd.

I leave DJ and walk slowly toward the line of policemen. I show one of them my pass and ask if he'll escort me to the Northwest Gate. As we reach the end of the street, the chanting grows louder and I see a thicket of placards beyond a second cordon of cops, uniformed Secret Service and Park Police. When I reach security, the mood is no less febrile.

While the agent runs my pass through a scanner, I try Reuben again, but still get voicemail. I WhatsApp him: *On my way in.*

The agent hands me my pass. I walk across the North Lawn to the North Portico, the chanting in my ears, the rain in my face, and show my pass again. I get waved through and take the elevator to the lower level. When the doors open, the lights are low and the floor silent.

I walk across the hallway and into Molly's office. She's left for the day.

As I step into mine, I sense I am not alone.

I turn to find Haight Graham, in a chair, pointing his pistol at me.

31

'*ARE YOU PREPARED TO COOPERATE FULLY WITH ALL APPROPRIATE authorities in disclosing how you came to track down Duke Gapes?'*

Graham lifts a buff-colored file from a pile of papers and places it next to the page he's just read from, a transcript of my polygraph.

He invites me to take a look.

The first shot shows me standing on the stoop of Ted van Buren's brownstone. In the second, I'm looking around, as if I know I'm being watched. In the third, I'm shaking TVB's hand and being ushered into the doorway. It was the night Hetta and I met Christy.

Even to me, I appear guilty as hell.

When faced with a subpoena for a client's medical records, it is a psychiatrist's or a psychologist's right to be able to claim privilege. Or at least it was. Under Section 215 of the Patriot Act, that is no longer an option, nor can any delay be made by the psychiatrist or psychologist to the execution of the warrant. In fact, almost all the options typically available to my profession are now illegal.

The Foreign Intelligence Surveillance Act and Section 215 also come with this beauty: a gag order prohibiting me from telling anyone I've received one, which means getting to speak to a lawyer is a luxury I can't expect. I am in the room with the table, the camp bed and the two-way mirror.

'Twenty-two minutes into your polygraph, Colonel Cain, you

were asked the following question: *Are there any reasons that might prevent you from legitimately fulfilling your duties as White House Medical Director?* You provided a negative response. That was a lie, wasn't it?'

I think back to our discussion in the tent. Graham knew about my drinking, and he knew about Hope's pregnancy. Both these facts were containable – even the Secret Service's suspicion that I'd been in a depressed mood state following my return from combat operations and had deliberately rammed the Kenworth.

But this changes things. If they've got TVB's patient notes and transcripts of any conversations he and I have had in the past week, then they also know that halfway through Georgetown I had a full-on breakdown, which never made it as far as my medical notes, and was absent from my background security check and from the subsequent declarations I made when I agreed to become the President's doctor. Even more damningly, it begs his next question: how did I get the job?

I wait, but it doesn't come.

Instead, Graham produces one of the three images Hetta, Christy and I withheld from his investigation: the guy who looks like Napoleon. There are a limited number of ways the Service could have acquired this picture. The first is via Hetta, who took it on her iPhone. The second is via Christy, who received it from Lefortz. The third is almost unthinkable: from Lefortz himself.

'Hart and I did not remove those images from the cabin,' I tell him.

'Then let me in on who did.'

'They were there when we kicked down the door. The following day they'd been removed and replaced. I warned you about letting the Army in, so if your guys didn't decide on a little sanitization of the evidence, you have a sizeable problem. Did you know that at least one of the forensics team wasn't with Army CID? A guy called Karl Dempf was masquerading as Army, but is some kind of comms specialist with a private military contractor called Triple Z Services.'

Graham remains unmoved. 'So, you don't know this man?' He points to the picture.

'No. Who is he?'

'Vladimir Ilitch. A Russian-Ukrainian national and friend of that other Vlad – Putin. He keeps a low profile. His interests span banking, minerals, pharmaceuticals and robotics. He also owns a couple of restaurant chains here and in Europe. And oh, I almost forgot: he's invested a great deal of money in emerging tech and particularly in areas that intersect with his principal interests – pharma and robotics. Imagine our surprise, then, when we find information about this man on Professor van Buren's hard drive.'

'That is simply not possible.'

'Oh, but it is. You see, your buddy Ted van Buren has received a great deal of cash from Ilitch's investment company.'

I think back to what TVB had been so excited about – his experiments into some kind of ultrasound that manipulated the brain's neurons – the prelude, he believed, to tech that would treat a range of mental disorders, including anxiety and depression.

'It is, in the opinion of this agency –' Graham looks again at the mirror, which confirms to me that Cabot is behind it, '– beyond coincidental that a man who has treated you for an illness – a *mental* illness you withheld from every agency tasked with vetting your appointment as White House Medical Director – is intimately associated with a Russian whose image turns up in the cabin. And for that image, along with two others, to have been removed without the knowledge of the investigative team.'

I am left alone with the light on, a bottle of water and a bucket in the corner of the room.

I have no idea what time it is – only that it's the small hours. They took my phone, and took my watch as well.

On the plus side, they don't know where Hetta is – at least, they didn't a couple of hours ago, when Graham left me to stew. He'd asked me where she was and I'd told him to go fuck himself – and Cabot at the same time; and that was the last supposedly human contact I had.

I've tried the door. It's locked. I've tried to sleep, too, but there's too much running around my head. So I lie on the bed, under the gaze of the mirror, and try to make sense of everything I've heard and where I see it all heading from here.

Ilitch, through some twist of fate, funds tech in which Ted is involved – not as crazy as it first appears, given that Ted is at the forefront of research in a field of technology that is designed to mitigate the physiological effects of trauma. But since there is scarcely an oligarch on the planet who doesn't have connections to his nation's security services, alarmingly the next link in the chain is Dmitri Sergeyev, a Russian intelligence agent.

As Cabot's three-ring circus has made bogus deductions about every other piece of evidence it's been confronted with thus far, I have no doubt it'll jump to the wrong conclusion about my meeting with Sergeyev – and all the arrangements for Moscow.

The irony is that Sergeyev almost certainly *is* on a mission – to learn anything he can about what makes Thompson tick. I saw him coming a mile off.

Whatever anyone says, our two nations are at war – a conflict being played out in the digital sphere, where the watchwords are dismiss, distort, distract, dismay.

James Jesus Angleton, the paranoid – almost certainly *clinically* paranoid – founding head of counter-intelligence at the CIA, once paraphrased the four Ds as an ever-fluid landscape, where fact and illusion merge . . . a kind of wilderness of mirrors. Which is what I entered when I stepped into St John's Church.

Cabot will keep digging until he can demonstrate that Reuben and I are not only in league with the Russian mafia, but also killed JFK.

So, unless I put a stop to this – right here, in this room – Cabot and Graham will blunder into the truth about *No Stone Unturned* and the next casualty will be Thompson's presidency.

I pull myself to my feet, run my hand over my unshaven jaw, stand up to the mirror, and make my confession.

'My name is Joshua M. Cain, Colonel, United States Air Force, and I lied so that I could become the President's doctor . . .'

32

I'M SHAKEN AWAKE, TO FIND GRAHAM'S FACE MILLIMETERS FROM mine.

'Get up.'

He hauls me off the bed. I have no idea how long I have been out of it.

'What's the time?'

'Oh dark thirty.' He hands me my watch and my phone.

'You haven't arrested him yet?'

'Who?'

'The President.'

'Funny,' he says. 'Save your breath. I'm surprised you've any left.' He throws me my jacket. 'Nice speech, by the way.'

In the Oval Office, Thompson is leaning against his desk, his hands clasped in front of him. He looks penitent. He is dressed in suit pants. The collar of his shirt is open. Behind him, through a gap in the drapes, a watery dawn is breaking beyond the trees.

Cabot is seated to his left. 'Thank you, Haight.'

Thompson looks shattered. For a moment I think it's because the dream has come for him again. 'Josh, I'm truly sorry. There's no need for this godawful charade any longer. A lie only begets more lies. I should have come clean the moment this thing started.

'You should know that I've told Director Cabot and Special Agent Graham everything – about the nightmares, your treatment of them, about No Stone Unturned. I also said I would tender my resignation forthwith.'

'And I said that would be quite unnecessary.' Cabot magnani-
mously waves his hand, as if to erase everything that has just been
said. 'We draw a line under this. Everyone has suffered enough.'

I hold Cabot's gaze. 'No resignations? No prosecutions?'

'No need.'

'Where's Reuben?'

'Safe,' the President says. 'Hart too.'

'We detained them, same as we did with you,' Cabot says. 'We
needed to be sure. We now are.'

Thompson turns to Cabot. 'Tell him, Tom.'

'An hour ago, PIAD's digital forensics lab got a lead on the
network traffic in the moments before Gapes was shot. The data
is now in: the system used to break the MPD's tactical radio net is
unlike anything we've seen before – quite beyond the capabilities
of any organization save one. Park that thought for a moment.'

Cabot comes and stands next to Thompson. Despite his diminu-
tive stature, there is something statesmanlike about him I've not
seen before. 'Our interests have always been aligned. My duty,
first and foremost, is the protection of the President. We're under
attack and the only way we're going to find out who is responsible
is if we work together – I mean, truly, properly, work together.
You, me, Reuben, Christy, Hart.' He looks at the President. 'All of
us.'

For the first time, Thompson meets my gaze. 'While you and
Hart have been busy, so have they. You need to listen to this.'

Cabot makes a signal to Graham, who walks over to the desk
and takes up position between him and the President.

'Jimenez's apartment. Forensics have wrung every molecule out
of the place and they've found nothing – no hair, no skin, no blood
beyond that of the victims that matches with anything intelligible
on a database. Which left us with only two pieces of tangible evidence: the footprint and the bullet casings.'

The footprint was a size-ten-and-a-half Nike Air – new, no
nicks or gouges on the sole or wear on the tread, which makes it
the shoe equivalent of a clean skin. The bullet casing came from a
Glock 19, a standard 9 mm.

The shooter fired five times, confirming what I heard from the stairwell. The working hypothesis is that our guy – the shoe size suggests a female assassin is unlikely, although not out of the question – was in the apartment with a gun to Jimenez's head when Anders showed; that he would have needed Jimenez's cooperation to lure the captain into the apartment.

Anders' suspicions ought to have been raised the moment he pushed open the door, because, as I'd discovered, the light was off. That must have been when he pulled the trigger – one shot to Jimenez's head and two to Anders' chest, within a couple of seconds.

I'm guessing my call to Lefortz rang a second before Gentleman Jim kicked in the door.

Graham says the assassin lost his cool at that point and stepped back into the blood that had begun to pool from Jimenez's head. He put his fourth and fifth shots into Lefortz then went for the fire escape. Lefortz staggered after him, but died before I reached him.

'Sunday,' Graham says, 'we asked the FBI for the best forensic technician they have and they sent us this kid from the Quantico Lab. First thing he does is check the casings for prints and DNA, but again, nothing. Even if the shooter had handled the rounds unprotected, the heat of firing the gun vaporizes any prints and cooks the DNA in the chamber, making it unusable.

'But moisture from the fingers of anybody handling the rounds will have corroded the surface of the brass. The lab can put a charge through the casing then dust it down with carbon powder. The current between the corroded layer and the uncorroded layer beneath it will attract the powder and reveal the print.'

'And?'

'And there *is* a print. It's only a partial and doesn't tell us jack, except that the shooter had eaten a processed meal within three hours of handling the bullet.'

'Because the salt content acted on the metal?'

Graham nods. 'So, we crunched every bit of CCTV in every Shake Shack, Five Guys, McDonald's, Subway and Burger King in a five-mile radius of the hit. We whittled down the list from a pool of eighteen hundred males during our window, till we were left with seven guys wearing size-ten-and-a-half Nike Airs. We followed them to their cars, ran their plates and eliminated a couple more. We tracked the others through the JOCC's license plate recognition cameras till we were left with four. Three of them amounted to nothing, but we tracked one all the way back to an underground parking lot in a building in Herndon.'

'Herndon?'

'Yeah,' he says. 'That was Hart's reaction.'

Herndon is filled with defense primes, telecoms giants, IT companies and security contractors. But I've only heard it mentioned once in the past week – when Hetta was telling me about the guy at the cabin identified from the three pubes he'd left behind in her bar of Camay – Karl Dempf of Triple Z Services.

'Triple Z Services is a private military contractor,' Cabot says. 'It didn't exist till a decade ago, but now it's turning over a couple of billion from all the jobs outsourced its way by the CIA and the DoD in Iraq, Pakistan, Afghanistan and Christ knows where else.

'So, now we got a guy from the cabin – and a guy we're ninety-nine per cent sure killed Jimenez, Anders and Lefortz, and both of them are with Triple Z Services.

'Something else. Triple Z had a former employee take them to court for alleged war crimes in Yemen. The case was held in camera. The mission was secret. This was five years ago. Your friend Charles Land of Collins Lovelock Land represented them. He got the case thrown out.'

No wonder Katya looked so damn scared.

'And who does Triple Z represent?'

'I'll let Hart explain.'

The Service, Cabot says, picked her up late last night – when she was on her way back to the White House after her meeting with her contact at the National Geospatial-Intelligence Agency.

'Is she OK?'

'Kind of. We just told her we had Lefortz's killers.'

And you watched as it went to work on her – the one thing that would have unzipped her like the bullet through Gapes's skull.

Cabot glances at the President, then me. 'I had my differences with Lefortz, and I've had my differences with Hart, but she needed to know – as do you, Reuben, Christy and the President – that we all want the same thing. We're going to get these bastards.'

'The guy at Geospatial came through,' Graham says. 'He told Hart he was able to match the image of the bunker. It's not on foreign soil at all. It's here. Part of a complex built on a former National Guard training area southwest of Salt Lake City.'

33

HETTA, REUBEN AND CHRISTY ARE WAITING FOR US IN THE Situation Room. I take a seat next to Reuben, who gives me a weak smile. The lights come down the moment the President is in position at the head of the table, flanked by Cabot and Graham.

Hetta moves to the podium and pulls up a headshot of an earnest-looking man in his late twenties or early thirties on the screen behind her. He has a full head of black, wavy hair and looks unkempt. One of his collars bends upward.

'Meet Dr Joel Schweizer. A computer scientist who attended Harvard between 2001 and 2003. This is a contemporary photograph, the best that we have. Two years after leaving, he founded a company called Sub-Quantum Dynetics, which dedicated itself to building the world's first commercially available quantum computer. Quantum computers aren't like classical computers. They are designed to solve unsolvable problems.

'Seven years ago, Dr Schweizer showed up on an unclassified contract run out of the Army Research Laboratory for a Holographic Information Transfer System, funded by Congress to test a hypothesis that information – hard, physical data – exists in a diffuse electromagnetic field at the quantum level of space: what you might call the fundamental level of existence. There is no hard evidence that data exists in this field, but the theory was first aired publicly by a man who worked out of the same department as Schweizer, a physicist named Dr Elliott Kaufmann. Kaufmann called this infinite repository of data the holosphere, and said he was working on the architecture of a coupling device – tech that Colonel Cain believes he meant to tap into it.

'For this heresy, Kaufmann got howled down by his peers. He then turned up at the Baltimore Central Institute of Technology the following year. Baltimore CIT led the work on the transfer system.'

'And Gapes?' Thompson asks. 'Where does he fit in?'

'The Army's science lab was sponsored by INSCOM, Gapes's taskmasters. To calibrate, to tune the system, one Stani Koori trained Gapes and others in the protocols of remote viewing. Then Gapes replaced Koori. There are photos of him wearing a helmet with electrodes that attach directly to the scalp. INSCOM put money into the transfer system because Congress said it had to match its investment in the resurrected remote viewing program.

'Judging by the Army Research Lab documentation, I don't think INSCOM was fully committed until Dr Joel Schweizer was contracted for the third-generation helmet.'

The timing is interesting, she adds, because from the moment he left Harvard to the moment he showed up on the paperwork, Dr Schweizer had gone rather quiet.

'From 2007, S-Q Dynetics was subcontracted to work at a place called the Multi-program Research Facility at Oak Ridge, Tennessee. The sponsors behind the facility are an alphabet soup of agencies with a vested interest in high-speed computing. Their aim, in fact, was to build the world's fastest computer. And, like so much sensitive government work, it involved both open-source and classified elements. The open-source part is how we know about the involvement of S-Q Dynetics. It also allowed for those rumors of quantum computer sales to intelligence agencies both particular and unspecified to filter out into the world.

'The classified piece, of course, was run by the NSA, whose target was the proliferating encryption arena that was allowing terrorists, criminals and bad guy states to talk to each other without fear of interception.

'In 2009, just after Oak Ridge announced it had developed the world's fastest computer, it brought down the shutters and restricted briefings on the program to no more than a handful in the intelligence community and Congress. But there were whispers that the NSA was on its way to the world's first exaflop machine – a supercomputer with enough speed to crunch the sum of human knowledge in less than a second. The only way to do that was by covertly adding a quantum-computing element.'

'So, when Schweizer joined Kaufmann in Baltimore,' Reuben says, 'your theory is that he brought the power of quantum computing to bear on Kaufmann's holosphere?'

'I think we can safely assume it's more than theory, Mr Kantner,' Hetta says. 'Schweizer knew Kaufmann. They worked out of the same building at Harvard, and I've followed enough audit trails to know when something ain't right. Everything at the Army lab was heading in one direction: the corroboration of the theory, Gapes's replacement of Koori, modest funding increases, money for a Gen 3 helmet, the display of data from the holosphere on some kind of visuals system ... when the funding was slashed, and a note appeared on the contract to say there had been a problem all along.

'Their mistake was shutting down Schweizer's computing company *and* Baltimore CIT. To avoid suspicion, it would have been better to keep them going, but my guess is they panicked when he ran.'

Reuben leans forward. '*Who* ran?'

'Gapes. Going AWOL was a cover story. They needed to make him invisible. But something spooked him and he hightailed it for real.'

'Until he announced his presence last week,' Reuben says. 'The sixty-four-thousand-dollar question, Hart: who are *they*?'

Hetta switches to a photo, taken at dusk, of buildings nestling at the base of a snow-capped mountain. Bright lights flare in the lens. I've seen it before.

'This is the Utah Data Center. Bluffdale, built on an old runway on a closed-off piece of government land beneath the Wasatch Mountains, south of Salt Lake City. It comprises four data halls, each half the size of the Pentagon, filled with servers. It's one of a number of NSA storage sites for the thirty trillion phone calls, emails, personal data trails and Google searches it's estimated to have collected from its surveillance activities since 9/11.

'A contact of mine at the National Geospatial-Intelligence Agency told me last night that six years ago construction began on an extension to the site in an arroyo out in the Wasatch. Unlike the other buildings in the UDC, this place is totally isolated and almost entirely underground.

'Geospatial believe it to be completely self-sustaining. It has its own water supply and gets fed two hundred megawatts of electricity, enough for a small town. Fuel tanks give it a week's worth of back-up generation. An image of this building is one of three removed without our sanction from the cabin, we now believe by a freelance contractor that's intimately connected to the NSA: Triple Z Services.'

Cabot leans in. 'Triple Z, we believe, Mr President, has been outsourced to handle the clean-up.'

'And you were followed from Bethesda,' Thompson says.

'Yes, sir.'

'By these people?'

'No, sir. By the Army. Their Criminal Investigation Division.' Hetta pauses. 'Not in the same league.'

'Agent Hart managed to apprehend a member of their surveillance team,' Graham announces. 'He's still being interrogated by the FBI agent who's heading up the task force charged with the church shooting investigation. Special Agent Wharton is passing data to us when he gets it, but it appears they were assigned to follow Hart and Colonel Cain by General Johansson.'

'Johansson? Of JaySOC?'

'Yes, sir.'

'And Wharton?'

'Wharton is a good guy, Mr President,' Hetta says. 'He and SAIC Lefortz shared a lot of history. In fact, Agent Wharton told Colonel Cain that Lefortz discussed some kind of investigation – a "probe" – commissioned by you. That he was working on it before he was killed. Does that make any sense to you, sir?'

Thompson looks up. 'A *probe*?'

'Yes, Mr President.'

'I don't know of any probe, Agent Hart.'

Hetta looks at him. 'You sure, Mr President?'

Reuben brings his hand down. 'Agent Hart, I'll remind you that you're talking to the President.'

'I know, Mr Kantner. I was merely—'

I touch her arm. 'Why don't we get back to Triple Z and the images that were lifted from the cabin?'

'OK . . . sure.' Hetta takes a moment to regroup. 'There are so many images on the walls, we believe they made a calculation we wouldn't notice that three of them had been swapped. But I'd photographed the cabin the night Colonel Cain and I first came across it and we were able to get the results to Christy Byford for further analysis.

'This is the place they've been trying to protect all along.'

With one of her looks, she lets me know she's done.

I pick up the thread. 'Here's what we think happened, Mr President. When the HITS helmet technology actually worked, INSCOM knew they were way out of their depth. So they gifted it to the NSA. And the next version of HITS, a black joint venture between INSCOM and the NSA, is just short of being fully operational.'

I point to the photo of the bunker.

'Three years ago, while Gapes was still convalescing from his burns, he told his mother they were sending him to the desert. We thought he was talking about Afghanistan, Iraq or Syria. He wasn't. He was talking about Utah. They needed him to calibrate the system.

'We also have an explanation for the dream-flashbacks. They were listed in the Army lab data as a side effect.'

'Jesus,' Thompson says.

'Gapes told his mom he was scared. Very scared. Nobody paid her any attention because she had dementia and, belt and braces, the Army bought the family's silence with a compensation package for what it had done to a traumatized ex-vet.

'This thing is so big, this . . . whatever this amalgam of the NSA and INSCOM calls itself, is so secret, it needed anyone they couldn't completely trust to vanish.' I reel them off. Kaufmann, Schweizer, Gapes . . .

The President brings down his hand. 'You're telling me they can *see* everything we're doing?'

Up till now Christy hasn't said anything. She touches his arm. 'That's precisely what Josh is saying, sir.'

'Right now?'

'No sir, not now. Soon.'

Six pairs of eyes turn to me.

'Since this started, Agent Hart and I have asked ourselves one question, over and over. If Gapes knew of a plot to kill you, Mr President, why didn't he give us chapter and verse?'

Thompson leans forward. 'You're not alone, Colonel.'

'Well, sir, Gapes knew if he went the WikiLeaks route, unveiling a technology that gives the intelligence community the means to hack into our movements, the world would have dismissed him, and it, as just crazy. So he decided to drip-feed us the data, having seized our attention in a way we couldn't possibly ignore.'

'Why?'

'Because black operators make errors when they're forced into the light. Look at Clarke's Crossroads. A master in the art of the hit took a step back and left us a bloody footprint. And this tech hasn't yet been perfected. Gapes knew there's a gap between the acquisition of data and it becoming intelligible to the end-user.'

'How can you possibly know that?' Cabot asks.

'Ten days ago, twenty-four hours before he mounted his protest at the church, Gapes shared his plans with a homeless vet, a guy called Steve at the Settlement, knowing that, in doing so, he was "unmasking" – blooming, in effect – on the system that's installed at Bluffdale.'

'What do you mean?' Cabot says.

'Gapes might have found a method of shielding his movements, but Steve hadn't. To fulfill his plan, for reasons that are still not entirely clear, Gapes needed to announce himself. Since this system evidently couldn't track him, his method was to shock it into awareness. He announced his plans to a wheelchair-bound vet and told him to *remember* them. He then pressed the guy's hands to his burned face so that the data imprinted. Since I've no doubt the system has some kind of early warning mode, this is the moment Gapes would have popped up on its radar screen. He was deliberately alerting it to his presence.'

'I have a confession to make,' Cabot says. 'Which I now see plays into what you're suggesting.' He clears his throat, a little self-consciously. 'The day you discovered the cabin, we received an anonymous tip-off that you and Hart had been operating off the books. That's why we hauled you in and polygraphed you.

'I think it was part of a damage limitation strategy these people triggered when they realized that we had moved a step ahead of them. I'm sorry, Colonel . . .'

Contrition from Cabot. You could hear a pin drop.

'You were saying, Josh,' the President says. 'About the technology having not yet been perfected . . .'

I nod. 'Hart and I found the cabin outside Blacksoil two days after Gapes popped up at the church. We followed a set of leads I believe were intended by him to keep us one step ahead of the system's ability to track us – his food, pieces of deer meat that he left in the basement of the church, part of a note we found there, and the collapsible canoe we think he used to covertly enter D.C. The crazy wall, as we called it, was filled with further clues.

'By the time the system realized we were there, Lefortz was already sending reinforcements. So they did the only thing they could: sent in a CID team. And not just Army, but Triple Z, black ops contractors who knew exactly what they were looking for and removed it. We all presumed there'd been a leak. There hadn't. Bluffdale had kicked in.

'The system wasn't operating cold by that point. It must have switched into some kind of tracking mode, because the lag between detection and intervention was twelve hours.'

The President frowns. Christy starts to scribble.

'The essential point is we now know its operational parameters:

twelve hours if it's running hot; twenty-four if it has to acquire a target from a standing start. To put it another way, Mr President, the NSA and INSCOM will know about the discussion we are having in this room within that frame. That's how long we have.'

'Mr President,' Hetta adds, 'gaining access to this site is going to be challenging. The video surveillance is visible from the geo-spatial imagery. There will be intruder alarms. Most of Western Utah is filled with military installations, some of which will provide this place with top-cover – active defense measures – in the event of a terrorist attack. There's a twelve-foot-high fence around the facility that can stop a 15,000-pound vehicle traveling at sixty miles per hour, which would rule out pretty much any kind of direct assault, except by helicopter.'

'And who do you suggest does this?' Cabot asks.

'It wouldn't be for me to say, Mr Cabot. That would be down to President Thompson. But if an assault were to be launched, sir, I believe it should be by us, the Secret Service.'

Cabot starts to laugh. 'You're fucking kidding me.'

'No, sir,' Hetta says. 'Four people are dead – five, if you include Gapes's recovery support specialist – and we have no reason to believe the killings won't continue. Gapes has said there is a threat to the President and everything he has either told us or fed us so far has turned out to be on the money. The Ilitch link – which extends to a professor of neuroscience at Georgetown, Edward van Buren, who is known to Colonel Cain – prompts us to believe that Gapes may be warning us of even deeper connections which are, well, kind of freaky.'

'An NSA or INSCOM link to the Russians?'

'Yes,' Hetta says.

'Why?'

'We really don't know.'

'I could run it past my liaison at the embassy.' Christy looks at me. 'With your buddy, Joshua. Colonel Dmitri Sergeyev. As well as being a spook, he's our link with their Special Forces on the WMD search-and-destroy front.'

She turns to the President.

'Go ahead,' Thompson tells her. 'But, Christy, I don't want any of this to rock my Moscow bilateral, you hear?'

'It won't,' she says.

'Let's you and me talk about this offline,' Reuben says to her. 'Finesse the narrative.'

'Do we have precedent?' Graham asks.

After his interrogation, Reuben looks as if he might reach out and strangle him. '*Precedent?* What the hell are you talking about?'

Graham flushes. 'For one agency taking down another?'

'We have no time for legalities,' I say. 'If we do, it will increase our chances of detection. And whatever action we take needs to be extremely tight. It's essential we move to detain General Johansson at Fort Bragg and the INSCOM RV team at Fort Meade at the same time as we make our move on Bluffdale.'

'You guys just focus on the NSA and Bluffdale,' Christy says. 'I'll take care of the military.'

'What assets do we have in Utah?' Cabot asks Hetta.

'A field office in Salt Lake City, but it's mainly administrative. We're going to have to bring our own units with us. I'd like to suggest we take two teams out of the Presidential Protection training cycle. Our only air assets in Utah are in the east: a couple of Hueys. Snake Ranch Mesa. Between Huntington and Green River.'

'Can it take a jet?' Cabot asks.

It has a seven-thousand-foot runway, Hetta says.

34

I FIND REUBEN SITTING ON A BENCH AMONG THE TREES IN FRONT of the West Colonnade. He's leaning forward, staring at the ground, smoking a cigarette, something I haven't seen him do in years.

He looks up and attempts a smile. I pull my jacket closer. It's almost freezing, and Reuben is just in a suit. His hand trembles slightly.

For a second or two, neither of us says anything. My head is filled with the rudiments of an assault plan. In ten minutes, Hetta and I will leave for Reagan, where the Vomit Comet is being readied for a departure under a false-file flight plan to Salt Lake City. A second jet is being prepared for rapid egress out of Baltimore for the ten members of the Presidential Protection Division's Counter-Assault Team, known as 'the CAT', who are being briefed by Graham at their training ground in Beltsville, MD.

Nothing we do may be communicated in any form, as we have to assume that the people listening to us will be tuned into our phones, our emails, our Internet searches, everything.

And if I'm right about the Kaufmann/Schweizer surveillance system, it will have picked up on the fact that Hetta and I have been to the contracts office of the Army Research Lab and followed the HITS thread as far as our conclusions about the holosphere.

Reuben, Hetta and I have taken the opportunity to lay a few false trails in our communications traffic to give the impression we are still deeply immersed in the investigative phase: Hetta at PIAD;

me, post-release in my office; Reuben in his. To get around the communications ban, Graham has driven to Beltsville to brief the CAT. He has put a small team of agents on my desk and Hetta's, who, between them, will work to a script – emailing each other, exactly as we would – to make them believe we're in D.C.

'Wish I was coming with you,' Reuben says between drags.

'Bullshit.' I sit on the edge of a white wrought-iron table, at which, in better times, I've seen the President, his wife and kids smiling in publicity shots. 'He needs you here. We need you here.'

'You think they know? I mean, really know? About everything? Our every move?'

'Yes, I do.'

He stares at the smoke curling from his cigarette. 'So, all his fears really did come home to roost.' He lets the stub fall and stares back across the Rose Garden toward the Oval Office.

'This may be something or it may be nothing, but the trail that led Hart to the INSCOM science program also led to your former boss, Tod Abnarth. He was the Minority Leader of the Senate Intelligence Committee when he learned the Bush presidency had duped him over the resurrected remote viewing program. All this was before your time, but only just. I'm telling you because Hart is onto it and, as you once told me, when she gets her teeth into something, she doesn't let go.'

'Abnarth knew about the science program that led to this?'

'More. He threatened to go public about the Executive Branch breaking all the oversight rules. Abnarth's quid pro quo was that INSCOM should place the science in the public domain, on the grounds there was never any need to classify it.'

'That's what I don't understand. Why did INSCOM comply?'

'I don't think they believed the science would ever work. They just wanted the committee's funding approval for the classified part – using psychics to support the Activity's hunt for WMD-toting terrorists.'

Reuben sits back and thinks about this for a moment.

'Abnarth and the President have history,' he says.

'I know.'

'Abnarth was the first politician to endorse Thompson for the Democratic nomination.'

'I know that too. So, let's not get blindsided. Talk to the President. He's a lawyer. He'll understand. There's got to be an explanation. Cabot's onside, but it won't take much for that to change if he believes we're hiding something else from him.'

I wait a beat.

'Listen. Back there, what Hart was saying—'

'What is it with her?'

'She's a good agent.'

'She was taking Thompson to task, Josh.'

'So there isn't a probe?'

'No. If there was, I'd know about it.'

'And you don't.'

'Fuck's sake, man.'

I've known Reuben long enough to tell when he's hiding something from me, and he isn't.

I hesitate. 'Do something else for me, would you?'

'Sure,' he says. 'Name it.'

'When they come for Johansson, the INSCOM leadership team, and Triple Z in Herndon, they're going to pull in Ted van Buren. I can't begin to guess how Ted's mixed up in all this, but I don't want Cabot and his goons putting him through the wringer. He's old and this will terrify him. Keep him safe until I get back. Then I'll handle it.'

35

FROM FIVE MILES OUT, IT LOOKS AS IF SOMEBODY HAS TAKEN A giant chainsaw and lopped the top off the mountain. The plateau, 1,500 meters above sea level, is dotted with pines and boulders, and a long, arrow-straight runway that cuts through the middle of it. The treetops have been dusted by a recent snowfall.

The field was built during the war to test stuff they didn't want anybody to see, and some of the infrastructure is still visible: two black hangars nestled amid a cluster of modern white buildings.

Two minutes after we land, we taxi up to one of the hangars and shut down. Our pilot steps into the cabin and opens the door.

Snake Ranch Mesa is a small general aviation field with a parachute club, and a couple of Gulfstreams registered to the billionaire businessmen who have wilderness lodges nearby.

The Citation Jet's air stairs flop to the ground. Graham, in jeans and a fleece, is waiting for us; his aircraft is more modern and at least fifty knots faster than the Comet. It's ten degrees colder here in Utah than it was in D.C. Hetta is in field-standard white and black. She shivers behind me.

'Follow me,' he says. 'We got here thirty minutes ago. Weather's turning. There's snow showers inbound. Let's push it.'

We jog across the apron and shimmy through a gap in the hangar doors, where I'm hit by a sound I haven't heard in a long time: the clink and rustle of people getting ready with purpose.

Two dark gray Hueys sit under the strip lights, surrounded by the assault team Graham brought with him from Beltsville.

He walks us over to a big guy in black tactical gear with his back to us. He's wearing a baseball cap, a T-shirt and a black nylon belt festooned with pouches. A helmet, a ballistic vest, a knife, a holster, a gas mask bag, half a dozen grenades and his weapons – an SR-16 and a SIG Sauer – lie on the ground behind him.

He turns. 'Colonel Cain.' His voice is a familiar baritone. 'John Hayden. We—'

'John Hayden.' I shake his hand warmly. 'Christ, you look a little different from the last time . . .'

'You two know each other?' Graham says.

Hayden smiles. 'We do. Since a certain zit-faced captain gave me a triage lesson outside of Ramadi. I was on the receiving end of a shell splinter that damn near took my arm off.' He holds it up to display a six-inch scar above the elbow.

He's still gripping my hand. 'Shit, it's good to see you, sir.'

'You too, John. You know Special Agent Hetta Hart?'

'Don't believe I do.' He lets me go and turns to her. 'Mighty glad to meet you.' He smiles, Hetta brushes her hair out of her eyes, and I feel something I don't expect somewhere in my gut.

Hayden gestures to the open door of the Huey behind him. On the floor is an Alice pack. 'That's our standard backpack, Colonel. You'll need to check it through as I'm guessing there's a shitload in there that's different from the last one you played around with.'

Graham taps his watch. 'Briefing in two, John. Let's go.'

'Ready our end,' Hayden says. He picks up his ballistic vest and slips it over his head. I make my way over to the helicopter.

I count off the essentials: a surgical kit with every kind of blade, probe and needle; different types of scissors, battle dressings and tourniquets; an IV infuser kit, saline, blood bags . . .

'OK, gentlemen, listen up. If I could have your attention, please.' Hetta's voice echoes beneath the hangar roof. She's standing next to a whiteboard with a hastily sketched picture of the target. The arroyo, which angles north to south. The rectangular bunker a third of the way up it. A fence where the arroyo ends and the valley floor begins. A guard-post. An access road between. The checkpoint.

The building itself. Pinned beneath the sketch is a blow-up of the image from the cabin, the gray roof of the facility stark against the salty white desert floor.

Hayden's assault unit comprises two five-man-strong tactical teams. They've also brought in two pilots with Huey experience. PPD agents are tasked to take a bullet for the President. These guys are different. If the shit goes down, the CAT is there – a few vehicles behind the Beast – to take the fight to the enemy. They train for every contingency, but they won't have trained for this: taking down a bunker guarded by ex-servicemen with much the same level of experience. This is the kind of op you'd normally give the SEALs, Delta or the Activity.

His men gather by the whiteboard.

Graham nods to Hetta.

'Before I left the White House,' she says, 'President Thompson handed me an executive order. We will touch down weapons hot; you have permission to return fire if engaged. Data on what we can expect is patchy. The nearest public land is five miles from the perimeter, so we reckon there's only a small security detail at the site itself. But the second we hit the ground, they're going to call in reinforcements.' She directs our attention to the paved road that runs from the bunker building to the main Bluffdale complex. 'And they're going to come right down this road. Your task is to hold the perimeter long enough to allow Colonel Cain and myself access to the building.'

Hayden stands behind his men, chewing on a match. He sticks his hand up. 'What happens then, Agent Hart?'

'I'll be honest with you. We don't know. We hope they're going to see that the game's up and do what we say.'

She looks surprised at the laughter from the floor.

She waits a moment. 'If there are no further questions, we're good to go. Weather is going to restrict our visibility on the way in and over the LZ, which isn't good, but on the plus side, it's going to fuck with them, too.'

Hayden's agents push the Hueys out onto the apron. Hetta and I clamber on board the lead craft, which will set down on the LZ between the perimeter and the building; the other, with Graham on board, will deliver its men onto the roof of the facility.

I strap myself into a seat behind the pilot and grab a set of headphones. Hetta does the same.

Hayden pulls the door shut. Snowflakes swirl around us as the pilot fires up one turbine, then the next. I close my eyes as fifteen years slide by – the only difference was that we'd used Black Hawks then, not Hueys.

We make a course adjustment at a waypoint north of a clapped-out junction town, clipping the southwest corner of the Uintah and Ouray Reservation.

The terrain switches from desert to forest and, as we flash over a large frozen lake, the CAT operator next to me waves at a guy fishing on the ice, then flips him the bird.

Hetta, eyes down, points to the map. We're heading for a valley with 3,000-meter peaks either side of it – our frontier with civilization. Beyond it lie the suburbs of Salt Lake City, an eight-lane stretch of Interstate 15 and the perimeter of the closed-off military training area that houses the Bluffdale site, the arroyo and our LZ.

Fifteen minutes later, my guts lurch as we crest a ridge and start to descend rapidly. There's a crackle in my headphones. 'Unidentified aircraft entering Class A airspace south of Sandy, this is Salt Lake ARTCC, please identify yourselves. Over.'

'Ah, Salt Lake ARTCC, this is Coyote Two-Three. We are a law enforcement flight out of Green River en route to Herriman requesting transit at flight level two-zero, estimated transit time—'

'Coyote Two-Three, you are about to enter restricted airspace. Request you immediate right turn, heading three-two-zero.'

We are now thirty degrees nose-down, hugging the slope. I crane my neck and see a patchwork of buildings and streets over the pilot's shoulder. To the left is Utah Lake. To the right, I can make out lines of ski-lifts on the slopes of the mountains to the east of Salt Lake City's southern suburbs.

'Coyote Two-Three, repeat: you are close to restricted airspace.'

We fly on.

'Make an immediate right turn, heading three-two-zero, repeat, three-two-zero.'

We shoot over the interstate, bank hard left, and I get a snapshot of a semi-circular cluster of large white buildings. They're so big, I could reach out and touch them.

The Utah Data Center.

We pull over a ridge and down the other side, using the terrain to mask our approach. High winds and snow buffet the Huey. Our pilot comes on the intercom: 'Thirty seconds to the LZ.'

Hayden slides back the door. Cold air rips into the cabin.

We haul over another ridge, make a turn above the bunker and come in low, pulling up in the last seconds to bleed off our speed.

Our skids bump along the sand. Hayden jumps out. Everybody else follows.

At the head of the arroyo the second team has already deployed onto the roof of the bunker. Two agents abseil to the ground and blow the steel door.

By the time Hetta, Hayden and I reach them they're already inside, probing with flashlights. The entrance is cold and dark.

Through the smoke, beyond a barrier fitted with biometric scanners, I spot a stairwell. The stairs go just one way: down.

36

A HIGH-TECH VERSION OF A VICTORIAN OPERATING THEATER, LIT by the glow of three Cyalume sticks.

Banks of seating extend three tiers up from a circular floor area. There are workstations for half a dozen people.

A three-foot-high circular plinth stands at its center. Bits of broken kit lie everywhere.

One of three large screens hangs on its wires. Two are on the floor, beyond repair.

Hayden raises his NVGs, jogs down a gangway, squats and runs a gloved hand across a six-inch-deep crater beside the plinth. Hetta and I stand next to him. The two others carry on sweeping the room.

'Fragmentation damage,' he says. The light from the Cyalume catches his breath as he speaks. 'It's still warm.'

I was wrong. They've refined the lag time: down from twelve hours to ten. *They knew we were coming, but only just.*

Feet tramp down the stairwell. Two CAT agents appear at the door.

'We got company,' one blurts. 'There's a fuckin' convoy of Humvees coming up the road. What to do, boss?'

Hayden gets to his feet. We'd preplanned for this. His voice remains calm. 'Secure the perimeter. Don't let them on site. Where's—?'

There's a muffled bang below us. The vibration shakes the floor.

I look at Hetta, then at Hayden.

He turns to his men. 'They want to parlay, fine. Graham's in charge. He can keep 'em talking. It's what he does. They want a fight, give 'em one.' He glances down. '*We* got company too.'

The two agents tramp back upstairs.

Hayden turns to Hetta and me. 'You both ready for this?'

He unholsters his SIG, racks the slide and hands it to me.

There's a door at the back of the room. Hayden pulls the handle toward him. I'm hit by the smell of electrical equipment. Blue, red, green and white LEDs blink in two large equipment racks. They extend floor to ceiling, and front to back. Four fan ducts, each the height of a man, are set in the wall behind a wire mesh screen. Their paddle blades are motionless.

We spread out. A flight of steps leads down from the end of the chamber. The acrid smell of the detonation rises to meet us. Wisps of smoke hang in the glow of the diodes and LEDs.

Hayden is the first to descend. Then Hetta. I follow.

The next level down is a duplicate of the one we've just left. Another flight of steps leads into the bowels of the facility. I wonder how deep the thing goes.

The two figures crouching between the racks on the far wall are barely visible and too busy doing what they're doing – assembling another charge – to see us. Against the thrum of the servers, they've heard nothing either. I raise my weapon.

Hayden yells: 'Right there, fellas!'

One of them rolls left, the other right.

Hayden and Hetta fire at the exact same moment.

Muzzle flashes light up the room. Bullets ricochet off the metalwork. There's a burst of return fire. Hayden staggers and hits the ground.

Hetta covers me as I crawl through a rack to reach him. I check his pulse, roll him onto his back and pull out a flashlight. He's taken rounds in the left shoulder and in his medial right thigh.

I tear open the top of his pants and a jet of arterial blood arcs past my face. I jam the palm of my left hand into the wound, stick the flashlight in my mouth and rummage through the pack for a wad of combat gauze. I shove it in the wound and press down with all my strength. Hayden screams.

Good. He's conscious.

I slip a tourniquet around his thigh. Working it with one hand takes too long. I pull it tight ten centimeters above the wound and shine the light in his eyes.

'John? You hear me?'

He nods.

'I need you to work the tourniquet.'

He nods again.

I'm guessing he's lost a liter of blood. If he loses another, he'll become confused, his pulse will weaken, his heart rate will jump, his systolic blood pressure will drop and he'll go into shock.

'Am I going to die?'

'I saved you before, didn't I?'

'Am I?'

'No.'

If I don't stop the bleeding in the next ninety seconds, though, he will.

I wrap his fingers around the end of the tourniquet and tell him to pull.

Still applying pressure to the wound, I reach into the pack and grab a pressure dressing. I let go of the flashlight, tear the wrapper with my teeth, unfurl the bandage and wrap it tight around the wound. I then elevate the leg by lifting his foot onto the pack.

Only now am I aware that the shooting's stopped.

'Hetta!'

She's gone.

I direct the flashlight beam onto the gap between Hayden's torso armor and the Kevlar protecting his upper arm. I cut open his shirt and the T-shirt underneath. The round has punched in and out, tumbling through bone and muscle. It'll be hurting like hell, but it won't kill him.

I glance at the thigh wound. The bleed's stopped, so I stick a fentanyl lozenge in his cheek and tell him to hold completely still. The fentanyl kicks in quickly and is as good as IV morphine.

'Josh!' Hetta's voice reaches me from across the room. 'We got a man down here. He's dead. The other guy's lost blood. Trail leads through one of the ducts. I'm going after him. Stay with Hayden,' she tells me. 'And keep your weapon close.'

I look around. In all the excitement, it's gone.

Hayden tugs at the sleeve of my jacket and points to his SR-16. It's lying where he dropped it, two meters away.

I get up, take a step toward it. Out of the corner of my eye, I see somebody silhouetted at the base of the stairwell. He must have worked his way behind Hetta, through the ducting.

I glance at the SR-16.

'Don't even . . .' the guy breathes. I can't see his face. It's in shadow. With his gun, he lets me know what he'll do to Hayden.

He spins me around, shoves his rifle into the small of my back and starts to push me up the stairs. Standing at the top, half in shadow, holding her gun in front of her with both hands, is Hetta.

The guy sees her too. He drops his rifle, grabs me around the neck and jams a pistol against my temple. 'I'll kill him,' he yells.

I look down. He's wearing a pair of Nike Airs.

'Josh?' Her voice is eerily calm. 'You OK?'

Is she kidding me?

He tightens his grip around my neck.

'You're going to be all right.'

Shut the hell up, Hetta.

'I'm going to get you out of this.'

He squeezes my neck so hard I can't breathe.

Shoot him, fuck's sake.

'You know who this guy is?'

I don't care. Shoot him.

'Tell me who he is, Josh.'

I can't. I can't breathe. Shoot him, shoot him.

'His name, Josh.'

I twist enough to allow me to gulp some air.

As Karl Dempf's body tenses, she fires.

*

The Humvees belong to a Utah National Guard unit. The territory on which we've landed, like the Utah Data Center itself, is leased from the military by the NSA. The twenty-five-man platoon had been taking part in an exercise on the other side of the ridge when they saw the helicopters land and drove over to investigate.

By the time we emerge from two levels below ground, accompanied by two CATs carrying Hayden on a litter, Graham has persuaded the unit's commanding officer to transport him to a military hospital outside Salt Lake City, supervised by one of their medics.

Hetta and I retreat to the entranceway of the bunker so that we can sitrep Reuben, but I'm stopped from making the call by Graham waving his cellphone.

'Guy from our local field office is on the line,' he says, like this is an entirely normal thing. 'Wants to speak with you.'

He hands Hetta the phone.

Hetta frowns. She looks at me and switches to speaker.

'This is Agent Hart. Who am I speaking to?'

'Rich Lewis, ma'am. Deputy Special Agent in Charge, Salt Lake.' His voice bounces off the concrete walls. 'You at the site?'

'The site?'

'The UDC at Bluffdale, ma'am.'

'Please state your business, Agent Lewis.'

'A man walked in here fifteen minutes ago. Says he has information to do with an investigation you're running out of D.C.'

'Is this a joke?'

'No, ma'am.'

'What else did he say?'

'Nothing. He'll only speak with you.'

'Name?'

'Say again.'

'What's his fucking *name*?'

'Oh . . . His driver's license says Jon . . . J-O-N . . . Silver. S-I-L-V-E-R. Forty-two. Says he's a contractor out there. He's real jumpy. Claims Silver ain't his real name too; says it's really Schweizer. Doctor Joel Schweizer. S-C-H-W-E-I-Z-E-R.'

37

SCHWEIZER IS NURSING A DAY'S STUBBLE. HE IS PALE, DRAWN and much older than he was in the photos we circulated in the Sit Room. From the rings around his eyes, it's clear it's at least twenty-four hours since he's had any sleep. His hands shake; he must be on some kind of amphetamine.

'You get every detail of what I know and built,' he says, glancing rapidly between us. 'But I need you to promise me immunity. And protection.'

The various acts passed by various administrations giving whistleblowers a measure of protection do not extend to private contractors, only to direct employees of the intelligence community, though there is no guarantee you'll avoid a jail sentence under the Espionage Act.

'I can get you an audience with the President,' I tell him. 'But first you're going to have to give us some indication of what you've got.'

'How about a list of every fucking contractor that ever worked on the Grid's software.' His eyes dart between Hetta's and mine.

'The Grid?'

Hetta puts her phone on the table and presses record.

'The Grid is what *it's* called. The *place* is called the Canyon.' He slides a USB stick across to her.

Hetta picks it up, looks at it.

'Encrypted, obviously. Names, dates, places. And a bunch of schedule data that includes a list of upgrades that will bring the system to full operating capability. You get all that when I'm in front of Thompson. Say yes and you get a sample now.'

There's nothing to discuss. I say yes.

Hetta leans in. 'How did you know to contact me?'

'I built a backdoor. I knew you were coming, maybe before you did. And before they did.'

'Who are *they*?'

'The people in charge.' He pauses. 'How much of it did they leave intact?'

'There's some fragmentation damage in what looks like a control center.'

'And the server chambers?'

'More substantial, but repairable.'

'It looks like they're trying to send a message,' he says.

'Who?' Hetta asks again.

'I have no idea. Really. The NSA contracts all this stuff out. I report to a manager, he reports to a supervisor, who reports to a technical director and only then is there likely to be any interface with the agency itself. Tracking who knew what and when is going to take weeks, months . . . years. Shit, the way they've compartmentalized the program, you may never fucking know.'

'So when did the evacuation order go out?' Hetta asks.

'Late last night. I got a coded notification not to show for work. The security apes have been jittery since Gapes showed up in D.C. The whole Canyon has been on standby to evacuate.'

'Why not do it sooner?' I ask.

'My bet is they were counting on containment, but like that kid with his pinkie in the dyke, the leaks became unstoppable. I live close to the site and saw your helicopters fly in.'

'What is the status of the system?' Hetta asks.

He says it's at what is known as Phase 4.

'Phase 4 isn't the all-up gig. It has a lot of bugs. There are – *were* – efforts underway to eliminate them. Right now, we still have to render the visuals. It can take a day, sometimes longer, for raw data to undergo the rendering process. And there are other flaws.'

'Like the fact it can't track certain people?'

'That's one of them.'

'Why can't it?'

He looks at me. 'Why can't it what?'

'Track them?'

'I don't know. I told you; it's what we termed an operational prototype. But . . .'

'Yes?'

'It appears that some people – a very few – have developed an ability to counter it.'

'*Counter* it?'

'As in jam, Colonel.'

'That, I imagine, included Gapes.'

'Clearly,' he tells me. 'Or they'd have found him.'

'Why'd he run?' Hetta asks.

'I don't know.'

'Did *you* know him?'

'I knew *about* him. After his AWOL stunt, everybody did.'

'What did they say?'

'That he'd done a Snowden. As in stolen a bunch of files. I never met the guy, but Kaufmann did. He and Gapes worked on HITS. Kaufmann was front-of-house. I was the interface guy.'

'The guy who used a highly developed quantum computing architecture as a stand-in for the brain's processing ability,' Hetta says. 'We managed to track your career as far as Oak Ridge.'

His eyes gleam. 'The subconscious part of the brain, the stuff we do without thinking, is, in essence, nothing *but* a quantum computer, Agent Hart.'

'Why the NSA?' she asks.

'After Harvard, I got to work on some of the coolest computers on the planet. Kaufmann took a different path. He'd spoken up for what he believed in – what the data was telling him. The establishment, however, took a more measured view.'

'So, they killed him, huh?' Hetta says.

'Psychic ability hinges on subtle differences in the way a psychic's brain is wired. Without knowing how they do it, Gapes and his trainer Koori pulled what the rest of us call psychic phenomena – ESP, clairvoyance, telepathy – from the ether, aka Kaufmann's holosphere.

'The holosphere turns out to be nothing more mysterious than an infinity of data points made up of sub-atomic particles that blink in and out of existence. When they blink out, we don't know where they go, except that they're somewhere beyond the bounds of classical space-time. When they blink back in, they appear as transient standing waves encoded with data.'

'So?'

'That's what the Grid does, Agent Hart – it taps data. Kaufmann's problem was believing the data was mystical – that it was pure consciousness – and should never have been weaponized. But the guy had done his deal with the devil. He'd taken the military's money, because nobody else would give him any, and when he told them he wanted out, they killed him. Made it look like a heart attack. Gapes took the only other way out.'

I nod. 'But after the helicopter crash, he was a wreck.'

'We calibrated the Grid in the same way we calibrated HITS. Gapes was incredibly gifted, but for the Grid's calibration process, and in light of his injuries, he worked best when there was somebody with him.'

A thought flickers somewhere at the back of my mind but fails to catch light. I ask him about the dreams and nightmares instead.

'Some people develop a resistance to being interrogated. When the subconscious part of their brain resists, for a reason we don't fully understand, they can develop psychological problems.'

Flashbacks that are so real they conjured what I took to be the truck that killed Hope coming at me on the road to Thurmont.

And the President's nightmares.

'Who was responsible for assigning targets?' Hetta asks.

'A cell back east.'

'Where back east?'

'I don't know. We provided it with a feed. The cell saw what we saw. My strong hunch is that it's buried inside the Cube.'

'Thompson is going to tear the whole thing down. You know that, don't you?'

Schweizer looks at me. 'You think?'
He shakes his head and laughs.

As soon as the Comet clears the Salt Lake Air Route ~~Con~~
trol Center, somewhere east of Colorado Springs, I put in a call to
Reuben.

I repeat what he will have got already in a sitrep from Cabot:
that the raid was successful, that 'the system' is no longer operational and that the mop-up operation under Graham – working
out of the Salt Lake field office – is ongoing.

I tell him that we have a key witness and that what he has to say
is for Thompson's ears only. Then again, Reuben *is* Thompson's
ears.

But I still have more questions than answers.

I don't know why Gapes ran.

I don't know how the threat he directed me to relates to the
President.

Nor do I know how it connects to the Engineer – or if the Engineer is even real.

I *do* know that the threat converges on Jerusalem.

And that somebody on the inside – somebody with a connection
to the Grid – didn't want us to know three things:

- About its existence;
- About a component for a nuclear weapon our own experts
  had trouble identifying;
- And about a Russian tech entrepreneur called Ilitch, an
  oligarch with a connection to Ted van Buren.

But, thanks to Gapes's trail of clues, I *do* know:

- About a technological breakthrough that can see events –
  past and present;
- That it messes with our thought patterns and produces
  strange, hallucinatory dream-flashbacks;

That there is a cabal within our intelligence community that went to great lengths to cover it up;

- That Thompson's nightmares started nine months ago; and this is when their interest in him began.

So, this is what I'm left with:

Why then?

And who are *they*?

'Josh . . . ?'

Reuben is still on the line.

'General Johansson and his staff are being held in a secure facility at Joint Base Anacostia–Bolling, as are all the other principal witnesses we spoke about.' It is past 3 a.m. on the East Coast and Reuben, like the rest of us, will have had little or no sleep. But I hear the relief in his voice, and, perhaps, a sense that things in D.C. are, at last, returning to a modicum of control.

Amongst the other principal witnesses are key INSCOM personnel, including Gapes's monitor, Cal Offutt; C-level executives of Triple Z; Katya; her boss, Charles Land; and TVB.

The concession I've got from Reuben is that I'll debrief TVB.

The joint base is on the east bank of the Potomac, across the river from Reagan National. It hosts a little-known Homeland Security compound with a below-ground suite for the covert detention and interrogation of terrorists. If the press does get a hold of it, Johansson is being questioned about historical abuse of PoWs in Iraq and Afghanistan.

There are sixteen agencies that make up the intelligence community.

Only around half a dozen of them have the power, reach and influence (a) to have known about the Grid, and (b) to have orchestrated the clean-up operation.

I list them: INSCOM, the CIA, the DIA, the Office of Naval Intelligence, the Intelligence Branch of the FBI and the NSA.

Their heads report to the Director of National Intelligence.

And the DNI reports to the President.

'We bring them all in – the whole damn lot of them – and we

put Cabot in charge of the round-up.' Cabot's the only person with connections to the intelligence community I actually trust.

'Where?' Reuben asks.

'Somewhere discreet and out of the way.'

'Which rules out Anacostia–Bolling.'

After a short discussion, we agree on Camp David.

'And if none of them talks?' Reuben asks.

'They will. If they'd wanted to destroy it, they would have. They need to negotiate, because they're not going to give it up.'

I open my eyes. Hetta is standing in front of me, holding two cups of coffee. I look at my watch. We're somewhere over the Great Plains – a little less than two hours before we land.

'Get any sleep?'

I shake my head. An hour has passed in a blur of half-formed thoughts and semi-lucid dreams about Schweizer, the Grid and how it came to be funded. She sits on the other side of the stained Formica and hands me a cup. I glance at Schweizer, out for the count in a seat across the aisle, a jacket half covering his chest and shoulders.

It takes her a minute to spell out what's on her mind.

'Are you angry with me, Josh?'

'Should I be?'

'I put two rounds in Dempf's head. Which was pretty close to yours.'

'Most people wouldn't have taken the shot. You did.' I take a sip of her coffee. It tastes terrible, but it does the job. I'm awake.

'I wasn't afraid,' she says.

'Good.'

'No. Not good.'

OK. Hetta Hart is trying to tell me something. I prop myself up on my elbows.

'I'm not asking for your professional opinion, you understand. I wouldn't want you to think—'

'Why don't you just tell me what's on your mind, Hetta?'

She brushes the crumbs of some agent's meal off the seat beside her.

'I told you about my brother . . .'

'Which one?'

'Mikey.'

'Which one's Mikey?'

'The eldest. The cop. I'd just graduated from Quantico. It was Thanksgiving. We were all home for the weekend . . .'

The Comet hits some turbulence. We clutch our coffees and wait till the shaking stops.

'Mom and I heard a shout. We were out back, talking. It was late. My uncle was closing up the bar. Mikey was helping. I ran into the bar and this addict's got a fistful of my uncle's hair and a knife to his throat and he's yelling at him to open up the register. Mikey's a meter or two away, pistol drawn. He's yelling at the guy to drop the knife, but the guy's screaming and yelling, too; he's completely off his head.

'And here's the thing, Josh. I know what to do – and it isn't what Mikey's doing, which is: *Drop the knife. Drop the knife. Drop the knife.* I have to take charge. And I got to do it now or my uncle's going to die. I step forward, Mikey sees me and shoves me out the way, because I'm just his little sister and I shouldn't be in the line of fire. And that's the moment the smack-head drops the knife, draws a thirty-eight and fires a round point-blank into Mikey.'

She pauses. 'I see what happens next in slow-mo. Mikey falling to the floor. The smack-head turning toward me. Leveling his gun. And then this weird thing happens. Time kind of stops.'

That's not so weird, I start to explain. The slowing of time, which is what some people experience, a review of their entire life, in the second before they think they're going to die, is unexplained, but some scientists believe it's another survival mechanism: the brain searching our life's experience to find something, anything, that can save us when the chips are down and there's no hope.

'You weren't afraid?'

'I've *never* been afraid, Josh. Of anything. Right from when I was little.'

'Tell me Mikey lived.'

'Yes, thank God.'

'And the guy with the knife?'

'An *ex*-guy with a knife.'

'You shot him?'

She nods.

'And your uncle?'

'Shaken, but OK.'

'How old were you?'

'Twenty-one.' She pauses. 'I've never talked to anybody about this. You think I should?'

That depends. 'Do you ever get intrusive thoughts?'

'No. But if I stop and think about it, I see everything as it happened – kind of like a snapshot – and that's not so good.'

This would have been the moment her superior autobiographical memory kicked in.

'Have you ever seen anyone about your OCD, Hetta?'

She looks at me.

'You have certain characteristics of obsessive compulsive behavior. OCD is a protection mechanism. You do what you do over and over to stop stuff you don't want – the really bad stuff – getting into your head. It may be better to have the OCD than the bad memories, but there are professionals I know who can help.'

She shakes her head and gives me a half smile. 'People at the first field office I worked used to have this joke about me behind my back, Josh. They called me the Gifted Gimp.'

Gifted.

'That's what he said.'

'That's what who said?'

'Schweizer said Gapes was gifted. But he also said, due to his injuries, calibrating the Grid worked best when there were two of them.'

I shake him awake.

Schweizer opens a bloodshot eye. 'Hey, we landing?' His stale breath turns my stomach.

'Who was the second psychic?'

241

'What?' He stares at me.

'Gapes was needed to tune the Grid. Koori had left. Who did he calibrate it with? You said the process required two of them.'

'I never knew the guy's name.' Schweizer hesitates. 'But Kaufmann told me he and Gapes had worked together. He was his monitor at INSCOM. It turned out he had a prodigious talent, too.'

Offutt.

Everybody who ever reported to the Canyon and left it – or, in Kaufmann's case, merely threatened to – has ended up dead.

Except for Offutt.

Which means he's still active – still working the program.

'After Harvard,' I ask, 'how did you get funded?'

'I applied for a federal grant.'

'And?'

'It gave me enough funding to develop the first-generation computer.'

'And, on the back of that, you started Sub-Quantum Dynetics?'

'Yes.'

'And then?'

'We built second, third and fourth-generation computers and won a contract under the Oak Ridge program. Cash got us through the next few years. We expanded, too fast, got into some trouble, and applied for another tranche of federal R&D funding.'

'Was this *after* you started working on Kaufmann's HITS helmet?'

'Yes.'

'Did you get it?'

'The grant? No. We didn't need it.'

'Why not?'

'Because in the interim we'd been recapitalized by a venture capitalist.'

'This VC,' I say. 'Was his name Vladimir Ilitch, by any chance?'

38

TVB STARES AT HIS HANDS, TURNS THEM OVER A FEW TIMES. After I've asked him the question, I watch his eyes as he takes himself back – to a time, I'm guessing, when life must have seemed pretty damn simple – especially if you've been staring at the walls of a cell. He's wearing the same sleeveless maroon sweater that he had on the last time I saw him. He looks bewildered – and utterly terrified.

'I was part of a trade mission that went to Russia after the Soviet Union fell. It must have been in '92. I was interested in experiments that had been conducted under the auspices of the Soviet Academy of Sciences in the area of trauma-induced depression – in particular, a device that had allegedly been developed by an academic called Kalunin to relieve the most radical symptoms. You may have heard of him, Josh. Professor M. M. Kalunin. Revered, even now, long after his death, as the father of modern-day Russian consciousness research.'

I invite him to tell me about Ilitch.

'Kalunin was ill. He had just months to live. Ilitch was a member of his staff and I barely noticed him.'

'Was he academic or administrative?'

'Administrative – something like an accountant.'

'Go on, Ted.'

'So, years later – I'm talking six, seven years ago – Ilitch contacted me. He'd become extremely wealthy on the back of medical equipment he'd sold all over the world and had diversified into IT

243

and other areas. He told me that consciousness research remained his abiding passion and, because of my work, wondered if there were opportunities for the two of us to collaborate. To be honest, I was flattered. Ilitch was neither here nor there, but I figured the link could be useful, because of his ties to Kalunin.'

'I thought you said Kalunin was dead.'

'He is. But Ilitch had married his daughter and she is – or was – the custodian of his personal papers.'

'So you and Ilitch co-developed tech that'd lead to break-throughs in the treatment of depression and, same time, you'd be able to review Kalunin's archive? That was the deal?'

'The open-source part of it, yes.'

'But that wasn't all . . .'

He nods. 'The Soviet military was all over Kalunin's work.' His brow furrows. 'Is that why I'm here?'

Yes and no. Ilitch is a person of interest, I tell him, in an ongoing investigation by the US Secret Service.

'Which links him to you and the guy they shot in the tower?'

'Yes. And me to you.'

'I see.' He stares at his hands again.

'Quid pro quo, Ted. How did Ilitch come to invest in your project?'

'It's a long story.'

'Tell me. Neither of us is going anywhere until you do.'

I am sitting on the bed next to him. Reuben, at least, has been true to his word. TVB's cell doesn't have carpets, but it has a bathroom.

'You've got to understand, Josh, in the consciousness field, the Russians are pre-eminent. No, let me correct that. The *Soviets* were. Iron Curtain scientists developed a set of theories about consciousness – unconventional ones – that would never have seen the light of day over here. Their insights into who we are, what consciousness is, and – most importantly – where it comes from, backed by decades of research and millions of roubles in state funding, are beyond any kind of understanding we developed in the West. Access to that data was – is – highly prized.'

'What kinds of insights are we talking about?'

'I have long believed, as you know, that it's possible to tune our minds through the development of technology to relieve symptoms of distress. But the Russians have been thinking this way for decades. Kalunin was responsible, almost singlehandedly, for a Soviet field of study – a unique area that looked at the integration of mind and machine. The Russians had a name for it: instrumental psychotronics.'

And so do we, I say to myself, as I look away. We call our damn version of it the Grid.

'*This* is why I went to Russia,' Ted continues. 'I wanted to see if there were areas of research in this field we could bring back to the US. Develop using US know-how. Collaborate on.'

'Were you successful?'

'No. He was too ill to do any business. We just talked, academic to academic, and we discussed some of the truly remarkable things he had been funded by the state to do.'

'Such as?'

'Many things. But the one area that sticks with me is the point at which the conversation turned to the survival of consciousness post-death.'

'In English, Ted . . .'

'What happens to us when we die.'

'Are you serious?'

'Yes, I am.'

'Like mediumship, spiritualism?'

'No, Josh. There's more to it than that.'

Damn right there is.

'What is it?' TVB says.

'The guy they shot in the tower was a psychic, Ted.'

'Do you think . . . ?' He hesitates.

'That you got caught up in something a whole lot bigger than you imagined? Yes.'

'What do I do, Josh?'

'Your trip to Moscow in '92 . . .'

'What about it?'

'You said it was part of a trade delegation.'

He nods.

'Which carried US government sanction.'

'Yes.'

'Who put it together?'

'The senior Democratic Senator from Wisconsin.'

Abnarth.

'Susan. Is she aware of what's happened?'

'No. She's on a flight to Nairobi.'

Now I remember: the dig she was preparing for in Kenya.

TVB looks terrified again. 'Is she going to be arrested too?'

'No.'

'What is going to happen to me?' he asks.

'You're going to get out of your arrangement with Ilitch, is what.'

'That may be easier said than done.'

'Why?'

'He's in Moscow. He's somewhat of a recluse these days.'

'Then email him. It doesn't matter how you do it, Ted, or how much it costs, but find yourself a good lawyer and kill the deal. Then forget any of this ever happened and get on a plane and go to Susan in Kenya – Susan who loves you and whom you love – and maybe, between the two of you, you'll decide that it's a good time to retire and live out your lives with the cats and the dogs.'

I call Reuben the moment I step out the elevator.

'Big problem,' I tell him. *Hetta was right.* 'There *is* a Russian connection.'

'Through van Buren?'

'No. Van Buren is collateral. Completely innocent. We can let him go.'

'Then who?'

'Where are you right now?'

'At Camp David. With the President.'

'And the DNI, the CIA Director, the other spooks?'

'They're either here or on their way. The moment you get here, we'll assemble at Aspen Lodge. You and Hart can brief them and if that fails to get their attention, we'll wheel your whistleblower in and see what effect that has.' He pauses. 'A Russian connection?'

'The Grid was part-funded by Ilitch. He's the son-in-law of the man who headed up the Soviet Union's research into psychic phenomena.'

'How can a Russian have funded an ultra-classified *US* intelligence program?'

'I think the NSA – or this cabal of intel agencies behind the Grid – has been laundering money through Ilitch to pay for it.'

'That is just way too un-fucking-believable,' he says.

'Think about it. The Grid is totally off the map, and yet it cost billions. Billions that don't appear on any congressional budget sheet.'

'But a Russian? Come *on*.'

'I know. It doesn't make sense. But there's another connection. Computers. Specifically, ultra-high-speed quantum computers. Ted van Buren, my professor, had been working on a project he's running out of Georgetown that analyzes brain waves in a way they've never been analyzed before. He was approached by an investor called Vladimir Ilitch. Ilitch's photo was one of the three that got removed and swapped in the cabin. There were three things in the cabin they didn't want us to see: the ballotechnic, the shot of the Canyon and Ilitch. The Grid uses highly sophisticated quantum-computing architecture. I think they used Ilitch's money to pay for early Grid hardware, tested it – it worked – then they shut down the companies responsible . . . Do I need to go on?'

There's a pause.

'Have you called off Jerusalem?'

'No,' he says. 'Thompson won't allow it.'

'Make him.'

'The conference is everything he's ever worked for, Josh. He won't.'

'That thing, Reuben, the spherical device that Gapes drew – the ballotechnic – it's a trigger for an H-bomb.'

'A *theoretical* trigger.'

'Yes, but a lot of this shit was theoretical and now we're not so sure.'

'We are. Christy's proliferation expert briefed us this morning. If our own nuclear weapons labs can't build a fourth-generation nuke—'

'Then we shouldn't just presume there's nobody else out there that can.'

I also relay to him what Hetta told me. A traditional H-bomb requires several kilograms of plutonium or uranium to initiate the fusion reaction. A Gen 4 weapon's nuclear material – pellets of deuterium and tritium – are measured in *grams*. Less, even. A terrorist could smuggle that in easy. Nobody would be able to detect it. *Nobody*.

Reuben once made a living on the Hill from his defense-level connections. He understands this stuff better than I do. 'The heat and pressure required to initiate the deuterium–tritium reaction is so great, the amount of explosive needed is easily detectable,' he says. 'Part of Thompson's insistence the conference goes ahead is based on the fact that we and the Israelis will deploy a phenomenally sensitive security system in and around the city that will make the movement of explosives impossible. And, of course, the conference is still months away. It's not ideal, I know, but . . .'

For a moment, it feels as if the line's gone dead.

'Reuben?'

'Yeah.'

'Your old boss, Abnarth, is up to his neck in this.'

Another silence. 'What do you want me to do?'

'Reel him in, along with all the others. We need to know exactly what he's up to.'

39

AFTER I'VE TOLD HIM AS MUCH AS HE NEEDS TO KNOW, OFFUTT walks over to the sink, takes off his glasses, runs the faucet and splashes water on his face. He then slumps on the end of the bed.

We're alone. His prison cell, two floors below ground, contrasts starkly with TVB's. There's the sink, a john, the bed and not much else. The walls seem to be impregnated with the stench of human waste. Only the chill air of the chamber stops it from overwhelming us.

I ask him how much Johansson knows.

'He got access to the data for his war on terror. That's all. He doesn't know where the data comes from. No warfighter is ever made aware of the source. By the time it's mixed up with all the other sources of raw intelligence, it's washed clean, made to look like it could have come from anywhere.' He looks at me. 'So what are my choices?'

'You don't have any. When we're done here, you, Hetta and I are going to head up to Camp David and brief the President. There's a helicopter waiting.' I pause. 'Tell me about the cell.'

He laughs. '*The* cell? There is not just one cell. The Cube houses dozens. Maybe hundreds. I have no idea how many. Everything was compartmentalized. Ours was focused exclusively on the WMD threat. Others will have been assigned to specific targets, all high priority and inaccessible by other collection methods. We're talking organized crime bosses, terrorists, Chinese and Russian strategic military planners, politicians . . . the list is probably endless. I just saw what I saw. My cell got a feed from the Canyon, same as all the others.'

'So, you don't know who would have targeted the President, or why?'

'The only people who would have known are the people who assign the targets, people we never got to see, and the operatives within the cell itself.'

He massages the skin on the back of his burned hand.

'Did he . . . suffer?'

'Who?'

'The President.'

I tell him: Yes. From a particularly debilitating dream.

'When?'

'More often than he'd like to admit.'

'Starting when?'

'Nine months ago.'

'Then that'll be the point of instigation. The Grid keys off events: intel we pick up on people or things that need verification when no other asset can provide it. If they were targeting him, something would have triggered a reason for wanting to get inside his thinking. You need to take a look at what was happening then.'

I get to my feet. *Nine months ago.*

The new administration had barely got started.

'Sit down,' he says. 'There's more. Calibration required me to ship out to the Canyon every few months. By now, Duke was there full time. Calibration was dull – it meant us wearing more sophisticated versions of the helmets they'd developed for the HITS concept demonstrator and for us to sit there for hours, while the computers were realigned and the engineers did their thing. The process could go on for a day, overnight sometimes, which is why it needed two of us, Duke and me. It's hard to maintain that level of focus for long.'

He rests the back of his head against the wall and closes his eyes.

'But on that day, the day before he ran, everything goes haywire. One minute, we're staring at a load of static on screen, the next we're watching a feed scrolling at a thousand miles an hour.

We see people, famous people, ordinary people, places I know and places I don't, historical events, wars – Vietnam, World Wars One and Two, stuff that goes back further, even; way, way back. It also starts to show events that *I* can remember, floods, earthquakes, volcanoes, the planes slamming into the Towers . . .'

He opens his eyes.

'And then the screens go black and I look left and Duke is standing in the glow of the emergency lighting, staring at the screens, still wearing the helmet. His eyes are open and moving, like the movie we just saw is still running, but it isn't, there's nothing to see, until, *boom*, suddenly the screens burst back into life again and so does the hologram they project onto the plinth when they need to show a target from multiple angles.

'There are images of the Wailing Wall, the gold cupola of the Dome of the Rock; churches, portraits of saints; and then . . .'

I lean forward.

'Then there's this guy waving at a crowd, and it's waving back, and I suddenly realize it's Thompson – *Senator* Thompson – only this is Jerusalem, and he's President.'

I hold up a hand. 'Wait a minute.'

Offutt stops and looks at me.

'You're talking about something that hasn't happened.'

'So?'

'You mean . . .'

'Yes, that's exactly what I mean. To the Grid, time is entirely fluid. Just as it is to a psychic. Totally meaningless. The holosphere is a perfect record of past, present and future events. The job of the Grid's processors is to bring the false positives down to a minimum so we know which future events are real.'

A bead of sweat trickles down my back. I ask him to continue.

'The picture switches again, and the viewpoint is somewhere above the Old City, in a building of some description, and we're face to face with this guy. He's talking, deeply, as if the fate of the world is at stake, and there's this flash, a burst of pure, intense white heat, the screens all disappear in a shower of sparks and Duke collapses.'

I scroll through photos on my iPhone until I reach the cabin sketch of the Engineer. I show Offutt the image. 'This him?'

Offutt peers at it, looks at me. 'Yes. Who is he?'

'You don't know?'

'Should I?'

'You told me your cell targeted the jihadist WMD threat.'

'So?'

'He's a bomb-maker with nuclear expertise. Goes under the nom de guerre "Engineer". Jihadists have been chattering about him for months. They're all telling each other he's going to ride at the head of the four horsemen and wipe away the unbelievers on a day that's going to make the Twin Towers look like a pre-game.'

I pause.

'And you weren't ever tasked with looking for him?'

I emerge with Offutt into a freezing wet day.

Hetta and Schweizer are waiting at the helipad. As we round the corner of a hangar, the wind picks up, throwing spray at us from the waves pounding the rocks off Hains Point. A hundred meters away a V-22 is warming up, one of the more recent additions to the presidential fleet: a 'tiltrotor' – half plane, half helicopter – able to take off and land vertically, thanks to two massive props on the end of its wings.

By the time I climb aboard, Hetta and Schweizer are already strapped in.

Hetta points to Offutt, cups her hands around her mouth and shouts at me over the engine noise. 'What's *he* doing here?'

'He's coming with us,' I yell back. 'I need him to tell the President what he just told me.' It's too noisy for a discussion. I mouth and semaphore the rest: *Tell you when we get there.*

Offutt straps in beside Schweizer. I strap in next to Hetta. We don headsets. There's a surge of power from the engines. The Osprey lifts into the air and in seconds is in full forward flight. I see the river recede and the Monument and the White House. I settle back into my seat as soon as we've crossed the Beltway.

Gapes fled with five thousand pieces of imagery on a flash drive. He managed to avoid detection by the Grid and made his way to the cabin – a place, due to its isolation, he knew nobody would ever find him.

From thereon in, he'd lost his tech bridge to the holosphere; but he didn't need it. He was a viewer – the best, everybody said – so he went back to basics. With pen, paper and an ability to access the signal line at will, he began to download his own data, sketching out everything he saw, filling in gaps, until he not only assembled a mosaic that spoke cryptically to what the Grid is, but delivered a warning: that without my intervention, apparently, the President is going to die in a conflagration in Jerusalem.

I stare out the window as we leave the suburbs behind, and think again about the muzzle flash in the blacked-out window of the office building beyond the labor union. The freeze-frame of the moment Gapes was shot by Jimenez. He knew he was going to die. And he knew it was the only way we'd listen really carefully to his message.

The day after the Grid meltdown, they took Gapes and Offutt for tests at a medical center within the Bluffdale complex. They were interviewed by a succession of suited types, but clearly military/intel, about what they thought they had seen. Was it real? Could the system have been hacked? At one point, Offutt heard one of the interviewers ask another whether it could have been 'reachback'. *Reachback?* He had no idea what that meant.

Duke remained calm throughout. Calmer than Offutt had ever seen him. At first, he thought they must have upped his drugs, but, looking back, he realized it was because he'd made up his mind. That afternoon they went back to the bunker to resume calibration. Some tests were made with a new helmet and, for twenty minutes, Duke was left alone – long enough, they figured later, for him to download what he needed on a drive. That evening, while taking the air outside the ward where they were running more tests on them, he gave his orderlies the slip, and vanished into thin air.

Ahead, through the rain, the rolling hills of Pennsylvania await us. What am I going to tell Thompson and Reuben? Gapes asked whether I believe the President to be a good man. I do, but there's something that he isn't telling me; and it isn't just about Abnarth – it's about two of the sub-panels in the sanctum that haven't yet revealed themselves to us – Church and *Pitnatsat*.

The implication of Thompson's sub-panel, 2B, is that he knows something about Church that he isn't sharing. If so, what does 'Church' refer to? A straightforward reference to St John's Church itself seems unlikely. Besides, I saw the way Thompson reacted when I asked him about it. He was lying. And '15ski', beneath the surface layer dedicated to the Engineer, has me completely beat.

The engine note changes. I hear the whine of hydraulics above us, as the Osprey's wings tilt toward the vertical and it begins its descent into Camp David. I look out the window. We're still a hundred meters up. And then I feel the shudder. We all do. Hetta grabs a hold of my arm. I glance at Schweizer and Offutt.

Offutt, who must have made as many trips in vertical lift aircraft as I have, looks panicky. We all turn toward the source of the vibration, which is coming from the starboard engine. There's a crackle in my headset. It's hard to take in what the pilot is saying, because a cacophony of horns and alarms suddenly bursts from the cockpit, but the words I catch are 'gearbox', 'failure' and 'catastrophic'.

'*What's happening?*' Hetta yells.

I snatch another glance out the window.

We're above a hillside covered in boulders and trees.

You get an engine failure on a helicopter, you contain it by decoupling the rotor and using the body mass to spin the blades as you fall, and flare off seconds before you hit the ground.

With a V-22, you lose an engine, it's still possible to fly thanks to a driveshaft that transfers power from the remaining good engine.

But when you get a gearbox failure the power transfer option isn't available.

I look back again toward the source of the vibration, which is getting worse. Then I look at Offutt. He pulls the straps tight across his shoulders and closes his eyes. Schweizer leans over and spews his guts across the floor.

We make a lurch to the right and I hear a voice in my head – not the pilot's this time, but someone else's – telling me to undo my seat belt, Hetta's too, and I reach over and twist the catch; first hers, then mine. A second after I do this, the engine makes a noise like a rattling toolbox. At the next lurch, more violent than the one that preceded it, the Osprey noses down and rolls. I grab Hetta and we fall from our seats, bouncing off the floor as we tumble across the cabin, until we hit the starboard wall just behind the forward bulkhead. The noise is unbelievable. Chunks of metal colliding within the gearbox as it rips itself apart. Schweizer screaming.

The voice urges me to reach beneath me and I grab something, a handle, which, with all my strength, I pull.

The door opens and I free-fall into the freezing air, dragging Hetta with me.

I see the stricken V-22 rolling to the right, upside down, and the ground spinning beneath me. I close my eyes, screw them tight shut, but still see the huge orange fireball and feel its searing heat.

The blast rips Hetta from my grasp.

I feel myself lifted by the explosion.

Then, happily, nothing.

40

A WARM WIND IS BLOWING IN OFF THE OCEAN. A FIRE CRACKLES.
Waves lap the shore.

I look up at the stars and see a million of them. Hope's hand is
on my shoulder. There's no anger in her voice. All is good.

I'm drowsy. The numbness envelops me again, except for a sen-
sation that's hard to describe, but it is boundless and timeless – like
the moment I first laid my eyes on her, the day we went to the
Mall – and I don't want it to end.

'Wake up, Josh.'

Wake up.

Now.

I open my eyes.

Above me, the branches of a tree are in flames. Thirty meters
away, one of the props of the V-22, its blades shattered, is still
chewing into the frozen ground, spitting clods of earth into the air.

A torn-off section of the tail-plane lies beyond it.

One of the fins, bent and twisted.

An arm, ripped free by the force of the blast, hanging from the
shredded stump of a tree.

I sit up. My vision swims.

A second later, a thought. *Jesus, I can move.*

I drag myself away. The moment I'm clear, one of the flaming branches detaches itself from the trunk and crashes to the ground where I've just been lying, showering me in sparks and embers.

I get away from the tree altogether and prop myself against a rock, where I carry out a body check. Move my left foot, then the right. Lift the left leg, then the right. The left gives me a moment of pain. I run my hand along it. No broken bones.

I touch my face. There's blood on my fingers.

My head hurts. My left leg hurts.

But that's all.

Slowly, I get to my feet, holding onto the rock for support. The engine has been through its death-throes and is now still. The heat is intense. The V-22 crashed on the hillside. There's fire and wreckage everywhere.

I shout to Hetta, almost blacking out with the effort. I hear nothing over the sound of the wreckage cooking off.

I start to walk, dragging my leg.

There's nothing left of the Osprey's nose-section; it's buried itself in the mountain.

I scrabble down the slope. The body minus the arm is Schweizer's. He's lying on his back, eyes wide. They tell the story of every second of the horror he experienced as the V-22 augured in.

A few meters away, Offutt's twisted body, face down, clothes torn off. I manage to put two fingers against his neck. No trace of a pulse. I turn around. No trace of the crew either. As I get to my feet, I feel the panic I felt when I could do nothing for the woman in the *abaya*.

Then I spot Hetta fifty meters down the slope. I stagger, trip and slide to a stop alongside her. As our bodies touch, she gasps, sucks down a lungful of air and opens her eyes.

Her hand goes up to her head. I tell her not to move.

'What happened?'

'You're OK. Lie back.'

'Anyone else get out?'

'No. All dead. Lie back, Hetta. And stay still.'

I reach into my pocket. My cell's still there.

I remove my jacket, place it over her. Check the signal.

One bar.

I dial 911. The call doesn't go through.

I stay online. If there isn't enough signal for a voice call, after thirty seconds the nearest mast will interrogate my phone. Request my GPS coordinates. Transmit them to the nearest first responder unit. Where might that be? Not relevant. The presidential fleet is equipped with the most powerful emergency locator transmitters on the planet.

'Josh?'

'Don't talk. Help's coming.'

'I'm cold.'

'Hang on.'

'There's a lot of blood on your face, Josh.'

'I know, Hetta. It's OK. Lie still.'

I hear a noise and see a familiar silhouette – a Black Hawk – through the trees, circling beyond the smoke.

I struggle to my feet, raise my right arm and wave.

As the helicopter banks toward us, my world goes into a spin and everything fades to black.

Book Three

Become the sky

41

I COME TO WITH A DRIP IN MY ARM, WIRED TO A MONITOR. MY left side is on fire. A nurse orders me to lie still. Time passes. Doctors come and go. I fall asleep again and wake up sometime later. My eyes adjust to my surroundings.

Dimly, I become aware of a shape at the end of the bed.

Reuben.

'Josh . . .'

'Where am I?'

'Bethesda. Navy Med.'

He tells me it's five days since the crash at Catoctin Furnace. Everything hurts, but I still feel myself smile at the crazy irony of the name of the location south of Thurmont where the V-22 came down.

I've been in an induced coma for part of the time to reduce swelling from the heavy concussion caused by the blow to my head.

Walter Reed National Military Medical Center – 'Navy Med' – is a stone's throw from my old stomping ground. From my bed, I can see the trees bordering the USU campus.

'How are you feeling?'

'Like I survived a crash.' My hand moves up to my head. 'How's Hetta?'

'Amazing, considering what you've both been through.'

'How long you been here?' I ask him.

He looks at his watch. 'I don't know. An hour or so.'

'Mr Kantner has visited every day since you came in,' the nurse says, as she leans over to check the tube from my drip is securely taped to my arm. She then leaves to go get a doctor.

'The President—'

'Don't go there, Josh.'

'I need to know he's OK.'

'He's OK,' Reuben says levelly.

'What happened in the meeting?'

'It never happened.'

'Because of the crash?'

He nods.

'Reuben . . .' I pull myself up the bed. 'There are some things you and Thompson need to know.' I focus with great difficulty on my discussion with Offutt. 'About Jerusalem.'

He holds up his right hand, cups his left hand around his ear and gestures with his eyes to the four corners of the room.

'We talk later,' he says. 'You need to rest.'

I shake my head and wish I hadn't. 'I need to get back to work.'

'No, Josh.' He holds out an envelope. 'You don't.'

I study him for a moment, then take the envelope and open it. Inside is a single sheet of Oval Office headed paper.

I force my eyes to focus. Thompson's handwriting is distinctive. *Josh, I am so very sorry for what happened. Please know that Jen, the kids and I are all praying for your continued recovery.*

'We are so grateful for all the service you have so selflessly provided . . .'

I put it down. Reuben is on his feet, staring out the window.

'Is Hetta relieved of her duties too?'

'That's not the way it's being classified,' he says.

'Oh?'

'You – she and you – need time to recuperate.'

'And then?'

'You'll be free to do whatever you want. You can go back to your patients. She'll be assigned to other duties, if that's what she wants.'

'Was that the deal?'

He looks at me. 'Deal?'

'With the people you gathered in Aspen Lodge?'

'Christ's sake, Josh. You almost *died*. Every doctor I've spoken to says it's a miracle that you and Hart came through. A few days' time, you'll be back on your feet. In a week, she will.' He pauses. 'Please, use the time to get some help.'

'Help?'

'Yes.'

'What does that mean?'

'The past two days, in your sleep, since they brought you out of the coma, you've been doing nothing except talk about Hope. As your friend, I am begging you, Josh. Rest. For as long as you need.'

He takes a breath.

'Actually, this isn't a request. It's an order.'

'Miracle' is a word I've heard a lot over the past forty-eight hours. I have shooting pains along my left side that baffle my physicians, as they correspond to the damage I sustained in the crash that killed Hope. My left leg, when I walk on it, is painful, even though the radiologists tell me that nothing is showing up on any scans – beyond the fractures that healed all those years ago.

Hetta and I speak on the phone, but exchange nothing more than our war wounds. She has a mild concussion, a dislocated shoulder, cracked ribs and a badly bruised ankle. I have not yet been able to see her in person, in part because I've been told by the doctors to move as little as possible, but mainly because there are federal agents posted at our doors. Officially, they're to keep the media out. Hetta and I are big news. But I can't escape the feeling they're really to keep her and me at a distance.

DJ's raincoat is draped over his right arm. In his left, he's holding flowers. 'She says hello.' He does his best to give me a smile.

'How's she holding up?'

'Pissed, since you ask.'

'She knows, then?'

'Yes. SAIC Graham came to see her this morning.'

'What's with the flowers?'

'I forgot she has allergies.'

He drops the stems into a jug of water at the foot of my bed.

'You probably heard that I've been pulled off the church shooting investigation,' he says after several beats.

I hadn't.

Gapes's security classification means the case has been handed to a special prosecutor in the Department of Defense. 'Where, as we both know, it'll get snuffed out like it never happened.' He looks at me meaningfully.

'Who's the investigating authority for the crash?'

'The V-22 is a Marine Corps asset. Where there's the remotest suspicion of sabotage, unlawful death, a national security breach or terrorism,' he says, 'the Bureau is normally involved. Not this time. The Navy's been given the investigating mandate.' He pauses. 'I'm *really* sorry.'

'What for?'

'You, me, Hart – we all got screwed.'

He heads for the door, stops, turns and hands me a piece of paper. 'Almost forgot. Doctor gave me this.'

I unfold it.

When I raise my eyes and draw breath he has a finger pressed to his lips.

The note is on the letterhead of the consultant who has been overseeing my recovery, but the writing, in black felt pen, isn't his.

It has an angular, familiar look.

Consulting Room. Third Floor. Now.

Hetta stands in the shadows to the left of the window. She's in mufti: faded denims, a white hoodie. Her right leg is encased in a ski boot; her crutches are on the table. DJ is outside, pretending to make a call.

The room looks like it hasn't been used for consulting in a while.

'How are you doing?'

'OK,' I lie.

'You see the news?'

I shake my head. 'No.'

'Your phone switched off?'

'I left it in my room. What is this?'

'Before the crash, while you were with Offutt and Professor van Buren, Wharton met me at Anacostia–Bolling. I told him that I needed two things. Everything that the Bureau had on Ilitch and everything SAIC Lefortz ever told him about the President's probe. Lefortz never told DJ what it was about, but, at Lefortz's request, DJ told him a bunch of stuff from way back that Justice, Treasury and the FBI had been doing to help the Ukrainian Government.'

'Listen, Hetta—'

'That's all I know. But it tells me the President has an interest in this that he hasn't communicated to the rest of us, and that this is what SAIC Lefortz was digging into when he was killed.'

'Hetta—'

'Thompson is going to Jerusalem, Josh. He announced it two nights ago in the State of the Union.'

'I don't want to know.'

'He's dropped the Moscow summit and pulled forward the conference to next month. Next *month*. What the fuck is wrong with you?'

'What is wrong with me is that by rights we should be dead.'

'But we're not.'

'The doctors are saying it's a miracle.'

'Not the word I'd use, but—'

'Hetta, this is all academic. Reuben's told me, and Graham's told you. We're off this case. And it'll be seriously detrimental to your health and mine if they think for a moment that you're still—'

She cuts me off again. 'Ilitch is half Ukrainian on his mother's side, Volga Tatar on his father's. The Tatars are a Russian Muslim people, Josh. Ilitch's father, a Muslim, was some kind of Soviet-era racketeer. There is a *big* Russian connection to all of this: Ilitch, the Orthodox Church in Jerusalem, the number fifteen.'

She pauses. 'In the late nineties, two Ukrainian weapons scientists were arrested for trying to smuggle nuclear material to Al-Qaeda. It was a sting. The FBI was involved in it. I asked DJ to look through the files. It was a part of the joint Justice–Treasury–FBI investigation. Among the materials that Al-Qaeda was trying to buy was something called a ballotechnic.'

She pauses to see if this registers with me.

'The thing on the wall of the cabin was part of a consignment of nuclear materials destined for an Islamic terror group more than twenty years ago. We've got to go see the guy.'

'What guy?'

'The guy who knows about this stuff. His name's Nils Bogarten. He works for the Stockholm International Peace Research Institute.'

'Hetta, nobody was meant to survive what we just survived. The people who brought our V-22 down aren't going to stop until they have taken care of the problem. And you and me are the problem. We're not going anywhere, you hear?'

It's useless trying to argue with her. She doesn't get it.

I tell her to wait two minutes before leaving the room.

Outside, I speak to DJ. If you care about her, I tell him, you'll get it into that thick, obsessive, OCD skull of hers that our every move is being watched and if we so much as *look* as if we're on the case—

He places a hand on my shoulder. 'Colonel – *Josh* – I already took care of it.'

She has a brother, he says. A brother who's a cop.

'Mikey.'

DJ knows Mikey. Mikey is a good guy.

Their plan is to drive Hetta up to Philadelphia tomorrow. Mikey is taking some leave. He won't let her out of his sight until she's better.

'And you?' he says. 'You look like you could use a little.'

'A little?'

'Time out from all this.'

I tell him I took the precaution of booking myself into a clinic – an out-of-the-way place four hours from D.C. on Delaware Bay, overlooking the Atlantic. I just about manage a smile.

'What?' he says.

'I helped to set it up.'

DJ ponders this irony for a moment before telling me he'll drive me there personally. After he's dropped Hetta with Mikey.

42

WE DRIVE NORTH ON THE I-95 IN SILENCE, WITH CHESAPEAKE Bay on our right for most of the journey.

DJ and I sit up front. I can tell that he's read Hetta the riot act, instructed her to stay with her brother, and that she's not happy about it. She sits in back, her leg stretched across the seat, radiating contempt.

We're somewhere past Baltimore when DJ, to break the mood, tells us that the upside of his removal from the Gapes inquiry is that he and his wife-to-be get to spend a proper honeymoon together.

'First time around?' I ask.

'Second.' He pauses. 'I was lucky. My first was a real good one. Lena and I shared twenty-five great years before she got sick. Cathy and Bernie were our neighbors. Bernie died five years before Lena. Cathy was her best friend, and helped me nurse her till she had to go into the hospice.'

He pauses again. 'It took Cathy and me a while to get together. I'm pretty sure, wherever she is, Lena's OK with it.'

I'm pretty sure too.

'Josh should take a leaf out of your book,' Hetta says. It's the first time she's spoken since we passed Baltimore's northern limits, around fifty miles back.

'How's that?' DJ glances into the mirror.

'You know how many years it is since *his* wife died?'

'Sorry for your loss,' Wharton says, turning to me.

Hetta leans forward. 'You said it yourself, DJ.'

'Said what?

'That Lena wouldn't have wanted you to stay stuck in the past.'

'She wouldn't.'

'So, why can't *you* move on, Josh?'

Wharton's jaw clenches. 'You're out of line, Hart.'

'Just saying.'

DJ adjusts the mirror so he can look at her directly. 'So, how many relationships you had that panned out?'

'I'm nothing to do with it. This is about Josh.'

'You can be so damned obnoxious at times, you know that?' DJ says.

'I'm trying to help.'

I turn and face her. 'So tell me. How the fuck does this help?'

'Well, I—'

'You don't simply move on.' Wharton softens his tone, but I can hear him still trying to tamp down his anger. 'Grief needs to make its own journey.'

'What does that even mean?' she says.

'It means it's personal. Everybody does what he or she does to get through it. It also means that being with Cathy doesn't mean I've stopped loving Lena.'

Hetta sits on this for a mile, maybe two, until the silence becomes deafening.

'And your new wife is cool with that?'

'Yes,' he says. 'She is completely cool with that.'

We pull up in front of a one-story house with a flagpole out front on a quiet street in Philly's northeast quarter.

DJ comes round the back and opens Hetta's door. She swings her leg onto the ground, stops, turns to me and touches my shoulder.

'Josh, hey, I'm really sorry . . .'

I look at her and nod. She gets out. Wharton, holding her case, walks her up to the porch where her brother is standing and

269

staring at us. Mikey isn't what I expected: he is short, wiry, balding and close to fifty. You'd never believe he'd survived a bullet. Just before she reaches him, Hetta turns and gives me a weak smile.

DJ and Mikey exchange a few words and shake hands. Mikey and Hetta then disappear inside.

Fifteen minutes later, DJ and I are heading south on I-95.

'I'm sorry,' he says, a couple of minutes after we cross the Delaware River.

'What for?'

'For what was said back there.'

'Don't be. It wasn't your fault.'

'Sometimes . . . Hart, she—'

'It's OK, DJ. Really.'

'I had no idea,' he says after we've driven on a while.

'About what?'

'Your wife.'

I know this isn't true. But I know, too, he's saying it for all the right reasons.

'It doesn't go away, does it?'

'No,' I reply.

We drive on.

'DJ?'

He turns, expecting me to say something about Hope or Lena. Instead, I ask him why he thinks Lefortz was interested in a couple of Ukrainians involved in the illicit trade of nuclear materials and components.

He gives it some thought. 'I don't think it was about the nuke stuff. I think it was about money. The real focus of the Bureau's work with Justice and Treasury was some kind of high-profile, cross-border money-laundering scam.'

'And that's what the President was interested in?'

'I think so. Lefortz implied that this probe was extremely close-held.'

It must have been. Even Reuben didn't know about it.

'And you and Lefortz spoke about it the night he died?'

'Yes,' he says. 'Right before he met you out at the airport.'

We drive on.

'He asked you to throw Bureau protection around a couple of our key witnesses that night, right?'

He nods. 'Sure. Your shrink pal out west and the lawyer who forgot the two of you ever met.'

'Would you be able to contact them without anybody knowing?'

'Sure. Why?'

'Because I need to disappear for a while.'

'I thought you . . . You mean . . . ?' His eyes narrow. 'Well, I'll be dipped.'

We don't exchange another word till we pull off Delaware Route One and turn into the Community Based Inpatient Clinic, a cluster of low buildings on reclaimed mudflats south of Dover Air Force Base.

A flock of wading birds, startled by our arrival, wheel above our heads. Their shrill cries fill the damp, cold air.

DJ walks me to the entrance where a nurse, in white, is waiting.

43

IT IS NO ACCIDENT THAT THE CLINIC IS A STONE'S THROW FROM
Dover.

At nights, I lie awake listening to the whine of jet transports
ferrying our troops around the world. By day, I sit with soldiers,
sailors and aircrew, many of them fresh from battle, most of them
sharing similar symptoms to mine.

There are few rules.

We're not allowed drugs or alcohol.

We can leave when we want.

What's said in the group stays in the group.

On Day One, I meet the first of my four therapists.

What I tell them is largely the truth. I describe my lability of
mood, my darkening thoughts, the sense I am on a slippery slope
that leads to a place I've already been. I tell them about the pain in
my left side that keeps me awake nights. I tell them, too, that it's
probably a blessing, because when I do close my eyes, I get a con-
flation of images: dead people mostly, the girl in the *abaya*, Gapes,
Lefortz, and the V-22, upside down, moments before it spirals
into the ground.

The two incidents I still can't conjure up are the ones I need to:
what happened in the V-22, and my final moments with Hope in
the wreckage of the Jeep.

I need a treatment to stop me from sliding down and they
know it. But after a week of prolonged exposure and cognitive
processing therapies that are proven to work the world over for the

kinds of symptoms that I have, they are surprised there's no improvement.

Halfway through the second week, I'm lying on my bed, in the darkness, eyes closed, when I hear a knock at the door.

It opens and the light flicks on.

I blink under the glare.

Mo Kerchorian is standing in the doorway.

We walk along a muddy path above the bay the morning after. Tankers carve in both directions through the gray, choppy waters between the river and the ocean.

Mo hasn't spoken to me since I called to apologize for the world of shit I dropped him into the night Lefortz was killed. But DJ has been quietly persuasive. I don't know what he said, or how he even got to Mo, but for the past week my buddy from Georgetown has been liaising with my therapists, checking on progress, or the lack of it, and guiding their strategy.

When they reported no improvement yesterday, Mo told them he would oversee my treatment directly and jumped on a plane.

'I told them your mood state and neuralgia are linked to the energy of multiple traumas which has nowhere to go but inward. To move forward, we have to expose those traumas to the light, allow your subconscious to make a meaningful narrative of everything that's happened, process it, then move on.'

He makes it sound wonderfully simple.

We walk on another hundred meters. I hear the mournful sound of a ship's foghorn somewhere in the distance.

'But your cop buddy told me there's more to it than that,' he says.

'There is.'

'And that it's not just about the pain.'

I hesitate, but only for a moment. 'I need you to recover some memories for me.'

'From the V-22 crash?'

'Not just that. From the Jeep.'

'OK,' he says. 'Speak to me.'

I hesitate. 'I'm worried you might . . .'

'What? That I might come to the conclusion you're crazy?' He laughs. 'Josh, I knew you were a fuck-up from the moment we met.'

I manage a smile, then tell him about the voice in my head – the voice that had told me to undo my belt, then Hetta's, and let go.

Not just any voice.

Her voice.

For all their independence, Community-based Inpatient Clinics are still military facilities and neither of us has any way of knowing who might be listening in. So Mo and I decamp to a Holiday Inn ten miles down the road.

We leave our phones in his car and unplug every device in the room. I settle into the armchair and focus on his pre-brief. His theory is that traumatic memories are held in every cell of the body. Mainstream medicine dismisses this as junk science, but assisted by an endorsement from our mentor, TVB, Mo's therapy has been adopted by the VA network – with the caveat that it remains 'experimental'. You say yes at your own risk.

Mo has immersed himself in my notes, including X-rays and MRIs going back years. When the V-22 crashed, he believes it triggered an acute reaction to my other unprocessed traumas: the dead baby in the *abaya*; Gapes's shooting; Lefortz's death. And my final moments with Hope in the wreckage of the Jeep.

He makes me count backward from ten and within a few seconds I'm under. I hear his voice, am conscious of sounds in and outside the room, but am suitably relaxed – in a state that desensitizes me to the acute feelings of anxiety that get in the way of answering the big questions.

We start with the night I went into Fallujah. The visceral feelings I tried to bury no longer rear their ugly heads. I must have processed those, at least. So we move on. It's the same with the deaths of Gapes and Lefortz. Mo grunts his approval. I hear him tap some notes into his iPad.

Now he takes me aboard the Osprey.

'Tell me what happened when the engine failed.'

Under hypnosis, it returns. Schweizer vomits because he knows what we all know: we're not going to make it. But at that precise moment I'm imbued with an enormous sense of calm. I feel Hope by my side. I hear her talking to me. Her voice is soft, soothing and clear. She tells me exactly what to do.

Undo Hetta's belt. Now yours. Trust me, Josh. Trust that it's all going to be all right.

Let go.

The V-22 rolls. We slide across the floor and hit the bulkhead and the fuselage wall.

Through the mayhem of the exploding engine:

Reach beneath you. There's a handle. Grab Hetta. Pull the handle.

The door falls away and we tumble into space.

We're thirty meters up, falling toward trees ready to break our fall. I glance right, see the V-22 seconds before it hits the ground, and brace myself for the impact.

Trust, Josh. I'm with you. Let go.

And then it's like the transmission stops.

The picture goes black. My breathing becomes labored.

'Relax, Josh,' Mo says. 'It's all right. What do you see?'

'Nothing. I don't see anything.'

'OK. Where are you?'

'On the ground. At the crash site.'

'Why can't you see?'

'I'm unconscious. But I can still hear and smell. Fire. Burning.'

'OK. Tell me what—'

'She's beside me.'

'Who?'

'Hope.' My voice catches.

Mo guides me. 'Keep talking. What's happening?'

'The V-22's cooking off all around us. She's lying right next to me. Talking to me. She's telling me that I need to go back.'

'Back?'

'Yes.'

'Where to?'

I try to make sense of it.

'To the night Jack died.'

'Jack?'

'Old guy. Lived with her mother. Hope really loved him.'

'Were you there?'

'Yes.'

'What happened?'

'He said something to her.'

'What?'

'I don't know. I couldn't hear. Right afterward, though, right after he died, Hope removed something from under his pillow.'

'What?'

'An envelope.'

'Do you have the envelope?'

'No. But I know what was in it. A photograph of Mac . . . and the other guy.'

'Mac?'

'Jack's nickname. When he was in the Marine Corps. In 'Nam.'

'And the other guy?'

'Jack's pilot. Freeley.'

'And Hope is telling you this is important?'

'Yes.'

'What else?'

'She's telling me she loves me. And . . .'

'And . . . ?'

'That she's sorry.'

'What for?'

'For what happened . . . to us.'

'OK. Let's move on. Ask her permission to go to the wreckage of the Jeep.'

I do as he says. My breathing becomes labored again.

'She's not letting me.'

'Why not?'

'Because there's something else she wants me to know. Something that's more important.'

'What?'

'She's taking me back. A long time back. To a night soon after we were married. We're on the beach. I built a fire. She's lying next to me. Her hand on my shoulder. Music's playing on the porch. That song she used to love . . .'

'What song?'

I feel myself drifting deeper.

' "Stardust".'

'By Nat King Cole?'

I shake my head. Smile at the memory. 'No. The first version. The Ella version. She absolutely loved it. Used to play it on our CD player. From our porch. We'd lie on the beach, night after night, letting it wash over us, as we watched the stars.'

'And that's where she wants to take you?'

'Yes.'

'Why?'

'I don't know.' Suddenly, I feel my whole body go tense. 'Something's happening, Mo.'

'What?'

'She's telling me I have to wake up. I don't want to. I want to stay with her, but she's shaking me.'

'*Josh?*'

Before he can bring me out of it, I snap to. It's so real, I roll off the chair onto the floor, convinced the flaming branch of the tree is about to fall right on top of me.

I go to the bathroom and take a moment to compose myself. I look in the mirror at the gray-blue eyes staring back at me. I'm still me and I'm still here and so is the pain. I limp back into the room.

'What did it all mean?' I ask.

'I'm not certain, to be honest.' He pauses. 'You want me to regress you again?'

I shake my head. I couldn't go through it twice. And I'm not sure it would do any good anyway.

'The therapy will continue to go to work,' Mo says. 'You may find it'll help loosen something in the days and weeks ahead. What it prompted, though, was interesting. You sure about that photo?'

'I'm sure.'

'In an envelope?'

'Yes.'

'Anything else with it?'

I tell him about the ankh, the tree of life and the silver, eight-pointed star.

'Interesting guy, this Jack.'

'Meaning?'

'The ankh and the tree are Jungian archetypes, Josh. You don't need me to tell you that. I don't know about the significance of the ankh, but the tree meaning is obvious. It's symbolic of your life. Roots that anchor you to the ground, branches that soar skyward, symbolizing all your hopes, your ambitions—'

'And the eight-pointed star in a circle?'

'I don't know. I'm not an expert on this shit, but these are very clearly messages from your subconscious.'

'It was like she was *there*, Mo.'

'Fella, I'm not denying she was real to you.'

'The envelope exists. I found it in a box of her things in a garage at her mother's place. Real, solid things. Are you telling me I'm being presented with objects manifested by my own psyche?'

'This is powerful stuff, Josh. Stuff you've never dealt with.'

He's avoided the question.

He looks at me. 'So you now have a choice. The hurt, your mood-state and everything you've described are linked. As a doctor, and your friend, I am bound to tell you what I think'll make you better.' He pauses. 'You can medicate. I can give you shit that'll help you get through the day; that will dull the pain in your side, too. But I don't think that's what you want to hear.'

'What's the alternative?'

'You know this better than me. You follow the advice your own subconscious is giving you. Go see the pilot.'

I have no idea where Freeley fits into all this, but a thought from the garage keeps replaying: *Gapes connects me to the President and the Engineer, Hope's portrait of Jack, and to a nickname I didn't know he had.*

'I don't even know if he's alive.'

Mo accesses the veterans register.

Colonel Nelson Freeley is seventy-eight years old and living in Vermont, close to the Canadian border. Five hundred miles away.

The distance isn't the problem. The fact that I may still be under surveillance is.

'As your therapist, I circulate a report that you're not well enough to present a threat to anybody except yourself,' Mo says. 'That what you need to recuperate, more than anything, is rest and some light travel.'

I nod.

Nobody – not even the intel community – is going to waste time on a washed-up nut-job.

44

THE DRIVE TAKES ME THE BEST PART OF THE FOLLOWING DAY.

As I head up through New Jersey and New York, the weather becomes progressively colder, the snow on the ground thicker.

Freeley's is a white clapboard Vermont house, overlooking a causeway leading to an island on the eastern shoreline of Lake Champlain. An old Plymouth sits on the drive and smoke rises from the chimney. The clear blue sky is crisscrossed with vapor trails.

I pull up next to the Plymouth and am about to switch off the ignition when there's a rap on the window. I turn and look into the ice-blue eyes of a tall, thin man with a neat white goatee. He has lost a lot of his hair since he and Jack were photographed next to their plane.

'You can't park here.' His voice is muffled by the window between us, but the message is clear. 'This is private property.'

I turn off the engine and wind down the window.

'Colonel Freeley?'

He blinks in the bright sunshine.

'Yes?'

'I'm the—'

'The President's personal physician, if I'm not mistaken.'

'The President's *former* personal physician, sir.'

His frown disappears.

'Well,' he says, as we shake, 'this is all rather extraordinary.'

'May I come in? I appreciate it's getting late.'

'Yes. Yes, of course.'

Freeley walks me through to the living room, where a fire crackles in the grate.

'Do we know each other?' he says.

'No, sir, we don't.' Through the plate windows that lead onto the patio I can see a woman in a thick coat and woolen hat, brushing snow off of a bird table. The yard looks over the frozen waters of the lake. 'You said, though, this was extraordinary—'

'Because I was talking about you to my wife only this morning. There hasn't been any news for a day or two . . .' He starts again. 'We – Alda and I – we were wondering if you and the other survivor . . .'

I tell him Hetta and I are both doing just fine.

Freeley wrings his hands, nods, and directs me to a chair by the fire. He invites me to call him Tom. Nobody calls him Nelson much, unless it's official or he's in some kind of trouble. He glances out the window at Alda.

I smile and thank him. 'I'm here for personal reasons. I'd be grateful if this remains confidential – just between us.'

'Of course.'

'It's about Jack Ackerman.'

He leans forward. '*Mac?*'

I nod. 'He was a friend. More than that.' *How to describe Jack?* 'My wife's stepfather. My wife . . . died . . . almost sixteen years ago. She and Jack were close.'

'I see.' He says this in a way that denotes more than a passing understanding of the things people do – the way they behave – in the wake of traumatic events. Having not fully rehearsed what I am going to say to him, I sense an opening. 'My doctors said it would be good for me to get my teeth into something . . .'

'Sure,' he says. 'A little family history. I'd be happy to talk about him. Mac was a great guy. An extraordinary guy. Truly.'

At that moment, his wife walks in. Alda is in mid-sentence – Tom needs to go to the store to buy some more birdseed – then sees me and stops. I get to my feet and Freeley does the introductions. When he tells her who I am, she melts. She vanishes into the kitchen, promising coffee.

'OK.' Freeley leans back. 'Where do you want to start? It's been a while since anybody asked me about Miracle Mac.'

'Excuse me?'

'I said it's been a while . . .' He sees my confusion and smiles. 'That's what we used to call him. All of us did. Miracle Mac was our talisman.'

'Your talisman?'

'Our good luck charm.'

I ask him to start right there.

The Hoi An incident wasn't the only time Mac cheated death. It didn't matter who he flew with. 'When you shared a cockpit with him,' Freeley says, 'you always knew you'd come back. In the end, none of us took to the air without rubbing one of his lucky charms first.'

'An ankh, a tree and some kind of star in a circle?'

He nodded.

'Which had the magic touch?'

'All of them did. But I got the impression it was the star that was special to him.'

I ask how long this ritual continued for.

'A year, eighteen months – the whole time VMO-3 was based at Da Nang East. It was quite a blow when he left.'

'Where was he posted?'

'It wasn't that straightforward,' Freeley says. 'A month or so after Mac and I got the Navy Cross, a couple of guys showed up from Washington. Well, I say that. In truth, I have no idea. They looked . . . official. Whatever, they took him away.'

'Why?'

'We just heard rumors.'

'What rumors?'

'A drug thing.'

'It was the sixties, wasn't it?'

'70, '71. To begin with, everyone turned a blind eye, but they clamped down when aircrew were found flying under the influence – though I don't believe Mac ever did.

'Morale plummeted, the attrition rate went up. In the end, we had to be deactivated and shipped back Stateside. I didn't see him again for four, five years. By then, we were based at Willow Grove, in Pennsylvania. I came home one day to find him on the porch. He was still in the military, but he looked a total wreck. I asked what he was doing, but he wouldn't tell me – said he *couldn't* tell me.'

'Where had he been all that time?'

'All he'd say was that he'd come east for something. He talked about meeting some people in D.C. Important people. That didn't make much sense either, but then . . .'

'Jack didn't always.'

Freeley gets up and shows me to his office. On the wall, along with photos of the kids and the grandkids, are several of the OV-10 Bronco with the snake and the knife on its fuselage. In one, he and Jack are smiling in front of it.

'How did he die?' Freeley finally asks.

'With great dignity,' I reply. 'Surrounded by people he loved.'

When I turn, there are tears in his eyes.

'It was hard seeing the way he was that day – the day he came back. It was like his brains had turned to mush. He was drinking . . .'

'Don't we all? War doesn't make sense at the best of times. And *that* war . . .'

Freeley shakes his head. 'Mac didn't drink to forget the past, Colonel Cain.'

It's a while before he speaks again.

'He drank in order not to see the future.'

45

I STAY AT A MOTEL DOWN THE ROAD AND HEAD BACK TO Washington before dawn the next morning.

I'm on a remote stretch of highway, across the New York state border, the sun is coming up, and I'm still thinking about Jack. I pull over and get out of the car. I'm a hundred meters or so from one of the many finger lakes that pepper the borderlands between the two states.

The air is freezing. A few pines, snow on their branches, are scattered between the road and the shore. There's no traffic, nothing except a light breeze in the trees to interrupt my thoughts.

And, suddenly, we're on the beach. It's a month or two after we bought the house. It's night, and it's warm. The waves are rolling in, the stars are out; a fire crackles beside us. Hope is massaging my shoulder muscles, transporting me to a place I'd like to visit more often, and she's talking about when Jack first came into their life.

'I was anxious about pretty much the whole world back then, Josh, but he took my fears away – about life, and about death.' She scoops up a handful of sand and lets the grains slip through her fingers. 'He used to tell me about the Shawnee, and their being in tune with nature. Jack sees connections in everything. He sees his ancestors in everything.'

'That's because Jack smokes a lot of stuff he shouldn't,' I say. 'When we die, we die.'

She claps me lightly on the back of the head, then leans forward and kisses me. 'If I go before you, Joshua Cain, which I hope I do, but not for a very long time yet, I am going to find a way of proving that you're wrong.'

The city is dark and rainswept.

I'm too tired to return the rental car, and pull gratefully into the last parking space outside my building. I look around as I pull my case from the trunk, but see nothing unusual. Mo's directive, which he emailed before he flew back to San Francisco, appears to have done the trick.

The apartment has the chill of disuse. Maybe that's because I'm out of a job. Reuben said I should go back to my patients. How can I? I'm filled with a sense of impotence and dread.

Unable to sleep and too distracted to watch TV, I go to the only place that offers any comfort. I sit and stare at the painting. A sliver of light from the hallway glints on Jack's ankh, tree and eight-pointed star. I don't know how long I've been staring at them before the room is filled with the scent of lemons. Hope's Ô de Lancôme. And I hear the voice in my head.

After Mo's diagnosis, I no longer know whose it is – hers or mine – but it doesn't much matter. *Are you just going to sit here, Josh, and feel sorry for yourself? Or are you going to get off your ass?*

'Doctor Cain? *Doctor Cain . . . ?*'

I open my eyes. The flight attendant smiles as she folds my table and returns my seat to its upright position. 'Sorry to wake you, Doctor, but we'll be on the ground in around thirty-five minutes. I thought you might want to take the opportunity to freshen up.'

I've been out for the best part of three hours.

I get up and go to the bathroom. My leg hurts, but I make a supreme effort not to let it show. My face, regrettably, is better known than I'd like it to be. Some of the other passengers stare.

Back in my seat, I flick between the two documents I was reading before I fell asleep.

One of them is the agenda of the international psychiatry conference where, the day after tomorrow, I will be keynote speaker. The other is the interim accident report on the V-22 crash, which was released by the Department of Defense while I was mid-Atlantic. It says that the right gearbox seized due to a key component failure, causing a near instantaneous loss of power to its rotor. Because the Osprey was decelerating, it didn't have enough forward speed for sustained flight, causing it to invert. It hit the trees and exploded on impact, killing the three crew, Schweizer and Offutt. Hetta and I had been thrown clear as it flipped.

There was no sign of sabotage, and inspection of the V-22 fleet uncovered no systemic flaw. I can still hear Schweizer's laughter in my head: the moment he said the President would never kill the Grid when he understood what it could do; that he'd want to build it bigger, faster, better.

I strap myself back into my seat and gaze out the window as the SAS Airbus's slow turn gives me a perfect view of the blue waters of the Stockholm archipelago. Southern Sweden looks bleak. Despite a few faltering signs of spring, there's still a lot of snow on the ground.

Thompson will go to Jerusalem in a few days. I've been immersed in articles on the conference's multi-layered security system. Initially developed by US and Israeli defense experts, Needle Eye – a series of concentric rings from the city perimeter to the convention center – has been enhanced by European, Russian, Chinese and Indian contractors, supported by their security services.

As a result, Saudi, Israel, Palestine, Iran and Turkey will join the US, the UK, France, Germany, China, India and Russia – twelve nations – in formal attendance. All their major faith leaders will be there too. Christy will remain in D.C. with the Vice President to dispense national security advice during the three days Thompson will be away.

Expectations are mixed, but hopes remain high and Thompson's ratings, at home and abroad, have taken off again.

46

THE HOTEL, PART OF THE COMPLEX WHERE I'LL BE SPEAKING, looks out across the harbor. Jetlag wakes me early.

I choose a route past the old City Hall, along the waterfront, through snow-covered parks and gardens, across an old bridge to an island beyond which the Baltic begins.

I follow signs to the Museum of Modern Art, a long building with a glass front, where I buy a ticket to the Chagall exhibition. Hope had so loved his work. He only just escaped the Holocaust, but it remains refreshingly optimistic. His subjects are mystical and magical: a man and a woman locked in an embrace above Vitebsk, Russia, the town of his birth; angels, mermaids and fairies; goats, bulls, flying fish and other animals, all painted in strange, highly improbable locations.

I stand in front of *Bestiaire et Musique* for no more than a few moments before hearing my name. Doctor Bogarten sports a black anorak and a woolen hat. We shake hands.

'I'm so grateful to you for having made time to see me, especially on a Sunday.'

He smiles. 'All this intrigue? How could I refuse?'

Nils Bogarten is a senior researcher at Stockholm's internationally famous peace research institute, and has agreed to assist me in analysis I am undertaking for a Washington think-tank on behalf of the FBI. Hetta identified him as the expert on the trafficking of nuclear materials by criminal gangs, especially from the former Soviet Union. DJ contacted him from a hot desk at FBI HQ.

'It would be impolite of me not to start by asking how you are.' Bogarten's voice is only marginally accented. 'It is quite an honor to meet you.'

We stroll from painting to painting as we talk.

'You have to understand, first off, the close relationship between criminal gangs and the Russian state,' he says. 'When the Soviet Union collapsed, certain corrupt officials attempted to get rich quick by using the Russian mafia as middlemen to sell nuclear materials. These middlemen were afforded protection by the KGB, now the FSB. They really didn't care with whom they traded either. I understood from your FBI colleague that this is a particular focus of your study.'

'I'm especially interested in a component known as a ballotechnic.'

He chuckles. 'OK, if this is the real purpose of our meeting, you can relax. I meant what I said. It is an honor to meet you, Doctor Cain, but the President's doctor – *ex*-doctor – making inquiries about nuclear weapons components on the eve of a conference in the Middle East, which the President himself will be attending? Has this resurfaced?'

I ask him to tell me everything he knows.

Bogarten takes a moment to study the painting we've stopped by – a self-portrait with seven fingers on each hand. 'In theory, ballotechnics have the capacity to trigger a fusion reaction in a nuclear weapon, but the pressure required to initiate that reaction is immense – tens of thousands of atmospheres.'

'So, we're not talking a conventional detonator.'

'Far from it. This material only *becomes* explosive when subjected to phenomenal pressure. As you may be aware, considerable mythology surrounds certain materials that were supposedly developed by the USSR during the Cold War. Ballotechnics, for example, are said to have magical properties when it comes to do-it-yourself nuclear weapons, but they have been dismissed by almost all the intelligence experts I know.'

'What do *you* think?'

'OK,' he says. 'There are three possibilities. One, that they *are* bogus – invented by conmen intent on duping gullible terrorists into handing over very large sums of money. This is the accepted version of the Ukrainian–FBI sting back in the day. The second is a canny twist: that they're the product of a disinformation campaign by intelligence agencies.'

'And the third?'

'The third isn't really an option.'

'Why?'

'Because it adheres to the old adage that disinformation works best when it is mixed with a little truth.'

'Meaning?'

'That the Soviets *did* develop this capability – or, at least, one on which the mythology is based.'

'Go on.'

'If that were the case, the weapons would be ... well, terrifying.'

'Aren't all nuclear weapons?'

'Just so. But these would be for a different reason.'

'Why?'

'They would be extremely small.'

'How small?'

'Baseball-sized.'

The seconds tick by.

'And yet ... ?'

'I'm a scientist, Doctor Cain. I put my faith in the laws of physics. Even if ballotechnics were real, there is no power – no power on this earth – capable of generating the pressures to trigger them. And no ballotechnic: no fourth-generation nuclear weapon. Whoever sent you, tell them their time and money would be better spent tackling the extremist ideology that produces the terrorists – not hunting for weaponry with little foundation in truth.'

I take a different route back to the hotel, through a kids' play area, and emerge onto the Strandvägen, which runs along the waterfront on the east side of the city. Inadvertently, I join a crowd of people, most of them head to toe in white.

Young and old mingle. Some carry placards. A man in a black waistcoat takes no notice of the cold as he bangs on a drum; another strums a guitar. The people around them – mothers, fathers, children, grandparents – are singing 'Give Peace a Chance'. Only the Swedes can turn a protest into a family outing.

A placard exhorts us to 'Seize the Moment'.

Another proclaims 'Scandinavians for A Free Palestine'.

A third promises 'Five Days to A Better World'.

I notice one emblazoned with the word 'Peace' in large yellow letters. The girl holding it is tall, willowy, with long blonde hair. A brown backpack slung over her shoulder. Fifteen meters ahead of me. I can't see her face, but I'm suddenly twenty-one years younger, in D.C., not Stockholm, with the woman of my dreams.

The crowd begins to slow. Ahead, through the trees, a four-story concrete and glass building comes into view. The Stars and Stripes flies from a flagpole above its heavily guarded gates. A dozen police cars with blue and yellow markings block the route to the end of the street.

A long-haired Swede with a megaphone clambers onto a concrete barrier and addresses us. I hear the words 'Thompson' and 'Jerusalem' and spot the girl with the placard again. She's ahead of me and slightly to the left. I still can't see her face.

As applause ripples front to back, she lifts her hand and waves to someone on the crowd's edge – a man: early thirties, tall, fair, serious-looking. He waves back and starts to weave his way toward her through the throng. In his left hand he seems to be holding a balloon, but, as the crowd parts, I see the string is attached to the wrist of a little girl, her face painted to look like a lion.

The woman kisses the man lightly on the cheek, then picks up the child and hugs and fusses over her. Something hanging from the woman's backpack catches the light.

I move closer.

It's a three-inch cross, crowned with a loop. An ankh, on a length of ribbon.

I hear the guy with the megaphone in the distance. The crowd claps. There's some jostling around me as people await the next speaker's arrival. I elbow my way forward, until I'm standing right behind the girl with the long blonde hair.

I touch her on the shoulder. She turns. Our eyes meet.

'Yes?'

I feel a crushing disappointment, then foolishness.

'I'm sorry. I thought you were somebody else.'

'You are American?'

She sounds like the stewardess on the plane. Grappling for a fragment of dignity, I ask her who these people are.

'We are peace activists from church groups across Sweden.'

She shows me a pamphlet. 'Would you like to take one?' Before I can answer, she thrusts it into my hand.

Ten minutes later, I stop at a cafe to warm myself with a cup of coffee.

A second before I consign the pamphlet to the trash, a logo at the bottom of page two catches my eye. A stylized tree.

I look again at the header, then at the paragraph below it, a quote from the Book of Revelation, 21:2 – *Then I, John, saw the holy city, New Jerusalem, coming down out of Heaven from God, prepared as a bride for her husband . . .*

Something echoes at the perimeter of my memory.

When Gapes went to the Settlement the night before he made his way through the sewer system to the church, he'd told Steve he was going to mount a protest everybody was going to know about.

He'd announced himself using the language of Revelation: *I, John.*

I glance back at the pamphlet.

Next paragraph. 22:1–2 – *Then the angel showed me the river of the water of life, as clear as crystal, flowing from the throne of God and of the Lamb, down the middle of the great street of the city. On each side of the river stood the Tree of Life, which bore twelve crops of fruit, yielding its fruit every month. And the leaves of the tree are for the healing of the nations . . .*

Twelve of them.

Twelve nations.

47

'POST-TRAUMATIC STRESS IS ONE OF THE GREAT SCARS OF OUR age,' Åke Lund tells the audience in his soft, lilting accent. 'Which is why we are fortunate to have with us our next distinguished speaker . . .'

The professor of clinical neuroscience at the Karolinska Institute has wild, chalk-white hair. He's in his mid-sixties, a two-time recipient of the Nobel Prize for Medicine.

The applause continues as I take my place at the podium. My water glass is charged. A technician checks the mike is working and gives me a thumbs-up.

I turn to check the title slide on the laptop is also displayed onscreen. 'The Ripple-Effects of Trauma – New Treatments', along with my name, in letters twenty centimeters high.

My talk is about the secondary effects of PTSD – how they act as a contagion upon those close to the primary; not about our returning veterans, but on their families: wives, husbands, children. I will speak about the phenomenon that led Hope, after months of living with *my* combat trauma, to become infected by it herself, without revealing the twist that has made it, for me, so tragic and personal.

'Ladies and gentlemen, it is a great honor to be here today. I am enormously grateful for the opportunity to be—'

My attention is drawn to the face of a man in the second row.

As I lean forward, my hand knocks the glass onto the laptop. The imagery flickers and dies, the glass smashes, I try to pick up the pieces and cut my finger.

The technician rushes back onstage, followed by a very flustered-looking Lund. He leans past me to speak into the mike. 'Please, ladies and gentlemen, please, let's take a short break while we get things back online.'

I scan the auditorium, but the man I saw has gone.

I need air.

I take a Kleenex from my pocket, wrap it around the cut, and follow the emergency exit signs down a long hallway, which takes me to a loading bay. Two delivery drivers are smoking and talking amid piles of empty cardboard boxes, plastic packaging and several giant waste collection bins. Neither pays me the slightest attention.

The door opens. It's the professor, a picture of concern. 'Doctor Cain? I am sorry. Perhaps it would be better if we were to reschedule your presentation for tomorrow.' He sees the wound on my hand. 'Maybe you are in need of medical attention. We have an excellent—'

'Thank you, Åke. It's just a cut. I need a few moments. I'll be fine.'

'Of course. Will you be all right to resume your speech in, shall we say –' he glances at his watch, '– an hour? Two?'

'An hour would be perfect.'

Moments later, alone with my thoughts again, I hear the door open.

I hadn't imagined it. Standing two meters from me is Stanislaw Koori, the man who trained Duke Gapes to remote view.

According to the file at the Army Research Laboratory, Koori was in his mid- to late sixties when he trialed the HITS helmet, which makes him seventy-five-odd now.

His accent still has a twist of Mitteleuropa, but is like nothing I've ever heard.

He reaches into his jacket, takes out a silver cigarette case and lights up an unfiltered cigarette, examining me with reptilian eyes.

When the Stanford Research Institute started the remote viewing program in the early seventies, on the back of all that CIA secrecy and money, Koori was one of a handful of psychics recruited to test the 'psi' phenomenon – whether we have powers that might be described as extraordinary: clairvoyance, telepathy, precognition and, strangest of all, psychokinesis, the ability to move, bend and break objects with the power of the mind.

Stani had come to the CIA's attention at some LA psi salons and spoon-bending parties. He had demonstrated an ability to score highly in all of these areas, which persuaded the Agency to throw more money at it because US Intelligence believed the Soviets were even deeper into psi than it was.

He drops the butt and grinds it beneath a brown-and-white brogue. 'There's no magic in roaming time and space. Boredom is the viewer's principal enemy. So when they asked if I'd like to test some kind of headgear that allows another person to see what the psychic sees, I was curious to know whether such a thing might be possible, even though it was clear to me the only person who believed in the project, at that stage, was the scientist himself.'

'Kaufmann?'

'His method of mining the data in which nature's memory is held is one of the greatest achievements of all time. Suffice to say, after a year or so of working on it, as the evidence began to build that this thing might actually work, I thought it would be wise to . . .'

He hesitates.

'Drop off the map?'

'In a manner of speaking. Some people call it retirement. I've never had much of a liking for excessive, Draconian secrecy, of which our government is so fond.'

'Then why are you here?'

He produces a sheet of paper and slowly unfolds it to reveal, in thick blue marker pen, a circle containing an eight-pointed star.

A month or so ago, while painting in his studio above San Francisco Bay, he spontaneously sketched this symbol in the bottom right corner of the canvas.

He hadn't remote viewed for many years, he says, but the reflex action that produced this was more than familiar to him. Back in the day, remote viewers used to call them 'ideograms'.

When the ideogram came through – sometimes it could be a squiggle, sometimes something more defined – the viewer and the monitor knew that the viewer was on the signal line, *connected*. That data from the target was about to come through.

'Three days later, I was in my apartment. It was evening, and I was getting ready to eat. I got a vivid picture in my mind of this same symbol, and did what I should have done the first time: I sat, quietly composed myself, and began to jot down all my impressions of the target – like I used to do.'

What came to him were images, feelings, of something hot, very hot, like an oven or a furnace. And the number 22.

He let Google do the rest. The V-22 Osprey flashed up, and the location of the crash. Then he found my booking at the conference.

Koori lives on the West Coast. He doesn't concern himself with current affairs much, but my name was familiar to him from the news generated by my encounter in the tower with the man he knew wasn't Matt Voss. He'd trained Duke Gapes, after all.

'I've felt nothing but guilt about that boy since I quit the program.'

'Why?'

'Because I knew they'd replace me with him, and that they'd turn our little tech demonstrator into something big, bad and operational.'

I say nothing.

He lights another cigarette and sucks in a lungful of smoke.

'The first-generation helmet that Kaufmann built really wasn't much to write home about. It used a classical computer in its bid to connect the hardware to . . .'

He pauses again.

'Kaufmann had this dumb-ass scientific name for it – he called it holosphere.' He brushes back what's left of his hair.

'Anyhow, it didn't work too good, but well enough for Abnarth to give him more funding to develop an improved model.'

I ask if he and Abnarth ever met.

'My, yes,' he says. 'The Senator was in and out of our lab all the time. More so when I told Kaufmann that something had changed with the integration of the quantum computer.'

'Changed?'

'It was trying to communicate with me.'

'But we're talking about a machine—'

'No, Colonel. We're talking about a channel via which the world of matter connects to the world of the immaterial.'

A breeze blows up through the loading bay.

Misty said her sister got calls from Duke while he was on the run. The idea was dismissed because of Lou's Alzheimer's.

But I now know they came at the point Duke was set to move from the HITS lab to the Canyon.

He told her he'd been in communication with his father, even though his father had been dead for years.

The suits who'd grilled Gapes and Offutt after the Grid's melt-down even had a name for it: *Reachback*.

No wonder he'd told his mother he was scared.

I check my watch. I'm back on stage in five minutes.

'And that's when you quit?'

'I know how this goes. I worked for the CIA and the military in the seventies. I retired. They brought me back to train a new generation of viewers after 9/11. I could see from Abnarth and Kaufmann's fixation that the *art* of remote viewing – *my* art – was about to become a science. I knew I had to quit before I got in so deep they'd never let me go.'

He reaches into his jacket. I think he's going for his cigarette case again, but he produces a small artist's sketchbook and flicks through it. Each page is filled with numbers, strange runes and symbols, but prominent amongst them are my initials, as well as renditions – in all colors and sizes – of the circle with the eight-pointed star.

'Native Americans wrote nothing down. Their ideas, their dreams and fears were communicated from one generation to the next through signs and symbols. The number eight represents balance and harmony. The circle represents protection. The star represents knowledge, particularly about things to come.'

He pauses.

'I guess you must know this now. They called it the Hope Symbol.'

Symbols. What Mo and I also know as Jungian archetypes. Deep subconscious messaging. After the talk, but before I leave the hotel for the City Hall ferry terminal, I sit in my room, kill the TV news, which is beginning to obsess about the forthcoming conference, and Google 'ankh'.

It was held by the early Christians as a symbol of eternal faith. The crucifix, which spoke of torture and death, was not adopted by the Church until the second or third centuries. The loop at the top of the ankh represented the soul, the cross below it the state of death. Together, they came to symbolize reincarnation.

The uppermost layer of Panel 4 had depicted my life and Hope's in the most intimate detail. The layer beneath had consisted of that single image of the scan – our baby girl.

But Gapes had layered the entire cabin with meaning.

Panel 4 *had* held another kind of meaning – spiritual meaning.

Not birth, though. Rebirth.

Why?

Much of what Koori had said resonated in me.

Along with the voice in my head seconds before the V-22 began its death-roll – *her* voice.

The cell-memory therapy session with Mo, in which I had heard her talking to me. In which she had directed me to the night Jack had died and to my memories of our time at the beach.

And, yesterday, the girl on the peace march.

The ankh hadn't been the only treasure on that old piece of leather: the Hope Symbol had been there too.

Jack hadn't simply turned up at the Five Pines by accident.

He had sought out Pam and Hope.

And the tree of life? Did it mean that somewhere deep inside of him, *Miracle Mac* – who'd had the power to protect his friends and see the future – knew that at some point I would wander into Hope's life too?

48

KOORI IS WRAPPED IN AN OLD FUR COAT IN BACK OF THE COVERED area of the upper deck. There are only three other passengers on the ferry: an old woman with a small, yappy dog, and a couple of punks – a girl and a boy – laughing as they neck vodka from a bottle.

Koori waits until we are several minutes underway before telling me about the four stages of what he has come to know as 'persistent consciousness' – states he has identified in the dead. This stemmed from his work on the remote viewing program at Stanford. None of it was provable in any scientific sense, he says, but came through as enough of a signal for him to have documented it in a paper for his paymasters.

'Stage One is consciousness in a transient state – consciousness which retains material attachments.

'Stage Two is consciousness that has shed these attachments – the part of us which comes to terms with things done and learned in this world; consciousness ready to evolve.

'Stage Three is consciousness that needs to learn from a higher plane – the many other planes of existence.

'Stage Four is when there's no more to learn from this life, or from the next, or from existence itself – when it has evolved so far it becomes one with what I call the substrate: the cosmos itself.'

We pass under a bridge and, for several seconds, the world plunges into darkness.

'Your wife is a new soul, Colonel, a Stage One. She still feels the need to commune with you.'

I guess he sees how much I'm struggling with this.

'I've known this to happen when there is a deep emotional attachment between two people, and when sudden death is involved.'

I tell him about Mo's cell-memory therapy session, and that, as a scientist, I'm inclined to accept his view that however real Hope's voice seemed to me, it's a construct of my subconscious.

Koori sighs. 'Our primeval relatives heard the voices of their dead ancestors in caves and forests. God spoke to them on mountaintops and on the wind. We have become so fucking rational, Colonel, that we think we know it all. But we don't.'

He pauses. 'If the full-up technology of the Grid is anything like the HITS demonstrator, then *it* chooses the time, the place and the individual with whom it wishes to connect. With HITS, it was subtle. It would send me an image only I would recognize.'

He pulls his cigarette case from his jacket.

'This used to belong to my father. A dear man I loved very much. Whenever HITS wanted to send a message specific to me, I would receive an image of the case on the heads-up display.'

'Its version of the ideogram?'

'Precisely.'

'And this would be followed by the message?'

'Yes.'

'What kind of message?'

'About what is to come.'

I think back to my encounter with Gapes in the tower. 'Duke told me he had found ground truth. I had no idea what that meant, until his monitor told me it meant I was the target. Why would he have targeted me?'

'Because he had information that was specific to you.'

I feel a sudden chill. Jack's portrait, finished somewhere else. Hope telling me – *demonstrating* to me – that she was still here and wanting to communicate.

He asks if I'm all right.

I nod. 'What about Jack?'

'I spent a long time this afternoon trying to form an impression of Jack, but my belief is that he has gone.'

'What do you mean, gone?'

'Evolved.'

'Like a Stage Two?'

'More like a Stage Three.'

'Why?'

'As you told me, Colonel, symbols carry meaning. They are deeply primal. But the subconscious is also a repository of other subtle forms of information that come to us from realms we really know very little about.'

He pauses again.

'I don't know if God is real, but if I were Him and I wanted to convey data, I'd do it in a way that our ancestors understood well. I'd do it via symbols. Symbols that carry meaning. The ankh, the tree of life and the eight-pointed star in a circle, taken together, tell me that Jack's purpose has to do with protection against a singularity. As he lay dying, he was trying to tell her. But she was too grief-stricken to understand. He was passing the role of guardianship to her. I believe he also knew she was going to die.'

I stare at him. 'Guardianship?'

'Some of us have a purpose in life and some of us have a purpose in death. Jack's purpose was to protect Hope. Hope's job is to protect you. We're *all* here for a reason, Colonel. Via the Grid, she found a means of passing the message to Gapes and now she is passing it to you, via coincidences and dreams.'

'What message?' I ask. 'And what the hell is a singularity?'

'Whatever Duke saw the day of the system meltdown,' he replies. 'Something that involves the President. Something that involves you. Something that consciousness itself wishes to convey with great urgency. Something to do with Jerusalem. Something . . . unprecedented.'

He looks out across the black water of the harbor and the lights of the city dancing on its surface.

'Now, for all our sakes, why don't you tell me what Duke showed you in that cabin?'

*

I reach for a sheet of paper and write down what Hetta and I found on the crazy wall:

Panel 1. (Rembrandt) Crucifixion > Ascension = **God.**
Panel 2. POTUS > Church = **Threat.**
Panel 3. Al-Mohandis (The Engineer) > '15ski' = **Proof.**
Panel 4. Cain's Life > Fetal Scan (rebirth?) = **Mac.**
Panel 5. Skyline > St Mary Magdalene = **Jerusalem.**

'Who is the Engineer?' he asks.
'Somebody jihadists believe will rid the world of us.'
'And fifteen-ski?'
'Shorthand. The word was transliterated from the Cyrillic: *Pitnatsat.*'
'And the significance of St Mary Magdalene?'
'The Russian Orthodox church on the Mount of Olives.'
Koori holds the note under the light.
'Oh, my.'
'What?'
'How best to explain this?'
He turns to me.
'Remote viewing is an imprecise art, especially when it pertains to the future. It is prophecy. But prophets don't see events with crystal clarity. They glimpse them.' He pauses. 'Duke is no different from Isaiah, Jeremiah, Ezekiel, Daniel – Jesus, even – all of whom, of course, are revered by Muslims as prophets too.'
'But this was shown to him by the Grid.'
'Yes. Jerusalem. Devastation. Judgment. Every element is there.'
The elements of Revelation.
'And the Russians?'
'The Russians have their place in end-times prophecies, too. Ever hear of the Church Committee?'
I nod. 'Set up after Watergate. '75?'
'And '76. Its brief was to investigate abuses of power by the FBI, CIA and NSA. It was named after the man who led it, Senator Frank Church, and blew the lid off of the intelligence community's

illegal mass surveillance of a swathe of the US population – since right back in the fifties. Stop me, please, if any of this is sounding a little too familiar.

'The most disturbing of their findings was a cache of CIA files nicknamed the Family Jewels. Most of them were destroyed when the Agency knew it was about to be subpoenaed.

'The Church Committee didn't know what to do with a lot of the contents. Some was classified, some just too damn weird. So it bundled everything into what came to be known in the viewing community as File 15 – the one they didn't make public.

'At Stanford, we used to refer to it as the motherlode. It held everything we were interested in: clairvoyance, telepathy, precognition, even clues to the remote viewing process itself. My guess is that Jack was a part of what the CIA called its behavior modification study. That they took him away to try to explore his gift for clairvoyance; to find out if they could exploit it. Jack would have testified to the committee for sure.'

'Is that it?'

'No. Our handlers always believed there was a Soviet equivalent of File 15. We searched all over for it in the seventies and eighties.'

'But didn't find it?'

'But didn't find it.'

I look at Panels 2 and 3. Church and *Pitnatsat*. 'Was Abnarth on the Church Committee?'

'He was a young staff member.'

'Did you know that when he became a senator, in '92, he sent a trade delegation to Russia, ostensibly to help US tech-entrepreneurs broker deals involving Russian-developed intellectual property?'

'No.'

I tell him about Ted van Buren's meeting with M. M. Kalunin, the man who'd been in charge of the Soviets' psychic warfare program, and their discussion about the survival of consciousness post-mortem.

The ferry begins to slow as we approach our destination, Hammarby Sjöstad, a waterside district on the edge of the inner city.

'If the Russians had an equivalent of File 15,' I say, 'if Kalunin had sight of it, what do you think it might contain?'

He purses his lips.

I try again.

'Gapes's cabin display contained multiple layers of meaning, to confuse the Grid – to allow our investigation to get ahead of the people monitoring us. The first layer was what we called the welcome message: *I saw the face of God. You shall too. Bear true faith. Hope. Pray.*

'The Grid depicted Jerusalem leveled in some kind of nuclear event at which President Thompson was present. It also grew out of experimental hardware that you and Gapes helped develop for the HITS program – with hardware that seems to have been financed by a convenient Russian venture capitalist.'

'So Duke found proof.'

'Of what?'

'Something involving File 15, or its Russian equivalent.'

I nod.

Something involving the Engineer.

'The Russian banker,' Koori says. 'What's his name?'

'Ilitch. Kalunin's son-in-law.'

'What else do you know about him?'

'Not enough.'

Koori reaches for another cigarette. 'Then perhaps I can help.'

We settle ourselves in the business center of a hotel overlooking the Hammarby waterfront, but not before I have passed through the lobby, where on the TVs, I catch more imagery of Jerusalem – the preparations being made for the arrival of the delegates.

At this time of night, few people are still up. I log on using a proxy ID and type in 'Vladimir Ilitch'. There's nothing to indicate that the man whose image Gapes placed on the wall of the cabin – a man in his youth, who bore a resemblance to Napoleon – would become one of the most powerful figures in modern Russia. There are no pictures, no narratives.

Nothing.

Except for this: Ilitch's generosity to the Russian Orthodox Church, which sits strangely alongside Hetta's assertion that his father was a Tatar Muslim. Ilitch has given billions to it. And in return, their praise for the oligarch you never get to see is fulsome.

If it weren't for Ilitch, the Cathedral of the Holy Trinity, one of Moscow's oldest places of worship, would have collapsed. It's been restored to its former Tsarist glory. The bill appears to have topped six hundred million roubles. He has also donated rare icons to the church, and given it millions more to distribute to the poor.

'I'll never get within a mile of him,' I mutter.

'So maybe you should try focusing on his wife.'

'I wouldn't get within a mile of her either.'

'If Ilitch were still married to her, you wouldn't.'

'They split?'

Koori closes his eyes. 'Recently. Rather quietly.'

'Do you see anything else?'

'Books,' he says.

'What?'

'Books,' he repeats. 'There is a connection between Sasha and books. She's also close to money. A place that's dripping with it.'

When I Google 'Sasha', 'Ilitch' and 'books', I draw a blank.

It's the same when I try 'Sasha', 'Ilitch' and 'author'.

The only thing that comes close is Sasha Mikhailovna, dealer in rare books off Tretyakovsky Proezd, in the heart of Moscow's Kitay Gorod district, right by the Kremlin. All I know about Mikhailovna is that it's a patronymic. When I Google the father of Russian consciousness research, I discover that Mikhail was M. M. Kalunin's first name.

The return ferry is a fraction busier than the one on the way out – half a dozen businessmen and women and a couple of late-night revelers making the journey back to the center of the city.

We're halfway there when Koori tells me I'll be putting myself at great risk.

'Is that a prediction?'

'No. It's a fact. For the past month, you've been off their radar screens. Cross that border and you'll light up like a beacon.'

I know.

'Is the future written?' I ask.

'Yes and no.'

'Meaning?'

'Research suggests that every moment we make a decision, the future splits. Simply put, in one version, there's an apocalypse in which Jerusalem is utterly destroyed. In another, there isn't.'

'Is this what we're being shown – the Apocalypse?'

'Are you religious, Josh?'

'Why?'

'In Revelation, technically the world isn't destroyed. The nations are healed by God's promise the curse will be lifted. That is the essence of the New Jerusalem. A world renewed. Reborn.'

'If the Engineer had managed to get hold of a nuclear device, would he be guided by that distinction? If he believes he's fulfilling a prophecy, wouldn't he go ahead and push the button?'

'I don't know.'

'What would it take?'

'Take?'

'For you to know.'

'More than what you've got,' he says.

'Stani?'

'Yes.'

'If you get involved—'

'I became involved the moment I sketched out that eight-pointed star.' He manages a smile. 'And retirement wasn't much fun anyway.'

I write down a name and address.

He studies it. 'Can I trust her?'

'Completely.'

We agree that I go east, he goes west.

49

DOMODEDOVO AIRPORT, MOSCOW. RECENTLY MODERNIZED, BUT not so you'd notice.

It's seven o'clock in the morning, still dark, and most of those around me have stumbled off flights from distant parts of the Federation and the territories of the former Soviet Socialist Republic: Irkutsk, Novosibirsk, Tashkent, Petropavlovsk.

When I finally get to the head of the line, I'm confronted by a blue-shirted officer of the Federal Migration Service. She's at least seventy, with gray hair molded like a bagel. She beckons me to the booth. I hand over my passport. She flicks through it till she finds the page she's looking for.

She spends almost a minute subjecting it to microscopic scrutiny, then looks up. '*Diplomatyeskii.*'

I nod.

She places Sergeyev's visa under a scanner. My passport had been couriered to my office the day of the V-22 crash. Molly had overseen its delivery to my apartment when she knew I wasn't coming back. Eyes down, the passport official says something to me in Russian, and gets irritated when I don't give an immediate answer.

'How many . . . days?'

'A week,' I lie. I don't want to give any impression of urgency.

She gives me the stamp. I'm in.

By the time I clear customs, I know that, as unsophisticated as everything appears, my details are already being scrutinized by the FSB.

I take the Aeroexpress and watch the sun rise over an endless succession of gray apartment blocks in Moscow's southeast suburbs. Steam vents from roofs. Factories belch smoke into a fine muslin layer of smog. Several centimeters of snow cover the ground.

I take a short taxi ride from Paveletsky station to my hotel, the Kempinski, across the river from Red Square.

I set off across the Moskvoretsky Bridge twenty minutes later, having showered, changed and wrapped up warm. Never having been to Russia before, I spend a minute or two appreciating my surroundings. I get out my phone, take 360-degree shots of St Basil's and the Kremlin walls, take several more of the Lenin Mausoleum and views over the Moskva River, then head to the eastern side of the square.

GUM is more a mall than a store. Its three levels are linked by escalators. Glitzy shops occupy each floor. I sit in a cafe, examine the tourist map I picked up at the hotel, then head for the restroom, enter a cubicle, lock it and sit down.

I run through every picture on my phone, expanding them as I go. Most of the people are obviously tourists. One guy isn't. Shaved head, black jacket and gray scarf. In my first shot I caught him unawares. He's looking straight at me. In all the others, he's turned away. I flush the john and wash my hands.

I spot a kiosk selling what look like hotdogs by one of the main exits. The vendor tells me they're called *sasiki*. I put down my map, count out fifty roubles, then sit on a stool and eat.

I exit by the nearest door, turn left, walk thirty meters, shove my hand in my pocket, make out I've forgotten the map and turn back.

As I step through the revolving door, the guy with the shaved head sees me, averts his eyes and keeps going, exactly as the manual has trained him to do.

I head back to the kiosk, pick up the map – josh about my forgetfulness to the *sasiki*-seller – and make for a different exit on the store's north side. I dive into a large group of tourists, moving with them down Nikolskaya Street, until I spot where I need to go.

*

Tretyakovsky Proezd is almost deserted. Like the undead, oligarchs come out at night.

Bulgari, Armani, Graff, Tiffany, Maserati, Ferrari are all here, but they're not what I'm looking for. I take another left into a street of perfectly restored pre-Revolution-era buildings painted in pastel shades of green and red.

The first store I come to sells icons; the second, classical paintings; the third, Russian porcelain. The sign above the doorway to the fourth reads 'Sasha Bibliofil Moskva'. Its interior is compact and redolent with the scent of leather, mold and preservatives.

The shelves, labeled in Russian and English, are packed with hundreds of rare, second-hand and antique books. Air conditioning ensures the sub-zero conditions remain outside.

A thin, pale girl with short black hair in a figure-hugging sweater and skintight jeans is tapping on an iPad behind a desk at the far end of the room. She looks up. There's no one else in sight.

'Speak English?'

'Little,' she replies. She puts away the iPad, taking her time.

'I'm looking for something to give to a friend. A memento.'

Her eyes narrow. A slight shake of the head.

'A gift.'

'This is *rare* bookshop.'

'I know.' I smile, and get nothing back.

'So, how much you like to spend?'

'Anything up to ten thousand.'

'Roubles?'

'Dollars.'

This prompts her to raise her sculpted eyebrows. She picks up the phone. A minute later, the door behind her opens.

The woman who comes through it has high cheekbones and naturally blonde hair, cut just above the shoulder. She's wearing a floaty smock and tight white pedal-pushers and her eyeglasses hang from a chain around her neck. Attractive, in her late forties, she's wearing no more than a hint of make-up.

'May I help?' Her English has little trace of an accent. 'I am the owner. Anya tells me you're looking for something rare.'

'Yes. A gift for a friend.'

'You're American?'

I nod.

'And you want a *Russian* book?'

'My friend doesn't speak it, sadly.'

'A translation, then? Of Dostoevsky, Tolstoy, Grossman, Solz-henitsyn? We have many. What kind of stories interest your . . . friend?'

'Universal themes. Complex characters. I'm sorry. I didn't intro-duce myself. My name is Joshua Cain.'

I extend my hand. She shakes it. Her palm is cold.

'Sasha,' she replies. A hesitant smile. 'But this does not help me nar-row the list. Russian literature, Mister Cain, is founded on universal themes and complex characters. But maybe I *do* have something. And it will not cost you the fortune that you mentioned.'

'No?'

'No. The state does not permit the export of books over a hun-dred years old without a special permit. Since you don't know that, I'm assuming you are not a collector. Are you here on business?'

'In a sense, yes.'

'What, if I may ask, does your friend do?'

'He's a psychiatrist. An eminent professor.'

'Then this is good.'

'It is?'

'*Da.* I have just received a copy of Lermontov's *A Hero Of Our Time*. The first edition of a 1958 translation by Nabokov. If your friend likes Russia, classical literature, and is American, then this maybe has everything that you – or he – might be looking for. Par-ticularly if psychiatry is his specialism.'

'Have you read it?'

'Of course.'

'And?'

'The central character is indeed complex. He is highly calculat-ing and manipulative, yet also cynical and sensitive.'

'Are we supposed to like him?'

'That is a matter of perspective.' She pauses. 'You think these are the kinds of themes that might appeal?'

'I don't know. Perhaps. If I could just *see* the book . . .'

She turns to Anya. They exchange a few short words. The girl opens the top drawer of the desk, removes a pair of white gloves, opens the door and disappears.

The sound of her footsteps recedes.

'You have a reference section, I see.'

'Yes.'

'I'd be interested in taking a look.'

'For your friend? Or for you?'

'For my friend, of course.'

'Then you will need to tell me a little more about him.'

'His passion is the study of consciousness.'

'I see.' She pauses. 'What is it that *you* do, Mister Cain?'

'I'm a physician and a psychiatrist.'

'I'm sorry. *Doctor* Cain. Then you must have views on this too.'

'I'm familiar with the territory, yes.'

'I come from a scientific family myself,' she says. 'My father was an academic. And this subject was very close to his heart. So, please, I am interested. Tell me.'

I cast myself back to TVB and our fireside chats.

'Where does the mind originate? Is it a by-product merely of brain chemistry? If so, what is memory? How do we store it? Does memory reside within us? Does consciousness? Or does it come from somewhere else? And, I guess, the truly big question: does consciousness persist after we die?'

'Tell me, Doctor Cain, have you lost someone close to you?'

Before I can answer, a door opens and closes somewhere downstairs.

Footsteps. Anya on her way back up.

Sasha turns to me. 'Doctor Cain, what is it that *really* brings you to my shop?'

Anya reappears, clasping the Lermontov in her gloved hands. She picks up on the electricity, glances at us both.

She and her boss hold a short, whispered discussion. Then, without a word to me, Sasha turns and walks from the room.

'Miss Mikhailovna says to tell you that she regrets she has no books that are of interest to you or to your friend. So as not to waste any more time, she says for you please not to come back.'

50

AS I CLIMB THE STEPS TOWARD THE ENTRANCE OF THE CATHEDRAL of the Holy Trinity, a young priest with a straggly beard tells me foreign tourists are encouraged to make a small donation to the homeless and the hungry. I get the feeling he has been posted to scout for trade and saw me coming a mile off. A wooden cross swings on a chain around his neck.

When we get to the door, he smiles and holds out a large silver collection plate.

I reward his efforts with a bunch of roubles, head inside and find a seat between two praying babushkas at the rear of the nave.

I unfurl a fact sheet from the Ilitch Foundation website.

Holy Trinity is the foundation's flagship, a model for its many other restoration projects. At the bottom of the sheet are some photos. They include a shot of the Church of St Mary Magdalene, which is familiar from the cabin. It overlooks the holy sites of the three religions and is a stone's throw from where conference delegates are now assembling.

I become aware that someone is standing behind me.

It's the young priest who accosted me at the entrance. He introduces himself as Father Yuri. 'Excuse me. English?'

I get to my feet. 'American.'

'I like to show you something.'

I follow him. At the entranceway, he points to the collection plate. 'Three thousand roubles! More than fifty dollars! This very, very good!'

I tell him I'm happy to help.

After he's finished pumping my hand, he asks me my name.

'Joshua? I like this. When I look for you, Joshua, I think you leave, but then I see you at back of church. As I come close, I see you reading about Ilitch restoration.'

I tell him the project interests me, particularly the one in Jerusalem.

'OK.' He claps me on the back. 'So, I do something for you.'

He leads me past a panel of icons to a screen displaying the various stages of the process.

No expense has been spared in the employment of cutting-edge twenty-first-century technology. Where it hasn't been possible to take castings from the original moldings, for example, digital images have been made of archive photographs and fiberglass facsimiles built using 3D printers. Yuri points out an angel's head high on the domed ceiling that's a prize example.

I ask him how I can make a contribution.

'Contribution?' He mangles each syllable.

'A gift.'

'But you make this already.'

'That was for the homeless and the hungry.'

I point to the picture of the Church of St Mary Magdalene in Jerusalem. 'What do you know about the work here?'

He peers at it. 'Little. Father Grigory. He know.'

'Who is Father Grigory?'

'Father Grigory is *nastoyatel*.' He pauses. 'How you say? Father Superior.'

'Please take me to him.'

'Now?'

'Yes. Now.'

'Father Grigory is busy man.'

'So am I. I want to make a sizeable donation.'

Yuri frowns.

I hold my hands wide.

We pass through a door that opens onto a narrow hallway.

A number of chambers lead off of it.

He stops at the second on the left, pauses, and knocks. A low voice answers. Yuri enters. I hang back.

A clean-shaven priest in a black robe and boxy headgear is sitting behind a desk in an office that's bare except for an inlaid gold icon of the crucified Christ on the wall behind him.

Father Grigory is in his late thirties. The cross hanging heavily from his neck is solid silver. He stares at Yuri, then at me. He's pressing a cordless phone to his ear with one hand and covering the mouthpiece with the other. He nods at Yuri.

I catch the words '*Yerusalim*' and '*Amerikanski*' in Yuri's response.

Father Grigory appears to give us a curt dismissal.

Thirty seconds later, Yuri and I are back where we started, in the entranceway.

When I ask what Grigory said, he simply repeats that the *nastoyatel* is a very busy man.

'He said you try come back tomorrow.'

My command of Russian isn't brilliant, but I am fairly certain that this is not what the *nastoyatel* said. The word I heard him use was *neudobnyy*. As I walk down the icy steps toward the pathway that leads to the river, I check a translate engine. *Neudobnyy* means 'inconvenient'.

A Range Rover and a Mercedes saloon – both so immaculately polished I can see my reflection in their paintwork as they sweep past – pull up at the base of the steps.

Two bodyguards leap from the Range Rover. One runs to the Merc and waits. The other clears a path through people milling around the entrance then speaks into his microphone. The first heavy opens the Merc's door.

A priest in a black robe and white headdress emerges. I hear someone close by whisper: 'Patriarch Nikolai,' and watch the closest onlookers dip their heads toward the Primate of Moscow, the head of the Russian Orthodox Church.

They pay little attention to the man who follows.

I have only seen that one picture of Vladimir Ilitch – on the crazy wall, from way back, when he was still a lowly accountant in the pay of the Soviet state. He is taller than I expected, but there's no mistaking him.

He checks himself in the reflection of the passenger window, sweeps his distinctive lock of hair away from his face, and slips on a pair of sunglasses. Flanked by his bodyguards, he puts his hands behind his back, drops his head, and strides into the patriarch's church.

51

THAT EVENING, IN MY ROOM, I WATCH THE WELCOME CEREMONIES that have taken place throughout the day in the center of Jerusalem.

Thompson flew in during the afternoon. After speaking to reporters at Ben Gurion International, he made his way to the Old City. There are pictures of his green and white helicopter touching down at the conference arena, a closed-off zone within spitting distance of the Temple Mount, where, tomorrow, amid a network of hotels and convention centers, the plenary and non-plenary sessions will get underway.

There are also images of him making his way on foot from the media center to the so-called Hall of the Assembly, from where the inauguration ceremony is now being streamed live.

He looks relaxed. Better, in fact, than I have ever seen him.

He smiles and waves. His shirt collar is undone.

Jennifer walks beside him, looking beautiful, though more . . . I don't know. On edge?

The crowd seems to love it, and him.

Security will be going apeshit.

Over a room-service meal, I watch a succession of political and religious leaders. When the commentator mentions that Thompson's will be the eleventh and final speech, I hit my laptop and check the news. India has dropped out. Floods in Kolkata have killed thousands and the government needs to attend to the crisis. For an irrational moment, I'm elated. Then the commentator drops in the fact the Pope won't arrive until the main plenary kicks off in two days' time.

The Vatican will make twelve.

There's a Bible in the bedside drawer. I go to Revelation 22:2, which talks about the tree of life and the healing of the nations. The next verse, as Koori told me, promises 'no more curse'. My eye is then drawn to 22:4: 'They shall see His face.'

I glance at my watch. Moscow is one hour ahead of Jerusalem. I dial Reuben.

We haven't spoken since his visit to the hospital. I'm surprised he picks up.

'You watching this?' he says.

'Yes.'

'And?'

'And what?'

'What do you make of it?'

'You're not with him?'

'No. I'm with the VP and Christy. We're caretaking while Thompson is in Jerusalem.'

'Reuben?' In my mind, I'm surprised he's not with Thompson.

'Yeah.' He sounds distracted. I can hear he's watching a TV or a monitor.

'Do you have a delegate list?'

'On me? No.' A pause. 'Why?'

'I want you to check a name.'

'Who?' Caution in his voice.

'Patriarch Nikolai, the head of the Russian Orthodox Church.'

A pause. 'Where are you, Josh?'

'Moscow.'

'The hell you doing in Moscow?'

'You remember our friend?'

'*Jesus.*'

'His foundation is carrying out a refurb of a Russian Orthodox Church overlooking the spot where Thompson is now.'

'So?'

'Check out the blast radius.'

'This is an open line.'

'It's a little too late for Opsec, Reuben.'

'Do the Russians know you're in-country?' He means the FSB.

'I imagine so.' I may have lost them during my walkabout, but they'll know exactly where I am now.

'The Patriarch?'

'If he's not on the list, you have a problem.'

'Why?'

'Because maybe he knows something we don't.'

The line goes quiet.

'Reuben?'

'Yes.'

'You remember the welcome message? *I saw the face of God. You shall too.* It's from the Book of Revelation.'

'So?'

'Gapes's next line told us to "bear true faith". From the oath we swear to uphold the Constitution. Against *all* enemies, foreign and domestic. He was warning us that the threat comes from both.'

I pause.

'And another thing. Revelation is attributed to John the Apostle. Gapes gave himself the pseudonym John when he turned up at the Settlement. He used the Church of St John to mount his protest. John the Apostle was a seer. He saw the future. Just as Gapes says he did.'

'Go home, Josh,' Reuben says wearily. 'This is crazy talk. I have done everything in my power to protect you. And I can only do so much.'

'Something's going to happen.'

'Go *home*, Josh.'

'Reuben—'

'Enough, damn it! I need to feed Thompson the rest of his speech. And you need to leave before somebody gets interested in this discussion.'

He hangs up.

I think about my options while I take a shower, and contemplate calling Stani. But he'll still be halfway to the US.

By the time I go back to the bedroom, someone has slipped an envelope with the Kempinski's logo under the door. Inside is a piece of plain paper with numbers printed down both the long edges of the page. The left-hand side starts with 39:6:13; 101:14:3; 170:35:18 and continues almost to the bottom. I count them. Twenty-four sets. The right set is shorter. Three numbers only.

I'm wondering what they mean when there's a knock on the door. I tuck the sheet quickly into the desk drawer.

'Yes?'

Room service.

I look through the eyepiece.

A man in hotel uniform holds up a brown envelope. I sign for it, tip him, and close the door.

I figure it has to be a lot easier to shoot me than to blow me up in the Kempinski, so I open it. It's a book. *A Hero Of Our Time* – the 1958 edition, translated into English by Nabokov.

There's a note in a delicate hand tucked inside the flyleaf.

Doctor Cain – Joshua – please accept this with my apologies, as a gift for your friend. A memento of Russia. With kind regards, Sasha.

I recover the list of numbers from the drawer.

I turn to page thirty-nine, count six lines down from the top, and trace my index finger past a couple of words until I reach the thirteenth letter, an 'L'. I write it down. I repeat the process twenty-four times until I'm left with two words and three sets of numbers.

Leningradskiy Prospekt 56.

Today's date, and a time: 21.30.

I look at my watch.

I have less than an hour.

52

I'M IN THE SUBURB OF SOKOL, SEVERAL LINE CHANGES AWAY ON the Moscow Metro and eight kilometers from the city center – not a poor district by any means, but a world away from the glitter of Tretyakovsky Proezd. Exhaust fumes hang in the air and stain the snow.

I take a left through a poorly lit park, avoid a group of drinking and smoking youths, and duck into a stairwell beside a dirty white apartment block to see if anyone is on my trail. When no one shows, I make for the street that runs parallel to Leningradskiy Prospekt, sticking to the shadows and steering clear of anything that looks like it could house a CCTV camera.

At the rear of No. 56, I ease past the barrier and a plethora of warning signs, and find my way to an open fire exit. I listen for a moment, then shine my cell's flashlight up the stairwell. The beam sweeps across a huge pile of cinderblocks, so I head down instead.

I push through a set of double doors into a basement partially illuminated by vehicle headlights filtered through rows of glass bricks at sidewalk level. I can see a candle flickering in the far corner.

'Doctor Cain?' A pause. *'Joshua?'*

I move closer. Metal workbenches are bracketed to the walls at waist level. Broken equipment litters the floor. The last vestiges of a laboratory.

'Were you followed?'

The candlelight throws uneven shapes across Sasha's face as she steps out of the shadows. My breath catches in my throat. Just for a moment, I'm looking at Hope. She's wearing jeans and a leather jacket. Her breath billows in the chill air.

'I don't think so. What made you change your mind?'

'If Vladimir taught me one thing, it is the value of due diligence. You are quite famous, online. It seems that we have both suffered. You rather more than me. I am sorry for the runaround – is that the word? I needed to take precautions. Vladimir is an unpredictable man. Anya has worked for him since we separated. Anything suspicious, she reports.'

My phone-beam picks out the remnants of old fires and half a dozen discarded syringes.

'Why here?'

'You need to see this place before they turn it into million-dollar condos.'

Intuitives. That's what they called them. People with the most extraordinary gifts.

When Yuri Andropov, the head of the KGB, decreed in 1971 that psychics should be drafted into the service of the state, schools, academies, universities and orphanages were scoured across the vast territories of the USSR for anyone with any gift that was out of the ordinary. It was the beginning of a top-secret recruitment drive that continued until the USSR collapsed at the end of 1991.

'They stayed here, in a dormitory, three floors above the laboratory.'

She glances up, then looks back at me. 'My father nicknamed them his *vorob'i*. His sparrows.'

'How old were you?'

'A teenager. Fifteen, sixteen, during the period Papa worked closely with them. I lived with my parents until I turned eighteen, which is when Vladimir and I married. You might wonder why, but he wasn't always the way he is now. Ambitious, yes, but not cruel.'

'The *vorob'i* . . . ?'

'My father would bring the little ones home so my mother could cook for them.'

She tells me about Kolya, who could slide a hand through a steel box and remove a key, a watch or a spoon from inside it. Andrei, who could extract a thought from her head and make it his own. He could put his thoughts into her head too. And then there was Artyom, who could bend iron bars by looking at them. Galina, who could turn lead into silver. And Vitaliy, who could see the future—

A noise.

In the shadows, somewhere behind her.

I point my phone-beam.

At the opposite end of the room to the stairwell, a couple of rats the size of cats pick their way through a pile of rubble at the base of a short flight of steps leading up to the *prospekt*.

I throw a brick at them and they scuttle into a vent.

Sasha holds up the candle and lights a cigarette. 'Back then, it didn't matter if you were an athlete, a chess player or a psychic – if you showed promise, the state took you to a school or an academy, groomed you, and turned you into something exceptional.'

The *vorob'i*, she says, were no different.

'And Vladimir?'

'Vladimir's job was to account for every last kopek the state provided for the many projects it funded my father to carry out.'

She blows a thin stream of smoke through her lips.

'This may sound strange, Joshua, but I don't know how he made his money. I am very sure, however, it involved the *vorob'i*.'

'What makes you say that?'

'When the USSR broke apart, my father was a sick man. He only had a few months to live. Vladimir was in the laboratory when his state sponsors, the KGB and the GRU, picked up the phones again.' She sighs. 'But in the new Russia, they want to know only one thing: how do we get rich?'

She drops the cigarette by her feet and glances up.

'I was helping my mother to nurse my father a few days before he died. It was evening, and Vladimir arrived to take me home.

When my father realized he was in the room, he asked my mother and me to leave the two of them alone. He wanted to talk to Vladimir about some business. I did as he said, but listened at the door.

'My father asked Vladimir about his plans for the institute. It was very important, he said, now that the state had been replaced by the new system – now the Cold War was over – that the *vorob'i* went home, back to their parents. But Vladimir refused to listen.'

'Why?'

'He told my father that they were now *imushchestvo*.'

'What does that mean?'

'Assets.'

A siren wails on the *prospekt*. She lights up another cigarette.

'That was when I realized how much he had changed. Whatever his former sponsors were out to get, Vladimir wanted to have it, too. And it frightened me very much. *He* frightened me.'

For a moment, I think she is going to cry.

'Sasha, are you aware of any payments made by Vladimir – any transactions at all – to a church in Jerusalem?'

I take a picture of the Church of St Mary Magdalene from my pocket and show it to her.

She studies it, then hands it back. 'No. His foundation is nothing but a facade. I guess you know that. It is there to make him look good. And, for sure, there are business advantages.

'There was only one church I know for certain he took a special interest in outside of his prestige project, the Cathedral of the Holy Trinity – and that's St Alexei's, a monastery in Sarov.

'Two years ago, I saw a letter from the episcopacy on his desk. The Bishop of Sarov acknowledging receipt of his donation. Vladimir slid it swiftly into a drawer and asked if I had seen it. I said no, of course. The next day, he asked me again. I told him I didn't know anything.'

'Did it have numbers?'

'It did. Hundreds of millions of roubles.'

'Vladimir is a Muslim, isn't he?'

'Yes. His mother was Ukrainian. His father was a Tatar, from the Volga region, who was killed in a gunfight in Donetsk in 1996. All his life, Vladimir has wanted respectability. Coming to Moscow, acquiring the habits of Russians – *being* Russian, being accepted, giving money to the church – that was his game plan.'

'Did he ever talk about someone called Al-Mohandis?'

She frowns.

'It means the Engineer. I don't know what it might be in Russian.'

'The same. *Inzheneer.*'

'A very striking individual. Dark hair. Pale skin. Blue, blue eyes . . .'

She shakes her head. 'I don't think so. Why?'

'Because I believe this man may have been an intuitive. And I think Vladimir may be using him for something.'

'Then it will be about money. Always it is about money.' She grinds her cigarette underfoot. 'His friends are very powerful.'

'Powerful enough to smuggle and trade nuclear materials?'

'If it pays, yes.'

'What about his relationship with your father?'

'My father was a very good man. It wasn't just the fate of the *vorob'i* that they fought over. Toward the end, they barely spoke.'

'Why?'

'Because he accused my father of withholding data.'

'What kind of data?'

'Data that he claimed belonged to the state.'

'Was he right?'

'No. Papa was a patriot.'

'Why did you agree to see me, Sasha?'

'Because of what you said to me in the shop.'

'About consciousness?'

'About a particular aspect of it. You asked if I thought it persisted when we die.'

'Do you?'

'Yes.'

'Why?'

'Because my father believed it. And my father was a very, very rational man.'

'He once spoke to my mentor about it.'

'The friend you were buying the book for?'

I nod. 'Ted van Buren.'

'I remember him. He came to visit Papa before he died.'

'Ted told me your father kept an archive. That you were its custodian.'

'Part of the conditions of the divorce was that I hand it to Vladimir.'

'Why?'

'He was obsessed with it.'

'Your father's *personal* archive?'

'Personal, but huge. Thousands of files. Very academic. Vladimir used to go through it. Always looking for something.'

'What?'

'I assumed the thing he accused my father of withholding.'

'What did he think we were capable of, ultimately?'

'My father?'

'Yes.'

'What do you mean by "we"?'

'We humans.'

'He told me we have barely begun to know ourselves.'

'Was he religious?'

'He grew up in an era in which the state sought to eradicate religion, Joshua. We lived well. It would have been dangerous, given his position, for him to have discussed it with us. But . . .'

'Yes?'

'Before he died, he said it was important – no, vital – that we lead good lives, because, in the end, it is we who judge ourselves.'

I'm about to ask her what he meant by this, when we both hear a noise.

A dog barks and a flashlight snaps on.

53

I PULL SASHA BACK TO WHERE I'D SEEN THE RATS – THE SHORT flight of steps leading up to the *prospekt*. I turn to see a German Shepherd at the base of the stairwell.

Behind me, Sasha is trying to force the door. I pick up a brick, tell her to step aside, and smash it down. The lock clatters to the floor.

The flashlight sweeps toward us. The dog snarls, bounds across the room and leaps at me. I bring the brick down on its head. The animal yelps, hits the ground and doesn't get up.

A second later, I am met by a blast of freezing air and the thunderous noise of the six-lane highway as Sasha kicks open the door.

She is through and out. I follow her.

It has started to snow. I look right and see the lights of the Metro station several hundred meters away. I grab hold of her arm and pull her toward it, but at that moment a group of men in long coats appear from a side street.

We turn and walk in the opposite direction, but the same thing happens. A man wearing a balaclava emerges from the basement. He is less than thirty meters from us, and holding a pistol.

I glance across to the far side of the *prospekt*, then pull Sasha through a momentary break in the traffic on the three northbound lanes. My leg almost gives out, but adrenaline forces me on. A truck barrels past. The snow catches in its headlights. A car swerves. Another blasts its horn.

We make it to the central barrier. I snatch another glance over my shoulder. Balaclava Man is where we left him – waiting for another break. I scan the southbound lanes, readying myself for the crossing, when I see two skinheads walking along its sidewalk toward us. There's no mistaking their intent.

Sasha spots them. Lets out an awful cry. 'I can't . . . If he catches me . . .'

One of the men in long coats steps into the slow lane of the northbound and holds up a hand.

It's gripping the butt of an automatic.

Tires squeal as the traffic grinds to a halt.

I turn back at the moment Sasha steps in front of a truck.

The driver slams on his brakes, but it still takes fifty meters to stop.

The vehicles behind do the same.

When I reach her, she's lying face up in the center lane. The flickering lights of the *prospekt* make her eyes sparkle, but only for a moment.

She's still alive.

I kneel beside her and brush a lock of hair from her face.

'Sasha . . .'

She's slipping fast.

Behind me, there's a commotion. Shouting. Barked orders. I take hold of her hand, feel her pulse. It's feathery. Almost gone.

'Stay with me, Sasha . . .'

Somebody grabs me and clamps a hand around my mouth.

They drag me up and backwards. I fight, I bite, I kick. Not because I know I can win, but because I have just heard the words that I used to my dying wife.

Stay with me.

Something unforgiving crashes down on the back of my head.

The Jeep is slewed across the road and the roof has been torn off. It's dark, except for the glow from one of the headlamps of the Kenworth, which has careered into a tree. Silence is now returning to this stretch of no-man's-land – a shortcut between the edge of town and the interstate. Then the cicadas resume their singing.

Hope's head has been thrown back. Her face is tilted my way. Her eyes are open. She's bleeding heavily. Part of the steering wheel has sheared off and driven itself into her chest.

I release my belt. There's a first-aid kit in the trunk.

I try to get out, but the left side of my body won't work.

'Oh, Josh . . .'

Her breath comes in tiny gasps. I can barely hear her.

'Don't . . .'

'I'm sorry.'

'Please. Don't speak.'

Tears are rolling down my face.

'No . . . Josh. It's . . . all right.'

I try to reach out to her. If I can just staunch the flow of blood from her chest . . .

'Hang on,' I hear myself saying. 'Help will be here . . . any moment.'

But help doesn't come.

I take her left hand in my right, the only part of me I can move. How did it get so cold already?

I look into her eyes. Feel her pulse weakening.

'Look at me,' I tell her.

She raises her eyes.

'Stay with me. Help's on its way.'

'It's OK . . . Josh. Everything's . . . OK.'

'Stay with me . . .'

I don't know how, but she manages to smile. 'Look,' she says.

I raise my eyes.

'See the stars . . . ?'

I look away. I have never seen so many.

And that's when she slips away.

54

I'm saying it over and over as I come to. My face is wet with tears. There's a patch of oil by my feet. I try to move, but I can't. All I can do is fractionally raise my head.

I'm in some kind of warehouse, tied to a chair. I blink under the lights. When the color kicks in, I see that the oil is blood. My right eye feels like somebody has been using it for target practice. The place is dilapidated, semi-abandoned. I've been stripped of my jacket and am shivering uncontrollably. I don't know how long I've been out. I glance through a hole in one of the shit-caked windows. I can see that the snow has stopped falling, but it is still night.

Sitting in front of me on some upturned wooden crates are three of the men I saw on the sidewalk. One of them clutches a wrench; another cradles a pistol. The third smokes while he stares at me.

I hear a car door open and close.

Footsteps.

A shadow falls across the concrete. The hairs lift on the back of my neck. The thug with the cigarette jumps up, but is waved back to his seat.

The Napoleon image in Gapes's cabin didn't do Ilitch justice. He's tall, and workouts – aided by a little surgical intervention – have driven away the pasty pallor of his youth. He has to be sixty-five, but his swarthy complexion makes him look younger. A cashmere coat is draped across his shoulders.

'What did you want with Sasha?' His voice, heavily accented, is unexpectedly soft.

'A book.'

He wags a finger.

The guy with the wrench gets to his feet.

'Well, of course. Colonel Cain, the ex-personal physician of the President of the United States, just happens to be in town on a book-buying spree.'

I say nothing. The guy with the wrench flexes his fingers around its handle, like a hitter getting the feel of his bat.

'I have good news for you, Colonel. My employees, as you can see, are only too eager to dispense some summary justice.

'Some are old enough to remember Sasha extremely well. Under the circumstances, I wouldn't consider it disloyal if any of them were to tell me that they felt a little angry at being in the presence of the man who killed the woman they once adored.'

'I didn't kill her.'

'We'll let the FSB be the judge of that. They are very keen to speak with you. Have you ever been to Lefortovo? No, of course you haven't. This is your first time in Moscow. The basement there used to flood, so I'm told. It doesn't any longer.

'It is no business of mine what they do to you there. But I imagine they will be interested in what you and Sasha had to discuss in the former laboratory of my erstwhile father-in-law, M. M. Kalunin. And will want to know, too, why you were keen to make a donation to a Russian Orthodox church in Jerusalem.'

He turns to the guy with the wrench, who takes up position behind me.

'The United States Secret Service is investigating you,' I blurt.

'So? Everything is negotiable. The FSB will wish to talk about this, too. Not that it will help you. The transcript of your discussion with Mr Kantner is already on the desk of the man waiting for you at Lefortovo. I have examined it myself. It clearly points to the fact that your visit here is unofficial. You may even be in breach of the terms of your visa.

'Things are changing in Russia, as they are in your country. We

330

too have a new president. Our security service, however, still adheres to the old rules. All of this can be discussed over the next few hours. But in two days' time, nobody is going to miss a doctor, even one as famous as you, who went for a walk in the wrong part of Moscow.'

I hear the scrape of a shoe on the concrete behind me, and brace myself for a blow that doesn't come. Ilitch turns and walks away.

Somebody grasps my arms and hauls me to my feet.

There's an unmarked van at the back of the building. A black Audi directly behind it, lights on, engine running.

They drag me across the concrete and throw me in the back of the van.

My face hits the floor. A moment before the doors slam shut, I catch a glimpse of Ilitch clambering into the back of his Mercedes.

We drive for ten miles or so on a road that bends to the right. It's freezing cold. I curl myself into a ball. The driver takes two more right turns and drives a hundred meters or so before he hits the brakes with such force I slam into the cab wall.

Yells from the front, the crashing of gears.

We fly into reverse.

A horn blares. We skid, hit something solid. Stop.

The driver's door opens. There's a shout and two shots.

From behind, a volley of automatic fire, more shouting, two more blasts.

The doors fly open and I'm confronted by a figure in a black balaclava gripping a pump-action shotgun.

He hauls me out. We're on a main road, in an industrial area. Watery yellow light bleeds from a lone streetlamp. The van has reversed into a bollard. Just behind it, slewed across the road, the black Audi is riddled with bullets.

The guy who's grabbed me is flanked by another, also masked. They drag me toward one of two gunmetal BMWs parked at the side of the road.

They throw me into the trunk and slam it shut.

We make a fast turn. Thirty seconds later, we're back at the interchange, and a moment after that, accelerating fast. This time, it's impossible to know which way we're going.

After another fifteen minutes, we turn off and drive for about a mile before coming to a stop. I hear the passenger door open.

The lid pops and I catch a glimpse of a three-quarter moon through the branches of a tree and a black-clad figure against it.

I try to get up, but the whole of my right side is numb.

The man says something and pushes me back into the trunk. Throws a blanket over me. Leans forward. There's something in his hand.

I know that voice.

The needle glints in the moonlight. He pulls up my left sleeve and jabs it into my upper arm.

I'm sinking.

But I know that voice . . .

55

I CAN SMELL DISINFECTANT AND BOILED MEAT.

I close my eyes and open them again. I didn't imagine it. I'm in the bedroom of what looks like a moth-eaten ski chalet, and Dmitri Sergeyev has put a mug of coffee on the table beside me. He says something to a man with a shotgun, who nods and leaves.

He reverses a chair and sits, arms folded on the backrest. He's holding an iPad. 'This *dacha* belongs to a buddy of mine from way back – old-school guy.'

I remember his English from our meeting at the embassy – precise and quaintly idiomatic.

'Far enough from Moscow, I hope, to keep the *siloviki* at a safe distance.'

'*Siloviki*?' I rub the back of my head.

'Corrupt politicians who have navigated their way to extreme wealth, often via the security services. Vladimir Ilitch has acted as banker for most of them – which is why you were on your way to an FSB cell at Lefortovo, and why, fortunately, we've been keeping a very close eye on him.'

'What do you want, Dmitri?'

'A little honesty.'

I prop myself up on the pillow and reach for the coffee.

'Five weeks ago,' he says, 'we intercepted a call to a cellphone tagged to the White House Chief of Staff, your friend, Reuben Kantner. From a business jet over the Southern Rockies, owned and operated by the US Secret Service.

'It reported a very recent raid, and instructed him to assemble the key players at Camp David. The caller, of course, was you.

'Approximately three hours later, you talked again, via your personal cell, from Joint Base Anacostia–Bolling. You referred to something called the Grid, which you claimed had been part-funded by Ilitch. You also mentioned Professor M. M. Kalunin, his institute, the program he'd worked on during the Soviet era, and Thompson's refusal to cancel the Jerusalem conference.'

He taps his iPad and hands it to me.

Cyrillic letters are interspersed among the telemetry running across the top of the screen. The shot is familiar. I can see the lenticular curve of the NSA's Bluffdale facility, the salt-white sand and, in the bottom right corner, the Canyon. A curl of black smoke drifts from a vent at the top of the bunker toward Salt Lake City.

'If you look very carefully,' Sergeyev says, 'you'll spot two helicopters on the ground, between the perimeter and the bunker.'

I've always been amazed at what you can see from space.

'Most notably,' he adds, 'this is the first instance we can identify during the modern era of one US federal agency taking down another.'

He lets me absorb this.

'Let us now cut to our presidents' scheduled meeting in Moscow – the trip that you and I were busy planning. The trip that was canceled the day after your unfortunate accident in the V-22.

'Your president spoke with mine on the telephone about this. He was polite and apologetic and explained his reasoning: that his priority now was to focus on the Jerusalem peace conference, where they should jointly make the announcement they would have made in Moscow.'

'What announcement?'

'I'm not sure if you knew this, Joshua, but Christy Byford and I liaised regularly on the WMD search-and-destroy mission.'

I did know. In the Sit Room, before we launched the Bluffdale mission, in response to Thompson's plea that the revelation of a Russian link to the Grid should not disrupt his developing relationship with his opposite number, Christy had told me she and Reuben were going to collaborate on a narrative for Sergeyev's benefit.

'What announcement?' I repeat.

'Judging by the call you made to Kantner, Joshua, you are already aware that Ilitch used every trick in the book to launder his and the *silovikis'* money. Donations to bogus charitable causes are just the tip of the iceberg. But he knew that even Sledkom – our generally toothless anti-corruption agency – would catch up with him at some point.

'So, six years ago, he began to invest his money in American tech. He and his friends didn't mind the risk, because they were confident of the protection your intelligence community gives to its top-secret programs in Silicon Valley and elsewhere. Russian mafia funding helps them avoid the scrutiny of your congressional oversight system.

'In Moscow, your president and mine were going to expose these strategies by the military-industrial complex to control a sizeable portion of your trillion-dollar defense and security budget, and thus maintain the cycle of threat, not just between our two countries, but globally.'

Graham's reveal about the encrypted Ilitch file on Lefortz's classified server suddenly makes sense. Lefortz, the most trusted guy in the White House, had been conducting the President's probe into this snake pit. And even Reuben hadn't known about it. *Why not Reuben?*

'The GRU and the FSB are engaged in a turf war also – have been for decades. Regrettably, not everyone in my agency takes seriously the oath they swore to protect our new leader. But I do. And he takes very seriously the relationship he has begun to forge with yours.'

'Who do you *really* work for, Dmitri?'

'My president, Joshua. My job is to watch his back. Which is why you and I find ourselves here. Because I'm struggling to completely understand the sequence of events we have already touched upon: the Utah raid, you of all people talking about the threat this place presented, the leaders of every US intel agency assembling at Camp David, and your V-22 crash. Then your president changing his mind about Moscow and unveiling the Jerusalem event.'

He pauses for a moment, and chews on his lower lip.

'Last night, Joshua, we tracked another of your calls to Kantner. You drew his attention to Patriarch Nikolai not showing up in Jerusalem, and to the blast radius from a church on the Mount of Olives. The blast radius of *what*? I suspect Ilitch and the FSB know, because they took the trouble to pick you up last night.'

He pauses again.

'So, if we're going to stop what you fear is about to happen, Joshua, you are going to need to tell me everything you know.'

The Soviet psi program left ours at the starting gate, Sergeyev says. While the CIA and INSCOM invested around $20 million on psi, his fellow countrymen spent around a billion.

All those schools, universities and academies scoured by the KGB for intuitives? All that money lavished on M. M. Kalunin's institute? Though multi-faceted, the institute's mission was dominated by one over-arching Cold War objective: the psychokinetic detonation of a US nuclear weapon on US soil.

We pull onto a two-lane stretch of road skirting the city of Nizhny Novgorod, and head into the leading edge of an east–west front that will take at least a day to blow over.

Sergeyev sits up front. Vasiliy, his shotgun-toting sidekick, drives. Between snow flurries, I get a fleeting impression of impenetrable forest, grime-stained ribbon settlements, faded road signs and the occasional skeleton of an abandoned Soviet-era vehicle. Behind us, there's a second BMW with Vasiliy's friends in it – the three other heavies responsible for springing me on the Moscow ring road.

We're heading for a place that used to be known as Arzamas-16. Its purpose was to design, develop and build nuclear weapons. The road signs now call it Sarov, but little else seems to have changed. It continues to be known as a ZATO: a *zakrytoe administrativno-*

territorial'noe obrazovanie; in essence, a closed military city. During the Soviet era, there were more than fifty ZATOs dedicated to the development and production of strategic weapons systems. Thirty years on, forty or so still remain.

Ilitch, Sergeyev says, made his first billion from Russia's vast mineral resources: titanium, magnesium, nickel, gold, copper, iron ore, platinum and diamonds. He had assets that could cut the costly upstream phase of the mining process from years to weeks. He sold his former sponsors in the KGB and the GRU – men who rubbed shoulders with Vladimir Putin and went on to share his investment strategies – on the idea of using the intuitives to pinpoint where to dig and drill.

The *siloviki* became his protectors – along with the upper echelons of the Russian Orthodox Church, which, in Putin's time, morphed into a de facto arm of the state, united in the suppression of unseemly non-Russian tendencies such as protest, liberalism and homosexuality.

Sergeyev's team is sifting through historic communications traffic between St Alexei's and Ilitch's foundation, as well as the files held by the GRU on M. M. Kalunin's institute. They are looking for pointers to, and connections between, the foundation and the monastery of St Alexei.

The monastery lies between the edge of the city and its northwest perimeter. Sergeyev shows me photos of thick, fortified walls, a moat, a drawbridge, towers at each of its four corners and cloisters where the monks live and worship.

I am about to go behind the lines in a country that is still at war with mine.

56

SERGEYEV PICKS UP DOCUMENTS TRANSMITTED TO HIM FROM Moscow at a field office outside Nizhny. They identify us as an inspection team with the 12th Chief Directorate, the branch of the military charged with nuclear security. I am a full colonel and Sergeyev is my deputy. FSB at the Sarov checkpoint will challenge us because they won't have any notification of a visit, but that's the whole point of a no-notice shock-inspection.

It's coming up to 6 p.m., but the snow, the low cloud and the smoke from Nizhny's factories make it feel as if we're still in the Dark Ages. Sergeyev leafs through the paperwork. I guess I shouldn't be surprised by anything in Russia anymore, but the fact that the GRU transmits things it wants to keep ultra-secure by fax is a good one.

'What do you know about Senator Abnarth?' he asks me suddenly.

'Nothing, except that his fingerprints are all over this.'

'As part of my job to understand Thompson, we needed to know whether his talk of justice, the desire for peace and his intention to dismantle the excesses of the military economy were real or for show. It was one of the reasons I was told to get close to you. And to try and fathom his relationship with Abnarth.'

I agree Abnarth is key.

Abnarth gave Reuben his first job on the Hill.

Abnarth, the dealmaker and kingmaker, the doyen of Washington's political scene, anointed Thompson.

338

Abnarth used to chair the Senate Select Committee on Intelligence.

Abnarth insisted that funds were appropriated from the secretly resurrected remote viewing program into the development of hardware for the exploration of consciousness.

'Is Abnarth in Jerusalem?'

Sergeyev nods. 'And it's unlikely he'd go there knowing somebody would detonate a bomb, don't you think? But maybe this has something to do with it.'

He passes me his iPad. Onscreen is a typewritten document entitled 'Toward a Unification of the Abrahamic Faiths'.

'A paper written by an idealistic twenty-one-year-old trainee lawyer and would-be politician with a master's degree in theology. It sets out, with some zeal, how the three great monotheistic religions – Islam, Judaism, Christianity – are just marginally different slants on the same faith.

'I have to say, as a piece of work, it is scarcely original – but embarrassing nonetheless, if you're running as the Democratic Congressman for the 37th District of the great, Bible-thumping State of Texas.'

I don't know how Sergeyev came by it, or how he knows it was Abnarth who made it vanish from the archives of Princeton, Thompson's alma mater, where it had presumably languished until he first ran for public office.

'Did Sasha voice the suspicion,' Sergeyev asks, 'harbored by her father's military paymasters at the time, that he had withheld certain aspects of his research?'

'Yes. She said Ilitch had been obsessed with their discovery. Why?'

'There's a seminary in New York City. The Church of St Simeon on the Lower East Side. During the Pope's last trip to the US, he and Thompson met there. You may recall the photos. A paparazzo managed to get shots of the two of them praying together. They were all over the papers.' He gives me a hint of a smile. 'Two days later, a call was placed between the Oval Office and the Holy See.'

The person who made the call, he says, wasn't Thompson.

It was Abnarth.

'We believe the recipient was Cardinal Rafaello Alonzo, the Pope's senior adviser. Abnarth said to him: "Do we agree?" Alonzo gave a positive response. We believe this relates to some kind of shared view, or a document, perhaps, that had passed between the Pope and Thompson when they went into that church.'

I think back to my hypnotherapy session with Thompson – the origins of his visceral antipathy to organized religion, his telling me that it was the destructive impact of faith that his administration was finally going to address. Their NYC love-in – that apparently spontaneous decision to pray together – was their second meeting. The first was while Thompson had been on the campaign trail in Dallas.

Did Thompson share his thesis at that point?

Or had this already been done by Abnarth?

'Here's something that puzzled both the GRU and the FSB,' Sergeyev says. He passes me several of the faxed sheets. Photographs, taken with a long lens, of the back of a very gaunt, thin man in a thick coat and fur hat, entering a church.

'Two years before the USSR collapsed, the Vatican and Moscow re-established diplomatic relations for the first time in nearly seventy years.

'Shortly before he died, Professor M. M. Kalunin walked into St Clement's, one of the only Roman Catholic churches in Moscow, during a mass. He took a seat somewhere near the front. He was followed and watched the entire time, of course.

'Among those in the congregation, sitting a few places from him, was the apostolic nuncio – the new ambassador. Nothing was seen to pass between the two men, but that doesn't mean that it didn't. Due to the nuncio's diplomatic status, we were unable to detain him, but Kalunin was taken in for questioning and searched.

'He admitted to nothing beyond a desire to feel close to God. If something *had* passed between Kalunin and the nuncio, I invite you to speculate on what that might have been. I also invite you to think about the circumstances we find ourselves in. We have three enlightened men in power – your president, my own and the

Pope – who will come together for the first time in Jerusalem. What might that mean, do you suppose?'

I don't know.

But I do know something.

As I'd sat in a cell several levels below ground questioning Cal Offutt, he'd asked me when the President's nightmares began. Because, he said, the Grid keyed in on events that were beyond the oversight of regular assets at the disposal of our intelligence agencies.

When the Pope and Thompson had disappeared into that church to pray, the intel community had no means of knowing what had passed between them.

Except for the Grid. The meeting had taken place in April. The President's nightmares had started a few days later.

My thoughts are interrupted by Vasiliy slowing to take a turn. I ask Sergeyev what's happening.

'I need a cigarette. And you need some air. The guards at the Sarov checkpoint work in eight-hour shifts. On a night such as this, even the best of them get a little careless at the end of a shift.' He glances at his watch. 'We'll stop here for a half-hour and arrive just before the handover.'

We pull onto the side of the road.

'You are my boss, remember, Joshua. And I need you to act like him. We only get one shot at this. Let us take a walk. There's something else I want to tell you.'

The forest is so dense that, a few meters in, there's barely any snow on the ground. The headlights of the two BMWs have all but vanished. In the glow of Sergeyev's cigarette, I see anxiety on his face.

'When you came to see me in the embassy, you asked about the photograph of me on the tank. Do you remember?'

'Yes. Taken in Chechnya.'

'In 2006 – the year you were fighting the insurgency in Iraq.'

He looks up as a few flakes manage to fall through the canopy.

'I fought that war, first as a lieutenant, then as a captain, fueled by a belief that what we were doing was right. Because the Chechens had violated our land and killed our people.'

He inhales deeply and exhales as he speaks. 'In September 1999, they hit four apartment buildings – two in Moscow, two in provincial cities. More than three hundred civilians died. Over a thousand more were wounded.

'Within a fortnight, President Yeltsin had ordered an all-out assault on Grozny, the Chechen capital. The slaughter was unbelievable. But I was high on anger. So were most of my countrymen. Half a decade later, approval ratings for the war were still through the roof.'

He grinds the stub of his cigarette underfoot and lights another. 'It wasn't until afterward that I was better acquainted with the facts. I began asking questions. About why we'd fought. Who had really gained from it. I even wrote a paper, but it didn't go very far up the chain. Or so I thought.

'A year ago, soon after the election of our new president, I was called to the Kremlin and asked if I would join a commission tasked with analyzing our defense-industrial complex and its value to the economy. I did. I was also able to look deeper into the origins of the Chechen wars.

'The answer to the questions I'd asked was now clear. It had been for a number of years to some journalists who are now dead. The person who stood to gain most was Vladimir Putin. Putin was in charge of the FSB when the apartment bombings took place. All the evidence points to the fact that they were authorized and financed by the FSB. Three months later, Yeltsin resigned and Putin was sworn in.

'Why am I telling you this, Joshua? For two reasons. First, your country doesn't come out of this well either. The origins of the Chechen wars go back to the end of our war in Afghanistan and the many active programs instituted by the CIA to foment unrest in the North Caucasus. To kick us when we were down. They helped to inspire the militancy that gave Putin the excuse he needed to start his war.

'But it doesn't end there. The people who carried out his

orders – the people who still do – are a cadre of young colonels you never see. The cogs in the machine. You have them, too. Ours are drunk on corruption, yours are drunk on winning; at beating the enemy, whoever he is, at any cost.

'Along the way, they have both lost sight of the fact that millions of people are paying the price. Along the way, too, some of them evidently decided that the greatest threat came from their own democratically elected leaders. My guess is when Thompson pulled in the heads of your agencies and they told him they had no knowledge of the Grid, some of them were telling the truth. This is the essence of the secret states our two leaders are committed to exposing. The essence of what has led us here.'

He gestures to the trees that surround us, digs into his pocket and hands me a pair of mirrored Aviators to cover the bruises around my eyes when we get to the perimeter. He flicks his final cigarette into the forest and starts to walk back toward the cars.

'Dmitri?'

He stops and turns.

'Excellent speech. Was it for my benefit, or yours?'

His eyes narrow. 'A little pep talk before we do what we now have to do.'

'You said there were two reasons.'

'The second is a little more personal.' His expression darkens. 'My family. The family you had the kindness to remark upon the day we met. They were killed in the second apartment bombing.'

57

A SIGN BELOW THE WINDOW PROHIBITS PHOTOS. THE FEMALE officer stamps the papers and hands them back. The guard passes them to the driver. They exchange words. The barrier swings up.

Vasiliy guns the engine. We pull up next to the booth.

Right beside the checkpoint is a three-man watchtower.

One of the guards leans over the parapet, a rifle on his shoulder, scanning the traffic going in. Sergeyev winds down his window. Smog and snow swirl in our headlights.

Sergeyev hands over our papers to the guard, who carries them to the officer in the booth. We watch her glance from one document to the next, then pick up the phone.

Ignoring the guard's barked instructions, Sergeyev gets out of the car, walks over to the booth and raps on the window. The officer looks up sharply and puts down her handset. The guard joins in the discussion. I can't hear what's being said. Sergeyev taps the top of his holster and points in our direction.

The guard starts walking toward Vasiliy's side of the BMW. He winds down the window.

The guard leans in. '*Dobry vyecher, Polkovnik.*' He's looking at me.

I know *polkovnik* means colonel. But that's all I know.

He says it again, followed by a bunch of stuff I don't understand at all. He's so close I can smell the meal he just ate.

I see Sergeyev making his way back.

He has our documents in his hand.

'*Neudobnyy*,' I say.

His face goes a shade paler, and he takes a step back.

Sergeyev gets into the passenger seat.

The barrier swings up.

'*Da vai*,' Sergeyev says softly to Vasiliy.

We drive. I'm still holding my breath. Then Vasiliy says something and Sergeyev starts laughing.

'Did you see the look on his face? I thought he was going to shit himself.' He slaps his thigh. 'The guard asks, slightly anxiously, what the 12th Chief Directorate thinks of their security arrangements. And you tell him they're *inconvenient*.'

Vasiliy joins in the laughter. I'm laughing too.

'*Inconvenient*. God, Joshua,' Sergeyev says, 'your talents are many and various, but I never had you down as a comedian.'

The sulfurous wind carries in more snow, sleet and hail from the east, and makes the glow of the monastery lights even more welcoming.

Sergeyev told the FSB guards at the checkpoint that any attempt to inform anybody, in any facility across the city, that we're on our way in, would be tantamount to treason; and that I, as the officer in charge, would relay this to the head of Strategic Rocket Forces on my return to Moscow. He's hopeful this will do the trick.

We'll see. He parks a member of his team among the trees, so he can monitor any calls on a scanner.

Two black-clad priests appear as we enter the courtyard.

We duck beneath an arch. Sergeyev shows them ID and they direct us toward a door at the base of a tower.

Sergeyev's phone buzzes as we reach the first floor. He listens for a moment. 'One of those priests is calling the abbot to alert him to a visit by state officials.'

Sergeyev listens again. 'They are still talking. Yefim is pinpointing the recipient.'

The cloister stretches ahead of us. A burst of hail drums on the roof tiles above our heads like machine-gun fire. A gust of wind through the arches rattles a row of pictures on the wall to our left.

Sergeyev pauses at the second to last of a series of doors, turns the handle and pushes.

The abbot discards his cellphone and struggles to his feet. Judging by the burst capillaries that crisscross his nose and cheeks, he's enjoyed the few earthly pleasures his Spartan surroundings have to offer.

Sergeyev gestures for him to sit. Two of his men file in and take up position either side of the desk.

After fifteen minutes, he leads me back into the hallway.

The abbot knows of no payments made by the Ilitch Foundation.

There's been no restoration work in the decade he has been here.

Nor has the name Ilitch ever been mentioned in any exchanges with officials at the Sarov episcopacy.

The name, in fact, appears to be completely unknown to him.

'You think he's telling the truth?'

'From a brief search of his files, they've found no evidence to the contrary. But without applying any more pressure, it is hard to be sure.'

He heads back inside and closes the door.

I raise the collar of my jacket and walk far enough along the hallway not to hear whatever exchange Vasiliy is about to have with the abbot, and then find myself drawn toward a chink of light on the far side of the cobbled yard. Steps down to a basement. I follow the aroma of incense.

The snow swiftly eradicates my footprints.

At the bottom of the stairwell there's another archway, and beyond it, a small crypt with three simple wooden pews and a stone altar. Two candles on it, which glimmer on the icon screens to their left and right.

A black-robed figure kneels to the left of the entrance, eyes closed, praying. I take a step back, but she hears me and looks up. I place my hand over my heart.

'*Prasteetye.*'

Sorry. It's all I know to say.

I retreat.

'Wait.' A soft command.

I turn. The nun is under five foot tall, in her late seventies perhaps, or early eighties, and wears the Orthodox headgear that's now familiar to me.

'English?'

I shake my head. 'American.'

'You are a very long way from home.'

'It sure feels that way.'

'Please.' She gestures to the pew beside her. 'You came to pray?'

I think better of lying, and say nothing.

'Stay.'

I look at her. It isn't just the word, but the way she says it.

She gestures again toward the pew. 'Just for a moment.'

I sit.

'What is your name?'

'Joshua.'

'Why are you here, Joshua?'

'We are looking for someone.'

'Who?'

'A Muslim. An engineer, maybe. We know very little about him, except that he has black hair and blue, blue eyes.'

'This is a Christian monastery, Joshua. There are no engineers here. And no Muslims.'

I nod and get to my feet. 'I'm very sorry for disturbing you.'

I'm back at the arch before she calls to me again.

'When hope is lost, Joshua, faith can still be found.'

I turn once more.

'Ask the abbot about this man.'

'My colleagues, they—'

'No,' she interrupts me. Her eyes burn brightly. '*You* ask him.'

I cross the courtyard. As I turn into the cloister, I feel broken glass underfoot. The wind has lifted a picture from the wall and smashed it to pieces.

I kneel beside the wrecked frame. Two photographs. The top

one is of a group of monks outside the walls. Some writing. 1911.
I'm guessing it commemorates the year the order was founded.
Below it is another of maybe thirty priests in two rows, one seated,
one standing, in the exact same spot, a century later.

I recognize the abbot, center front, leaner than he is now.

Then my gaze is drawn to the man on his right.

I turn and run to the abbot's quarters. When I enter, Vasiliy has
his pistol drawn. The abbot looks terrified.

I put the photo down on his desk.

'Ask him who this is.'

'Who is he?'

'Just ask him.'

Sergeyev turns to the abbot. There's a brief exchange.

'OK, he remembers this man.'

'He's no longer here?'

'He left, maybe eight or nine years ago.' Sergeyev pauses. 'He
uses a word to describe him that's quite hard to translate.'

'Try me.'

'*Osobyy*. It means—'

The abbot starts to speak again.

Sergeyev talks over him. 'His name was Danilovsky. From Dagestan, in the Caucasus. One of our southern Muslim republics.'

'*Muslim?*'

'Yes. Before he was orphaned, the boy's given name was
Magommed.'

By now, the abbot is babbling and won't stop.

Sergeyev translates.

'Soon after he was placed in the care of the monastery, the boy
converted to Christianity. Maybe the monks forced him, maybe
not. The abbot doesn't know. This was before his time. In any
case, as a young man, Magommed Danilovsky trained here.'

'As what?'

'As a priest. He had a reputation for curing the sick.'

'*Osobyy*,' I say to Sergeyev. 'What does it mean?'

He thinks for a moment. 'Special, I guess.'

'So, he trained as a priest *and* a doctor?'

The abbot shakes his head.
'*Nye doktor. Inzheneer.*'

As we're heading back across the moat, Sergeyev's cell goes. He stops, listens, puts it back in his pocket. His men are waiting for us in the cars. As a precaution, the abbot is coming with us.

'Moscow,' he says. 'They think they're onto something. A pattern in the traffic between the Ilitch Foundation and the Orthodox compound in Jerusalem.'

'What kind of a pattern?'

'Around six months ago, for three weeks, blocks of text were transmitted from a single desktop to an office used by the foundation to coordinate its restoration works. It's impossible for us to decrypt it without a key, but all the blocks begin with a G and comprise letters and numbers that never exceed 256 characters. This pattern is characteristic of digital data converted into a 3D model and consistent with programming language that's used only in computer-aided design.'

'What does it mean?'

Sergeyev shakes his head. 'This I don't know.'

As I follow him to the cars, I remember Yuri at the Cathedral of the Holy Trinity. He invited me to study the fiberglass mold in the ceiling, high above the altar. The angel's head.

Everybody has agreed that it's impossible to smuggle a piece of kit as sophisticated as a nuclear trigger into Jerusalem, because the Needle Eye system will pick it up miles before it gets to the city.

But an intuitive doesn't need explosives. He needs a small, perfectly built sphere he can rapidly collapse – a ballotechnic – which delivers enough heat and pressure to kickstart a tritium and deuterium chain reaction.

58

TIME WAS WHEN I THOUGHT I'D NEVER SEE HOW THIS CAME together, but I use the silence in the car to build it into a coherent pattern: a rehearsal for what I'll say when I get on a phone at the GRU's field HQ outside Nizhny and cough up my guts to Reuben and Christy.

This is how it plays. Thompson comes to office with an agenda of radical reform. He's going to make a lot of people really pissed, but he doesn't care, because fighting injustice is hardwired into him. It always has been.

In his crosshairs is the part of the military-industrial complex that's been beyond oversight for far too long, which he believes is as much responsible for conflict as it is for defending us against it.

He launches a probe, not knowing at this stage that a large part of the black world of US intelligence operations is funded by a cabal of organized criminals in Moscow, and places it in the hands of a man he trusts, literally, with his life – Special Agent in Charge Jim Lefortz.

At the same time, he opens up a backchannel line of communication with the Pope, a man who hasn't been beyond ruffling a few feathers himself.

There is a chance, the two men agree, for the world to hit the reset button, especially now that a radical reformer is also in place in Moscow. But it's going to need all the tact, charm, secrecy and guile that Robert S. Thompson can muster.

In the background, his mentor, Senator Abnarth, has told him about technology the intelligence community has been working on, which, though in its infancy, has the capacity not just to listen in on people, but to see what they're doing, anywhere in the world, in quasi-real time.

Does the operational technology exist, based on what Abnarth saw in an Army weapons lab almost a decade ago, before the tech was demonstrated and they brought the shutters down?

The President doesn't know, nobody does. Not even Abnarth, because all trace of it has somehow disappeared off the map.

When the nightmares begin, Reuben contacts me, desperately concerned about the sanity of his boss.

Thompson and I click, and I'm brought on board.

We veer off the ring road toward Moscow.

I glance at my watch. It's coming up to midnight.

According to the abbot, Danilovsky was nine or ten when he came to the monastery – a single photograph, retrieved from his files, depicts a lanky, raven-haired, blue-eyed boy – one of the very last children, I imagine, to have been recruited under Kalunin's intuitives program.

He may have been one of the assets Ilitch used to prospect for diamonds and precious metals. He certainly had other gifts.

The abbot had heard how, as a young priest, he used to lay his hands on the sick; that there'd been talk of miracles, even.

Six years after the fall of the USSR, Danilovsky lost both of his parents in fighting between separatist Muslim guerillas – Islamist hardliners invading from neighboring Chechnya – and native Dagestanis defending their homeland from radicalism.

He remained at the monastery, at an orphanage that had been established there after the war, a legacy of the many scientists who'd died of radiation-triggered sicknesses in the ZATO.

The boy went to university locally when he was eighteen, to train as an engineer, and because Sarov, as it is now, does nothing other than design, develop, build and maintain Russia's nuclear arsenal, for sure this is where his skills lie. He then became a priest – the ultimate cover for an operative in a sleeper cell.

We can arrest Ilitch. We can arrest all of his cronies. But this isn't going to do any good. All it requires is for one word of the clean-up operation to leak and the Engineer will trigger the bomb.

We can get word to the conference, but we both know that any move to evacuate Jerusalem will also result in him detonating it.

'So,' Sergeyev says, 'we need to get someone into the city who can find this man before it's too late. There are effectively two candidates for the job: me, and you. And I have to choreograph the arrests of Ilitch and his *siloviki* network in Moscow.'

I tell him that's OK. I'd come to the same conclusion.

'Thanks to their friend Ilitch, the FSB are looking for you at every port, airport and border crossing, Joshua, so we are going to have to smuggle you out. But it is when you get to Jerusalem, my friend, that your troubles will really begin.'

He's right. We can't alert the Israelis; they'll start to evacuate the city. And if the Engineer, the *siloviki*, or their allies in the US intelligence community get even a hint of this, our story can only have one ending.

This isn't a negotiation. There will be no warning. There is no deal to be done. The cabal also wants to hit the reset button. It doesn't like Thompson's vision of the world. It likes chaos and fear. It *needs* them to survive and thrive. The Engineer will detonate the bomb, radical Islam will get the blame, the world's security apparatus will swing into high gear, we'll build more guns, bullets and bombs instead of schools and hospitals, and a century after two world wars that killed a hundred million people, we will have learned nothing.

So, where is the device?

And when will he trigger it?

Ilitch's words echo in my head. *In two days' time, nobody is going to miss a doctor, even one as famous as you, who went for a walk in the wrong part of Moscow.*

Sergeyev tells me the Pope arrives tomorrow.

'He lands at Ben Gurion and goes straight to the Hall of the Assembly. His address is scheduled for midday. Thompson speaks directly afterward. This will be the point of maximum impact.'

I look at my watch.

Israel is an hour behind Moscow.

If he is correct, we have a little less than thirteen hours.

'Between here and our field office,' Sergeyev says, 'there's an old fighter base. Angelskoye. It has not been operational for many years, but it has a long and usable runway.'

He looks at the dash. 'In approximately forty minutes, a jet under charter by my department is going to land there, and you are going to get on it. The flight plan says you're a diplomat with data for our conference delegates. Israeli air-traffic control requires we provide them with a code word. Yours, my friend, is Omega.'

Vasiliy has not uttered a word since we came back through the checkpoint. He says something now to Sergeyev.

Sergeyev listens intently. 'There's a car behind us. Impossible to know who, but one of the monks may have raised the alarm.' He speaks again to Vasiliy, then turns back to me. 'We cannot afford for them to follow us to the airfield. And there may be checkpoints ahead.'

'How far to the airfield?'

'Close. Two more exits off the highway.'

We come off at the next ramp and pull onto the curb at the edge of a bend. Trees on both sides of us. A break in the snow. A light mist has descended. The second BMW, with the abbot in it, pulls up behind us. A couple of Vasiliy's friends emerge from the rear doors, weapons at the ready, and disappear into the forest. Yefim, the driver, flicks off his headlights. Sergeyev gets out, runs over and holds a rapid-fire discussion with him.

'What now?' I ask.

'We wait.'

At this time of night, there is no traffic. As I watch through the rear window, a set of beams appears from the direction of the ramp.

We move slowly through the darkness. There are flashes in the trees. I hear what sounds like fireworks.

Vasiliy rejoins the empty highway and accelerates past a hundred before he switches our lights back on.

59

WE GET WAVED DOWN BY A MAN WITH A FLASHLIGHT – SOMEBODY from the private security company hired by the local authorities to keep kids and crack-heads off the site pending its redevelopment into Nizhny's new terminal. A glimpse of Sergeyev's ID and we're through, navigating the weed-ridden roadways and former barrack blocks.

Vasiliy drives slowly. The road opens onto the airfield. We stop and get out. Night turns into day as the guard brings up the flare path.

I hear engines in the distance, above the wind.

To the north, lights blink below the cloud base and then rock as the jet is buffeted by crosswinds on its final approach. Moments later it barrels past us, then veers onto a taxiway and comes to a halt twenty meters from where we're parked.

Airstairs drop beneath the tail and a guy with stubble-length blond hair and a white, short-sleeve shirt with two bars on his epaulettes bounds down them.

He speaks to Sergeyev then turns and shakes my hand.

Sergeyev tells me Vadim is ex-Air Force, now a major in the GRU. A man I can trust. I'm about to make my way toward the steps when he puts a hand on my shoulder. 'How do I contact you?'

'I imagine that you and Christy already have some pretty secure protocols.'

He grins, exposing his gold incisor. 'As secure as can be.'

'I hope that she will now have been alerted to the fact that I've spent two days in Russia. Tell her as much as you need to. Whatever else you need to say to me, route it through her too.'

He gives me a bear hug and I follow Vadim.

'I meant to ask,' Sergeyev yells over the whine of the spooling engines. 'In the monastery, who told you about the photograph?'

'A very helpful nun,' I yell back.

Two minutes later, we pull into the clouds and bank hard toward the south.

60

WE'RE SOMEWHERE OVER THE NORTHEAST MED WHEN VADIM shakes me awake.

'Message from Sergeyev,' he says, handing me his phone.

Joshua – I trust you have slept. I have some more data for you.

Danilovsky left Sarov nine years ago. As a boy, he trained there for a special mission, and still has the ability, using the energy of his mind, to collapse a ballotechnic and trigger a nuclear weapon.

He went initially to Dagestan, a village called Dalukhani. There are reports of a priest answering his description returning to his birthplace, re-embracing the faith of his people and committing himself to jihad. Some say it's here that he took on the nom de guerre Al-Mohandis.

Next set of sightings: Iraq, coinciding with the rise of ISIS, then from all around the Caliphate – first Syria, then Yemen, Egypt, Somalia, Sudan and Niger.

We believe he entered Israel through Gaza, and have to assume the presence of a fully assembled hydrogen bomb somewhere in the city, built by Vladimir Ilitch with a 3D printer, and the support of the *siloviki* and your own intelligence community.

One more thing. The abbot tells me there are no nuns at St Alexei's. Never have been. Get some rest before you reach Jerusalem, my friend. You're going to need it.

I look up to see Vadim beckoning me toward the cockpit.

As I squeeze through the door, the co-pilot turns, smiles, and shakes my hand. His name is Oleg. The sun is up. We are between Turkey and Cyprus, two hundred miles from Ben Gurion, closing on the Israeli coast.

I take the jump-seat and reach for a headset.

'Tel Aviv Identification,' Oleg says into the radio, 'this is Moscjet Two One Two, flight level three-nine-zero, squawking one-six-six-four.'

The response crackles in my headset. 'Moscjet Two One Two, Tel Aviv Identification. Request standby on One-Two-One, Decimal One.'

Oleg switches to the new frequency.

'Moscjet Two One Two, One-Two-One, Decimal One, Moscjet Two One Two, standing by.'

'Moscjet Two One Two, go ahead.'

'Please be advised we are a diplomatic flight with a VIP on board for the conference talks in Jerusalem, codename Omega.'

'Moscjet Two One Two, Tel Aviv Identification, understood. Be advised that Iron Dome is active.'

Vadim and Oleg look at each other.

'What's Iron Dome?' I ask.

'The Israelis' missile shield,' Vadim says.

'For protection against short-range artillery rockets,' Oleg adds. 'Normally it is switched off. But because of the conference it's active, I guess.'

Another crackle in my headset. 'Moscjet Two One Two, this is Tel Aviv Identification. Please repeat name and identification of your VIP. Over.'

Vadim indicates to Oleg that he has the mike. 'Moscjet Two One Two, VIP's codename, as stated, is Omega, repeat . . .'

'Understood, Moscjet Two One Two. To proceed as cleared to Ben Gurion, we need your passenger's *actual* name. Over.'

I think for a moment, as we continue to head toward Israeli airspace at six miles per minute, then signal that I have the mike and dip the transmit button. 'Tel Aviv Identification, VIP's name – *my* name – is Colonel Joshua M. Cain, and I am required—'

The controller jumps in before I can finish. 'Thank you, Omega. Stand by.'

I look again at Vadim. There's an interminable pause.

Then: 'Moscjet Two One Two, Tel Aviv Identification. Continue as cleared to Ben Gurion, landing on Short Runway zero-three, two-one. Be advised you are cleared through Iron Dome and your ground party is waiting for you by the old Israel Defense Force cargo ramp east of the runway. Shalom, Omega. Welcome to Israel.'

Fifteen minutes later, we thump down and taxi to the site of the former IDF base.

I clamber out of my seat while Vadim is still shutting down the jet and make my way toward the back of the plane, where the airstairs are already starting to deploy. I exit as fast as I can into the glare of the apron and the rising temperature.

Hetta is at the wheel of the waiting Suburban, hair tucked into a baseball cap, eyes hidden by Ray-Bans, her freckled face angled toward the sun.

61

HETTA STEERS THE SUBURBAN OFF THE RAMP ONTO ROAD 1. THE
signs all point to Jerusalem.

'The Engineer has built a bomb,' I say.

She keeps her eyes on the road. 'There's no way anyone could
smuggle one in.'

I envy her conviction.

'All they have to do is smuggle in the deuterium and tritium.
Neither carry a signature on their own. Ilitch can do the rest with
a 3D printer.' I pause. 'Why are *you* here?'

'PIAD liaison with Presidential Protection.'

'On whose orders?'

'Cabot's.'

'Cabot's here?'

She nods. 'A message came in two hours ago. Secret Service eyes
only. From Christy. My orders are to pick you up and bring you in.
To avoid a diplomatic incident. Stop you doing anything stupid.
Everyone's seriously on edge. If the Israelis get even a whisper of
this, they'll scrub the conference.

'But the consensus is, nothing can get through. You'll see the
security arrangements when we hit the Needle Eye cordon.'

'Consensus?'

'The considered opinion of our multi-agency intelligence cell.'

'The CIA director. The head of the NSA. The DCI. Are any of
them here?'

'No. Cabot is the only person of any seniority with intelligence connections.'

'That's something, at least.'

'Meaning?'

'We can trust him. Cabot isn't going to sacrifice himself for the intelligence cabal that put this together.'

'Cabal?'

'Us and the Russians.'

Her eyes narrow.

'The Russians?'

'I was in Stockholm, Hetta. I saw Koori.'

'Gapes's trainer?'

'Koori went back to the US. He briefed Christy. I went to Russia.'

She breathes in sharply when I remove my glasses and show her the dents on my face.

'I met Ilitch.'

There's a line of vehicles ahead.

A policeman with a baton is directing ordinary traffic to the two right-hand lanes, diplomatic to the left.

A barrier that looks like a toll booth stretches across the highway – a thing with walls and a roof.

The diplomatic lane is empty. The volume in the others is already building.

A set of lights instructs us to slow and then stop.

A scanner sweeps from front to back, checking out the exterior and interior of the SUV for anything with a signature that looks weapon-like, while a mass-spectrometer takes micro samples of the air.

The merest trace of explosive, biohazard, or a nuclear or chemical material would be flagged to the heavily armed cordon beyond the barrier.

A green light invites us to drive.

I wait till we're accelerating again.

'This device is different. It doesn't need explosive. It's a high-precision, compact nuclear weapon, tiny, potentially, with a yield somewhere in the five-to-ten-kiloton range – enough to destroy half the city. The printer builds the casing to the tolerances required. The Engineer makes it go bang by collapsing the ballotechnic.'

'How?'

'With his mind. He has trained for this since he was a kid.'

She turns and stares at me. 'Fuck you, Josh.'

I point to my face again. 'Believe it or not, this is evidence-based.'

We pass through a cutting. The road narrows from three lanes to two and drops into a valley. I can see tall buildings on the distant hillside.

'Christy's team has compiled a dossier of all the intel on the Engineer. She doesn't believe he's for real.' She pauses. 'Nobody does, Josh. They think he's blowback, like Johansson said – a myth we created, returning to haunt us.'

We slow again. Another checkpoint. A soldier spots our plates and waves us into the left lane. Hetta powers down her window and hands our documents to a guy with a submachine gun. CCTV cameras scan our movements and facial expressions for anything that suggests we might have something to hide.

The spectrometers provide their usual back-up.

We're waved through, toward a cluster of vehicles. Soldiers milling about. Motorcycle outriders. Guys in suits and shades watching the road and the skies.

'What about the President?' I ask.

She pulls in. 'He remains to be convinced, too.'

I spot the Beast, five vehicles ahead.

'You've got five minutes,' she says.

Hetta and I clamber into the back of the Beast. Cabot and Graham flank the President. Christy's brief sits on his lap. I know Sergeyev's dossier on the Engineer will have been passed to him too.

I give them the missing piece to their puzzle: the Russian determination since the seventies to find someone with the talent to trigger an explosion by psychokinesis, the power of thought.

'Insane,' Graham says. 'We have covert WMD inspection teams at key points who've scoured the city, including the Mount of Olives, for a chemical, biological, radiological, nuclear or high-yield device. They're still out there, patrolling, backed by some serious SEAL support, five minutes, max, from any point they need to reach within the city. Trust me, Cain, there's no trace of one.'

Cabot nods, but I can see that he's less convinced.

I lean forward. 'This isn't a conventional nuke. It's a fourth generation weapon with a vengeance. The initiator – a thing called a ballotechnic – is chemically inert. And on their own, tritium and deuterium don't emit detectable radiation. A Geiger counter in the Hall of the Assembly would get more excited by the exit signs. But when subjected to high pressure, that all changes.'

Thompson's jaw clenches. 'This initiative is the reason I became a politician. It's the culmination of everything I've ever worked for. Everything I've dreamed about.'

I sense the ghost of Kit Harper at his shoulder – the kid who threw himself under a train to get away from Pastor Green and his other tormenters at the Southern Cross, the reform school Thompson was sent to by his parents as a fourteen-year-old.

'If I leave and there is a bomb, I'm the worst kind of coward. If I leave and there isn't, I'll be a laughing stock.' His gaze falls on each of us in turn.

'So,' Cabot says, 'we don't have a choice. We have to find him.'

I nod. 'We know the Engineer's name is Danilovsky, and that he's from Dagestan. He's thirty-five years old. There's a photograph of him as a priest from around a decade ago. And the sketch from the cabin.'

'If we circulate them, we risk alerting the Israelis,' Cabot says. 'It'll trigger an evacuation of their key personnel. That happens, it gets flagged by the intelligence community. And picked up by Danilovsky. Then, *boom*.'

'There are in excess of fifteen thousand delegates.' Graham's voice rises an octave as the implications of our task sink in. 'Including two thousand clerics.'

'The device itself,' Cabot says. 'What are we looking for?'

'Something around the size of a baseball,' I say. 'Most of it is made up of the trigger mechanism, the outer shell – the ballotechnic. The core – which contains the nuclear material – is no bigger than a thimble.'

I look at the President. 'When are you onstage?'

'A little over seven hours.'

'And the Pope?'

'Directly before me.'

I share my view that it's highly unlikely the Engineer will detonate the bomb until he has both star performers in his sights. And the Pope doesn't land at Ben Gurion for another three hours.

Cabot rolls up his sleeves. 'OK, so we put the delegate list back under the microscope.'

'And then some.' Graham turns to Hetta. As liaison between PIAD and the President's protection detail, she must mastermind the hunt.

'OK. So let's get back to the Hall.'

Cabot glances significantly at us both. We can pull in around a dozen other Secret Service personnel, but they don't get to know what we are doing.

Hetta and I return to her Suburban and hitch ourselves to the back of the motorcade. We're joined by four Israeli motorcycle outriders, who fire up their lightbars and sirens.

At the city's outer limits another huge sign directs regular traffic to the left, badged conference vehicles to the right.

I'm filled with the dread I felt after returning from Vermont, when I sat in the guest room with Hope's ghost and Jack's portrait.

The outriders ignore the stop lights at the next junction, wave other road users out of the way, and the motorcade peels off to the right, toward the Hall of the Assembly.

I tell Hetta not to follow.

She brakes as the lights turn red.

'This isn't right. Gapes directed us to the Church of St Mary Magdalene.'

'You heard Graham. There's nothing there.'

'Then we need to look again.'

'No. They need our eyes-on in the Hall of the Assembly.' She indicates right, grips the wheel and stares resolutely at the lights, waiting for them to change.

'Why did Lefortz assign you to me that night?' I ask. 'At the tower.'

'I happened to be on duty.'

'Happened to be?'

'OK, he said you needed protection.'

'But why you? You weren't Presidential Protection. You were PIAD. A threat analyst, not a bullet catcher.'

She drums her fingers on the rim of the wheel. 'I don't know.'

'He told me. You were the only person he could trust. Thompson had charged him with a clandestine probe into the misdemeanors of that part of our intelligence community which is beyond oversight, and using Russian mafia money to fund the Grid and other deeply classified programs. Thompson knew his world was about to turn dark; that the knives would be out for him.

'There was no one he could trust except Lefortz. And no one Lefortz could trust except you.'

She glances at me.

'I'm asking you to trust *me*, Hetta, the way he did.'

The lights change.

She cancels the indicator and makes a left.

62

BY THE EAST WALL OF THE TEMPLE MOUNT, ACROSS THE KIDRON
Valley, a narrow road leads up to the Mount of Olives. The sign
says Al-Mansuriya Street. We take it.

At this hour, and with all the security in the central part of the
city, there are only a handful of tourists making their way to the
holy sites and even fewer going to the Mount of Olives itself.

Fifty meters up, there's another checkpoint. A couple of Israeli
soldiers emerge from behind a stack of sandbags, flag us down,
check our passes, smile at Hetta and wave us through.

Hetta takes the turning a hundred and fifty meters further on,
but a set of gates stops us from going further.

We park and get out.

A sign in Russian and English lets us know we've reached the
Church of St Mary Magdalene in the Garden of Gethsemane and
that it opens at 9 a.m. I try the gates. They're padlocked.

I stare through the two-centimeter-wide gap. Beyond a grove of
trees, I spot the gold domes. A warm wind carries the scent of
earth and pine. Birdsong breaks the silence, and somewhere distant a *mu'ezzin* calls the faithful to prayer.

I haul myself to the top of the gates, turn and give Hetta my
hand. Once inside, we make our way through the trees to the steps
at the base of the entrance.

I am contemplating my next move when the doors open and a
nun appears. We stare at each other for several moments.

Hetta walks up the steps and produces her badge.

The nun peers at it over the top of her glasses. 'God *damn* it,' she says under her breath.

All of a sudden, I'm in New Jersey.

Hetta looks like she's been slapped in the face. 'Who are you, ma'am?'

'Sister Martha. And you're trespassing.' She stares at Hetta's ID. 'This is the third inspection of our church in as many days.'

'I know, ma'am. I'm sorry. My associate and I, we were hoping we could come in and take another look around.'

'I just *said* . . .' Sister Martha checks herself. 'Of course. Forgive me. You're doing your job. My sisters are at prayer. *You* may enter, but he can't.'

She gestures behind her to the singing I can now hear beyond the thick wooden doors. 'No men allowed during the liturgy.'

Hetta turns and hands me her phone. 'Read this. Christy's intelligence assessment.'

She follows Sister Martha inside. The door bangs shut.

I walk into the garden and sit on a wall that looks out over the Old City. I open the attachment and scroll down.

Christy's team has used a form of artificial intelligence – machine learning – to sift Engineer sightings over the past decade.

Some of the references come from classified assessments; others from open-source accounts: papers, blogs, websites, Twitter feeds, Facebook. They've been fed back into something like the pattern-mining search algorithm we used to scan the images from the cabin.

The places name-check against many of those identified by Sergeyev: Iraq, Syria, Yemen, Egypt, Somalia, Sudan. Christy's geeks plotted the sightings against accounts of unrest. They'd matched his reported movements against shootings, bomb blasts, riots: all the usual trace elements of high- and low-intensity conflict.

And they discovered the opposite of what they expected.

The locations he appeared to have visited were remarkable for their absence of violence.

Which is what led Christy and her team to conclude that we were chasing a ghost. Johansson's blowback. That the Engineer really was a myth.

And the chatter? All those snippets picked up from the jihadist community in the backwaters of the Web?

She doesn't know.

I do, though. Cover, deliberately planted. The cabal kicking over its traces.

Only, I can't prove it right now. I can't prove anything.

I look up. Beyond the Dome of the Rock – the spot where Muslims believe Mohammed was taken to heaven – I can make out the Hall of the Assembly.

It's coming up to six-thirty. In an hour, Thompson and his fellow leaders gather in preparation for the day's agenda.

At nine, the Pope lands.

At eleven, he arrives at the venue.

At midday, he makes his speech.

Then Thompson takes to the podium.

I stare out across the Old City, then turn and look back up the Mount to its summit.

What do *I* see?

Through the trees, a tower.

The doors of the church open. Four or five doves perched above the entrance take flight as Hetta rushes down the steps.

'Nothing,' she says when she reaches me. 'I told you. The place is clear. Just a bunch of nuns.'

Sister Martha reappears.

'What in God's name are you looking *for*?'

As Hetta draws breath to answer, her phone vibrates in my hand. I look at the screen. Graham. She takes it and walks to a part of the garden where she won't be overheard.

Sister Martha comes and sits next to me.

'How long have you lived here?' I ask.

'Fifty-three years.'

'Where are you from?'

'Hoboken. You?'

'No fixed abode.'

'And right this minute?'

I manage a smile. 'I was thinking about the priest at my father's funeral. He spoke about Jesus coming like a thief in the night. I was twelve. I had no idea what that meant – I still don't – but I've just remembered that this is the place Christ spoke those words.'

'Yes,' she says. 'The day and the hour unknown. Therefore, keep watch, because you know not on what day your Lord will come.'

She takes my hand in hers. 'What's your name?'

I tell her.

'Do you believe in God, Joshua?'

There's a noise behind me.

Hetta bounds around the corner of the church. 'Josh,' she blurts, seemingly oblivious to Sister Martha's presence. 'We've got to get back. Graham is going nuts and Cabot wants to kill us.'

I let go of Sister Martha's hand and stare back up toward the tower.

Do I believe in God?

The very first words Gapes spoke to me.

Hetta shields her eyes against the sun. 'What is that?'

'It marks the spot where Christ ascended. We're looking in the wrong direction, Hetta. With all those spooks looking over our shoulder, Duke would never have pointed you and me straight to it. He's aimed us toward the zone, and left the rest to us. Do you have a secure line to Christy?' I get to my feet. 'I need a place name on the Iraq–Syria border.'

'Something's going to happen, isn't it? I feel it.' Sister Martha takes my hand in hers again. 'Don't you?'

The Orthodox Church compound we glimpse through another set of locked gates comprises a chapel, a convent and a hostel. Hetta and I haul ourselves over these too, and drop to the gravel. When I look up, I see a beautifully simple stone church and, behind it, four stories high, arches on each level, stark in the bright white sunlight, the tower.

We walk toward it, past the church and up a flight of steps.

I give the door a tug, expecting it to be locked. It isn't. The hinges groan as it swings open.

We take a last look around. Nothing stirs. We head inside. The stairwell provides a glimpse of the level above. A breeze gets up and rushes past my face.

I stop.

'What is it?' Hetta asks.

'He's here.'

'How do you know?'

'I feel it.'

'Feel what?'

'What I felt when I stepped onto the ladder at St John's. Moments before I climbed into the bell chamber with Gapes. He's here, I'm telling you.'

I step forward.

'Josh, wait.' She draws her .357 and indicates I should tuck in behind her.

But this doesn't feel right. I indicate that *I* should go first.

She frowns, shakes her head. 'We need to do this by the book. Call back-up.'

I agree. But the strangest instinct is telling me that *I* need to do the negotiation. And that there is no time to waste.

If the device is at the bottom end of the low-yield spectrum, Hetta might survive if she's able to shelter somewhere in the shadow of the Western Wall, but her refusal to entertain this in our lightning-quick discussion makes it academic.

My fallback position is to point out that the SEALs – or whoever is tasked with taking down a nuclear-armed terrorist – will take ten minutes, maybe less, to get here, and she will need to liaise with them when they arrive.

Which means I get to go on up.

She looks like she's about to argue, then says, 'Here, you'd better take this,' and hands me her .357. 'I've got a back-up in the vehicle.'

63

YES, SISTER MARTHA. SOMETHING EXTRAORDINARY IS GOING TO happen. I feel it, too.

I'm on the second level when I hear what sounds like bell ropes vibrating in the breeze. I stop and listen, straining to hear over the hum of traffic in the valley. It's coming from somewhere above me.

I move up one more story, clasping the Beretta with both hands, stop and listen again. This time, it's more distinct. Not the bell ropes. A low murmur. A voice.

I look at my watch. The second hand has stopped. I must have damaged it when I jumped off the wall. What do I do when I get to the top? Do I shoot him? I look at the gun and place my foot on the step that will take me up to the final level – the level from which the murmur has become the sound of a man at prayer.

When hope is lost, Joshua, faith can still be found.

I set the gun down. It makes the slightest of clinks, metal on stone.

The murmuring stops.

I reach a doorway, take a breath and step through it, into the bell chamber.

A warm wind blows through the eastern arch. A man, taller than me, is standing in the far left corner. He is wearing the black robe of a monk or a priest. His back is to me. His head is bowed.

A backpack sits on the floor in front of him.

'You're here,' he says in English. His accent is somewhere between Russian and Arabic.

'I'm not armed.'

'I know.'

He turns.

Pale skin, bearded, framed by flowing black hair. His blue eyes have an intensity Gapes's sketch captured precisely. They seem to look right through me, into the depths of my soul.

I glance at the backpack.

'You're afraid,' he says.

'Of course.'

'Fear kills our ability to think – but you don't need me to tell you that.' He inhales deeply. 'So let us agree not to be.'

He leans back against the wall and lowers himself to the floor. 'This isn't going to end the way you think it is.' He gestures in front of him.

I hesitate.

'*Itfadl*,' he urges. *Please*.

I sit too.

We are less than a meter and a half apart. He turns and gazes out across the city.

'The fifth *surah* of Verse 32 of the Holy Qur'an tells us: *Whoever saves a life, it is as though he has saved the world.*' He looks at me. 'Do you know this verse?'

'Yes.'

'How?'

'From Iraq.'

He studies me.

'I'm a doctor. I was supposed to save lives there.'

'And did you?'

'Not enough.'

The breeze rises. He turns his face toward the arch and breathes it in.

'What do you know about me?'

'Your name. Where you're from.'

'What they made me do?'

'Yes.'

'And why I am here?'

I hesitate. The backpack is sitting between us. I can't take my eyes off of it. 'What does it take to trigger the bomb?'

'The same energy it takes to save a life.'

'What does that mean?'

'It means there comes a time when the two go hand in hand,' he says. 'It means also that I am here for you.'

'Me?'

He stares beyond the arch again. The silence starts to vibrate in the space between us.

'You said you are a doctor.'

'Yes.'

'And yet it is very clear to me you are the one in need of healing.'

'My wife ... I ...'

He raises his hand and holds his thumb and forefinger fractionally apart. 'You know, don't you, not even this much separates you.'

I nod. *Yes. But without her, life has lost all meaning.*

He shakes his head. 'No, Joshua, it hasn't.'

I hadn't told him my name. I hadn't even articulated the thought. 'Mind games, Danilovsky?' I glance again at the backpack.

'Close your eyes,' he says.

'Is this the end?'

'No. The beginning. Close your eyes. For Hope. *Pray.*'

My skin prickles. The wind drops.

I do as he says.

'What do you hear?'

Nothing, except the rush of blood in my ears.

'Listen,' he says.

I breathe in and hear it: a heartbeat that's not mine.

I open my eyes.

I'm standing on the porch of our beach house. Hope is beside me, her head tilted to one side as she considers the brushstrokes she's just applied to her canvas. The portrait of Jack. Not the work in progress in my guest room, but the finished portrait from the cabin.

There are tears in her eyes. She turns to me, smiles and brushes the hair from her cheek.

I breathe in her perfume, a gentle undertone to the scent of the ocean. Feel the breeze on my face.

Oh my God. Am I dreaming?

'No, Josh.' She takes my hand and lifts it to her face. 'I've been here all along. You just haven't been able to see me clearly.'

'Jack's portrait?'

'You knew what it meant as soon as you opened your mind.'

'The voice?'

'Of course.'

'In the V-22?'

'And all the other times you've needed it.'

I don't dare move. If I take my eyes off of her, even for a second, I'm going to wake up.

'What is this place?'

She smiles. 'What does it feel like?'

'Home.'

She touches my face. 'It is home.'

'The little girl holding the balloon. On the peace march in Stockholm. Is she . . . ?'

'Beautiful. Just beautiful. Her father's daughter.'

'Where is she?'

'Out playing. With friends. We're together. You, me, her. And we're happy. I promise. Where we were – where you are – is where we learn, where we grow. And it's so very nearly over.'

'What is?'

'What you have to do.'

'I don't want to leave. I want to stay. With you.'

'You don't need me, Josh. Not anymore. Not in the way you think.'

'You're wrong.' My voice catches.

'You have the courage to do this,' she says.

'Do what?'

'To finish it.'

I shake my head. 'No . . .'

'It's OK.'
'We haven't talked enough. I—'
'What is there to say?'
'I'm so . . . sorry . . .'
'What for?'
'For the crash. For . . . everything.'
'None of that matters. Really.'
'It matters to me.'
'Let it go. It wasn't you.' She pauses. 'And it wasn't me.'
'Then . . . what . . . ?'
'It was something we had to do.' She leans forward and kisses me. 'Trust, my darling. Everything is going to be all right, because it was meant. You. Me. All of it. Didn't I always tell you about the people who were going to live because of you? Well, now's the time.'

She looks around us.

'This will be here – we will be here – waiting for you. But right now you have to go back.'

She reaches out to me. 'It's all right, Josh. It's all right.'

I take her hand and the world slews.

When I open my eyes, everything rushes at me in high definition.

The Engineer is standing in the corner of the room.

The component parts of the ballotechnic are stacked neatly on the backpack by his feet. It resembles a child's puzzle. There's hardly anything to it.

'Do you understand now?' he says. 'That's how much she loves you, Joshua. That's how much I . . .'

He stops, listens, his head cocked to one side.

'What is it?'

'They're here.'

'Who?'

'The people who are preparing to storm the tower.' He looks at me. 'It's time to go.'

I glance at the disassembled pieces.

'You're giving yourself up?'

'Yes,' he says. An unearthly light shines in his eyes and the wind rushes in, bringing with it the chant of the *mu'ezzin*.

And something else.

The music of the bells. Church bells.

'Come,' he says. 'Take me to them. Before the killing begins.'

The breeze stays on my back as we start down the steps. The Engineer is beside me, a pace or two to my right. I am aware of the rising temperature outside, but in the tower, it remains cool. The shooting pains in my side have gone. And I know they won't be back.

On the third level, I glance down. The gun is exactly where I left it. As I step over it, I glance at my watch. It's working again.

The sounds of the city grow louder the further we descend.

When we reach ground level, the Engineer is about to step outside.

I place my hand on his shoulder. 'Best I go first.'

'And if they shoot?'

'They're less likely to shoot me than you.'

I tell him to shed his robes. He's wearing jeans and a T-shirt underneath.

'Lose the T-shirt too.'

He takes it off. I place his clothes in a pile at the bottom of the steps. I then open the door a crack and shout for Hetta.

'*Josh?*'

Her voice is muffled. She must be thirty, maybe forty meters away.

'Yes.'

I still can't see her.

'I'm coming out, Hetta. I have Danilovsky with me. He's unarmed. The bomb is at the top of the tower. He's disassembled it. Send somebody up. He's coming with me.'

I fully open the door and lead the Engineer outside.

A guttural command crackles across the courtyard: '*Down! Fuckin' down!*'

375

My momentary hesitation is met by a chorus of yells. *'Down! Or we shoot!'*

'On your knees!'

'Do it now!'

'Now!'

A second later, my face is in the dirt. I hear the crunch of their feet on the gravel.

'Stay still!'

'Don't fucking move!'

Somebody kicks my hand away from Danilovsky's.

The muzzle of an assault rifle is drilled into the back of my neck, and I'm yanked to my feet. There are around ten of them, in black tactical gear.

I glance right as the butt of an M4 catches the Engineer in the side of the head. He drops to his knees. Somebody rabbit-punches him in the kidneys. He gasps for air.

I'm head-locked. I can't move.

I hear boots tearing up the tower behind me.

'Hey!'

Hetta's voice. She chambers a round and the effect is instantaneous. The guy who has my neck in a vise lets me go.

To my right, the Engineer has curled into a ball. Hetta is standing a meter and a half away, her aim alternating between the head of the black-clad SEAL who's been kicking the shit out of him and the head of the guy who's been holding me.

'Secure the prisoner,' she says. 'Any of you sons of bitches so much as lays a finger on him, I swear I'll shoot you myself.'

One of the SEALs pulls Danilovsky to his feet.

Another takes his arms and pulls them behind his back.

A third cuffs him.

I take several steps back to a low wall. I watch them take the Engineer away. A minute later, Hetta comes and sits beside me. 'What happened up there?'

'I don't know.'

'You don't *know*?'

'He was waiting for me.'

'On the first level?'

'No. At the top.'

'That's not possible, Josh. You were in there for barely a minute. We got lucky. One of the SEALs' patrols was passing at the bottom of the Mount when I made the call. They showed up seconds after I left you.'

She looks at me. 'Is there something you're not telling me?'

I'm spared from answering by her radio.

She glances up at the tower and says: 'Go ahead.'

'Agent Hart?'

'Yes.'

'The deuterium–tritium pellet. It's missing.'

The Suburbans are parked up outside the gates, no more than fifty meters away. Hetta launches herself toward them. I'm right behind her. As we round the corner, five agents, alerted by the same message, are leaping out of two of the other three vehicles.

The middle one's doors are closed. Nothing is visible behind its blacked-out windows.

The lead agent tugs on the rear nearside handle. It won't give. Hetta is five meters behind him. I'm three paces behind her.

There's a flash from inside, so bright the agent is hurled to the ground.

I see what looks like a photographic negative of Hetta by the door, weapon drawn. She puts two rounds into the lock and pulls it open.

'That is not possible,' she says. 'That is *not* fucking *possible*.'

The interior of the Suburban is clear. Not a trace of flash burn. Not so much as a wisp of smoke. The two escorts are on the rear seat, heads in their hands. Both of them are yelling they can't see. I glance down. A pair of locked cuffs sits between them.

And Danilovsky has vanished.

64

THE PLENARY THEATER – THE MAIN STAGE WITHIN THE HALL OF the Assembly – holds almost eight thousand people. Multiple rooms lead off it, each hosting a non-plenary event.

The Secret Service has established its command post behind the stage. The atmosphere in the airless black hole is close to panic. The silence is only broken by the whir of computer fans, the hum of the air-conditioning units, the clack of keyboards. A fluorescent strip casts cold light on the desk.

Half a dozen agents, plus Hetta and me, are sifting through security badges on our laptops. Another half dozen are running the live CCTV footage through the monitors, while their algorithms explore the facial features of the delegates.

A man who can vanish from under the noses of the Secret Service will have little difficulty making himself invisible in a gathering as large as this. But as Cabot said in the Beast, we don't have a choice.

What remains of the bomb has been couriered to our embassy, where every detail has been photographed. The imagery is being pored over by technicians at Los Alamos and Lawrence Livermore right now.

The question is a simple one. Can the Engineer initiate a thermonuclear reaction of deuterium and tritium without the ballotechnic, the weapon's trigger mechanism?

I glance at the monitor above Hetta's head, where the Holy Father is reading his speech in occasionally halting English.

He's dressed in white, and the lights glint on his round glasses. His words are displayed in five languages below close-ups of his face on screens to the left and right of the stage.

Every now and again he looks up and smiles.

'For too many years, religion has been at the heart of conflict,' he is saying. 'I have said this many times before, but peace isn't only about the absence of war . . .'

As the CCTV tracks toward the stage, I catch a glimpse of Thompson in the front row, and beside him, the top of Cabot's head. Several other Secret Service agents are clustered around them. Jennifer is there, too. And the Russian president and the General Secretary of the UN.

We've had to do this by disconnecting our machines from any communications source, so we remain unobserved. This means it's taking time.

Hetta pushes back her chair, rubs her eyes and tips some cold coffee down her throat.

'Three and a half thousand security passes,' she says.

Four and a half thousand to go.

And that's just for the Plenary.

There's a sudden and palpable shift in the mood of the auditorium.

'It is impossible to stay silent on this issue . . . any longer.'

The pontiff takes a sip of water.

'In 1992, the Vatican acquired information collected by the former Soviet Union on what were termed "offensive consciousness experiments" – how to develop the mind as a weapon.

'This is not the time or place to discuss the morality of this venture. Suffice to say it provided my predecessors with a remarkable insight into the true nature of consciousness. What this seemed to suggest was shocking to them – perhaps to us all – because of its implications for the Holy Catholic Church, indeed, for religions everywhere . . .'

He goes on to describe the substance of my exchanges with Sergeyev, the essence of which, it is now clear, was acquired by the

Vatican – and subsequently buried – when M. M. Kalunin met with the apostolic nuncio in Moscow shortly before his death.

The experiments, the Pope adds, involved readings by psychics of the make-up of basic sub-atomic matter – elementary particles. No matter how many particles they examined, their attention was always directed to the moment of Creation, and to a blueprint of an infinite number of universes preceding our own.

The cameras pan across the audience. People shift in their seats and turn to one another. Even I can feel the air of expectation.

'As you know, I have tried many, many times to bring together the theology of the Holy Catholic Church and the building blocks of science. There is no reason, I believe, why well-founded theories on the origins of the universe and the evolution of species should be in conflict with the most fundamental tenets of our belief.'

Murmurs ripple from the front to the back of the auditorium like a Mexican wave.

Hetta goes back to examining the badges.

'By themselves, the Soviet tests might mean little. But for many years, I have been uneasy with the idea that a benign God would give us only one chance at salvation. And whilst I know that Jesus Christ died for the remission of our sins, I struggle with the idea He died for Christians alone. And we all wrestle, at various moments, with the big questions: about the meaning of life, why we are here, our place in Creation. God's purpose. *Our* purpose.'

He takes another sip of water.

'A little under a year ago, I held my second meeting with the President of the United States of America. Robert Thompson, as many of you know, is a lawyer with a background in theology.

'In my first meeting with him, Senator Thompson, as he was then, told me he had written a paper while at Princeton outlining the underpinnings of the three Abrahamic faiths – Judaism, Islam and Christianity – and asked me whether, in my view, there would ever be any hope of reconciling their differences.

'Not unnaturally, I hesitated at the suggestion. But it made me think. And, in the course of discussions with my closest advisers, including the many cosmologists whom we fund to carry out research at our own Pontifical Academy of Sciences, I was told of the existence of the Soviet experiment, and how we had come by our knowledge of it.

'This led me to initiate my second meeting with President Thompson in New York City last year. When we were able to be alone together, he outlined the vision he harbored for the creation of a safer, better world, and I told him of the feeling I and my advisers now shared – that the idea of *pre-existence* felt right.

'Since then, it has been pointed out to me many times that pre-existence – not just of universes, but of the soul – was a belief held by the very first Christians. And that this belief was driven out because it removed the need for our intercession, the intercession of the Church, between man and God.'

There is an intake of breath across the auditorium. Several African bishops get to their feet.

'Please, please . . .' The Pope raises a hand. 'I am so nearly finished.'

The protesters settle back and an uneasy silence descends.

'It was while we were praying together, alone in the Church of St Simeon, that President Thompson said: "What if I were able to deliver the proof that you need?"'

Whatever he says next is lost in a howl of protest.

'That is *way* too much of a coincidence.' Hetta is staring at her laptop. 'Take a look.'

I peer over her shoulder. A forty-something guy with a beard and short fair hair stares at me from the screen.

'His badge code says he's a contractor, name of Axel Lydon. But check out his left eye.' She hits a key and the image expands.

I move closer.

A keyhole-shaped blemish in the iris. A coloboma.

'What are the stats on that?' she asks.

'Approximately one in thirteen thousand.'

'And we see two in as many months.'

I look again. The beard is distracting and there may have been some surgery to reduce the prominence of the brow, but it's Voss the guy MPD originally told us was Gapes, no question.

'Everybody,' she yells, 'listen up. We have a situation here.'

The dozen agents in the room stop what they're doing.

'We have *two* potential targets in the building – Danilovsky and this guy.' She turns her laptop around so everyone can see.

'Voss. Master Sergeant Matthew L. Missing, without trace. Afghanistan, five years ago. According to his file, he was part of a fourteen-man Marine Special Operations Team. That's all we know for sure, because our information may have been manipulated.'

'Manipulated?' a PIAD agent with a round, sweaty face shouts from the back.

'Altered, Agent Gibson. And thank you for volunteering.'

'Me?'

'Yes, you. We need to verify Voss's specialism. We need to know where Axel Lydon sprang from. And we need both those things the day before yesterday.'

'How?' Gibson says.

'Your next stop is the National Security Adviser.'

'It's . . . it's five-thirty in the morning in D.C.,' he stammers.

'You think she's not watching this? Call her. *Now.*'

She throws me a radio and an earpiece.

Then we're out the door, heading for the Plenary.

We enter the auditorium to the left of the stage.

The pontiff is making his way back to his seat and Thompson is heading for the lectern.

There is only mute applause as the Pope sits down.

A crackle in my ear, then Graham's voice asking Hetta what the fuck she and I are doing. I spot him in the wings, to the right of the lectern.

'Switch to the back-up channel,' Hetta says.

I dig into my jacket. Graham is mid-sentence when he gets cut off.

'Gibson – are you reading me?' Hetta says.

Gibson acknowledges.

'Anything from Byford?'

His voice is strangulated. 'No. She's not answering.'

'Then try her on another line. Hurry, for Christ's sake!'

Thompson steps up to the mike.

'Ten years ago,' he begins, 'our military made a small-scale attempt to explore human consciousness. Nobody gave it much hope of achieving anything. Today, however, I am able to report that it succeeded, and spectacularly so . . .'

I start walking up the right side of the auditorium, scanning the crowd. Hetta does the same on the left.

'We now have proof,' Thompson says, 'that physical existence is made up not just of matter and energy, but of information – data that never dies. A perfect record, burned forever into the hard-drive of reality, of every molecule of matter, of every event, of every emotion, of every thought anybody ever had.'

I feel the restlessness of the audience.

'Now imagine,' he continues, 'what we would know – what we might *do* – if we could access this data. What it might tell us about our planet; about the origins of the Universe. About *us* . . .'

He pauses. 'Well, this is exactly what we've done.'

A few people begin to clap, then think better of it.

Thompson waits a moment or two. I carry on up the steps, trying to look into every face, but there are so damn many . . .

'This discovery, of course,' Thompson says, when some semblance of order has returned, 'has come at a price. Because what it gives us is unprecedented capability.

'We, the United States, now have the means to know what you did yesterday, to know everything that your parents did, and their parents before them. Soon, we will be able to do this in real time, to see everything you do, as you do it; and everything you think.'

As the implications of what he has just said filter through the language barrier, some people toward the front get to their feet. A few of them start to shout and to heckle.

Hetta and I have made our way to the back of the auditorium and we've seen nothing. I tell her I'm heading back toward the stage. She stays where she is.

'Unknown to my administration, or to any administration, this system was developed and financed as a special-access program – in the black – beyond the oversight of our Congress. It was financed using money laundered off the back of criminal activity in another nation state. That nation state was Russia.'

The whole place goes silent.

'For the past year, I have been working with my friend and colleague, the President of Russia, to expose this activity, whose purpose can only achieve one thing: a perpetual cycle of mistrust, of simmering conflict between our two nations, and many other nations of the world. And it is certainly not the only program to have done this.

'I am all for secrecy, in certain circumstances, but too much of what we develop militarily exceeds what is appropriate and affordable. And as the acquisition of this system has demonstrated, it is open to serious abuses of power.

'As a research tool, its technology will enable us to see that the differences that we believe divide us – of race, color and creed – are simply not there. They don't exist.'

He pauses.

'As a surveillance tool, however, this system is beyond anything that has ever been built in the name of decency and honor, and should not be placed in the hands of any one nation.'

He pauses again.

'It is for this reason that I have taken a decision. As of today, I am handing over the Grid, as we call this technology – lock, stock and barrel – to my good friend the General Secretary of the United Nations.'

He steps down from the podium and takes his seat next to his wife, the Pope and the Russian President.

Anybody who hadn't been on their feet before is now.

Some are cheering, others are yelling. Some are shouting abuse.

Chaos in the room where we're hunting for a killer.

65

I'M ALMOST BACK AT THE STAGE WHEN I HEAR GIBSON'S VOICE IN my ear. 'Agent Hart, we have the data.'

I have difficulty spotting Hetta over the heads of the audience. She's stopped, head bent forward, one hand pressed to her ear.

'Matthew Voss was the ops team marksman. And Axel Lydon is listed as a cyber-security specialist. Strictly backroom.'

'And he's here on whose authority?'

'Approval came through in the past hour. From the White House.'

My heart stops.

I see Gapes in the tower. Hear his words from behind the mask. *There's a plot to kill the President. It is well planned, advanced, and will be well executed, unless you move to stop it.*

Gapes was shot by a sniper from the window he'd sketched on the crazy wall. He hadn't just seen the future, he'd shaped it.

An act of self-sacrifice.

His final clue.

I look up.

Right at the back. Above Hetta's head. In the rear wall. Two tiers of windows. For stage lights. Projectors. Christ knows.

An upper and a lower tier.

Hetta sees them too, and bolts through the emergency exit.

I hear her breath sharp in my ear as the adrenaline kicks in. She's crashing up steps. A door bangs open.

'What's he waiting for, Josh?'

I don't know.

The crowd is on its feet. I can't see the President. He's lost in a sea of heads and hands. The noise is deafening.

I dip my head toward my lapel mike.

'Where are you?'

'Second level. A hallway, doors leading off.'

Thompson appears on one of the giant screens. He's shaking hands with the Pope and the Russian President. Still the huckster from Texas with the people, acknowledging their response. Good and bad, he doesn't care.

In my earpiece, Hetta catches her breath. 'Is he on this floor or the floor above?'

I glance at the two tiers of windows.

The only view I have of Thompson is still onscreen.

And if I can't see him, nor can the Special Ops marksman.

'Hetta, he doesn't have line-of-sight.'

'What?'

'Voss. He can't see the target. He must be on the lower tier.'

I hear her crash down the steps and throw open a door.

'Hallway, same as the floor above. Doors off.'

A bang as she kicks the first of them in.

'A storeroom. Clear.'

I turn.

Thompson is getting to his feet.

I pull my radio from my pocket, switch channels.

'Graham, this is Cain. Get Thompson to sit the fuck down!'

I'm met by a wall of static.

The President steps back onto the podium. He looks up from the lectern. Sees something.

I turn to my right.

A man on his feet. Tall and dark. Short hair. I can't see his face, but I'd recognize my companion from the tower anywhere, from any angle. He's wearing a suit. A loose-fitting jacket. No tie. He takes a step down toward the stage. Then another.

Three members of the Presidential Protection team see him too. Graham, making his appearance from the wings, is one of them.

Thompson reaches for his glass of water. His hand is shaking.

'Hey!' Graham shouts. 'You! Back in your seat!'

The Engineer keeps on going.

Graham doesn't know who he is. Nobody does.

In my earpiece, I hear Hetta kick in another door.

'Clear! What's happening?'

'It's the dream,' I murmur.

'Say again.'

'It's the President's dream.'

I start moving again, also toward the stage. Some people are still on their feet; others have sat back down as it becomes clear Thompson isn't leaving the Plenary.

I push past a group of priests, who are standing in the aisle arguing about what's just been said. I'm still three rows back.

'Hey!' Graham yells again. He moves forward, placing himself between his boss and the Engineer.

Graham slips his hand inside his jacket. 'I said—'

Thompson steps out from behind the lectern. Two Secret Service agents move too slowly toward him from the wings.

'It's all right,' Thompson's voice booms over the PA. 'Let him come.'

All eyes turn to the intruder. His hands appear to be clenched, but I can't see if he's holding any kind of weapon. An unearthly light seems to shine from his eyes – the look that I'd seen in the tower. He's an automaton. Unstoppable.

I push past a cardinal and attempt to vault the front two rows. I almost make it, but my foot catches a backrest and I sprawl between them.

I look up as the next part of the story unfolds, exactly as Thompson said it would.

One of the agents attempts to pull him to safety. Thompson resists. The Engineer reaches the stage. They look at each other.

The Engineer opens his jacket, reaches inside it.

Graham raises his weapon.

A crash in my ear.

Hetta, kicking in another door.

A shot.

The high-powered bullet punches through Graham's upper body. Blood sprays across the screen behind him.

A scream from the crowd, then: 'Hey, you!'

Hetta in my ear.

The Engineer steps to his right, in front of Thompson.

He turns, sees me. Then looks up at the back of the auditorium. His eyes close. He spreads his arms wide.

Two shots, so close together the second sounds like an echo.

Hetta's voice in my ear: 'Nailed him, Josh. But not before he fired. The President, is he . . . ?'

I don't hear any more. My earpiece falls to the floor as I get to my feet and rush for the stage.

The Engineer's lying face up, taking short, sharp breaths. I pull back his jacket. The entry wound is tiny, but the damage is irreparable. A crimson flower blooms from his punctured heart.

'Stand away, Colonel.'

An agent's voice, somewhere behind me.

'Stand away! He may be wearing a belt.'

I ignore him.

As I touch the Engineer's neck, his eyes open. The face that has haunted me since I was first confronted by him at the cabin – and maybe even before then – now gives me a look of infinite kindness.

His skin is still warm but I can't find a pulse.

'Joshua . . .'

'Shhh . . . Don't speak.'

'It's all right,' he says softly.

'Somebody get me a first-aid pack!'

'It's all right . . .'

I lean forward until I can feel his breath on my cheek.

'I am you . . . Joshua . . .'

'What?'

'I . . . am . . . *you.*'

He somehow finds the strength to raise his hand.

Holds three fingers in front of my face.

As I pull his devastated body toward me, I see the disciple falling backward out of Rembrandt's *Raising of the Cross.*

I plead with him to hold on.

But my friend is dead before I can gather him into my arms.

66

TWO HOURS LATER, THOMPSON STANDS SEVERAL STEPS BEHIND A lectern on which someone has hastily hung the presidential seal. The impromptu press conference is taking place in the suite on the top floor of his hotel, a block away from the Hall of the Assembly. Flashbulbs fire. TV lights have been rigged. Hetta and I watch on a monitor in a protection suite along the hallway.

'Mr President! *Mr President . . . !*'

Shouts, yells. Everybody trying to fire in the first question.

'Hey!' his embattled press secretary cries. '*One at a time!*'

It's my old friend, Molly's nemesis, Joe Seitz.

'We will be issuing a full statement in the next hour. In the meantime, President Thompson wishes to make a short statement of his own.' Seitz ushers him forward. 'Mr President.'

Thompson steps up to the mike. 'There will be a full inquiry into these events. Three people are dead. The identity of two of them is unknown at this time. Tragically, the third, Haight Graham, is the second White House Special Agent in Charge to have been killed in the line of duty in the past two months. Words cannot express my sadness at this loss. Jennifer's and my thoughts and prayers are with him and his family at this time . . .'

His words tail away as hands shoot skyward.

'Mr President! Has it been confirmed that the man who rushed at you was holding or wearing any kind of explosive device?'

'No, that has not been confirmed.'

'Did he have a gun?'

'No.'

'Any idea who he was?'

'Not at this stage.'

'Or why he appeared to step into the line of fire?'

'No.'

'Where were you taken in the aftermath of the incident?'

'Somewhere safe.'

'Who fired the shots? The Secret Service says it wasn't them—'

'Hey. What did I say?' Seitz wades back in. 'One at a time.' He pauses. 'And if you have a question, please give us your name and affiliation.'

He picks out somebody at the front.

'Mr President, Carolee Stanley, CNN. Was the announcement you made today scripted before you took to the stage?'

'No, it wasn't. And for this I must apologize to my media team.'

'They didn't *know*?'

'No. And they deserved better. It was ... spontaneous. My decision.'

'Your decision alone?'

'Not entirely,' Thompson concedes. 'The delicate liaison between us and the Vatican has been greatly assisted these past months by Senator Tod Abnarth, the only person I know with the experience and skill to broker an initiative of this kind. The Senator, being a prominent Catholic, already had strong ties with His Holiness.'

'The son of a bitch *planned* this?' Hetta whispers.

'Abnarth must have warned him that something like the Grid was out there.'

'Yeah?'

I nod. 'Between them I think they took the decision to flush it out of the shadows.'

'Sure as shit did that.'

Thompson directs his gaze to another part of the room. 'Yes?'

'Mr President, Mike Honniker, *Washington Post*. First off, are you all right, sir?'

'Shaken, but OK. Thank you, Mike.'

'You said the guy who came at you was unarmed. And yet

footage appears to show him reaching into his jacket for something.' Honniker checks his notes. 'So, if it wasn't a bomb or a gun—'

'It was an envelope, Mike.'

'An envelope?'

'An old photograph of a kid holding a box.'

'A what?'

'A wooden box. With a lid.'

'Any idea who the kid is?'

'Yes.' Thompson pauses. 'The kid is me. It was taken when I was at school. In ninth grade.'

'Do you know how he came by it?'

'Not yet.'

'Maybe the guy was sick. Have you considered that possibility?'

'We're considering everything, Mike. The Secret Service is all over it. Forensics are working the angles. As soon as we know any more we'll share it with you. But in the meantime, sick isn't what I'm thinking. Unless sick means sacrificing your own life to save someone else's.'

He scans the sea of faces and picks out a Reuters reporter.

'Are you able to summarize, in just a few words, what you think the breakthrough you announced actually means?'

'It means, after too many years of an escalating arms race in the field of mass-surveillance, that everybody gets to see what everybody else is doing. That is why I am handing it to the UN, for the benefit of every nation. I believe we are about to enter an era of zero secrecy. I will leave you to speculate on what a world without secrets will mean, but I believe it will herald a paradigm shift in the development of both domestic and international relations.'

Another chorus of yells.

'WE HAVE TIME FOR TWO MORE QUESTIONS!' Seitz bellows. 'Yes, Eli.'

'Eli Harper, Mr President, CBS. If this was a classified program, how did you – or the Executive Branch – get to learn of its existence? And a follow-up, if I may. Does this have anything to do with what we are hearing out of Washington as we speak: about a series of raids launched by the FBI and the Secret Service on several facilities owned and operated by the National Security Agency, as well as a number of other US intelligence agencies?'

Thompson takes a step back. 'How did we learn about it? Too big of a deal for today, Eli. Joe Seitz and his media team will brief you on the salient details as soon as they become available.

'In answer to your second question, I issued orders ninety minutes ago for a number of key individuals within the NSA, CIA, INSCOM, the DIA and some of our other intel agencies to be detained under the Patriot Act for questioning about the unauthorized development of this system. There will be further arrests over the coming days, weeks and months.

'Again, I will leave Joe and his team to brief you further, but you may want to check with my Russian counterpart and his team. I understand there were also a number of significant arrests by the Russian authorities across Moscow today.'

'We're getting unconfirmed reports of arrests within the White House too,' Harper says.

'There has been only one arrest,' Thompson says. 'That of my Chief of Staff, Reuben Kantner.'

This, inevitably, triggers another deluge. Seitz says that he will brief on this delicate development in due course.

'Last question,' he says, surveying the forest of hands.

Thompson shields his eyes from the glare as he sweeps the room. 'Yes. Right at the back there. Your question, please.'

'Thank you, Mr President. Avi Keller, *Haaretz*. I am a security correspondent here in Jerusalem. We are picking up reports of an incident that allegedly involved your security people at around seven o'clock this morning on the Mount of Olives. The area was closed to public access for several hours.

'Is this something you're aware of? And the Israeli authorities? Was it terrorist related? Does it have anything to do with what just took place in the Hall of the Assembly?'

Thompson throws a glance at Seitz. 'I'm out of time, I'm afraid, but Joe and his team have your questions, and I know that they'll get back to you as soon as they possibly can.'

67

THERE'S A BUZZ AND A HEAVY CLICK. THE NURSE PRACTITIONER, a heavy-set guy who's introduced himself as Bass, pushes open the door. I step inside and am greeted by a strong smell of bleach.

The NP asks if I want to be accompanied.

I tell him that won't be necessary. I've known the patient half my life. He closes the door. Bolts slide and locks tumble.

It is more than a week since Reuben's arrest and in that time he has twice tried to take his own life. His mental collapse is due to a condition that has been diagnosed as involutional melancholia.

The psychiatrists here at South 3 – the mental health unit attached to D.C.'s Central Detention Facility in the South East district of the city – have stabilized him, but his condition remains grave. They have agreed to my request for a visit in the hope it will help him 'reverse himself out' of the illness, and prepare to take steps to fully recover.

My onetime brother-in-arms is lying on a bed of sorts secured to the far wall, in white hospital pajamas. His back is to me. The cell is free of protrusions and under observation 24/7.

Reuben doesn't move. I watch the rise and fall of his breathing for the longest minute of my life.

'Did you give the order to kill Gapes?'

'No. They pulled me in after the Bluffdale raid, when everything began to unravel.'

'So, the V-22, that was you . . . ?'

'No. But I signed off on it.'

I manage to keep my voice level. 'And Voss's security pass?'

'Voss was perfect casting. Have your marksman take down the terrorist with the bomb on live TV, thus demonstrating the lunacy of the President's peace initiative. Then take down the President. Two birds, one stone.'

Jesus . . . He was allowed into the Plenary because they wanted him there. And he went because he had seen what they had in mind.

'How did they get their hooks into you, Reuben?'

'Because they *knew*,' he says.

'About Iraq?'

'About *everything*.'

He rolls over and looks at me. His skin is puffy, his eyes red-rimmed. 'One shitty, tiny slip, Josh.'

He's talking about the family that died in Fallujah, and his subsequent cover-up of the tragedy.

'Why didn't you go to Thompson?'

'And have them leak what happened to the press? My career would have been over. Or worse. You saw what they did to Gapes. Lefortz. Anders. Jimenez.'

I did see what they did to Gapes. And Lefortz. I had a ringside seat. At a time when I hadn't realized that the President's dream wasn't a dream at all, but a prophecy.

'You need to focus on getting better,' I say.

There's something manic about his laugh. 'What the fuck for?'

'Because things can change.'

'Yeah? Like how? I'm going to jail for a very, very long time.'

'That doesn't mean your life is over.'

'Is this you talking, or God? I get confused.'

'The President is pushing for a full congressional hearing – an opportunity for the facts to emerge. There will be a trial, too, of course, but you know Thompson. The Oval Office is more about truth and reconciliation these days than judgment and retribution.

'You have no idea how things will play out, Reuben. None of us does. But in a year or so, when the Grid is back online, there will be no hiding place. From hereon in, everybody will need to be mindful of what they say and think.'

I clamber into the Lexus. The engine is running, the heater on full.

'Well?' Hetta says.

'He's not good.'

'Do you care?'

'Yes. Strangely, I do.'

'Fuck, Josh. Sometimes I don't know if I'll ever get you.'

'He came close to killing himself. Would you feel better if he'd succeeded?'

She appears to give this quite a lot of thought as she maneuvers the car right then left onto Massachusetts Avenue.

'No,' she says eventually.

'I didn't want to say this to Reuben, but something that Kalunin told his daughter has stuck in my mind. He said that on the Day of Judgment, we judge ourselves.'

'What does that mean?'

'I think it means a number of things.'

'Like?'

'Like, we have to take personal responsibility for our actions. But also, shit happens.'

Like nuclear weapons and the World-Wide Web.

Like not being able to wind back the clock.

Like the holosphere is real. It's here. And soon, we'll need to learn how to live with it.

Hetta pulls up close to where I've parked, around the corner from the Supreme Court. I thank her for the ride.

I'm heading to my mother-in-law's place for a couple of days. Since I got back I've felt a yearning to be close to Pam. There are some things I have to tell her. And I have Hope's painting in my car. It belongs at the Five Pines.

I also have this feeling that there may be clues to Jack's past hidden in the one thing nobody would ever have thought of searching: his old Impala.

'Josh?'

'Yes.'

'I'm sorry for all the things I said.' Hetta hesitates. 'About Hope. Sometimes, I can be a little . . . You know . . .'

'The traffic wasn't all one-way.'

'What does that mean?'

'I've been a little obsessive myself.'

'Will you be back?'

'In a few days.'

'Then?'

'How about dinner? Or would that be . . . inappropriate?'

'No.' She smiles. 'I'd like that.'

Then: 'Josh?'

I turn.

'There's something different about you. Funny –' she smiles '– I never noticed till now.'

'My leg?'

'Yes.'

'It's . . . better.'

I've been meaning to tell Mo too.

As I make my way north, out of the city, the horizon widens.

Inquiries are underway into the acquisition system that, for decades, has allowed our defense and intelligence agencies to buy weapons and services beyond the scrutiny of our elected officials.

The probes will examine how former government employees like Duke Gapes, Matt Voss and Karl Dempf were able to drop off the map in support of activities like the Grid and Triple Z's assassination agenda.

Thompson has promised that – like the Church Committee and the Rockefeller Commission formed on the back of Watergate – these inquiries will be transparent. All their findings will be made public.

The irony, of course, is that the conclusions will emerge around the time the Grid is back online.

As Thompson made clear, its control and development will come under the auspices of the UN – and it's anyone's guess where this will lead. Opinion seems to have polarized. Those of us brought up in the shadow of the Cold War are fearful and cynical. The next generation, for the most part, have embraced it.

Since Jerusalem, a permanent peace camp has been established in Lafayette Square under the banner 'No More Secrets'. Thompson sees it every morning when he goes to work.

Meanwhile, the ramifications of arrests here and in Russia persist.

A 3D printer was located during a search of the Ilitch Foundation's office in Jerusalem's Old City. Thompson's defense advisers are in crisis mode over what to reveal about Gen 4 nuclear weapons and the capacity of psychics to initiate the fusion process.

There is still considerable debate about whether this is even possible. The advice of our labs remains that it isn't. And, based on what's been passed to us by the Russians, there is no evidence that anybody has achieved the psychic collapse of a ballotechnic initiator.

No trace of the DT pellet was ever found. The Engineer really was unarmed. Which leaves the cabal unraveled. They were relying on him to tick the suicide bomber box.

The Secret Service says his body was disposed of at sea, like bin Laden's. No grave, no martyr's shrine.

But all kinds of stories have emerged online, some of them, apparently, peddled by sources within the Service: that there never was any burial at sea; that the Engineer's body simply vanished from the morgue where it was taken after the shooting.

As to his past, the press has many more questions than answers.

It seems that wherever he traveled, his focus was entirely on healing division. There are tales of cures and miracles.

The media haven't yet tracked him back to the Iraq–Syria border, but there's a good chance, when they do, that they will come across the incident Christy Byford shared with me, prompted by Hetta's request to the Department of Defense for details of Gapes and Offutt's Black Hawk crash.

The Engineer was in Ma'a Helwa – the tiny border village of Sweet Water – when the gunship fell to earth.

What did Gapes see? What did I?

I have revisited the events of the past three months many, many times, and what happened in the tower will never leave me. I know that somewhere – in a realm science has yet to find the words to describe – there is a place where Hope, our daughter and I *are* together; a place that is separated by the thinnest of membranes from the plane we insist on labeling 'reality'.

It is here, perhaps, that we judge ourselves, as Kalunin put it, against all the thoughts, feelings and emotions that are laid bare for all to see, ourselves included, in the holosphere.

If this is the case, perhaps we will all think twice about the pain that we inflict before we go right ahead and do it.

According to the data Kalunin handed to the apostolic nuncio, evolution isn't just the fundamental impulse of species, but of existence itself – which was also divined by the intuitives who'd 'viewed' the information held within the particles that subtend everything we see and touch. If the data is correct – if, at the end of our universe and all the others that have preceded it, it gets 'read across' to a new one, encoding it with lessons learned – then, I guess, a *rebirth* of some kind has to take place.

Perhaps, too, consciousness operates on the same principle. We live and we learn. And we die. But it lives on. I haven't asked him yet, but maybe this is what Stani was trying to tell me on the ferry: the four stages of consciousness he'd mapped for the spook scientists at the Stanford Research Institute.

It is here, meanwhile, as Hope had said, that we learn; where we grow.

I think often about the Engineer. I always will.

As he lay dying, what was he trying to show me?

Proof of what?

Proof of the deeper reality Thompson promised to deliver via the Grid?

Or something deeper still?

The romantic in me wonders how close he came to saying, as he lay at the foot of the President's podium, 'Forgive them, Father, for they know not what they do.'

Before visiting Reuben, I spent time with Thompson in the Oval Office, just the two of us. I found him thoughtful, but excited by the opportunities that lie ahead.

I asked him what he made of the Engineer trying to hand him a photo of the box he had made at the Southern Cross.

'Do you believe in co-agency?'

I told him I wasn't even sure what that was.

'I don't speak about my time at the Southern Cross because it was profoundly upsetting. You saw that during our hypnosis session. Even as a kid, it got me to thinking about the insanity of man's inhumanity; and, doubly insane, how its more twisted advocates called upon religion to justify their deeds.'

When he showed no sign of continuing, I'd prompted him. 'Co-agency . . . ?'

'One night I started to pray for the strength to stand up to Pastor Green, and the wisdom to deal most effectively with people like him.'

'What happened to the box?'

'I still have it. It goes everywhere with me.'

He walked over to his desk and opened a drawer – the same drawer, three months previously, from which he'd removed the Daily Brief with its details of the slaughter of the innocents in Yemen.

He placed the box on the table between us and invited me to open it. A comforting smell of wood and polish greeted me as I lifted the lid. Inside was a piece of frayed paper – a page from a school notebook.

'The morning after I prayed, I went to the school library,' Thompson said. 'Every volume had a religious theme, except for one. A collection of poetry. It fell open at a particular page. "Only Breath", by Rumi, a thirteenth-century Persian. I read it, and wept. I wrote it out and tucked it in there. That's what you're holding.'

I started to read.

> *Not Christian or Jew or Muslim, not Hindu,*
> *Buddhist, Sufi, or Zen. Not any religion*
> *Or cultural system. I am not from the East*
> *Or the West, not out of the ocean or up*
> *From the ground, not natural or ethereal, not*
> *Composed of elements at all. I do not exist,*
> *Am not an entity in this world or in the next,*
> *Did not descend from Adam and Eve or any*
> *Origin story. My place is placeless, a trace*
> *Of the traceless. Neither body or soul.*
> *I belong to the beloved, have seen the two*
> *Worlds as one and that one call to and know,*
> *First, last, outer, inner, only that*
> *Breath breathing human being.*

As I handed the box back, Thompson turned to me. 'I still think of Kit Harper, you know, the kid who threw himself under a train because of the torment meted out by Green and his henchmen. I have tried since to honor his passing, Josh. To let him know that his life—'

His voice caught as he looked away and returned the box to its drawer.

I thought back to what Stani had told me. That some of us have a purpose in life and some of us have a purpose in death. But that we all have a purpose . . .

Before parting, I shook him warmly by the hand, then became suddenly aware that I was holding on too long. 'Just one more question, Mr President?'

He nodded.

'When did you know for sure that the Engineer hadn't come to kill you?'

I'll never forget his smile.

'Afterwards,' he said.

*

I look up. Over the steering wheel, I see the rolling hills of Pennsylvania.

Co-agency was an idea that Thompson had become familiar with at Princeton. It described the way God acts in the world when we align our will with His.

Like Rumi, the Engineer had been raised a Sufi.

But he'd also been brought up a Christian.

In searching for anything else that linked him to Thompson, I came across another of Rumi's poems, which included the Engineer's final words to me:

Say I Am You.

And at that point, something shifted in me.

I realized, finally, that the connectedness and the physics were one and the same, and that they were bonded by a thing each of us at some fundamental level knows and understands.

A thing called love.

And with that shift came something else.

The knowledge, at last, that I am free.

Dramatis Personae

Tod Abnarth – Senator; Reuben Kantner's former boss

Eric Abram – WWII veteran; sold Josh and Hope his home on the point

Jack Ackerman – Hope's surrogate father

Tobias Anders – Captain, Special Tactics Branch, Metropolitan Police Department, Washington, D.C.

Arturo – sidekick of Pastor Green, the Southern Cross (Thompson's school)

Nils Bogarten – WMD expert, Stockholm International Peace Research Institute

Misty Buckhannon – Lou Gapes's sister; Duke Gapes's aunt

Admiral (Retired) Christy Byford – President Thompson's National Security Adviser

Tom Cabot – Director, US Secret Service

Josh Cain – The President's doctor and White House Medical Director

Hope Cain – Josh Cain's wife

Katya Dedovic – Lawyer at Collins Lovelock Land, Washington D.C.

Karl Dempf – Consultant/mercenary with Triple Z Services; ex-Army Afghan vet

'The Engineer' – Jihadi terrorist

Colonel Nelson 'Tom' Freeley – Former Marine Corps flyer, Vietnam

Duke Gapes – Ex-Marine

Hank Gapes – Duke Gapes's father

Louisa 'Lou' Gapes – Duke Gapes's mother

Haight Graham – White House Special Agent in Charge; Lefortz's successor

Pastor Green – Principal at the Southern Cross

Kit Harper – Thompson's classmate, the Southern Cross

Hetta Hart – Special Agent, intelligence division, US Secret Service

John Hayden – Head, Presidential Protection Division's Counter-Assault Team; former US Army, Iraq

Reverend 'Isaac' Hayes – Director, Georgetown Presbyterian Mission (a charitable shelter for the homeless), Washington D.C.

Vladimir Ilitch – Moscow-based oligarch

Raoul Jimenez – Sniper, Special Tactics Branch, Metropolitan Police Department, Washington D.C.

General Zan Johansson – Commander, JaySOC (Joint Special Operations Command), US Army; organizational head of the US's 'war on terror'

Professor M. M. Kalunin – Russian academician; Ilitch's father-in-law

Reuben Kantner – Chief of Staff, the White House

Heather Kantner – Reuben's wife

Dr Elliott Kaufmann – Physicist at the Baltimore Central Institute of Technology; colleague of Schweizer at Harvard

Dr Mo Kerchorian – Progressive psychotherapist; studied with Josh under Ted van Buren at Georgetown

Stanislaw Koori – 'The world's greatest psychic'

Charles Land – Senior partner at Collins Lovelock Land, Washington D.C.

Jim Lefortz – Special Agent in Charge, US Secret Service, the White House

Sister Martha – Nun at the Church of St Mary Magdalene

Marty – Security guard, office building on 16th Street

Mikey – Hetta Hart's brother and cop

Sasha Mikhailovna – Ilitch's wife

Molly – Josh Cain's personal assistant

Patriarch Nikolai – the Primate of Moscow; head of the Russian Orthodox Church

Major Cal Offutt – US Army; former colleague of Duke Gapes

Dr Kate Ottoway – Forensic pathologist, Office of the Chief Medical Examiner, Washington D.C.

Pam – Hope's mother

Dr Joel Schweizer – Computer scientist; colleague of Kaufmann at Harvard

Joe Seitz – Assistant Press Secretary, the White House

Colonel Dmitri Sergeyev – Military Attaché, Russian Embassy, Washington D.C.

Steve – Paraplegic ex-Army vet, the Settlement, Washington D.C.

Robert Thompson – The President of the United States

Jennifer Thompson – The First Lady

Ted van Buren (TVB) – Associate Professor, Department of Medicine, Georgetown University; Josh's mentor

Susan van Buren – Professor of archaeology; TVB's wife

Vasiliy – Sergeyev's sidekick

Matthew Voss – Ex-Marine

DJ Wharton – Special Agent, US Federal Bureau of Investigation

Cody Wyatt – Small-time criminal, Blacksoil, West Virginia; former friend of Duke Gapes

Acknowledgements

The Grid had been in my head for a long time before I began to write it, and so remembering everyone who has helped me along the way is an imperfect and risk-filled endeavour.

First, I am indebted to my friend, the writer and playwright Simon David Eden, for his advice at key junctures of the narrative. Simon's insights – his gift for plot and character especially – helped me at moments when I really needed it. To have the guidance of another writer during what is essentially a solitary undertaking was an extraordinary gift. My pal, and Helena, thank you.

Martyn Forrester, another great friend and writer, was also very helpful early on in the story, as was the eminent psychiatrist and physician Professor Gordon Turnbull, whom it has been my privilege to know for over a decade.

Jeannie BB kindly provided very helpful 'US back-up', Mike M was constantly on hand with his own unique brand of sage and strategic advice, and James and Sara and the team at Plastic gave very generously of their time (and bottom line) in putting together a phenomenal 'teaser'.

For her behind-the-scenes support, my heartfelt thanks to our angelic friend Celia and her amazing 'hit list', and to our many other friends who provided me with 'weekend refuge' when I wasn't writing in my urban eyrie: Susie C-T, the Swinburnes, David and Mary, Eddie and Amanda and, of course, Fiona and Baz.

Andrew and Jane, Ian and Zuhra, Sue Q, Sal, the DGs, Sophs and Jonathan, Micci and Lee, the DWs, and Foxy were – and still are – a source of huge support; as were – and are – Kevin, Gavin and the Optima team. Huge thanks, too, to my friends Robert M. Knight and Maryanne Bilham Knight for their extraordinary and wonderful photographs.

And a special thank-you to Chris – without question, the world's greatest bank manager.

I am indebted to Susan and Tom for – respectively – their

knowledge of international conferences and negotiating safe passage through Iron Dome, as well as a number of people – many going back to my *Jane's* days – who helped to provide *The Grid*'s technical underpinnings.

And I couldn't have gone on this journey without the love and help of some very special people who very sadly are no longer physically with us: my father, my step-parents, Sylvia, Baz, and Giles.

To that end, I must also thank Ingo Swann, the original remote viewer; also his sister, Murleen, and niece, Elly, for welcoming me into their lives. It has been a huge joy and a privilege getting to know you.

I could not have written *The Grid* without having first read a great deal about remote viewing and the nature of consciousness. I am indebted to many authors for their insights, though none more than Hal Puthoff and Paul H. Smith. The latter's *Reading the Enemy's Mind* is a truly remarkable account of the RV program from its inception, which is why I acknowledge him – and the book – on page 197.

For a starter on consciousness and the physics of reality, I strongly recommend the works of the person who got me started: Ervin Laszlo.

On the publishing front, *The Grid* wouldn't exist but for the incredible team at Transworld: Bill Scott-Kerr, Janine Giovanni, Eloisa Clegg, Sally Wray, Ella Horne and the many unseen others who pulled it together across editorial, marketing and design. A big thank-you, too, to Steven Maat at Bruna; my foreign rights agents, Nicki Kennedy, Sam Edenborough and Jenny Robson at ILA; and – at The Soho Agency – to Mark Lucas, my agent and friend of more years than I want to admit to. Mark, I owe you: first, for not batting an eyelid when I ran the idea past you, but most of all for the care, love and attention you invested in it – and therein, huge thanks to Mindy, too.

Nor, of course, would *The Grid* exist but for my family: my extraordinary and wonderful mother, Hilary, my equally wonderful sister Kate and brother James – and *their* amazing partners and children.

And finally, to Ali, Lucy and Will. Thank you, too. My love for you guys knows no bounds.

Nick Cook is a bestselling author, documentary filmmaker, and a former senior editor for *Jane's Defence Weekly*. His groundbreaking *The Hunt for Zero Point* detailed his ten-year investigation into efforts to crack the Holy Grail of aerospace propulsion: anti-gravity.

His TV credits include *Billion Dollar Secret*, a two-hour documentary that he wrote and presented for the Discovery Channel and Channel 5, and *An Alien History of Planet Earth*, for The History Channel and Channel 4.